CANAL
PUSHERS

ANDY GRIFFEE

CANAL PUSHERS

Orphans
Publishing

First published in Great Britain in 2019 by Orphans Publishing
Enterprise Park, Leominster
Herefordshire HR6 0LD

www.orphanspublishing.co.uk

A Cataloguing in Publication record for this book
is available from the British Library

Hardback: 978 1 903360 31 6

Printed and bound by Clays Ltd, Elcograf, S.p.A.

To Helen

THE JOURNEY
OF THE JUMPING
JACK FLASH

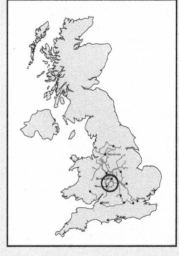

Birmingham

(2)

Kings Norton   (4)   Hockley
                     Heath
         (3)
Tardebigge   (5)   Kingswood
         (7)
    (2)   Stoke Prior   (5)
                        Wootten
    Hanbury   Wawen
                          (5)
(5)
    Worcester   Stratford

KEY

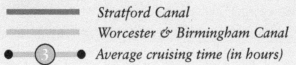

Stratford Canal
Worcester & Birmingham Canal
Average cruising time (in hours)

The lone fisherman sat on a sturdy plastic box that was covered by the rainproof cloak that draped down around him. Its strangely pointed hood added to the impression of a man-sized bell-tent and hid almost all of his face from both sides of the canal towpath. He held a single solid-looking fishing rod out in front of him and a landing net on a pole lay on the ground by his feet. But the fisherman barely glanced at the small fluorescent orange float that bobbed gently on the water a few metres away. Instead, his eyes flickered constantly from left to right and back again. The hook dangling below the water was wholly absent of any bait.

To his left, the dark canal swung around a bend and out of sight towards The Commandery museum, a civil war battle headquarters once used by Charles II. The canal then flowed on behind the remains of the Royal Worcester porcelain factory before opening up into Diglis Basin and its small floating village of boats, near the point where a deep lock allowed the canal to join the River Severn. In the other direction, the canal stretched away towards Worcester city centre where the noise of cars and late-night revellers could still be heard in spite of the lateness of the hour. The fisherman checked his watch and smiled to himself as the nearby cathedral's clock tower chimed midnight.

Would he be lucky again tonight? It was a calculated risk to set up camp in such a populated area – but it was one which would prove his audacity. Characterless new-build apartment blocks surrounded the basin and there was regular pedestrian traffic along the towpath. However, this particular stretch was shrouded from onlookers by mature trees and bushes on both banks, and the proximity of pubs and clubs meant there would be no shortage of potential victims. He knew how to be patient and then, when the time came, lightning quick and decisive. He knew that one day his boldness and skill would have people shaking their heads in wonder at

1

his achievements. The fisherman hunched his shoulders under the cape and congratulated himself on possessing the patience of an experienced angler waiting for his first catch.

He heard the man before he saw him. An empty drink can kicked by a foot made a tinny sound before it sailed into the centre of the canal and landed with a soft splash. With a stab of excitement, the fisherman saw a dark figure to his left, silhouetted by the faint glow of streetlights and car headlights from the road bridge just beyond the bend. The wait had paid off. The fisherman could not make out any of the man's features, but he could tell from his weaving walk that he was heavily drunk, or drugged, or both. He was slurring to himself in maudlin self-pity.

'Bitch... thas wa' she is... bloody bitch. S'not my fault. S'not my fault. Got to have some fun... but no money... all gone... all gone...'

The man only registered the fisherman's presence on the towpath at the last moment. He lurched to a halt, his legs automatically spread wide to prevent himself falling over. His body swayed forwards and backwards in an automatic attempt to overcome his intoxication and stay upright. Up close, the fisherman could see he was a burly man of average height in his mid-forties, dressed cheaply in some off-white training shoes, grubby jeans and a dirty quilted jacket.

'Sorry, pal... did na see you.'

The fisherman grunted whilst checking quickly along the towpath behind his victim and then in the other direction. There was only a short window of time to strike. He stood up swiftly, lifting his fishing rod and swinging it forcefully with both hands in a sweeping circle behind him and over his head. The thick bottom of the rod smashed into the man's back before he could make sense of what was happening. The momentum of the rod sent the drunken man stumbling onto the brink of the towpath.

'Wha' the —!'

But the fisherman was squarely behind his victim now and, holding the rod level with both hands, he forced the man forward. He watched his victim's arms windmilling as he tipped head first into the cold black water. The sudden splash sounded deafening and the fisherman knew that he had to act quickly. He threw down the rod and picked up his landing net. The struggling man gasped for air as the sobering effect of the icy water replaced his inebriation with panic as he tried to make his way to the bank, coughing and spluttering with the effort. They always made that mistake. It was a split-second life-or-death decision. Strike out for the other bank or return towards their nemesis? And they always, always returned to their nemesis – the stupid bastards.

As soon as his victim was close enough the fisherman looped the landing net over the man's head and pressed down as hard as he could. The net and the man's head sunk quickly below the water's surface. The fisherman twisted the net in a couple of circles and kept his arms stiff and strong, as he had learnt to do. The thrashing below the water and the steady stream of bubbles slowly subsided. When he was sure it was over, the fisherman untwisted the net and pulled it back. The canal was silent again. The fisherman removed his cape, dismantled his rod, picked up his box-seat and the fishing net and, giving one last glance at the mirror-like surface of the black, still water below him, walked away.

CHAPTER ONE

It was a narrowboat, sure enough – and a pretty long one. The brochure had said sixty-four feet but the sun-faded photograph of its profile in the chandler's window now seemed to barely do it justice. Standing on the little half-round rear deck next to the tiller, *Jumping Jack Flash* seemed to stretch forward to eternity. The parallel lines of the flat shiny roof converged way off in the far distance at the level of my midriff. A short chimney stack poked through the roof and I could see little brass-mushroom shaped domes before it. Her black metal hull felt heavy and solid beneath my feet. A masked and manically grinning jester adorned one side. He was dressed in a diamond-patterned all-in-one skin-tight suit and he was crouched with knees akimbo and both arms straight down in front of him as though he was leaping froglike up into the air.

She was moored to some rings set into the towpath and facing a small fleet of other boats, which were bunched together picturesquely safe and snug on pontoons. This did little to reassure me that I could safely detach my boat and motor away. My potential new home had assumed the apparent dimensions of an oil tanker.

I dragged my eyes away and refocused on the acne-scarred young man next to me.

'... so, that's the thing to remember. Turn the key in sequence and you'll have no problems starting the engine, even when it's bloody cold in the winter.'

'Sorry – what sequence?'

The kid stared hard at me, unsure if I was joking or just stupid. He hitched his skinny jeans a fraction higher than his groin, but the broad white waistband of his branded underpants was still in plain sight. He decided I was just stupid, glanced at the time on his mobile and patiently repeated his instructions.

'Turn the key to this mark and hold it for five to ten seconds. It'll beep at you. Then turn the key to start and when it does, let the key go back to the run position.'

Just three things to remember. I thought I could manage that, although Debbie would probably beg to differ. Ex-wives tend to do a lot of differing. I did as I was told and the engine coughed, caught and began rumbling with a reassuringly deep and regular rhythm. Diesel fumes seeped up out of the boat and mixed with the crisp autumnal air before quickly dissipating.

'Anyway, as I said, there's a book in the kitchen with everything you need to remember.'

'Isn't it called a galley?'

'Yeah, well – call it want you like. The book is by the sink – which is still called a sink.' He flicked his long fringe away from his eyes, whilst avoiding mine in case I took exception to his banter. But it was fair enough. I was being an arse.

'Sorry. Look you probably want to get off. Don't worry, I'll read the book before I go. I've got all evening. And I've got your number if I need any help. It's fine.'

'S'okay,' he said, although his face suggested otherwise. 'But are you sure you'll be all right? It's a lot of boat to handle all on your own as a beginner. Especially at locks.'

He was right to doubt me. I doubted myself.

'I've got a mate coming along with me for the first week. I should be somewhere I want to stay by then and like I told your boss, if I still like it after a month's rental, I'll buy it.'

It was either that or live in a tent, but I didn't tell him that bit.

'Well, she's a sound boat, like I said. I saw her out of the water a couple of months ago and she's had a good all-round overhaul and tidy-up. Engine's sound too – for her age.'

I held out my hand as a hint that I'd had enough advice from an adolescent. He accepted the hand briefly, gave the hatchway one last look around, killed the engine and jumped nimbly onto the towpath.

'Well, I'll be away. Good luck then, Jack,' he said dubiously and sauntered off, a hand in each pocket, presumably to hold up his trousers.

I confess it was the boat's name that had first attracted me to her. I'm a sucker for serendipity and it shared my first name. But the second-hand price had come a close second. My ex-wife had given me a small advance on half the value of the house, fixtures, fittings, car and cat. A month of cheap hotels had already heavily dented it and another mortgage was out of the question. I wasn't in a hurry to do all that 'worldly goods' stuff again, but I also didn't have a job. *Jumping Jack Flash* was going to have to be hearth, home and maybe even my office for a while.

I scooped up the cardboard box of food and drink from the deck and moved down into the boat's cabin. Welcome to the seven-feet-wide waterborne corridor where I would attempt to live my new life. I tripped on the last of the steep narrow steps below the hatchway and just managed to stop myself falling. My first overwhelming impression was of shiny over-varnished pine and the musty smell of stale air combined with a whiff of damp and diesel fuel. There were two tiny wardrobes on either side of the steps below the stern hatchway with large holes drilled at head height rather than handles to open and shut them. Beyond this I found two very narrow single beds on either side of the gangway. Cheap polyester sheets in a sickly shade of lilac had been folded over a few thin-looking red blankets. Undaunted, I pressed on through my new domain. The single beds had a swing door between them and immediately behind that was a door on the left leading into a small bathroom with sink, toilet and shower. It was a snug fit. The bathroom was sealed in what looked like a continuously moulded piece of grey-white plastic so that it functioned as a wet room – presumably as long as you kept the toilet paper dry and hidden away in a cupboard under the sink. The fixtures and fittings, especially the tiny rubber sink plug on a metal chain, reminded me of childhood caravan holidays. I tried the aeroplane-style flush, watched the weak trickle of water into the pan and made a mental note to buy a toilet brush.

A double bed came next, open to the gangway with its base facing the bathroom and its shiny pine headboard up against the dividing wall which formed one end of the kitchen (or galley). At least this boasted a duvet rather than the unwelcoming sheets and blankets of the single berths. It did look thin, though. I mentally congratulated myself on bringing a decent sleeping bag. The kitchen opened out into a living space with four small but comfortable and well-used easy chairs and a small dining table. The metal chairs tucked underneath it reminded me of the black and white photograph of Christine Keeler straddling one with no clothes on. The kitchen and living space comprised about half of the boat's interior and felt generous for a two-man crew. I wondered if Will would accept one of the small single berths or whether he'd insist on tossing a coin for the comfort of the double.

Most of the interior fittings were made out of pine that had been slathered in layers of shiny varnish. In the sleeping quarters the windows were small, round portholes and there were larger caravan-style windows in the galley and saloon letting in a paltry amount of light in the gathering gloom of a chilly English evening in the Midlands in late September. All in all, though, I wasn't too disappointed by my initial exploration. Many land-locked living quarters in my limited price range would be a lot worse and they would have neighbours you couldn't sail away from.

I dumped the box of groceries next to the tiny stainless-steel sink, found a plastic wine glass in the cupboard underneath and poured myself a generous glass of Argentinian Malbec. Beyond the living space another door had a small metal sign saying 'foredeck' and I followed it out onto the pointy end of the boat, where wooden bench seats faced each other on either side. This, I decided, was where I would be spending a lot of time – weather permitting. It was the nautical equivalent of a suburban patio but with even less maintenance hassle. Although, I reflected, some plants in pots might be nice. I imagined Will at the helm and myself cosily ensconced on one of the benches, legs stretched out in front of me, a glass in hand, happily watching the countryside slowly pass by.

The boatyard at Wootton Wawen was quiet save for an occasional duck quack and the hum of cars using the busy A-road that ran nearby. My teenage friend had explained that summer changeover weekends were 'manic' as holidaymakers came and went, but that there was hardly anything to do on a mid-week Wednesday in early autumn. His boss who owned the boatyard and a number of hire boats, including *Jumping Jack Flash,* usually disappeared from Monday to Friday at this time of year but he had emailed me photographs of the boat a few weeks earlier. He had been hiring it out to holidaymakers for five years, but its shortage of berths made it unprofitable so now he wanted to sell it and buy a larger boat that could take extended families or groups of friends, even the odd stag or hen party. He had given me a much-reduced rental charge for the next four weeks in the hope that I would take it off his hands for good. I swung my legs sideways onto the outside bench and leaned back once again to consider my life darkly through a wine glass.

Jack Johnson, forty-five years old, divorced, jobless, childless and with nothing more to show for twenty-five years of work and twenty years of marriage than a rented canal boat. Cheers. I shivered, my mood matching the temperature of the evening and the dampness of my surroundings. The wine wasn't working so I topped up my glass to give it a second chance.

When in doubt make a list: one of Deb's rules in life rather than mine but, what the hell? Problem one: money. The cash from the divorce settlement would just exceed six figures but it wouldn't last long with nothing else coming in. Scratch problem number one. Make it number two. Problem number one: bitterness and heartache. It had to be confronted. Six months after moving out and three months after the divorce, I was still struggling to come to terms with the end of something that had once been so fine. In the absence of funds for a psychotherapist, I had tried to find my own words for the mixture of sadness and regret, but it still sat heavily in my gut, like the aftermath of a particularly bitter and noxious cocktail.

How did the two freewheeling American Studies students who had first made love in a campervan parked in a Cornish layby, and got married five years later, become such strangers to each other? The decades had blurred into each other and were now reduced in my mind to Deb's meticulous photo albums. Occasionally I'd flick through them at speed to create a flipbook flash-frame movie of holidays, barbecues and other people's weddings and christenings. I imagined this might be what a drowning man saw as his body carried him down into the increasingly cold and dark watery depths.

Three years of expensive and ultimately unsuccessful IVF treatment had taken their toll on both of us. My weekends had been spent doing subbing shifts in London for a national tabloid. Deb's weekends had been without me. I'd spent long tedious weekdays alone when Debbie was out working for a small independent bookshop that she loved passionately. By the end, we had both been simply numb. Silent apart from the minimum of communication necessary to stay efficiently sheltered, fed and watered together. There had been no shouting, no recriminations, nothing thrown through the air. Perhaps there should have been. Anything would have been better than the slow-motion agony of realisation and finally acceptance that your lover, spouse and friend no longer wanted to be with you – and vice versa. It was hard to self-diagnose the residual pain from it all. It wasn't fatal. But it lingered, like the constant nagging ache of an infected molar. Moving on.

Okay. Problem number two: money. Done that. Nothing had changed in the last five minutes. Problem number three: employment. There was no doubt that I needed to start writing or subbing again. My relatively well-paid weekend editing shifts had petered out with the takeover of the paper by a new and ruthless cost-cutting corporation. I had vague notions of contacting the local newspapers in this part of the country to see if they had any vacancies. But I suspected they were already one-man-and-his-dog operations, failing to compete against the internet, paying a pittance to desperate media studies graduates and unlikely to welcome a forty-five-year-old hack with open arms and an open chequebook.

Nevertheless, it was hard to shake off romantic notions of a life lived on a picturesque canal backwater supplemented by occasional glamorous foreign assignments for the Sunday broadsheet colour supplements. It would be hard to find more peaceful surroundings than the ones I now found myself in. The boat was admittedly a bit shabby, but it wouldn't take too much effort to make it a comfortable and cosy retreat from the hurly-burly of daily existence and the nastiness of the real world. I imagined myself as an occasional globe-trotting columnist, returning from the world's hotspots with my smart new leather luggage to a bucolic canalside existence where a single malt waited for me by the wood-burner whilst a casserole simmered in the cosy orange glow of the wall lights. However, this time my wishful thinking refused to take wings and divert towards a sunny upland. So, I parked it and moved on to problem number four: hunger.

At least I could do something about that. I swung back off the bench, grabbed a coat, and made my way out of the hatchway. I was just about to step across onto the towpath when I noticed that the boat that had been moored behind me had now been moved back onto the pontoons. There was no real reason to move *Jumping Jack Flash* but a wine-fuelled wish to tinker with my new acquisition was whispering in my ear. How hard could it be to simply reverse the length of the boat? I walked along the towpath, undid the mooring rope at the bow, coiled it and threw it onto the boat. Then I walked back to the stern and realised that I had forgotten the sequence to start the engine. No problem, the instructions were down in the galley. I ducked down inside, found them and came back to the hatchway. But as I looked back along the boat's roof, I realised the bow was now drifting outwards and away from the towpath. Damn! Maybe I should have started the engine first? I ran back along the towpath, but the bow was now at least two metres from the bank – too far to risk trying to jump back on board. Moreover, the gap was slowly continuing to widen. It wouldn't be long before the boat pivoted 90 degrees and blocked the entire canal. I ran back along the towpath, jumped onto the stern and rushed to the bow where the rope was a mess of coils on the deck. If I could throw the rope onto the towpath, I could sprint back and pull the bow back in, I thought. My first three attempts ended with the rope sliding back under its own weight into the water. Each time, the task became harder as the gap continued to widen and the rope became heavier. I was now blowing hard and feeling pretty stupid as I pulled the wet rope back for the third time. Shit! What should I do?

Suddenly I felt the boat shudder and heard the engine growl into life. Surprised, I looked up and saw a figure at the stern raise a hand to me in acknowledgement. The boat moved backwards a short distance and then the bow began to move back in towards the towpath. I stepped back across the narrowing gap and tied the line to the mooring ring as the engine was turned off. The boat was back in its original position. I strolled as nonchalantly as I could back towards the stern.

A slim black-haired woman was bending to tie the rear mooring rope onto its original mooring ring. She stared coolly at me with big dark eyes as I approached. She was hard to age – between twenty-five and thirty perhaps? She wasn't tall, maybe five feet two or five feet three, and she was wearing a big chunky-knit woollen jumper. A large blue rucksack was on a wooden bench nearby with a slug-shaped khaki kitbag on the floor next to it.

'Uh, thanks very much,' I said. 'I owe you one. She's a bit of a handful for one person.'

The woman straightened. The knot of her mooring rope looked a lot neater and more secure than mine.

'Depends on the person's experience, I suppose,' she said drily.

I coughed to cover my embarrassment and stepped onto the stern. 'Yes, well, I've got a mate coming tomorrow to help me. I'll just lock up and then I'll buy you a drink.'

I turned to lock the two small doors but found that no matter how I turned the key, they would swing back open with ease.

'There must be a knack to this,' I said helplessly.

'You need to close the hatch cover first.'

'Sorry?'

She sighed heavily and approached the stern. Her hand was outstretched as she stepped on board and I meekly gave her the keys, which were attached to a ball of cork by a small length of cord. She reached forward and pulled the top hatch cover all the way back and closed the doors so that the door catches caught under the cover. She turned the key and pulled on the door handle to make sure it was locked before putting it back into my hands.

'Not much point having locked doors if someone can just get in through the roof,' she said. I realised what a complete idiot I had been and stuttered my thanks again as she nimbly hopped down and took her seat on the bench alongside her rucksack. Red-faced and sweaty with embarrassment, I nodded at the nearby pub.

'That's two drinks I owe you.' She stretched her legs in front of her, crossed them at the ankles and linked her hands behind her head.

'Thanks. Maybe later. I'd like to enjoy the peace for a moment.' I lingered awkwardly until she narrowed her eyes at me and added, 'Don't let me stop you.'

The Navigation was a cosy old-fashioned place with swirly red carpeting and a lot of dark wood. A wood-burning stove was throwing out a bit of heat. Posters for jazz and skittle nights suggested it was trying hard to attract a regular clientele but, like most pubs, it had probably been confounded by the motorists' fear of the breathalyser, the smoking ban and cheap supermarket cans of powerful lager that were swigged at home in front of the TV.

It was seven o'clock and there were just two customers in the lounge bar, so I had a wide choice of built-in settles to choose from. The elderly couple watched me walk up to the bar in silence and then resumed their staring into the middle distance. The woman behind the bar pulled me a pint of bitter and took my order for steak and chips with a smile that failed to reach her tired eyes. I retreated to a corner under a cheaply framed cartoon of dogs on their hind-legs playing snooker. The couple opposite me avoided my eyes. He occasionally sipped his half of beer and she sipped her sherry. It wasn't a very cheery place at that moment.

Ten minutes later, the door opened and we all looked expectantly at it. It was my canal-path rescuer. I half stood to offer her a seat at my table but she gave a slight shake of her head, quickly scanned the space and made for a settle two down from my own, pushed her bags under the table and returned to the bar. After returning with a glass of white wine she sat down, carefully folded a newspaper in front of her and began to work on a crossword. It was as though a force field closed around her. Her whole demeanour suggested that company of any kind would not just be unwelcome, but fiercely unwanted.

My steak and chips arrived quickly. It was standard pub fare, but I was hungry and set to. Almost immediately, my mobile phone's ring tone disturbed the silence. The startled elderly couple gave me a furious glare.

'Jack?'

'Hi, Will.'

Enter stage left William Simpson, Esquire, also forty-five and my oldest friend and drinking partner. We had relied on each other to survive a grim boarding school education on a remote wind-blasted site on top of the white cliffs of Dover.

Will was barely tolerated by my ex-wife but loved by many other women. This was mainly due to the shameless exploitation of his choirboy looks, lustrous blond curls, and a strong-shouldered build combined with a flat belly that somehow managed to survive his self-indulgent lifestyle. Will was an occasional film actor, occasional stage actor and a regular sponger off the previously mentioned collection of adoring women.

'Hey Jack, my man...'

I knew that tone of voice so well.

'You're not coming are you?'

William Simpson, stage name Bill Simpson, known to me as Will and the least trustworthy friend in existence. He was about to strike out again, just as he had countless times over the decades. Would I never learn?

'Well... look... I'm sorry, Jack. I know I said I would, but something's come up.'

'Your prick presumably? That makes a change.'

'Ahhh, c'mon, Jack, don't be like that. I think I'm in love, you know. She's amazing, and she's just been given a lead part in Bristol that comes with this amazing loft apartment on the waterfront. She needs me, Jack. Her play opens this week and she's a bundle of nerves, you know? I told her that I'd promised you a week but she's falling apart, Jack... and she's so young but with so much promise. She really needs me more than you – and she's a lot better-looking! But I am sorry, Jack.'

'Yeah, you said, you bastard,' I snapped. 'One week is all I asked. One week to help me get this bloody boat somewhere that I can stay for a while. Thanks a bunch, mate.'

I suddenly became aware that my voice was raised, but I knew I was in a serious fix without him. My stomach churned with trepidation at the thought of having to handle *Jumping Jack Flash* single-handed. I couldn't even reverse it a few feet or lock its bloody door.

'Jack – I knew you'd understand. And what good would I be on a boat anyway? I get seasick, you know.'

'Will, it goes at four miles per hour and the water is completely flat. This boat is about a mile bloody long and I can't handle it on my own.'

I heard someone talking to him in the background. The words were indistinct, but I could tell that it was a young woman's voice.

'Listen, Jack, I've got to go. I just wanted to warn you I wouldn't be there in the morning. I'm really sorry. I'll catch up with you soon, matey, honestly, but Susie's need is greater, you know? I'm sure you'll find someone else to help.'

'Fuck off, Will.'

The woman behind the bar had been trying to ignore my angry one-sided conversation and regrettable language – but she locked eyes with me as I threw the phone onto the table and reached for my drink. The elderly couple decided they'd had enough excitement for one evening, gathered their coats, dutifully deposited their empty glasses on the bar and left.

My phone pinged to indicate an incoming text.

> Sorry mate, W xx.

I decided to ignore it and sulk. Debbie had always thought it was one of my most well-honed skills.

Fuck, fuck, fuck. I was fucked! *Jumping Jack Flash* loomed outside in my imagination, all sixty-four feet of her in red-and-black paintwork, defiantly tied to the towpath and silently challenging me to even try to manhandle her out of the boatyard on my own, let alone take her any kind of distance. I pictured the painting of the jester on her side. His wide grin now seemed more like a leer of mischief and mockery at my misfortune. The gods laugh when men make plans. Did Jumping Jack know something that I didn't? My mind raced. Maybe I could pay the teenager to help me for a week? Would his boss let him? Fuck. Something stronger than beer was called for. The unreliable bastard. I should have known. In truth, I had always known. That was Will – the only reliable thing about our friendship was that hope kept triumphing over my experience of him.

The woman behind the bar looked slightly less bored this time as I demanded a large Teachers with one ice cube. Two young couples came in as I was being served and headed straight for the pool table. She returned my change and immediately began pouring four pints of lager for them without being asked.

My rescuer, the slim dark-haired woman was looking at me as I turned to return to my table. She didn't smile but she didn't look away either. Nevertheless, the force field still seemed to be firmly in place. I sipped my whisky and fumbled with my phone as a distraction from the realisation that my overloud whining at Will had probably painted me as even more hopeless.

'Mind if I join you?'

I looked up in surprise to see my rescuer approaching my table. She didn't wait for me to reply but pulled out the chair opposite me and sat down with her arms folded and her calm, no-nonsense eyes fixed on mine.

'Um, hi. Again. Sorry for the swearing. I had some bad news. Would you like that drink now?'

'Yes, please.'

I liked the direct way that she accepted, without any fuss or simpering gratitude. I also very much liked the way she looked but that was probably getting ahead of myself.

'Same again?'

'Yes, please. Sauvignon. Medium.'

I collected a glass of wine from the bar and took it back to my new companion.

'Thank you.'

She swallowed the dregs in her other glass and leaned over to put it on an adjoining table.

'I'm Jack. Jack Johnson.'

She smiled but didn't shake my hand. It was a nice smile with very neat and even white teeth but for some reason it wasn't mirrored in her eyes.

'Jack Johnson,' she repeated. 'JJ?'

'If you like. And you are?'

She hesitated for a bare second and then extended a hand with an elegant gold bangle around the wrist.

'I'm Nina.'

'"Feeling Good"?'

'Sorry?'

'Nina Simone – "Feeling Good". Great song.'

She looked genuinely puzzled.

'Nina Simone – amazing jazz and blues singer. Sorry, before your time maybe?'

'Oh yeah. Sure.'

She sipped her wine, so I sipped my whisky and tried to think of more sparkling repartee. Nina beat me to it.

'So, your friend has let you down?'

'Ah... yes. Yes. He has. Sorry for the swearing – again. He's an unreliable swine but yes... I'm a bit stuck now. I was relying on him to help me get this bloody great boat out of here to a more permanent mooring. Now it seems that he's had a better offer.'

'Yes, we all heard,' she said. 'I could help you.'

It was a statement rather than a question. If this was a movie, I thought, this would be one of those moments when everything goes into freeze-frame and time stands still for several seconds. But it wasn't and all I could do was gape. Bloody hell.

'Um... sorry, did you just say you could help me, err, again?'

'Yes.'

Her coolness was very impressive, I thought. The less she said, the more I babbled.

'Gosh. Well, that would be great. I was hoping to travel for a few weeks and look for somewhere where I can moor up cheaply while I get my life back together. I'm thinking of buying the boat if I like her. I need somewhere to live.'

'Sounds like a plan,' she said without a hint of a smile.

'Yes, that's it, a plan. Who knows what'll happen? But that's the plan. So, what are your plans then, Nina?'

'Nothing much.' She nodded back at the rucksack and the khaki kitbag on the floor by her table. 'I'm just travelling around.'

'So, you would really help me with the boat?'

'Yes. If you can't even shut the door, I imagine you're going to need quite a lot of help.'

I decided to ignore the comment and ride my luck. 'For a week?'

'Maybe.'

That was good enough for me. It was time to move before an evil fairy appeared and burst my bubble. I drained my glass.

'Right. Come on then. I'll show you *Jumping Jack Flash*.'

CHAPTER TWO

I tossed and turned most of the night, slipping in and out of consciousness, vaguely aware of a dream that I returned to in disjointed phases, but which I failed to remember on waking properly. It might have been mildly erotic though, as a morning glory accompanied the grey dawn light which came through the porthole opposite my bed. It cramped my progress to the bathroom, and I had to slant my naked body in order to achieve the only possible angle for relieving the pressure on my bladder. My manhood quickly deflated to its normal state of affairs as I tried to pee quietly, with one hand on the wall above the toilet and my heels against the door. Then I activated the underpowered flush, hurried back as quickly and quietly as possible and pulled on a pair of shorts and a sweatshirt with Stanford University fraudulently emblazoned on it. I lay back on my bed and pondered the mystery that was Nina. The journalist's mantra rattled through my head – who, what, where, when, how and why? Who the hell was she? What was her story? Where had she come from? When would she want to move on? How much did she know about boats? And why would she just up and volunteer to join me? No answers were forthcoming no matter how much I turned these questions over in my head, so I headed to the galley where I lit a gas ring to make a pot of tea.

A thin veil of mist clung to the water, but it was still just about warm enough to sit outside in the weak sun and enjoy the stillness. The oak tree immediately above the boat's foredeck had left a modest carpet of brown and red leaves in the well between the two benches. There was no sound from the offices of the hire company and its car park was empty. I opened the plastic instruction manual for the boat and spent half an hour reading the theory of how to start and stop, how to moor up, how to use locks and how to avoid smashing into other canal users. It all seemed reasonably simple on paper – though I feared that trying to steer eighteen tonnes of wood and metal might prove a lot more challenging. There was a drawing of the boat's layout at the back, so I took a photo of it on my phone and emailed it to myself.

Then I looked ahead of our current route with the help of a small pocket-sized book called *The Canal Companion: Severn & Avon, Mid-Worcestershire Ring and Cotswold Canals*, published by J.M.Pearson & Son Ltd. It showed that our boatyard was a mere seven and a half miles from Stratford-on-Avon in one direction, whilst the centre of Birmingham lay in the other direction, about eighteen miles away where the Stratford Canal, which we were on, met up with the Worcester & Birmingham Canal. I suspected that neither direction would provide me with the semi-permanent berth of my dreams, but I decided to explore a bit whilst I had an apparently competent companion to show me the ropes.

'Good morning.'

I slopped my cold tea in surprise. I looked up from the foredeck to the roof above my head to see a bare pair of feet and ankles at my eye level. Further up, a brown pair of calves tapered into a close-fitting pair of royal blue shorts just above her knees. A light blue rugby shirt had its sleeves rolled up to the elbows. It was casually expensive leisure wear that didn't suggest it belonged to someone who had been living rough on the road for any length of time.

'Nina! Good morning. Sleep well?'

'Yes, fine thanks.' Her freshly brushed hair was drawn back into a pony tail and she looked well rested.

'Tea?'

'Yes, please. Milk no sugar.'

So far, my new crewmate hadn't shown much appetite for extensive conversation, but I still lived in hope.

'Aye, aye, Cap'n, one mug of tea coming up.'

'Oh God, let's not do all that nonsense shall we?'

I stopped short in the doorway. 'Sorry?'

'All that old seasalt crap. This is a narrowboat, for God's sake.'

Her level tone and clipped pronunciation gave no hint of anger or frustration. It was a simple rebuke in the brisk no-nonsense tone of someone who knew her own mind and wasn't going to take any shit. I touched my forelock and did my best pirate imitation, rolling back through the door.

'Aye, aye, Cap'n, one mug of tea coming up, pieces of eight, pieces of eight...'

When I returned Nina was stretched out on one of the benches, her ski-slope nose tilted upwards to try to catch some warmth from the early morning sun. She took the mug of tea but brushed aside the plastic instruction manual that I tried to give her with it.

'I told you, I've done this before,' she said crisply. 'Lots of times in fact – on family holidays in the Broads and on the canals since I was a girl. I know my way around.'

Family boating holidays made sense, I thought, along with ski chalets, a pony in the home paddock and a prefect's badge at an expensive girls' boarding school.

Then, perhaps conscious of the need to make more of a polite effort, Nina relented with a small sigh.

'It's wonderfully peaceful. Restful. That's probably why I was drawn to that bench last night. *A la recherche du temps perdu.*'

I reflected that she must have had a good education. The average bum didn't rattle off references to Proust like that in excellent French. Encouraged by this sudden willingness to share her background, I seized the moment.

'Really? Tell me more. You didn't grow up around here then? Did you have a big family?'

She fixed her unblinking dark eyes on mine, folded her arms with the mug still gripped in her right hand and sighed again.

'Look – let's get a few ground rules established.' Her whole manner suggested a head-girl bringing an unruly third-former to heel. I unconsciously straightened my back. 'You shouldn't feel the need to tell me your life story and, just to be clear, I'm absolutely not going to tell you mine – at all – ever. Understood?'

I nodded.

'And don't touch me – at all, ever – or any of my things. Okay?'

'Now look here...' I began, affronted at the suggestion. But she wasn't finished.

'And whilst we're at it, if you don't cut out that pirate crap I won't last a day, let alone a week on this boat. It's so terribly boring and predictable.'

As temporary captain and the potential owner of *Jumping Jack Flash*, I felt it was time to reassert some authority.

'Would there be anything else?' I said, hoping that the sarcasm in my voice would strike home. I hoped in vain.

'Yes. What time do you want to leave?'

And so, with the ground rules firmly established by her and grudgingly accepted by me, we briefly plotted our route to Stratford using the brand new little handbook that I had bought in the boatyard's shop. Nina didn't offer an opinion on either direction of travel and simply shrugged her acceptance when I suggested a short detour south before reversing our route and heading back towards the bright lights of England's second city. We would head a short distance to Bancroft Basin, in the centre of the international tourist magnet that is Stratford-upon-Avon. I had vague notions of going to the theatre – if the price of tickets wasn't going to bankrupt me. Nina might be persuaded to thaw out a bit under the influence of the Bard's poetry. With a bit of luck, we might coincide with a romantic comedy rather than a grim tragedy; it seemed that both of us needed cheering up a bit. Within an hour we were setting off. My authority was further eroded as Nina calmly called orders from the tiller, where she had started the engine without any obvious fuss, whilst I scrambled along the towpath to release the rope. I threw it onto the boat and followed her instructions to push out the bow before clambering back on board. She skilfully pulled her stern rope free of the towpath, pulled it in, coiled it neatly and eased the boat forward towards the ridiculously narrow-looking entrance of a metal aqueduct that led away from the boatyard's large turning area. Temporarily redundant, I took a moment to register that I was also casting off from my previous life into a whole new unknown future.

Perhaps Nina caught my mood as she flashed me a rare smile and then furrowed her brow in concentration as she made small adjustments to the tiller and throttle to line the boat up with the metal trough which spanned the A-road. In under a minute, my new home was gliding about twenty feet above the roofs of lorries and cars that were beginning the commuters' rush hour on the road below. Already, I felt the busy everyday world slipping away from me. A curious mixture of emotions was taking hold: an eagerness for the adventure that lay ahead and the new chapter I was about to begin, coupled with a peaceful sense of separation from all the unhappiness of the past.

'JJ?'

I immediately liked the familiar way the letters rolled off her tongue. 'Yes, Nina?'

'Coffee now, please... and you need to tidy up that rope in the middle.'

My place in the pecking order having been quickly established, I dutifully set about carrying out my chores. The coffee made and served, I obtained permission to move to a perch on the roof in the middle of the boat to watch the countryside slowly slip by. I pondered the enigmatic woman at the helm. For a start, I thought, there seemed to be very little doubt that her real name was *not* Nina. Anyone called Nina would surely be fully aware of the famous blues singer of the same name. And when I used her name, there was also the fraction of a second that it took her to respond. Fair enough. If she wanted to be private it was up to her. But journalists are born curious and I was born with ink in my blood. Just why was her privacy so important to her? Was there something in her past that she didn't want me to discover? Or was she hiding from someone? Running away from something? So far, she had declined to open the door even a chink on who she was and where she had come from.

I looked back at the object of my curiosity. She had found a small wooden box to stand on, so she could get a clearer view along the length of the boat to the bow and beyond. Her face looked relaxed, eyes focused past me on the sweeping left-hand bend of the canal and the first of many very narrow small stone bridges. This sent me scurrying back to join her at the tiller. We passed under it confidently but with barely six inches of water to spare on both sides. At some stage I knew I would have to be taught how to manage the boat for myself, but for the moment I sensed that she wanted to be left alone and that there was no rush to begin my education so I made my way through the boat's interior to the bow. As a semi-contented loner myself, I was more than happy to respect Nina's need for space but that didn't prevent me from puzzling over her history.

I stretched out on my back on the roof, my feet towards the bow, and stared up at a grey blue sky streaked with thin lines of cloud, like the shimmering silver markings on a freshly caught mackerel. The regular low thrum of the boat's engine and the slow pace continued to be very relaxing as the countryside slowly slipped by. We passed a handful of moored boats, most of them shuttered and locked. One boat appeared to be occupied; different-sized pots of straggly herbs lined the deck, coal was stacked under tarpaulins and a line of well-worn washing waved lazily in the breeze. There was no sign of life on board as we passed apart from a small dog of very mixed ancestry who appeared at its bow to yap excitedly at us. Was this a glimpse of my own future? Moored up in some quiet canal backwater, living as cheaply as possible but gradually going feral, losing contact with society and smelling of dampness, coal smoke and cheap whisky? I shook the thought away. It didn't have to be like that. For every canal dropout there were countless people enjoying the freedom and companionship of the open waterways in their colourful and cosy floating homes. It made complete sense to join them, I thought, once I had learned how to operate the boat for myself.

Nina, who now had the little map book trapped under a mug by her side, had called a short warning to remain prone as two more small bridges came and went. Then she shouted: 'Lock and aqueduct coming up.'

I sat up to see the route ahead barred by a single large wooden beam stretching across the canal. A solid looking lock gate met the waterline. Nina began slowly drifting towards the left-hand bank until it was almost grazing the boat, pushed the throttle lever into reverse and then quickly into neutral before hopping ashore to tie up front and back.

'Right then, our first lock. I'll walk you through it and then afterwards you can hop off and get the next one ready and I'll stay on the boat and take it in. Okay?'

I considered giving her an 'Aye, aye, Cap'n' for a millisecond, but settled for the less provocative, 'Sure thing.'

Nina put the shiny metal windlass in my hand and we walked up to the lock and looked down into its wet and slimy emptiness. She pointed to a little stone lip at the rear of the lock, immediately below the single gate. 'That's the cill,' she said. 'And that's the warning.' She pointed to a painted line at our feet. 'You've got to make sure the boat is far enough in front of that line not to get the stern stuck on the cill as the water goes down or you'll end up with the boat at forty-five degrees and water pouring in at the front. Not nice if it goes wrong. People have died.'

I nodded nervously, only too happy for someone else to be in charge of the boat for now. She talked me through winding the paddles open on the top gate nearest the boat so that water rushed into the lock and its level rose up to ours. When the two levels on either side of the gate were even, I pulled and pushed the gate open with a grunt and watched as Nina brought the boat carefully into the lock. Then she ordered me to close the gate behind *Jumping Jack Flash* and drop the paddles. Nina stepped back off the boat and called me up to the bottom gate, where I wound up the paddles and the water in the lock began to rush out. Nina quickly hopped back on board before the boat descended too far and edged it forward of the painted cill warning marker.

The stone walls of the lock slowly reappeared as the top of Nina's head descended below me. When the water levels on both sides of the bottom gate matched, I pushed it open, closed it behind the boat and wound down the paddles carefully under Nina's instruction. Nina held the boat steady so I could easily hop back alongside her at the tiller, where I returned the handle to its plastic pouch and went back to my perch on the roof. How the hell could anyone manage all that lock business as well as steer the boat on their own? And I was yet to see a whole flight of them.

From my position I could appreciate the approach of what looked like an enormously long iron trough spanning a natural valley some twenty or thirty feet below. The towpath continued along the aqueduct for about 500 feet, but at a lower level so that the heads of any walkers would have been almost level with the water. I glimpsed a quiet road, a railway line and a gentle river running down the length of the valley, all bisected by the red-brick towers that held our bridge and its canal water high up in the air. Nina was also taking in the gently undulating landscape that had opened up so suddenly it was startling. It was gratifying to see such an amazing feat of engineering.

'Pretty amazing,' I called and was rewarded with a nod and a smile – it felt like progress of a sort.

The verdant rolling hills of the Warwickshire countryside stretched away in both directions for a while longer before we entered a patch with densely packed elder and willow trees on both sides. Some of them trailed plastic bags in the lower branches that dipped into the water, hiding the edge of the canal from view. The canopy of trees above blocked out the sun, casting a chilliness over the stretch of water, which felt oppressive after the open vistas of the aqueduct. One tree boasted the tattered remains of a plastic Jolly Roger flag, probably the detritus of a rowdy all-male boat or stag party – but I didn't feel that pointing the pirate flag out to Nina would be wise.

Onwards we drifted, our wake barely disturbing the foliage at the canal's edge, the propeller turning slowly and lazily but with sufficient force to keep us moving at a slow walking pace. I suspected we were travelling at even less than the 4 mph speed limit but Nina clearly wasn't in the mood to rush anywhere and so I wasn't either. This, I thought, might be just what the doctor ordered after the painfully conflicted emotions of the divorce and the stress of losing a frenetic job dominated by hourly deadlines, surly demanding bosses and unreliable IT. I could see how easy it would be to succumb to the extraordinary tranquillity of these old waterways. It was hard to imagine that these were once the country's vital arteries for trade and business, busy with boats transporting their heavy loads of raw materials and manufactured goods up and down the country. The last canal I had travelled on, in Amsterdam, had been used in almost equal parts for tourism and transporting supplies. We had been on an ill-fated weekend trip that Deb had suggested as a way of 'reconnecting'. It had rained constantly. We had stayed in an expensive but unspectacular modern hotel and most of the other tourists were wrapped in cheap see-through plastic cloaks. We returned home even more wistful and sad than we had been when we set off. I remembered one of our only shared moments of laughter came from the pre-recorded commentary on the canal tour boat, which joked that the canals of the Dutch capital were three metres deep, 'with one metre of water, one metre of silt and one metre of old bicycles'. I wondered how deep the water that we were travelling on now would be. There were no clues in its cold and inky blackness.

We had been travelling for about an hour without coming across any boats going in the opposite direction. The school break had ended and the summer holiday traffic had clearly come to an end. It was still only mid-morning when I climbed down through the forward door, rinsed out a couple of mugs and put the kettle back onto the gas hob. The sensation of travelling inside the boat was very different, especially in this darker more enclosed stretch of the canal. But I looked about me again and realised that I already felt a surprising fondness for my surroundings. I saw how the boat's designer had worked cleverly to combine the cupboards, flat surfaces and furniture in a way that was efficient and practical in such a confined space. Perhaps I could envisage this being my home for a while after all, at least until I could afford something more permanent. Just then I felt the side of the boat nudge the bank and heard the note of the engine change before it was switched off and replaced by almost complete quietness.

Nina ducked her head through the rear door.

'Okay if we moor up for a bit? We should still make Stratford pretty easily by the end of today.'

'Of course. Coffee?'

'Thanks.'

Nina slipped into one of the easy chairs and put her bare feet up on the one opposite whilst taking out the elastic band which held her pony tail in place, shaking her shoulder-length hair briskly and re-twisting the band. I busied myself with a cafetiere, mugs and milk from the little fridge and decided to wait and see whether she would break the lengthening silence first. Surprisingly, she did.

'So... I wonder who the Stones fan was?'

'Sorry?' Pull yourself together, Jack, I told myself. You're always apologising to this woman.

'*Jumping Jack Flash* – it's a Stones track. I wonder who named the boat after it.'

'Ah yes, I see. Some middle-aged rocker who traded in his electric guitar and vinyl collection for a post-retirement adventure I expect...'

She nodded and sipped her coffee. 'So, you don't think Mick or Keith once owned a canal boat then?'

I calculated that our short trip must have relaxed her a lot if she was making her first effort at humour with me. I gestured around the interior. 'I think they'd have had a few more mirrors and leather banquettes.'

'And a much bigger fridge for all the booze,' she added, 'and some leopardskin touches somewhere.'

'No, I can't see it myself. The only celeb I've read about being on a canal boat was Harrison Ford. I used to work on a national newspaper at weekends and a nice picture came in from a stringer of him waving from the front of a boat.'

'So – you're a journalist?'

I almost reminded her of her golden rules but then remembered that she had said that I didn't need to feel obliged to tell her my life story, not that I was banned from doing so. If this was turning into a conversation, I might have an outside chance of finding out some minimal facts about my new companion. But for the moment, it felt like good tactics to let her do the fishing. I risked slumping into one of the other armchairs myself as I replied.

'Yes. Not very successful, I'm afraid, and out of work at the moment. And quite recently divorced,' I added as an afterthought. I avoided looking at her. 'I've got just about enough money from the split to buy *Jumping Jack Flash* if I like it. It's something new and different, which I need at the moment and it'll be a very cheap home for a while.'

'And do you?'

'Sorry?' There I was apologising again.

'Like it? The boat. Enough to buy it?'

'I'm not sure yet. I've got a month to make up my mind. She's pretty roomy for one person. And there's even space for guests,' I added, 'not that I'm expecting many. And I've enjoyed this morning.'

'Mmm... me too,' she said. 'But if you don't know anything about canals, what made you try this out?'

'Money, mostly. I can't afford to buy a house and a rental would eat up my savings and as for a static caravan or mobile home...' I pulled a face. 'I agree with the Frenchman, hell is other people. I subbed a feature about how more and more people are living on the canals near Bath – it's causing a bit of a problem, apparently – but I thought it might work out for me. I like the idea of just moving on when I get bored with a place. But we'll see.'

Nina nodded thoughtfully. 'But you'll still need to buy diesel and food and logs or coal,' she said, indicating the little stove between two of the armchairs. 'And pay for a permanent mooring.'

I nodded. 'Sure, but nowhere is completely free, is it?'

'No... nowhere is free.' Her words seemed to carry more meaning than I'd suggested, and she trailed off into a lengthy silence. Again, I left her to break it first.

'Look, do you mind if I take off for a run? Just for an hour,' she said. 'I'll pick up some lunch if I see a shop and then we can go on into Stratford this afternoon. The book says its only about four miles from here – so that's only about four hours when you take into account the locks.'

'Sure. I'll cook tonight, though. So just a sandwich or snack will do me fine.'

She slipped down the boat to her room and I managed to be loitering on the stern deck when Nina reappeared in the front hatchway and jumped out onto the smartly tended towpath. She had a baseball cap on, a green running vest and some tight-fitting black leggings which stopped just below her knees. A well-used pair of running shoes, short white socks and a tiny red rucksack completed the outfit. She gave a wave over her shoulder and then, kicking her heels high behind her, bounced off briskly in the direction that the boat was pointing – towards Stratford. As I watched her go, my mobile rang.

Mrs Deborah Johnson, ex-wife of this parish. We were still just about on speaking terms – especially as I was still waiting for my half of the divorce settlement. I answered.

'Hi, Jack? How are you?'

'Hi, Deb. Yes, okay thanks. How about you?'

She ignored my question. It was one of her traits that I had come to find deeply annoying.

'So where are you then? Did the barge thing happen?'

'I think you have to call them narrowboats,' I said. 'But yes, it sort of happened.'

'What do you mean sort of? Where are you?' She sounded needlessly suspicious and snappy, but I took a deep breath and remembered the money.

'Well, we're about four miles from Stratford. Just pulled in for a coffee. It's going fine. Very peaceful. Very therapeutic. Very slow. Very cheap.'

'We? So, Will actually fronted up? I'm truly amazed.'

I sighed. Deb and Will had never enjoyed much respect for each other. As an unhappily married man, I would probably have covered his back, but as I was now an unhappily unmarried man it didn't seem worth the effort.

'Actually no. He let me down last night. Rang up to say he'd had a better offer.'

'Oh really? That's such a surprise. He's such a stupid unreliable self-centred prick. I've always —'

'I know,' I quickly interrupted. 'You've mentioned it a few times over the years.'

'Yes, well. So, how are you managing on your own?'

'Well, I'm not on my own. I managed to find a crew, just for a few days to help me out. So, it's going fine.'

Deb pounced on this snippet of news faster than a Jack Russell onto a baby rat.

'Really? How did you find him? It is a him, isn't it?'

'Um... it's a woman, actually. She was in the pub when Will rang. And she offered her services.' I realised how this sounded, even to an ex-wife, and gabbled on. 'She's very nice, a bit posh... and very private. She's called Nina. But she knows all about boating so she's more captain than crew at the moment. But I'll pick it up as soon as possible.'

'Nina?' Deb's tone was striving for amusement but came across as a bit strained. 'Is she pretty as well as obviously very available?'

'Deb, please!'

'No, you're right,' she said briskly. 'None of my business. So is she?'

'Yes, stunning actually. She looks like a model. She should be on a catwalk – or a film premiere red carpet somewhere. She wears a designer bikini made out of mink-fur when she's on the tiller and everyone faints when we go past.' I was annoyed. 'Honestly, Deb! She's just very nice and I don't really know a thing about her. But she's helped me get the boat going and that's about it for the moment.'

'Well, it all sounds a bit odd to me. A woman hanging round in a pub offers to join a strange man on a strange boat, just like that?'

'Yes... exactly like that. She no doubt has her own reasons but I haven't got a clue what they are and she isn't saying.'

'But you could be an axe murderer.'

'Deb, you know I'm not an axe murderer.'

'Yes, but *she* doesn't know that.'

'Deb, this is silly.'

'Well...' she sniffed dubiously. '*She* could be an axe murderess then. Do you really know nothing at all about her?'

I nearly told her she didn't have the right to comment on my life any more but bit my tongue. It was actually quite nice to confide in another human being and, after all, I shared many of her questions about my secretive companion.

'So where is Nina now?' she asked.

'Out for a run and picking up some lunch.'

'Sporty *and* domestic... aren't you the lucky one, then?'

'Deb, can I just say, you're sounding a tiny bit jealous.'

She snorted. 'Ha! Don't flatter yourself, Jack Johnson. Is she wearing a wedding ring?'

'Oh... ah... I don't know. I haven't looked.' And curiously, I hadn't. I had never developed such a habit during my marriage to Deb. For all its faults, our relationship had remained entirely faithful on my part and, I was pretty sure, on her part too.

'Oh God, Jack. You really are useless. I can't wait to tell Mary about this.'

'Bloody Mary' was Deb's vile and vindictive best friend who had never forgiven me for refusing to snog her once at a very drunken party.

'Yeah, well,' I said. 'Good luck with that. Look, I must go. I've got scuppers to sweep and cabin boys to keel haul. Thanks for the call.'

'Be careful, Jack. I want to know how this all pans out.'

'Yeah sure,' I said, whilst thinking to myself – don't hold your breath.

She disconnected fractionally before me, but I could still sense her suspicion and intrigue. I leaned back in the armchair, closed my eyes and fell asleep to the sound of a late-season wasp beating its head relentlessly against one of the portholes. I knew how it felt.

I woke with a dry mouth and a sore neck as the engine began turning over and I sensed the boat moving out into midstream. But by the time I'd had a pee, swilled water over my face in the tiny bathroom basin and combed my overlong mess of hair, we seemed to be pulling in again and coming to a halt. Climbing up the hatchway's steps, I saw that we had moved forward a short distance and come to a stop behind a line of five or six moored boats about two hundred yards from a road bridge.

'Wilmcote,' called Nina from the stern. She was still in her running gear. 'It's a nice little place with a couple of pubs. I've had a jog around. I thought maybe we could get a sandwich.'

I stuck up a thumb, jumped off to secure the bow's mooring rope and then strolled down to the stern deck. She ducked down into the boat and called up from her cabin.

'I'll just have a quick shower. See you in ten minutes at the first pub you come to.'

The hatchway cover slid shut from below and then I heard the door to the bathroom being bolted emphatically from the inside.

I shrugged, patted my pockets for phone and wallet and set off towards the bridge along the side of a small railway line. The village began almost immediately on the other side of the bridge with houses either side of the small road that crossed the canal. On the right I noticed a cluster of signs outside an ancient-looking timber-framed farmhouse with gables. Moving closer, I saw that they announced the building as 'Mary Arden's Farm – the childhood home of Shakespeare's mother'. I struck on for the pub, which I could now see up ahead at the far T-junction. Sure enough, it was called the Mary Arden and I wondered what the long-dead farming woman might make of her twenty-first century celebrity status courtesy of her world-famous son. All the outside tables were empty, so I decided to perch myself at one and wait for my lunch guest before ordering drinks.

Within minutes, Nina came striding into view. She was dressed as she had been before her run and with hair still damp from the shower. She slid in beside me and fished a tenner out of her rugby shirt's breast pocket.

'Glass of dry white wine and a wrap or a sandwich, please, with some kind of meat in it.'

Prompted by my conversation with Deb, I now noticed that there was a plain but expensive-looking band of platinum around the second finger of her left hand. I pushed the note back across the little round table's rough wooden surface.

'My treat. Wages in kind.'

She shrugged, re-pocketed the note and rolled her head around on her neck, loosening her neck and shoulder muscles.

I had a little think whilst I was being served at the bar and came back prepared with my opening shot.

'My ex-wife rang whilst you were out running.'

'Oh yes,' she replied, wholly dispassionately. 'So you're still on speaking terms?'

'Sure, well, growling terms, anyway. We're still friends – or trying to be. At least until I get half the money,' I confessed. 'She was very intrigued to hear about you.'

'Yes, I imagine she would be.'

'She couldn't work out why you'd suddenly help out a strange man who might be an axe murderer.'

She furrowed her brows at me. 'Are you? An axe murderer?'

'No. I'm pretty sure I'm not.'

'That's all right then. So, she doesn't need to worry about me, does she?'

'No, no... of course not.' I sipped my draught bitter to gain some time. 'But she was very curious about who you were and where you'd come from and why you're helping me out.' I coughed nervously, 'And whether you were married.'

She gave a slight wince which was followed by a very long cool stare. 'Yes, she was curious wasn't she, JJ? Well, if she rings again you know what to do, don't you?'

'What's that?'

'You just explain the ground rules to her, don't you? Cheers.'

CHAPTER THREE

The sun came out full and bright during our lunch, so it seemed wrong not to order a second round of drinks and enjoy the unseasonal heat on our faces. The little front garden of the pub was a picturesque suntrap. The tranquillity of the village street reminded me of dusty and seemingly deserted French villages where everything stood still for three-hour lunch breaks. The almost total silence was undisturbed by us as we both caught the mood of the moment and dozed over our drinks.

We agreed not to have a third drink without discussing the idea and meandered slowly back over the bridge and down to the boat. *Jumping Jack Flash* sat low and solid in the water, basking in the sunshine; its upper black and red paintwork was hot to the touch. Jumping Jack's manic leer was topped by a pair of piercing blue eyes that seemed to follow you eagerly as you went past.

Nina had warned me about the flight of eleven locks at Wilmcote, which we would shortly have to navigate on the final stretch of canal into Stratford. But the sun, food and drink combined to give me little enthusiasm for such a mid-afternoon burst of activity. Nevertheless, I was surprised when my tentative suggestion to stay berthed where we were and head for Stratford on the following morning was quickly accepted. We headed for our separate beds but her siesta lasted longer than mine and so I grabbed a small backpack and headed off to find some food for dinner.

I retraced our steps to the pub and the small village store almost opposite it. Next to the door, sitting on the floor, was a pale gaunt-young man with a scruffy brown terrier on his lap. The dog looked alert and clear-eyed in contrast to its owner, whose eyes were dull, hair long and matted and his clothes dirty and ripped. He was wearing a long tweed coat with unfashionably wide lapels – probably a charity shop find. As I went to move past him, he swivelled on his backside with surprising quickness and straightened both legs, putting his big clumsy black boots up against the far doorframe. He was now blocking my path into the shop.

'Hey!' I exclaimed.

'Yeah, hey there,' he said, whilst dropping his feet to the floor and standing up, the dog now held under one arm. 'Pleased to meet you. I'm Sam.'

I reluctantly took his outstretched hand and said, 'Hi.' But when I tried to extract myself he refused to let it go.

'Ah, come on. I told you my name, didn't I?' He had a faint northern accent, but it was hard to place, unlike his manner, which was straight out of the street handbook of passive-aggressive begging. I pulled my hand free.

'I'm Jack. Pleased to meet you. Now, I need to do some shopping.'

Sam positioned himself and his dog squarely across the doorway.

'So, yeah, shopping,' he said belligerently. 'Nice is it, when you've got the money to go shopping? Maybe you could spare me some cash so that I can go shopping too?'

Now, I'm all in favour of charitable giving. I've even been known to stop in the street and have a long conversation with earnest and polite young chuggers wearing T-shirts for Oxfam or Unicef or other worthy organisations. But I really didn't like this brand of begging by physical intimidation. Nor did I understand it. It was hard to age this guy but he couldn't have been more than mid-twenties. He was at least five inches shorter than me and a hell of a lot more scrawny. I had lost my last ever fight when I was in my early teens at school but I was pretty sure I could handle Sam if it came to a push and a shove. I brought my face up close to his sharp features, tried to ignore his ripe breath and stale body odour and smiled.

'No, I don't think so, Sam.'

He met my stare. Then he began to gabble a short breathless speech into my face at breakneck speed.

'Why's that then, Jack? If you don't mind me asking? I mean, in the great scheme of things it's not much to ask, is it? A few quid to keep me and my dog alive? Maybe a few quid more so I can indulge myself? Why not then, Jack? Will you miss a fiver? A tenner? Will you really? I saw you and your girlfriend having lunch. Nice lunch, was it? What did that cost, then? Hey? You on a boat, then? Having a nice holiday? Then what, Jack? Back to a nice three-bedroom house in a nice little cul-de-sac and a nice fucking tedious job so you can have another nice holiday next year? Is that it? I'm giving you a chance, Jack... to do something great in your mediocre life. You can give me some money, Jack, because I need it more than you. And you can feel good about that – or bad. Who gives a shit? Hey? I don't care how you feel. That's your business. But your money is my business at this moment... and you really ought to give me some, Jack. You really should.'

The torrent of words gathered pace even as he was speaking. A white fleck of spit appeared in one corner of his mouth and his eyes gleamed madly. During the final sentence he had begun prodding me hard in the chest with the grubby forefinger of his free hand. It hurt. The guy was unhinged or drugged – or both. I had had enough.

'Piss off.'

I pushed him roughly and he half fell to the floor, grabbing his dog with both hands and hitting the ground pretty hard on his shoulder and back. The dog gave a frightened little yelp. I moved past into the darkness of the shop. I half-expected him to follow me but having glanced round quickly, I reassured myself that I was alone. The fracas had caused a rush of adrenalin, so I took several deep breaths to calm myself down. Then I picked up a wire basket and toured the small number of aisles, loading up with milk, bread, wine and the ingredients for a pea and prawn risotto. I paid the young girl at the till, took a deep breath and headed for the door.

Sam was back in his previous prone position. I stopped at his feet, a carrier bag in each of my hands.

'Is your dog okay?'

It was on his lap and he was agitatedly stroking it with both hands. He didn't say anything.

'Look, I'm sorry I pushed you. Is your dog okay? Are *you* okay?'

'I could do you,' he said quietly. 'I could do you for assault. You attacked me. I could report you to the police.'

I should have been angry but instead, when he looked up at me, I was appalled to see tears streaming down his grubby cheeks. I squatted down so that my head was level with his.

'Look, I'm really sorry, Sam. I didn't mean to upset you or hurt you, or your dog. You wouldn't move out of my way and you were, well, you were being aggressive.'

Far from aggressive now, his face looked completely crushed and crumpled. He half sobbed, half sniffed and wiped his eyes with the baggy sleeve of his coat. His dog's saucer-like eyes were fixed on mine – large, brown and fearful. Its ears were pinned back.

'Oh, for fuck's sake. Look, come over to the pub with me. I'll buy you some food and a drink.'

He met my eyes, wiped his own again and nodded quickly once. Then he picked up his dog and trailed behind me to the table that I had previously occupied with Nina.

I left him there and went inside, ordered him a pint of cider and a steak pie, chips and beans from the bar and poured a half-pint glass of water into a plastic ashtray for the dog. I gave Sam the cider and told him some food was coming. He took a long swallow, nodded passively and sat quietly as did his dog. He was seriously messed up if his sudden mood swings were anything to go by. All trace of the angry stream of consciousness had gone and so now had his tearful episode. The food came, accompanied by a doubtful look from the young waitress.

'So, are you living rough?' I asked.

He paused, two chips and a smear of ketchup on his fork.

'No. I've got a room in a cottage near here with some people. But they're all in Stratty today.'

I imagined his friends in Stratford, with their own dogs and well-worn hard-luck stories targeting tourists before returning with loose change or foreign currency to be spent on... what? Cheap super-strength booze and drugs probably.

'Nice dog. What's his name?'

Sam didn't bother finishing his mouthful before replying.

'Eddie – he's young.' The dog looked up at the mention of his name and was rewarded with a piece of gristle from a cube of beef.

'Where d'you come from, originally?'

'Manchester. Salford.'

'Why d'you leave?'

'Fell out with my parents. Mainly my dad.'

The food was disappearing fast and with metronomic regularity now.

'Why was that then?' He looked at me.

'Why're you interested all of a sudden? You gay?' The question took me by surprise. 'No... no I'm not.'

'It's okay. I am. Well, bi anyway. Dad didn't like it. Threw me out.'

'So, you came south?'

'Yep, walked down the canals,' he said with a hint of pride. 'Slept rough mostly. Picked Eddie up a month ago. He'd been dumped in a box. Met Jazzer and stopped here.'

'Are you on drugs?'

The aggression returned instantly. 'Hey! What the fuck's that got to do with you?'

'I'm just curious. Honestly. People walk past people like you and sometimes they give them money or food, but they all secretly wonder what their story is. They want to know how they came to be sitting there with just a few coins and a dog to their name... and most of the time they're too shy or frightened or busy to ask.'

'Yeah, and d'you want to know why?' He pointed a dirty fingernail at me. 'Because they're all shit scared that it could happen to them.'

Sam finished his glass of cider and used his knife to scrape every last smear off his plate. Then he licked the knife clean.

'That was great. Thanks. Can I have some money too?'

I shook my head in disbelief at his front.

'Maybe. Answer a few more questions.'

He sighed, turned exaggeratedly, put his head on one side and smiled with patently fake enthusiasm.

'You can have a question for a pound. As many questions as you like. The more the better.'

'Are you on drugs?' I repeated.

'Whenever and wherever I can get them. That's a quid.'

'What came first? Being thrown out of home or the drugs?'

'It was just the scene, okay? When I was fourteen I went to Canal Street for the first time and discovered loads of men wanted to buy me. It was great money – especially the all-nighters in their big flash flats. But a couple beat me up. My mum found the bruises and my dad found the cash. But I kept going back. Sometimes they'd take me to their places and we'd have some blow. Then the business kind of dried up. I wasn't a nice cute little kid any more. But I had other habits by then…' He shook himself. 'That's worth two quid – so you owe me three.'

'How old are you?'

'Nineteen and that's four quid.'

I was shocked. He looked at least five years older.

'Why don't you get clean? Get some help?'

'Is that a question?'

I nodded. I was genuinely curious.

He just laughed. 'Don't want to. Life's too short.' He laughed again. 'Five quid.'

'What's your surname?'

He looked suspicious. 'I'm just Sam, okay? I won't charge you for that,' he added with a clear sense of his own reasonableness. The little dog had been tied to his chair with a length of frayed string for most of the lunch, but it was bored now, whining, sighing and quietly talking to itself. Sam bent down and lifted it back onto his lap but there wasn't a scrap of food left on the plate for it to lick.

'One more question...'

'Go on then.'

'I've got a boat nearby with a bathroom. D'you want to get cleaned up in some hot water?'

I expected a derisory rejection, but his bloodshot eyes actually seemed to water-up with emotion.

'You sure you're not gay?' he asked.

I shook my head. 'I'm sure.'

'Well, okay, yeah... thanks. That'd be good.'

He forgot to charge me a pound for the extra question.

During the walk back to the boat Sam told me there was no running water in the ruined cottage where he was squatting, but that there was a tap in some ruined outbuildings where they could fill a bucket for an occasional strip wash.

'Hot water,' he said dreamily, 'that's the biggest thing I miss from home. And me mam,' he added, as an afterthought.

I told him to wait on the towpath while I warned Nina that we had company, but the boat was empty. Her bags were still on board, though, so I knew that the crew hadn't abandoned ship in my absence.

I showed Sam the bathroom, checked the water was running hot and left him to it. Nina reappeared whilst he was still in there. She registered the noise of the shower and the steam escaping from under the bathroom door, but she only raised an eyebrow in enquiry.

'His name's Sam and this is Eddie.' The little brown dog was sniffing for his owner by the bathroom. 'Sam was begging up in the village. He's just cleaning himself up.'

She nodded slowly, scooped Eddie up off the floor and sat down in an armchair.

'You enjoy picking up waifs and strays, don't you?'

'Is that what you are, Nina – a waif and stray?'

She tipped her head sideways in thought. 'Sort of, yes, I am, at the moment.'

She fondled the dog's small triangular ears and it stretched out luxuriously along the gap between her closed thighs, his head balanced on one of Nina's knees.

'Well... at least Sam told me a bit of his life story, unlike you. Although I did have to pay him for it.'

She laughed, a nice sound but a rare one on the basis of our relationship to date.

'Really? How much?'

'A pound a question... and some of the answers were very short.'

'Hmmm – good tactics. I'll give it some thought but I don't think you could afford me. So why would you want to know his life story?'

'Just curious, I guess. Always have been. Probably why I went into journalism.'

'It doesn't feel like much of a reason, though.'

'Are we talking about Sam now, or you?'

She laughed again. But any reply was interrupted by the bathroom door swinging open and Sam reappearing with a towel around his waist and another draped over his shoulders. The bare flesh of his stomach and legs had an unhealthy blue-white hue and he was very thin. A tattoo started just below his belly button and ran down below the towel's hem.

'Oh, hi,' he said, eyeing Nina with his dog. 'Sorry. Just wondering if I could get some privacy and get dressed out here? It's a bit cramped in there.'

'No, you'll have to manage in there,' I replied. Nina raised an eyebrow at me, but Sam muttered something unintelligible and retreated back into the bathroom.

I lowered my voice. 'I'm not a complete pushover. He'll steal whatever he can if we leave him down here on his own.'

Nina shook her head in apparent sadness at my overly suspicious mind and took Eddie out onto the stern deck, nuzzling his head in the crook of her neck as she went. Sam reappeared five minutes later, dressed, face slightly pink and with an outstretched palm.

'You still owe me a fiver.'

I fished a ten-pound note out of my wallet and gave it to him. 'Keep the change.'

'Thanks very much,' he said, checking it and pocketing it very quickly in the back of his trousers.

I escorted him out onto the deck where Nina handed over Eddie – somewhat reluctantly – and they jumped down onto the towpath. Then he and the dog shambled off, back in the direction of the village. 'See you around,' he said with a raised hand, without looking back.

Nina and I watched him and Eddie go down the towpath in silence. From behind, I noticed the little dog's tail was slightly bent, as though broken in the middle. The two of them looked like a pitiably matched pair. Just as Sam reached the bridge, a dark blue Land Rover pulled to a halt next to him with a squeal of brakes. Sam leaned into the passenger's window and began talking to someone. I watched him reach into his rear pocket, take something out and hand it through the window. Then he put something back in his pocket again and stepped away whilst the Land Rover gunned its engine and roared off in a cloud of blue smoke. However, after no more than ten metres, it stopped and reversed just as quickly. Sam scooped up his little dog, opened a rear passenger door and got in. Then the Land Rover shot off again and was out of sight in a flash. Nina looked at me questioningly, but I just shrugged.

We both pottered companionably around the boat for a few hours. I attempted a cryptic crossword in the newspaper, started reading a previous holidaymaker's novel and eventually fell asleep. When I woke I noticed my crossword had been completed and Nina was chopping onions and crushing two large bulbs of garlic. The evening meal was uneventful but as we settled down in the failing light with more wine for her and a whisky for me, she asked me to tell her what I had learned about Sam. I told her the few facts that I had paid for.

'So that's it really. Poor sod. But I don't imagine it's an untypical story. I couldn't believe how young he was when he told me his age.'

'Yes. I imagine you age quickly with that kind of lifestyle,' she said quietly.

'Short life expectancy too,' I reflected and sipped my drink.

I checked the BBC weather for a localised forecast – colder but staying dry – and looked at a couple more websites before powering it back down and going for a final pee and to brush my teeth. As I finished clattering around I heard the quick repetitive sniffs of a person who had been crying coming from the other side of Nina's bedroom door. I almost instinctively knocked on it to ask if she was all right but stopped myself. Her fierce desire for privacy had been strongly expressed and it felt right to respect it, even if she was in some distress. So I padded back to bed and worried about her until I eventually fell asleep.

The fisherman sat on his plastic box. Once again, the line below his small orange float was bereft of any bait. He had spent most of the day meandering up and down the stretch of canal between Wilmcote and Stratford looking for the perfect spot. This was a much quieter stretch of water than the location of his last killing but it was still close enough to Stratford to get a reasonably regular number of walkers and runners going past. An attractive woman had jogged past him twice on her own just before lunchtime and he hoped she might decide on another late evening run. He had never killed a woman and the prospect excited him. He had parked his car at an industrial estate on the edge of town and finally decided on a lonely spot with no streetlights or buildings nearby. This stretch of canal was in the middle of a flight of locks where no boats had been moored for the night.

The fisherman gathered his plastic cloak about him. The strange pointed hood looked sinister, like he was a member of the Ku Klux Klan. Patience. It was all about patience. While he waited he congratulated himself on his achievements so far. Five 'accidental' deaths by drowning. Five! And there hadn't been a breath of suspicion voiced by anyone. His method was foolproof. His careful preparations and the choice of his victims meant that the only risk was being discovered in the middle of the act – and he'd make sure that didn't ever happen. He would go down in history as one of the greatest killers of all time. That would serve them right, wouldn't it? His bitch of a mother and all those teachers who said he was lazy and stupid and wouldn't amount to anything. He would show them. And those bastards at work. He'd show them all that he was clever and powerful and not to be messed with. The fisherman checked his watch. 11.30 p.m. There was only a tiny sliver of moon tonight and even that was regularly hidden by low cloud. Perfect conditions. *He could already tell that he would be successful tonight. When he was nervous a painful ball of tightness gripped the back of his neck where his spine entered his brain but tonight there was no such pain. He felt relaxed and sure of himself. But as time passed he began to worry. Nobody had passed him since a middle-aged couple with a black Labrador at 10 p.m. Maybe he was fooling himself. Maybe that was why he had no pain tonight. Maybe it was just too quiet – too far away from the pubs and clubs. It was doubtful that the lone woman runner would be out on another run this late in the evening.*

As usual, he heard the man before he saw him emerge from the darkness to his left. This one wasn't being particularly noisy, but the fisherman heard him clear his throat and spit out phlegm. He reeled in his line so there would be one less thing to do and pretended to check the hook. Then he checked to his right and across at the other bank but there was no one else in sight.

The man came towards the fisherman. He looked thin and hunched over against the cold, both hands deep in the pockets of his big woollen coat. One of his knees kept buckling uncontrollably though, a sure sign that he was ripe for a swim. He saw the fisherman and immediately speeded up and swayed towards him.

'Spare me some change, mate,' he slurred.

'Yeah, go on then,' replied the fisherman, standing up and reaching into the pocket of his cape.

Encouraged, the man closed the distance between them and stood expectantly with a hand outstretched, palm upwards. The fisherman pulled his own hand out of the cloak and reached out to the man. But instead of emptying cash into his outstretched hand he grabbed it and violently yanked the man forward over the edge of the canal.

His victim hit the water hard but came up fast, coughing and spluttering with both eyes wide open and showing a lot of white. This one was younger than the fisherman had first thought but his heavy coat and big boots would weigh him down. The landing net swiftly covered the boy's head and, with the heavy-duty metal frame resting on both shoulders, he was pushed back under the water. The fisherman twisted the net round twice, checked left and right again and then locked his arms, pressing down hard to force the thrashing mass to stay below the waterline. The struggling stopped after two minutes but this time the fisherman could risk making quite sure and he waited another two minutes before unwinding the net and pulling it back up. The top of the man's head surfaced briefly but then slowly sank back down into the depths of the inky black water.

The fisherman anticipated this one being found quickly as there was bound to be canal traffic using the flight of locks the following day which would disturb anything under the water. He had already taken off his cape and slung the strap of his box over his shoulder when he saw the dog. It was some kind of young brown terrier just sitting on the towpath and watching him from a short distance away. He should have seen it earlier. Should he try to kick it in the water? No – they wouldn't expect to find it there unless the man had been carrying it when he fell in. Should he try to catch it with his keep net? Definitely not. If he was seen with the dog people could eventually connect him with the dead man. He shrugged. Dogs don't talk and what could be more natural than a poor pet abandoned on the towpath where his master had accidentally fallen in and drowned? The fisherman set off towards Stratford and the dog slunk around him to sit on the towpath and stare at the flat empty expanse of black water where his friend and master had disappeared.

CHAPTER FOUR

It took a couple of locks on the Wilmcote flight for us to work out a system but then a routine quickly slotted into place. The locks were close together so I would walk along the towpath, which was the width of a car, make sure the water level in the next lock matched ours, swing open the single gate and Nina would steer the boat in. Then I'd close the gate behind her and open the bottom paddles, watch Nina and the boat sink down to the next level of water, swing open the gate at the Stratford end, close it behind her, drop the paddles and walk briskly down to the next set. At first she went too fast and caught up with me. But then she realised it was best to take it really slow and give me time to prepare the next lock so that she could go straight in without having to stop at the bank or try to keep the boat static in midstream.

There were a few cyclists, mid-morning joggers and dog walkers sharing the well-kept towpath with me who all called out a cheery good morning without exception. I reflected on how a canal towpath seemed to be such a nice and friendly place. It was colder than the previous day but still dry and that morning I had heard a radio weather presenter refer hopefully to this benign early autumn as an Indian summer. Nevertheless, the temperature was still falling as were the leaves, which carpeted the surface of the canal in places.

Nina brought the boat into the bank after the eleventh and final lock and I hopped on to join her by the tiller for a reasonably lengthy ride along a deserted stretch of canal before the town's eastern outskirts came into view. Another lock took us on through a rash of industrial estates where chain metal fences contained the detritus of small manufacturing firms. Other office-based companies had also sprung up along the canal's route with rows of company cars lined up outside small box-shaped buildings that seemed to have been designed to be as cheap and functional as possible. The business buildings slowly gave way to houses and shops and even a large supermarket as we moved on into the heart of Stratford-upon-Avon.

Until now, we had seen no other boats, but a pair came out of a cruising boatyard and Nina skilfully edged over to one side so that they could pass us by, port side to port side. Both had middle-aged couples at the helm with the smug contented looks of the retired and comfortably pensioned. They gave us good-natured waves of acknowledgement. After three more bridges and four more locks we crept under two very busy road bridges and the canal suddenly opened out into the expanse of Bancroft Basin. A restaurant boat, a floating art gallery and an ice cream boat were moored up close to the basin's entrance and opposite them were some pontoons which fish-boned out from the left-hand bank. Four of them were occupied by boats like ours. Nina thrust the tiller right over to one side and deftly switched between forward and reverse until *Jumping Jack Flash* had pivoted through 90 degrees and could edge alongside one of the pontoons. I jumped ashore to fix the ropes whilst Nina shut down the engine.

I grinned up at her. 'Very impressive. Well done.'

She grinned back with a little show of pride. 'The trick is to keep it slow and have the tiller pushed right over whilst you go forward and backwards. It was fun – but you had to do all the hard work coming down.'

'I needed the exercise more than you,' I said, ruefully patting the beginnings of what I feared would be my middle-age paunch.

'You do,' she agreed.

Now the business of manoeuvering and mooring was over, I looked around at our location and its surroundings properly for the first time.

We were slap bang in the centre of town and the peace of our previous night's mooring had been replaced by the constant hum of traffic, the regular high-pitched beeping signal of a nearby pedestrian crossing, shouts and screams from children playing on the nearby grassland and the occasional honk of swans and the quack of ducks. This clearly wasn't going to be suitable for anyone seeking privacy or tranquility. A gaggle of smartly dressed young Japanese tourists had lined up to watch and were excitedly photographing us; crowds of people were scattered all around the basin, pushing wheelchairs, eating picnics at benches or just standing and gawping. Facing us, across the grassland and a small road, stood a line of shops and cafes, which would enable us to restock the boat's provisions very easily, I thought. The cold air carried the smell of beef burgers and fried onions on the breeze.

The red brick façade of the Royal Shakespeare Theatre loomed up on one side with a new glass-topped tower at one end. Ahead of the boat, a statue of William Shakespeare, with his bald pate, moustache and goatee beard, was giving a thousand-yard-stare whilst holding a stone skull. He was probably trying to ignore the scores of visitors taking selfies with him, I decided. The steady flow of traffic over the nearby bridge would certainly be interrupting the great man's thoughts. There was no doubt our stay here would have a noisy backdrop.

I had read that my hire boat's Canal & River Trust licence meant we could moor in the basin for free. After asking Nina to put the kettle on, I set off to double-check that this was the case at the floating information centre at the end of the basin and to pick up a map of Stratford. The coffee was waiting in the pot when I got back and we sat companionably in the stern, sipping from our mugs and watching people who watched us back.

'I thought we might see if we could get some tickets for tonight,' I said, nodding in the direction of the theatre.

'What's on?' she asked. 'Comedy or tragedy? I'm not in the mood for tragedy.'

'Neither am I. But actually, it's historical – Henry V, Agincourt and all that.'

'I could be persuaded to go once more into the breach,' Nina said, 'but I really doubt that you'll get any tickets at this late stage.'

That was good enough for me.

'You leave that to me,' I said, quickly flinging the dregs of my coffee over the side. 'Back in an hour or so.'

I picked up a jacket and headed off to try to buy some culture. The Japanese tourists at our bow had been replaced by an extended family of tall and well-fed Americans who parted courteously to let me through. At the theatre, a friendly young woman at the ticket office told me she might be able to let me have two seats, but she wouldn't know for at least an hour.

'We have a seventy-two-hour limit on refunds,' she said. 'But we might be making an exception tonight. There's quite a big group and some of them have got food poisoning so the trip organiser is waiting to see if it wears off or not. He's got to get back to me by one o'clock or they get charged whether they come or not.'

I headed off to a nearby pub for a pie and a pint where I tried to recognise the cast of actors and actresses on walls crammed with old black and white publicity photographs.

I still wasn't sure what I was hoping for from this theatre trip. Nina was obviously well-read, and on the most basic level I hoped that the theatre would distract her from whatever was troubling her – because something obviously was. This opinion wasn't solely based on hearing her crying to herself the previous night. Her whole manner was one of a deep and lingering sadness that she was being momentarily distracted from by the effort of concentration needed to drive the boat. Moreover, my curiosity was even greater given the ferocity with which she fended off even the mildest of enquiries about her past, present or future. Perhaps an evening with the RSC might sufficiently relax this attractive and intriguing young woman to open up a bit?

I made sure I was back at the ticket office ten minutes before the one o'clock deadline with a spaniel-like eagerness written across my face. Sure enough, the gods were smiling – on me, at any rate. The tour party had full-blown food poisoning and a dozen tickets had been returned. They were expensive seats, but I cheerfully handed over my credit card to have three figures' worth of digits deducted from it. I carefully tucked the tickets into my wallet, thanked the young woman and took my booty back to the boat. Nina deliberately echoed my earlier words of congratulation at her boat manoeuvering skills, 'Very impressive. Well done,' finished her lunch of pre-prepared salad in a plastic container and announced that she was going to 'wander round town'.

'Want some company?' I asked hopefully.

'Okay – why not?'

We began to plot our way around the town centre streets, ticking off the 'houses of historical and architectural interest' and joining the queues of tourists to enter a couple of them. Some churches came and went, including one where we spent a happy ten minutes watching a student who was on his knees doing a brass-rubbing of a medieval knight. We completed a ramble along the river Avon, watched some people throwing bread at the swans and then cheered along some practice heats by a local rowing club – the singles zipping along in jerks like water boatman insects and the eights powering along in energetic unison.

Slowly, as the afternoon wore on, and as we kept all our conversation in the present, Nina began to visibly relax. She began suggesting where to go next rather than allowing me to lead. She even joined me in a game of guess the tourist's nationality.

I pointed to a pair of statuesque white-blonde older women. 'You first.'

She wrinkled her head in concentration.

'Sweden – definitely,' she said.

'Nope. Norway.'

She squared her jaw. 'Only one way to find out.'

She marched confidently up to them, dragging me reluctantly by one arm. The couple laughed and confirmed they were visiting from their home in Stockholm. Nina punched the air and then my arm.

'Six-four to me. Do you give up?'

'First to seven and the loser buys the ice creams,' I suggested.

She looked around competitively and pointed at a large Asian family group of four or five different generations. 'Anglo-Indian.'

'Final choice?' I said.

'Hmm. Or Anglo-Pakistani?'

'Choose.'

'Okay – Indian.'

'And I say Pakistani.'

Nina almost ran over to the group, full of childish excitement and chatted briefly with a young mother with a baby in a sling on her front. Then she turned around, gave a huge grin and pointed me at the nearby ice cream boat. I shook my head in mock grief and trooped off to get two cones. By the time I returned she had found a small boat doing tours along the Avon and back and bought two tickets. The boat was about to leave so I had to run with an ice cream in each hand as she laughed and urged me to go faster. Breathlessly, I jumped on board to a small cheer and round of applause from the other passengers, including Nina. She helped herself to an ice cream, pushed her chocolate flake into mine and led the way to a couple of empty chairs in the stern.

We dipped under one arch of a long old stone bridge and some riverside homes appeared on the far bank, their long sloping gardens and lawns stretching down to the river. She studied the first one closely.

'That's a five.'

'What?'

'Five out of ten.'

I looked at the house, which looked palatial and immaculate to me. As someone with barely even a boat to live in, it also looked to me significantly beyond the financial reach of most mere mortals.

'It's a nine from me.'

She opened her mouth in mock disbelief and pointed at the next home as it slipped past. 'Six – but only because it's got a cute little boathouse.'

'Ten.'

And so we progressed upriver, scoring each house in turn, with Nina always going first and me always adding at least two points to her valuations. Her put-downs were pithy and deliberately snobby.

'Just too, too mock-Tudor, darling.'

'Probably belongs to a successful hairdresser.'

'Ughh... look at the colour of those window frames.'

'Trying just too darned hard.'

'Plastic children's play equipment and a plastic greenhouse – minus two.'

She was funny, relaxed and sharp – a new Nina that I had not encountered in the past forty-eight hours. Other passengers were listening in to our game and quietly smiling at Nina's damning judgements. For an apparently homeless lady-of-the-road, she had a very high threshold when it came to residential properties. Many of these riverside homes would easily cost more than a million pounds but they failed to meet her exacting standards. Once more I reflected that she must have had a privileged upbringing. She was certainly no stranger to the finer things in life.

As the boat turned to cruise back in the opposite direction, Nina fell silent to study the sparsely populated banks, her arms spread flat, her fingers interlaced and her chin lowered to rest on them. This time we travelled on past the centre downriver alongside some water meadows towards a weir and lock, before turning again and returning to our point of departure.

'That was fun,' she said as we disembarked. 'Although you are a man of remarkably poor taste when it comes to houses.'

'Perhaps,' I conceded. 'It's probably connected to my lack of readies to buy them with.'

'Oh no, you're wrong there. You don't need money to appreciate quality and style.'

'But you do, maybe, need to have grown up and lived in big houses to judge them quite so harshly?'

She stopped and looked me squarely in the eyes.

'That, Mr Johnson, sounds like a question rather than an observation and, as such, may constitute a breach of the golden ground rules.'

'Ah yes, the ground rules.' I sighed heavily. Nina laughed and moved on two paces ahead of me back towards our own much more modest floating home.

As we crossed the lawns and flower beds that bordered Shakespeare's statue, another boat was just arriving on the other side of our pontoon. A trim grey-haired couple in their sixties, dressed in matching blue and white striped sweaters, were preparing to moor up. Nina and I stepped forward to share the tying-up duties.

'Very good of you, thanks very much,' said the well-spoken woman in the bow as I completed a figure of eight around the cleat on the pontoon. 'Have you been here long?'

'Just since this morning,' I replied.

Nina busied herself with the padlock on our hatchway whilst I retied the rope so that it was tighter and neater.

The woman's husband joined her. 'We would have been here hours ago, but they closed the canal further up to fish out some poor soul who'd drowned,' he said.

'We had to moor up for ages,' the woman complained.

'How inconsiderate,' I muttered under my breath.

'Ambulance, police divers, the whole works,' said the man. 'You didn't see anything when you came down this morning?'

'No, nothing. It was a clean run. Where was this?'

'Middle of the Wilmcote flight,' said the woman. 'Oh gosh.' She put her hand to her mouth. 'I wonder if he was already under the water when you went past?'

'It's a wonder you didn't bring him up,' said her husband, somewhat ghoulishly. 'Propeller and movement of the boat, that sort of thing.'

It might well be a wonder, but I didn't like to dwell on the idea and I didn't want this grim news to spoil our happy afternoon.

'Yes, well, we must get on I'm afraid. We're going to the theatre.'

'Us too,' said the man. 'We're running bloody late now. Might see you later then. Enjoy the show.'

Nina had already switched on the yellow wall lights in the main cabin and was brewing a pot of tea. The table was laid with cups, saucers and a little plate of biscuits. A handful of coal in the stove had quickly brought the temperature up to single-layer level. Mozart's clarinet concerto was playing quietly on the radio in the saloon. She looked up as I came down into the boat. 'What were the neighbours saying?'

'Nothing much – tales of their epic voyage. They're going to the theatre too.' I was damned if I was going to risk spoiling Nina's newfound cheerfulness with news of a drowning on the canal that we had travelled down only hours earlier.

'Well, if we're going to eat before curtain up, we'll need to get a move on. Need to change.'

She took her mug of tea down to her berth. Shortly afterwards I heard the shower going. I slipped a clean jumper over my shirt, ran my fingers through my hair, rubbed the toes of my only decent pair of shoes against the back of my trouser legs and reckoned I was ready for a cultural night out.

Nina reappeared from behind the swing door and, at once, I felt intolerably shabby. She had a white collared shirt on with both of the top buttons open to reveal a grey pearl hanging from a simple gold chain necklace. A tapered black skirt and elegant heels completed the simple but chic ensemble. Once again, I wondered about her luggage and what thoughts had prompted her choice of contents to pack.

'Wow, I feel underdressed.'

'Don't worry. The lived-in look suits you. Come on. I'm hungry.'

I was relieved to see that the couple next door were still inside their boat as we left. I showed Nina back to the pub where I'd had lunch; my selfless research had indicated it was popular as a pre-theatre watering hole.

'The Black Swan?' said Nina as we approached and she saw the pub sign.

'The locals call it the Mucky Duck.'

She laughed and fate continued to smile on us as a tiny window table emptied just as we walked through the door.

Nina sipped her large glass of chilled New Zealand Sauvignon and then voiced my unspoken thoughts.

'Thanks for this afternoon. It was fun. I came here once on a school trip to the theatre. But we didn't see any of the town and it was a lifetime ago.'

I nodded. 'Me too. I must have been fifteen or sixteen. I came up with an inspirational English teacher and his few favoured pupils. I suppose it would be frowned on now, but I think he just wanted us to have great cultural experiences. He took us up to West End theatres too. We happy few were the hardcore of the school's drama society.'

'What did you do?'

'Oh, *Waiting for Godot* once – in upper sixth. It was one of our A level texts so it seemed a good thing to do. Helped me to quote reams of it in the exam. It was the only one I didn't screw up. I wanted to do law but ended up in journalism. Definitely a close escape.'

'Go on...' she encouraged. I was happy to oblige.

'I was Vladimir and my best mate was Estragon. That's Will, in fact, the deeply unreliable actor who let me down with the boat. One of us had a real memory problem on the night – or maybe it was both of us. I think we did half of one whole act twice. But I don't think anyone noticed – it's so bloody repetitive anyway. The scary old army major who taught German fell fast asleep and was snoring with his head tilted right back in the first row.'

'Do you remember any lines?'

'Lots, actually.' I sipped my pint of Doom Bar bitter. 'The nihilism struck a chord with my adolescent self at the time. *They give birth astride of a grave, the light gleams an instant, then it's night once more.*'

She let the bleakness of the words sink in. 'And do you still believe that?'

'*But that is not the question*. Then it goes on, blah, blah, blah, something, something, something... *Yes, in this immense confusion one thing alone is clear. We are waiting for Godot to come.*'

Nina put her hands together in mocking applause.

'Although of course, Godot never comes, does he? A bit like your friend Will! I haven't ever seen the play, but I know that much.'

'True. The waiting is the whole point. Bit of an anticlimax really.'

'Just like life then?' This time Nina took a gulp of wine and her eyes seemed to fill with moisture.

'Oh, I don't know,' I added hastily. 'Even if the light only gleams for an instant, well... you might as well make the most of it.'

Just then, thankfully, the food came. Nina had grown more thoughtful and reserved again after this flurry of slightly one-sided conversation. But she cleared her plate of its fillet of bream, new potatoes and salad and as we strolled the short distance across the road to the theatre she grew bright, cheerful and chatty again. The crowd was already quite dense; a mixture of school parties running amok, smartly dressed middle-aged, middle-class regulars who strode through the foyer with practised familiarity and tourists eagerly taking in the scene for the first time. I paid for a programme, handed it to Nina and we went through to the stalls just as the doors opened and tickets began to be checked. It took about twenty minutes for the audience to fill the theatre and settle. Whilst the excited hum of conversation became louder as the audience grew bigger, Nina and I paid particular attention to any couples taking their seats and speculated whether they were lovers, happily married or married and having an affair with their theatre companion. The first couple was easy – our clearly happily married neighbours from the marina. They spotted us and gave us a friendly wave. After we'd giggled companionably over the first five pairs she turned to me.

'But, of course, you can be a lover to the person you're married to, can't you?'

'Yes, of course,' I said. 'When I said lovers, I suppose I just meant unmarried.'

'Hmm... Mr Johnson. For a journalist you have a distressingly slipshod attitude to language.'

'I'm a damaged divorcee,' I admitted.

'Marriage can be the expression of ultimate love,' she declared firmly, bringing our game to an end.

Then the house lights dimmed, a disembodied voice reminded everyone to turn off their mobile phones and we were into the play. I stole a glance sideways at Nina as the chorus entered for the prologue. The actor was familiar from some TV drama or another, but Nina's face was rapt with attention as he asked whether this cockpit could hold the vasty fields of France. He finished with a plea: 'Your humble patience pray, gently to hear, kindly to judge our play.' I was to remember this quite vividly afterwards.

A couple of grey-beards dressed anachronistically in double-breasted business suits rattled through the opening scene, which set out the political background of the story, and then King Henry strode onto the stage with a collection of dukes and attendants. He was a head taller than the others and dressed in the khaki camouflage of a modern-day British army officer. I heard a sharp intake of breath beside me. I looked at Nina. I could sense she was visibly trembling and even in the darkness I could tell that her face had gone deathly white.

'Nina? Is something the matter?'

I reached for her hand, but she snatched it away. She was still staring at the stage, her mouth and eyes open. I followed her gaze. What was the matter? It was Shakespeare, for God's sake. Did Nina know one of the actors? Was he the cause of her current retreat from the world? The actor playing the Archbishop of Canterbury was well into his opening scene, explaining to Henry at tedious length why he was justified in waging war against the French. Like Henry, the nobles were all in modern-day army dress – ankle length black boots wrapped in puttees, desert camouflage trousers and green jumpers with shoulder and elbow pads. The setting was that of a modern war-room rather than the palace of a fifteenth-century king. I didn't have much time to ponder what the problem could be because Nina suddenly rose up from her seat with a muffled sob of apology and began pushing past the people in our row of seats. I trailed helplessly in her wake, whispering apologies as I tried to keep pace with her rapid exit. I heard the action on stage falter and then resume as the disturbance in the audience came to the attention of the cast. Once clear of the seats and in the aisle, Nina ran up the wide carpeted stairs and pushed her way past an attendant with a noisy bang of the swing doors. I followed her through and managed to grab her arm above the elbow as she tried to retreat further down the corridor.

'Nina... what the hell?'

Two theatre attendants, one man and one woman, bore down on us.

'Sir, madam... you really can't just leave like that. You disturbed the whole performance.'

I ignored them.

'Leave me alone... let me go.' Nina twisted in my grasp.

'Nina! What's the matter? For God's sake, are you okay?'

'Sir, perhaps you should take your hand off the lady?'

'Mind your own fucking business.'

'Now then, sir, we won't tolerate abuse to our staff.'

'Security to door four, please.'

'Nina?'

'I repeat, security to door four, please.'

Nina's distress was disturbing to witness. Tears were rolling down her cheeks and her beautiful dark eyes were dribbling black mascara. She seemed to be hiccupping and sobbing at the same time. I felt as if she would fall to the ground if I let go of her arm.

'Now then, sir, let's let go of the lady, shall we?'

Two strong hands reached round from behind me and broke my grip. Nina almost collapsed into the woman attendant, who wrapped an arm round her and ushered her away around a corner and out of sight. I was spun round to face the black T-shirt, broad chest and shaven-haired person who represented 'security'. He was even taller than me, almost twice as wide and half my age. I took a deep breath as his muscle-knotted arms kept my own arms pinioned on either side.

'Look, I'm sorry, okay. My friend was distressed. I don't know why. She just ran out of the play and I'm trying to find out why.'

'It looked as though she was trying to get away from you, sir.'

The male attendant who was loitering nearby said, 'Shall I get the police, Ralph?'

Ralph smiled nastily. 'Well, that's up to the gentleman and whether he's going to leave the theatre quietly now.'

I quickly figured that Nina wouldn't be hanging around for long and that my best chance of being reunited with her was to wait by the main entrance doors.

'I'm going,' I snarled, and managed to shake myself free. Ralph and the male attendant closely stalked my every step on the walk to the main exit. I looked right and left for Nina as I went but there was no sign of her. Outside, I peered at the boat in the distance and although it was quite far away, I couldn't see anyone moving near it. Ralph stationed himself just inside the door with his arms folded, watching me with an unblinking and well-practised hard-man stare. After half an hour of pacing up and down outside, I went back inside to speak to Ralph.

'Look, can you just tell me if my friend is still here, please?'

His eyes bored into me once more and he shook his head slowly.

'Is that a no, then?' I asked. 'Or are you just trying to convey that you think I'm a wanker?'

'That wouldn't be polite, would it, sir?'

'No, it wouldn't. Look, I was here with a friend. Something in the play upset her. She ran out. I tried to catch her, to comfort her and then you waded in.'

I took my wallet out of my back pocket and fished out my four-year-old membership card for the National Union of Journalists.

'You should know that I'm a bona fide journalist on a national newspaper and I'll be making waves about this place's standard of customer service unless you answer me, okay?'

His eyes narrowed even further as he looked at the card. I kept it firmly in my hand, one thumb carefully positioned over the expiry date. 'It's a simple polite question. Is my friend still here or not?'

He thought it over; I could almost hear the cogs grinding between his ears. Then he turned away from me and muttered something into his headset. There was the indistinct crackle of a reply and he turned back round.

'The lady has left the building, sir,' Ralph said. Then he stepped up close, craned forward so that his mouth was over my right shoulder and whispered, 'So, now, why don't you do us all a favour and piss off too?'

This time I took his advice. I ran back to the boat. Both Nina and I had a key but as I got closer I saw the hatchway was still shut and there were no lights on inside. I slumped onto a bench nearby and rubbed my face vigorously. What on earth had just happened and where was she?

CHAPTER FIVE

A vibration in my back pocket sent me scrambling for my phone, but even as I pulled it out I realised it couldn't be Nina. At no stage had she asked for my number, or even indicated that she had a phone herself. It was Deb. I groaned inwardly. I was in no mood for a jolly catch up with the ex-wife, but I was also feeling confused and lonely after Nina's tearful exit. It might be good to talk – even to Deb. I pressed the little green icon.

'Hi,' I said sullenly.

'Hi, Jack. So, how's the big adventure going? Where are you?'

'Oh, you know, it's okay. We're moored up in Stratford-on-Avon.'

'We? So, the mysterious lady crew-mate is still with you.'

She didn't exactly stress the word *mate*, but the monosyllable had a particular emphasis.

'Yes... well, no. Actually, she seems to have disappeared in the last hour.'

'Oh, Jack. What have you done?'

'Nothing. Absolutely nothing. I took her to the theatre and she suddenly went ballistic about a minute after the curtain went up. Something really upset her and she stormed out with me trailing after her. Then I was held by security for a bit because they thought I'd upset her in some way and by the time I was released, well, she had just vanished.'

'That all sounds pretty weird.'

'Yes, it's all very strange.'

'Nina's done a runner,' Deb stated slowly and thoughtfully. I wasn't surprised that she had remembered Nina's name. She had that kind of attention to detail when it came to my failings.

'Well, not quite. She hasn't been back to the boat – all her things are still on it. She honestly seemed quite upset and I haven't a clue why. She'd been pretty happy all day...'

'Oh, really? So, you've been getting to know each other quite well then?'

I was starting to regret accepting the call. Deb wasn't being at all sympathetic or even thoughtful about the situation. If anything, she just sounded a bit jealous and, as usual, I was on the defensive. I reminded myself that we were divorced and ploughed on.

'We had a pretty good day in Stratford, yes. But she's a complete bloody mystery, to be honest. I don't think Nina is her real name. I know absolutely nothing about her and she's kept it that way for more than forty-eight hours now.' I was cross now. Cross with myself for having this conversation, cross with Deb for the way it was going and cross with Nina for walking out on me. 'She refuses to say a thing about herself, anyway.'

'Some women use mystery to keep a man interested Jack.'

'Deb, sometimes you talk so much crap...'

I heard an indistinct mumbling in the background and broke off.

'What about the wedding ring, Jack?' Deb asked then. 'Did you look?'

My hackles rose. Someone in the background had planted the question. 'Is someone there with you, Deb? It's Bloody Mary, isn't it? Snooping around as usual. Have you got her listening to all this on the bloody speaker?'

'Don't be silly, Jack. Mary's a good friend to me.'

'Yeah well, Mary, if you're listening and enjoying this, get a bloody life of your own, you vulture. Bye, Deb.'

I furiously punched the little red icon and stuffed the phone back into my pocket.

I felt it vibrate again but ignored it.

Two pissed and half-dressed teenage girls staggered past, giggling and holding each other up as they weaved along the towpath. I watched them stagger close to the edge with some apprehension. They looked so young and vulnerable. I wondered suddenly if I would be more or less anxious about a son or a daughter, if I ever had children of my own. The seemingly endless expense and stress of IVF treatment had put me off the idea, but I knew my sperm was fertile and perhaps one day it might still happen. The two girls continued towards the lights of the town, balanced precariously on vertiginous heels and shrieking with laughter.

These thoughts brought on a fresh wave of anxiety about Nina and her own vulnerability. I pondered my options. Should I find the local police station and report her missing? They'd probably laugh in my face: she'd been gone for barely an hour. I didn't know her surname – in fact I probably didn't even know her real *first* name – she'd walked off in a perfectly sober state, under her own volition. She was distressed, but that was just my word. The theatre management might tell a different story. No, it was probably not a good course of action at this stage. I considered going to look for her. I could wander the streets of Stratford all night to try to find her. But it seemed a bit futile trying to find one woman in a town of 25,000 people. She could be anywhere. On the other hand, if I didn't try I would feel awful. She had a key to the hatchway and if she returned to the boat she could always let herself in. I decided to go out again.

Clearly, Nina had wanted to be alone for a while. What was she likely to do to calm down? Go somewhere peaceful, a church perhaps? Or just go and swallow a few stiff brandies? There was no shortage of pubs to do that in. But she would probably avoid the Mucky Duck on the basis that this would be the first place I'd look. Without much hope I walked over the large sweep of grass to the pub where we had enjoyed dinner and did a quick tour of its darkest corners. There was no sign of her. I stopped at the bar for a drink. The situation called for something strong. I had a large Laphroaig with a splash of water and then another before making my way back to the boat. A number of theatregoers had spilled out for an interval cigarette and a low hum of chatter reached me. I swerved off to join them in the unlikely event that Nina had returned for the second half but there was no sign of her. Ralph's arm-folded and mountainous presence was still just inside the doors and made it impossible for me to check any further inside. So, I re-traced my route back to *Jumping Jack Flash,* which remained closed up, dark and empty. The jester's mocking leer was starting to annoy me now.

I unlocked the hatchway, slid it back and walked down the steps past the two single beds, one of which still had Nina's bags on it. I very deliberately put on all the lights, poured myself another glass of whisky, kicked off my shoes and stretched out on the double bed. I lay there for an hour, my mood swinging from frustration to anger to worry and back again.

Finally, I poked my head out of the hatchway, took a long slow circular look around and decided to give up for the night. I pulled the hatchway closed without locking it, had a lengthy pee, stripped off leaving a pile of clothes on the floor, killed all the lights except for the one above Nina's bed and collapsed into my own. The whisky and the warmth of my sleeping bag quickly sent me into a deep sleep. At one stage I was vaguely aware of the couple next door returning to their boat and at another I registered loud shrieks and laughter as the pubs and clubs emptied. The nagging awareness that Nina was missing didn't prevent me from sleeping but it did prevent me from achieving any kind of deep unconsciousness.

Then suddenly I jolted awake. The mattress had dipped and a body pressed itself against my left-hand side. My sleepy confusion cleared quickly and I realised it was Nina – largely from the smell of her Jo Malone red roses cologne. I had familiarised myself with it after she had left the bottle on a shelf in the bathroom. I took a deep breath and turned my head towards her. She was lying on her right-hand side with both her hands tucked under her head. Her big dark eyes were looking straight at me from the ghostly pallor of her face.

'Sorry.'

I wasn't sure if it was an apology for rushing out of the theatre, for waking me up or for lying on my bed without an invitation. It could have been all three or none for all I cared. Nina was back. She removed her left hand from under her head and stretched it across my chest. My own arms were cocooned inside the sleeping bag leaving me frustratingly powerless to move or respond in any way. Her voice was little more than a whisper.

'Don't move. I just need a hug.'

I forced my body to relax and took some deep slow breaths to recover from the surprise awakening.

'Where've you been?' I asked quietly. 'I've been worrying about you.'

'Just walking about. The play upset me.'

'Yes… obviously.' I tried to keep my voice quiet and level. 'But why, Nina? What was that all about?'

She tightened her arm around my side and then released it.

'Thank you for worrying about me,' she said quietly. 'But I don't want to talk about it. I'm okay now. Can I just lie here for a bit?'

I thought about struggling free, sitting upright and demanding an explanation but I knew I would get nowhere by forcing the issue. She was reaching out for the first time for some kind of comfort and that was progress in itself.

'Sure,' I whispered. 'Take as long as you like.'

She nodded her head very slightly and closed her eyes. I was wide awake now, staring at the long thin panels of the wooden ceiling a few feet above me in the darkness. A silver slice of moonlight shone through a chink in the curtain that partially covered the porthole opposite my bed. I could easily make out Nina's features as her breathing steadied into a slow and regular rhythm. Her arm across my chest was a dead weight now with no hint of a grip. I needed to turn on my side to return to sleep but I stayed on my back, reluctant to disturb her. The same instinct prevented me from pulling my wrist free to check my watch, but I guessed it must be about three a.m.

I must have drifted off after a while because I jerked awake for the second time as the mattress moved. It was lighter in the cabin now and I could hear the dawn chorus warming up outside. I pulled my watch in front of my nose and registered 05:15.

'Nina?'

She must have been standing in my pile of discarded clothes. She put an index finger to her lips.

'Shush... get some more sleep. It's still early.'

She left and I listened as she undressed and climbed into her own bunk. The narrow line of yellow under her door went black as she clicked the light off.

I have to confess that once she had gone my thoughts began to stray into what might have been. Whilst Nina slept next to me, my only concern was that she recover her equilibrium and that I didn't disturb her. I had felt fraternal about her close physical presence in my bed. Now that she had gone, I all too quickly conjured up a fantasy in which she had walked up to my bed naked and confident and happy. In my imagination, she had squirmed down into my sleeping bag and her lithe body had moulded itself to mine, the fresh dark red lipstick she had worn to the theatre leaving small marks all over me, like the smudges of ricochet marks on a squash court's walls. I shook my head vigorously from side to side. *Pull yourself together, Johnson, you sad old bastard.* These were the mad unbidden thoughts of the very early morning and I was instantly ashamed of them.

I remembered a feature article that I had subbed for the paper once and smiled to myself in the dark. It explored the notion that the average man thought about sex every seven seconds. The author had worked out that this amounted to 500 times an hour or 8,000 times during sixteen hours of a day's wakefulness. Who knew what the rate was when we were asleep? It had seemed ridiculous to me and I had gone searching online to check the facts. I recalled stumbling across a report that said researchers at Ohio State University had given a group of eighteen to twenty-five-year-olds handheld monitors to measure how often they thought about sex, food and something else. The little bastards weren't quite as horny as the story suggested. But they still pressed their sex buttons nineteen times a day on average, or once every 1.26 hours. I chuckled at the memory of the writer's annoyance when I suggested he incorporate the research I had found into his piece. But we quickly made up over a pint after work and I remembered a vigorous debate over whether older men would think about sex more or less than younger ones. Some of the female subs had argued that older men probably did it less and so thought about it more. The writer and I joined forces, reasoning that older men were wiser and more rounded people who had other things to think about – like mortgages, jobs and dependent children. The evening had deteriorated into widespread drunkenness and, somewhat ironically, I remember Deb gave me a frosty reception and an even colder back when I crept into bed later that evening.

Eventually, my random and meandering thoughts receded and I managed to drift back to sleep again. I woke at eight o'clock to the sound of people talking as they walked past the boat and the murmur of the rush-hour traffic inching its way into town. Nina poked her head around the corner of her swing door.

'Hi,' she said brightly. 'I'm going to Costa. Fancy a large bucket of Americano?'

There were grey smudges of tiredness under her eyes but no other signs of the previous night's trauma. My voice, however, sounded several octaves lower after too much whisky and too little sleep. 'Yes, please. Cold milk.'

'… and no sugar. See you in a bit.'

The tiredness of my disturbed night and slight hangover mostly slipped away with the water of my hot shower. I was dressed and smoothing out my bedclothes when Nina returned bearing two newspapers, two huge cardboard cups of coffee and a bag of muffins. She put her spoils down onto the table and sat down. The events of the previous night hung in the air, unspoken between us.

'Nina...' I began. She turned to face me with a sad smile, her head tilted to one side.

'Nina, I'm sorry but I need to know why you were so upset last night. It really freaked me out and I'd like to help if I can.'

She sighed heavily, stared down at the floor for a bit and then looked up at me. Her usual feistiness had gone but she still managed to be direct and to the point.

'I'll tell you if and when I'm ready to, Jack. You were very lovely yesterday and I loved our day together. The play upset me – let's just leave it at that. I needed a hug and you gave me one. Or you could say I helped myself to one anyway. I'm sorry you wasted your money on the tickets. I'll pay you back.'

She put one hand on top of one of mine as I opened my mouth to protest.

'Please, Jack... just give me some space. This boat is a lovely little safe haven for me at the moment and I think I'm being useful, which is a good feeling. That's all right with you, isn't it?'

At least this was now a plea for privacy rather than a peremptory order. Her vulnerability was disconcerting. I squeezed her hand and took mine away.

'Okay. It's maddening but okay. If that's really what you want.'

She surprised me by leaning forward and touching my forehead with her lips. 'Good man. Now then, national or local?'

I took the *Telegraph* whilst Nina held onto the *Stratford Herald* and we made our way out onto the foredeck's benches with our coffees and muffins. It was a little chilly, but I welcomed the fresh air.

'Oh, listen to this,' said Nina almost at once. She was looking at the paper's front page. '*Police are seeking the public's help to identify a young man whose body was found in the Stratford Canal yesterday.*' I wonder where he was found?'

I nodded at the boat opposite us. 'The couple next door were held up by the police activity yesterday afternoon. I didn't want to say anything after our lovely afternoon and, well, before we went to the theatre.

Pretty depressing stuff. We were already moored up here when it was all going on though.'

'Oh.' She read on. *The body was spotted in a stretch of canal at the Wilmcote flight of locks by a dog walker who alerted the emergency services. A police spokesman said: 'A post mortem is to be carried out and the coroner has been informed. We are checking our missing persons records and ask that anyone with any relevant information contact Stratford Police Station. The man is thought to be aged between late teens and mid-twenties and was wearing a long tweed coat and black boots.'*

She stopped.

'Poor sod,' I said. 'Horrible way to die.'

Nina was staring at me.

'A long tweed coat,' she repeated. 'Jack, you don't think…'

I stared back at her, perplexed. Then I realised the full horror of what she was thinking. My stomach flipped in sudden apprehension.

'Sam. Sam was wearing a long tweed coat. And black boots. And he's the right age.'

Nina looked at the story again.

'It doesn't say anything about a little dog. Maybe it isn't him.' She paused. 'But the dog could have run off… or been drowned itself.' She looked up from the paper, her eyes wide. 'Oh my God, Jack. We need to check he's okay. We need to find out if it was Sam.'

Deep down, I had a terrible sense that it was. 'How though? We know hardly anything about him. We don't even know where he lives. He just talked about some old farm cottage and he was probably squatting there.'

'Well, we can tell the police that. They can make enquiries.'

I nodded. She was right. 'I think he was hitching a lift after he left us,' I said, remembering the blue Land Rover.

'It could have been more than that,' she replied quickly. 'He seemed to know them, don't you think? They seemed to swap something over.'

I pictured Sam's thin young face, changing so quickly from aggression to self-pity and then grinning with cunning as he answered my questions for a pound a time outside the pub. I remembered him demolishing his free lunch and pint of cider. I remembered him telling me about his life in Manchester and his clear fondness for Eddie, the little brown terrier. Had we really cruised down the canal yesterday morning, totally unaware that his skinny, pale and lifeless body was lurking somewhere in the silt and weeds under our hull, being stirred and disturbed in the water's murky depths by the blades of our propeller? And if it was Sam, how did he end up in the water?

It took half an hour and two disgusting cups of coffee from a vending machine before the coroner's officer arrived in the police station's reception and introduced himself. Sergeant Brian Milk conformed to my cub-reporter memory of his particular breed of police officer. He was in his late fifties, carrying a lot of extra weight and he probably had a long and largely undistinguished career as a lower-ranking detective behind him. He had no doubt been carefully chosen as a coroner's officer for his no-nonsense organisational skills and his sensitivity with grieving relatives. His heavily creased face and buzz-cropped grey hair suggested an air of lived-in competence that had seen it all but without the overly cynical air cultivated by most of his former colleagues in CID. He wore a dark grey baggy suit, a shiny red-and-black striped tie and big black shoes with toecaps and rubber welts that could only have belonged to a police officer or a security guard. He referred to a slip of paper that the receptionist had completed.

'Mr Johnson and Mrs... ?'

This was interesting. Was I about to learn my crewmate's real identity? I couldn't suppress a small grin of enjoyment as I turned to look at 'Nina' with one heavily cocked eyebrow.

She didn't bat an eyelid, however. She took his outstretched hand firmly and replied, 'Just call me Nina, please. I'm a friend of Jack's... uh, Mr Johnson. Just here to help if I can.'

Sergeant Milk looked at me quizzically but then shrugged and nodded.

'So you think you may have an idea who the body in the canal is – or was? Is that right?'

We were all still standing in reception. A few other people were sitting, leaning back against the wall and listening intently, whilst trying not to make it obvious.

'Perhaps we could go somewhere a bit more private?' I asked.

The sergeant squeezed the bridge of his nose between his eyes with a thumb and index finger. It could have been exasperation or just a sign of tiredness, but he simply nodded again and said, 'Yes, you're right. Come this way, please.'

Sergeant Milk punched a number onto a keypad and took us through a door, along a corridor smelling of bleach and into a small room labelled IR (3). He slid a small wooden board on the door from right to left so that 'unoccupied' now read 'occupied'. Then he motioned us both to hard chairs on one side of a metal-topped table that had been bolted to the floor and sat down opposite us. He pulled a biro out of an inside jacket pocket and held it poised over the scrap of paper with our details on.

'I'll get a proper statement later if it's needed,' he explained when he saw me looking. 'Just tell me what you think you know, please.'

I gave brief details about how Sam had been begging outside the village shop in Wilmcote with his dog. How I had taken pity on him, bought him lunch, asked him about himself and taken him back to the boat where he had met Nina and cleaned himself up before clambering into a blue Land Rover. I described Sam and his clothes as best as I could and passed on the few details he had shared about his past. I also mentioned the tattoo we had seen below his navel.

Sergeant Milk jotted down a few notes as I spoke and Nina stayed silent. When I finished, he looked at her.

'Anything to add Miss... er... Nina?'

'It was a nice little dog. A brown terrier. I think it was called Eddie.'

'Hmm. Well, there was no sign of a dog at the scene, I'm afraid, but from what you say, it could be him. The description seems to tally and you were moored up not too far from where he was found. Just wait here, please.'

The sergeant came back with an official statement form and leaned against the wall whilst I sat at the table and wrote down what I had already told him. He read it through, signed and dated it and, after I did the same, he folded it in two and put it into an inside jacket pocket.

'Now, I'm sorry to have to ask you this, Mr Johnson, but it's our best chance. I need you to try to identify the body.'

Nina gave a sharp intake of breath, but I'd suspected this might be coming.

'Just me? Or both of us?' I asked.

Sergeant Milk thought about this for a minute. 'Why don't you both come? Then if you're in any doubt, sir, we can ask the lady for a second opinion. But hopefully we won't have to ask you, Miss.'

It wasn't going to be a pleasant experience, but Nina nodded.

'I'll need to make some arrangements – then I'll come and fetch you from your boat later this morning.' He glanced down at his paper. '*Jumping Jack Flash*, tied up in the basin, is that right?'

Nina and I made our way slowly out of the police station. We were both feeling pretty shaken. It seemed likely that I was going to come face-to-face with Sam once more, but this time on a mortuary slab. I had managed to go through life without ever seeing a dead body in the flesh. The ordeal of the viewing was going to be grim even if it didn't turn out to be Sam. I seriously hoped it wouldn't be Sam, but I also hoped that a second opinion wouldn't be called for and that Nina wouldn't have to share the unsettling experience.

We arrived at the local hospital a few hours later in Sergeant Milk's unmarked car. There had been no conversation during the journey. We were too preoccupied, anticipating what was to come. The hospital no longer had facilities for surgical operations and there was only a very limited accident and emergency service. Sergeant Milk explained that an operating theatre at its rear had been maintained for autopsies and the cold storage of bodies until they were released for burial or cremation. He parked his car in a space reserved for staff behind the main building, put a card saying 'Police Business' on the dashboard and let us in through an unmarked door. He then asked us to wait in a corridor before disappearing through a second unmarked door, where we heard him talking to another man. Sergeant Milk reappeared after a few minutes, fetched a chair from along the corridor for Nina and ushered me through to the next room. The smell of formaldehyde was overpowering. A large metal tray with a slight slope and a drainhole stood on solid chrome legs in the middle of the room, but my attention was immediately drawn to what could only be a covered body on a trolley next to it.

'Over here, please, Mr Johnson.'

A man dressed in a light blue smock and trousers stood behind the body. I barely took in his appearance as I moved towards the trolley, my eyes fixed on the sheet covering the body's head.

'Ready?'

I took a deep breath and nodded, my heart pounding. The attendant reached both hands forward onto the top hem of the covering sheet and brought it down so that a neat fold lay across the corpse's neck.

There was no question about it.

It was Sam.

The flesh on his face, which had been an unhealthy grey in life, now had a ghostly blue-white pallor and his sharp, lean features were puffy, his nose and cheeks artificially swollen, his high cheekbones much more rounded. His eyes were closed but his hair still hung down in a mess of matted ropes.

Sergeant Milk coughed. 'You mentioned seeing a tattoo on his body when he had a shower on your boat? Is that right?'

I nodded, too wary to speak in case my voice let me down.

Sergeant Milk nodded to the attendant, who covered the face once more and then raised the bottom of the sheet up over Sam's scrawny white legs, exposing his shrivelled penis and his torso just above his navel. The tattoo I had seen disappearing below the waistband of Sam's towel had been the start of a dragon's tail that twisted and spiralled into a head, gaping mouth and forked tongue that pointed downwards on his lower groin.

I nodded again.

'Mr Johnson, you're sure this was the man you met at Wilmcote, called Sam?'

'It's him... there's no doubt in my mind. There's no need for Nina to see this.'

Sergeant Milk nodded. 'Thank you, sir. You can come away now.'

I turned away from the body and paused for a second before I left the room, trying to swallow the bile rising up in my throat and push back the nausea. Nina looked intently at me as I came into the corridor. I just nodded sadly and she came forward to give me a hug. I hugged her back while the sergeant looked on patiently. We separated, still under his scrutiny, and waited for him to tell us what would happen next.

'Thank you for your assistance, Mr Johnson. Now we've got a lead on who he was, I'm going to have to go out to Wilmcote and do a bit more asking around. I need to see if I can get a surname. Find out where he was living, if I can.'

'Well –' I broke off to cough. My tongue could almost taste the chemicals that had smelt so strongly in the autopsy room. 'If there's any more help you need?'

'I think we can take it from here, sir. But if anything else springs to mind, please give me a ring.' Sergeant Milk fished two business cards out of a plastic container and gave us one each. 'Now, I'll take you both back to your boat.'

As we drove back, Nina in the rear seat and me in the front, I asked when the inquest would be.

'Next week if I can get a firm identification.'

'Do you think it was an accident?' I asked.

Sergeant Milk looked at me sideways.

'Probably. No sign of suicidal intent at present. And he had more than enough booze and drugs in him. He could have missed his footing easily in the dark.'

'He didn't seem to have any money for drink and drugs,' I replied.

'No, sir. But you gave him some money, didn't you? Amazing what these people can buy when they know the right people... or the wrong people, rather.'

I was annoyed by the sergeant's dismissive reference to 'these people' and disturbed by the implication that I might have inadvertently helped Sam to his doom, but I stayed quiet and chewed my lip.

'Will I be needed at the inquest?' I asked eventually.

'I doubt it, sir. Your statement should be sufficient. It'll all be pretty much cut and dried once we know exactly who he is.' The sergeant quickly corrected himself. 'Was. You say he mentioned family in Manchester? We'll want to find them and let them know.'

'I'd still like to attend. I didn't spend much time with Sam, but I liked him. I was wondering...'

'Sir?'

'Well, perhaps we could drop Nina at the boat and I could help you try to find out who he was back at Wilmcote?' I could sense Nina bristle at the idea of being left out but, until I discovered the cause of her distress, I was reluctant to involve her in another ugly situation. I could also sense the big policeman was drawing breath to refuse my request, so I pressed on quickly. 'I know the shop where he hung around and I might remember something else which helps you.'

'Well, it's pretty irregular, ' he rumbled, 'but it might be helpful. Thank you, sir.'

Nina put her head forward to the left of my headrest and hissed into my ear. 'Why can't I come?'

Sergeant Milk pretended not to hear. I turned round and gave her a firm look.

'Too mob-handed,' I said. 'I'll brief you later.' She pushed herself back into her seat and folded her arms crossly.

Five minutes later we were stopping the traffic briefly to let Nina out onto the road near Shakespeare's statue. I tried to avoid her furious look as I quickly hopped back in and we pulled out to head out of town.

CHAPTER SIX

Sergeant Brian Milk's stomach was rumbling. I could hear it from the passenger seat. He was a careful police-trained driver, so he signalled well in advance of the layby. He changed down carefully through the gears and pulled up just behind the burger van and a handful of parked cars. I joined him at the hatch. It was almost lunchtime but there was no queue and I was peckish too in spite of the disquieting visit to the mortuary. We ordered two burgers with onions and brown sauce.

'So then, on holiday are you?' he asked while the meat sizzled and spat on the hotplate.

'No. Not really. I'm trying out the boat before I buy it to live on.'

The sergeant gave me a shrewd look. 'And the young lady? Your girlfriend, is she?'

It was interesting that he had automatically assumed we weren't married even though Nina was wearing a wedding ring. Then I remembered Nina's reluctance to give him her surname and guessed that he thought we were having some kind of illicit affair.

'No, she's just a friend who's helping me move the boat around.'

The sergeant had seen *Jumping Jack Flash* when he came to fetch us. 'Aye, she'd be a handful for just one person true enough.'

The burgers were flipped to brown their other sides. 'Are you talking about Nina or the boat?' I said, deadpan.

He laughed and I felt myself warming to him.

After swallowing his last mouthful of burger, the sergeant belched quietly and I started sipping scalding hot tea, which tasted of polystyrene.

'We should have enough to go on to find out who the kid was,' he said thoughtfully.

'He told you he was living in a run-down cottage somewhere near Wilmcote and had a friend called Jazzer. Shouldn't be too hard to locate.'

He pulled out his smartphone, punched in his security code and accessed the latest of his photographs. I tried not to be too interested in what he was doing but he saved me the bother with a shrug and turned the screen towards me. Sam's young puffy white features stared back, his eyelids open and his skinny shoulders bare. 'Just in case we need it.'

It must be very difficult, I reflected, not to become blasé about death when you were dealing with it on a daily basis; to retain real compassion and sympathy for the survivors. I wondered what the burnout rate was for such officers. Most seemed to do it at the end of their careers. Perhaps a lifetime in such a role would be just too much. Ten minutes of the formaldehyde was more than enough for me. We had just got back into the car when my own mobile phone rang. The number was unrecognised. The sergeant pulled his hand back from the ignition key and waited for me to take the call.

'Hullo?'

'Jack? It's Nina. Remember me?'

So, she did have a phone hidden away along with goodness knows what else in her voluminous kitbag. I decided to ignore her pointed question.

'Nina, hi. What's up?'

'I got your number from the boat hire documents. I've been thinking about the dog, Sam's dog, Eddie.'

'Hang on a mo… I'm putting you on speaker.' I pressed the speaker icon and turned up the volume. 'Sergeant Milk is listening too. Go on.'

'Well, I was wondering what happened to Sam's dog,' she continued.

'Like I said,' the sergeant said with a sigh, 'there was no sign of a dog when the body was spotted or at any time during the recovery process. And we were there for at least two hours.'

'Yes, I know,' Nina persisted. 'I was just wondering though whether you had checked the local dog rescue centre?'

Sergeant Milk sighed again and crushed his serviette into a tight ball.

'No.' He was speaking at me rather than towards the phone. 'I've been a bit busy trying to find out the dead lad's real name since you came into the station. And even if the dog is out there, it's not going to help me much, is it now? Not unless it can speak.'

'I suppose not,' she said.

'Nina, I think we need to focus on Sam so that we can let his family know what has happened,' I said.

'Yes – well that's what you are doing isn't it?' she shot back. 'So I might as well do something useful too. Do you have any objection to me checking it out? I'd like to know if the dog is okay.'

Sergeant Milk looked at me and I hunched both shoulders to indicate 'what harm can it do?'

'Jack? Sergeant? Are you there?'

'Okay, Miss. I don't see why not. If anyone's found him running around as a stray, the station might have a record. I'll check it out when I get back.'

'Thanks very much,' said Nina, sounding genuinely excited. 'I'll dig out the number of the dog rescue centre and see if they've got him.'

'Aye, you do that,' grumbled the sergeant quietly.

'See you later, Nina.' I grinned and hung up. It sounded like she was on a quest and that would be a harmless distraction from whatever was distressing her.

We parked in the centre of Wilmcote and the sergeant stretched his large frame with a grunt as he got out of the car. We walked over to the shop. The same teenage girl was behind the counter, vigorously chewing gum and examining her dark blue nail varnish. It was a weekday so she couldn't still be school age, I thought, but not far off. Despite the late September temperature, she was wearing a pair of cut-off denim shorts fraying at the knees and a crop-top which exposed her slim midriff, complete with a black navel ring. She flicked a heavily lacquered fringe out of her hair as we approached.

'Hello, Miss... on your own today?'

She registered the sergeant's lack of shopping bag and his cheap shiny suit and quickly looked me up and down too.

'The manageress deals with reps. I'm not allowed to. And she's out. Sorry, you'll have to come back later.'

Sergeant Milk pulled out the warrant card with his photograph on it and showed it to the girl.

'I'm a police officer. What's your name?'

The girl almost stopped chewing her gum, but not quite. She didn't change her slouched position either, but he had her attention.

'Gina... Gina McQuiggan. I haven't done nothing,' she said sulkily.

'It's all right. Didn't say you did, did I? I'm trying to trace a young man who was found dead in the canal. We think he may have lived round here. He hung round outside the shop asking for money. He had a little brown dog and um... what do you call them? Dreadlocks.' There was something comical about the way he pulled imaginary tresses of hair down from his grey crew-cut head.

'Dead?' she said, coming out of her slouch and standing up straight behind the counter, her heavily made-up eyes open wide.

'Afraid so... yesterday afternoon. We need to find out who he was, Gina. Any ideas?'

She pulled the gum out of her mouth and began rolling it between her thumb and index finger.

'Yeah, sure. He'd hang around scrounging outside the shop. The boss wouldn't let him in, but I gave him old tins of meat for his dog a few times. I never really spoke to him. He smelt a bit. He turned up about a month ago. I don't know his name, though... honest.'

Sergeant Milk nodded. 'Any idea where he might have been living?' He quickly corrected his verbal clumsiness. 'Staying. Any idea where he could have been staying?'

Gina shook her head. 'They're all posh twats round here. Can't see them putting him up. And he hasn't been in any of the council bungalows or I'd know about it.'

The sergeant stayed quiet. Good coppers, like good journalists, know when to shut up and be good listeners.

'He must have been staying round here somewhere, though, because he was always going past or dossing down outside. A lot of the customers didn't like it, but what can you do?' She put the gum back in her mouth and began chewing vigorously again. 'Maybe he was on one of the farms. They take people on for fruit picking and stuff.'

A bell above the door pinged as an elderly lady came in. She was wrapped in a green quilted jacket and pulling a wicker basket on wheels.

'Hello, Gina,' she called out in a firm well-spoken voice.

'Hello, Mrs T,' Gina called back.

The woman tilted her head back to look directly at me and Sergeant Milk. 'Good afternoon,' she said sniffily, before vanishing along the aisle closest to the door.

'So what farms are we talking about?' asked the sergeant.

Gina looked blank. 'Well, it's the countryside, innit?' she said. 'There's loads of 'em.' She gestured vaguely with an arm movement that swept from east to west. 'Me and Mum have only been here a year. What a boring dump. Can't wait to go back to London.'

Mrs T was now approaching the counter, a few tins of soup and dog food in her wire basket. Gina turned to her.

'This is a policeman, Mrs T,' she said self-importantly. 'He says that lad with the little dog who begged outside has been drowned in the canal. He's trying to find out where he lived.'

Mrs T looked Sergeant Milk up and down and then began emptying her basket onto the counter. 'It was a rather nice little dog,' she conceded. 'It looked like a Border terrier. But probably full of fleas and worms.'

Sergeant Milk allowed himself to raise an eyebrow at me.

'Yes, well, it's the lad we're concerned with, ma'am, rather than the dog. He may have had parents in Manchester. We need to find out who he was, so we can let them know.'

'Awww,' said Gina sympathetically. She began to swipe the barcodes on the tins against the till.

'Drood Cottage,' said Mrs T.

'I'm sorry, what was that?'

Mrs T turned to look up at the police officer.

'He was staying at Drood Cottage. It's a wreck of a place in the woods on the edge of Chester Farm. There's a few of them living rough there. I saw some smoke in the chimney when I walked past with Ted a few times. That boy was sitting outside with that dog on his lap.'

'Ted?' asked the sergeant.

'Yes, Ted.' She looked at the sergeant as if he was particularly slow. 'My chocolate-brown Labrador. Of course, Ted completely ignored the other dog. He always does,' she added with satisfaction. 'He's very particular about who he sniffs and who sniffs him.'

Gina finished swiping the last of the tins. 'There you go,' she said. 'Mrs T knows everything that goes on round here.'

'I rang the Major about them. But he said the cottage didn't belong to the farm. I always thought it did because it's so close to their fence. But apparently it was just abandoned when the old lady who lived there died. That was twenty years ago, and it's been falling down ever since.'

Mrs T clearly didn't regard herself as resembling an 'old lady' in any way, I thought.

'The Major?' the sergeant asked.

'Major Jones owns Chester Farm,' she said with an air of fast-diminishing patience. 'He won't know them, of course. But I imagine the others at the cottage might help you. I really wouldn't advise you to go bothering the

Major. He really gets very fierce about any uninvited visitors, very fierce indeed. And anyway, you're not really dressed for it.' She allowed herself a secret little smile, then turned to Gina. 'Thank you, dear.' Her beady eyes had already registered the price on the till and she pulled a debit card from a small leather purse, touched it onto the pay point device and then swept out, pulling her shopping basket along behind her.

'Quite a character,' commented the sergeant.

'Aww, she's lovely really. Got all her marbles, has Mrs T. She's always out walking with her dog, so she sees everything that's going on. If she says the boy was staying at Drood Cottage, then he was.'

'So where is Drood Cottage then?' asked Sergeant Milk. 'Or Chester Farm?'

'Search me,' said Gina. 'You should have asked Mrs T. I've heard some terrible stories about that Major, though,' she added with a shudder.

I was intrigued to hear more but the sergeant had already darted back out of the door, doubtless to try to catch Mrs T and her trolley. But when I got outside there was no sign of the elderly lady, or her brown Labrador, for that matter. Her movements were clearly as quick and sharp as her mind and her manner. Sergeant Milk sighed heavily, checked his phone for messages then nodded towards the pub. 'Maybe the landlord'll know,' he said.

As we headed in towards the public bar a ping sounded on my phone.

'I'll catch you up,' I said. I showed my phone the index finger of my right hand to give me access and stabbed the text message icon. It was from Nina.

> No dog's home in Stratford. Any stray dog found with no tag/microchip is sent to Birmingham. Trying to get hold of local dog warden. Fingers crossed.

The sergeant was leaning against the bar when I entered. A middle-aged man in an apron stood waiting behind the bar to take the order. The only other occupants were two men sitting at a corner table with half-drunk pints of bitter in front of them. Ex-military, I thought, taking in their short back-and-sides haircuts, their muscular frames and their smart-casual dress. Both had check shirts underneath crew neck sweaters and black jeans tapering down to two pairs of well-polished boots.

'Yes, gentlemen, what'll it be?'

Sergeant Milk ordered a pint of bitter shandy and a ploughman's lunch and I did the same. The barman said he didn't know the whereabouts of Drood Cottage and so we took our drinks to a table near the other two customers. Sergeant Milk nodded at them.

'Alright,' one of them responded without a smile.

The sergeant took a gulp of shandy. 'Don't know if you can help me? I'm looking for Drood Cottage. D'you know it?'

The pair exchanged a glance and the stockier of the two spoke first.

'Oh aye?' he said in an unfriendly manner. 'I don't think it's for sale.' His mate snorted with laughter and added, 'You'd need to spend a pretty penny on that place.'

The first one continued. 'Aye, we know it. It's close to our boss's land. Who wants to know?'

The sergeant ignored the question. 'Would that be Chester Farm, run by a Major Jones?'

The two looked at each other again. Their body language changed. They both now seemed to be wired and tense.

'What do you want at Drood Cottage then?' asked the stockier one.

'Police business,' said the sergeant. The men stiffened even more but the sergeant gave no outward sign of noticing their change in demeanour. He pulled out his phone, punched in his security key, brought up the picture of Sam's face and slid it onto the other men's table.

'We're trying to find out a bit more about this lad,' he said calmly. 'He was pulled out of the canal yesterday. Family in Manchester, apparently. I've been told he was staying at Drood Cottage.' Two closely shaved chins bent over the phone. Eventually, the stocky one looked up, speaking slowly.

'No. Never seen him before.'

'Nor me,' said the other, quickly following his friend's lead. Too quickly, I thought.

Sergeant Milk took his phone back.

'Well, perhaps you can kindly point me in the direction of Drood Cottage?' he asked.

The barman came over and put down some cutlery and a sharing platter of cheese, bread and pickles in front of us both. As he did so, the two men simultaneously drained the substantial amounts of beer in their glasses and stood up to go.

'Drood Cottage?' said Sergeant Milk again, taking a hefty bite out of a pickled onion.

'Look, it's a bit difficult to find,' said the stocky one. 'It's down a path, about half a mile into the woods. It's on its own.'

The sergeant looked directly at him. 'So how do I get to this path?'

The man was almost squirming in his anxiety to get away. His partner had already detached himself and was waiting impatiently by the door.

'Out on that road for a few miles, turn left at the first crossroads... go on past the signpost for the drive down to Chester Farm on your right and you'll see a bridle path sign on the right after about a mile. You'll need to park there and walk.' He looked down at the police officer's footwear. 'You have to go down a steep hill, cross a stream and go up the other side... might be a bit damp.'

'I've got boots in the car. Thanks very much.'

The man turned to go but the sergeant stopped him.

'Just a minute, will you?' He pulled out a scrap of paper and a biro and asked the man to repeat the directions whilst he jotted them down. The other man had now left the room and a vehicle horn impatiently demanded that his friend should join him.

'I've got to go,' the man said. 'Work to do.'

'I won't keep you,' the sergeant said. 'Thanks again.'

'Something you said?' asked the barman, clearing the glasses. Somewhere in the background, I heard a diesel engine accelerating away at speed.

The sergeant shrugged and bit into a chunk of Cheddar.

'Ex-army, are they?'

The barman nodded. 'They work for the Major, so they must be. Don't give much away though. I don't even know their names. They pop in a few times each week for a bite. Never say much though.'

'That's Major Jones, is it?'

'That's right, up at Chester Farm. Big spread he's got. Miles and miles of those plastic tunnels. But he never comes in here, thank goodness. They say he's got a nasty temper on him. Trigger-happy, you might say. And he wouldn't like our dress code, would he?'

'What do you mean?' I asked, remembering that Mrs T had said something similar.

The barman chuckled to himself and began polishing an ashtray. He looked up at us, his sole customers and winked. 'Just don't go calling there unannounced, if you know what's good for you,' he warned.

Before we could ask any further questions a woman's voice called from the other bar and the barman slipped out in its direction. My phone pinged again. It was another text from Nina.

> Tracked down warden and he's got Eddie! He'll bring him to the boat. Result!

I sent back a thumbs-up emoji and slid the phone over for Sergeant Milk. He finished his bread and cheese, swallowed the remainder of his pint and wiped his hands on a paper napkin.

'Nice to get a proper lunch break,' he said with satisfaction.

'I thought that the burger from the van was lunch?'

'Looks like you've got an extra crew member, with four legs,' he remarked nodding at the phone.

I decided to call it a one-all draw and we headed back to his car. Back in Stratford, the sergeant dropped me off close to the basin. A call had come in demanding his presence in another part of town so it seemed that finding Drood Cottage would be a task for another day. I found Nina lying prone on her narrow bed, one hand behind her head and the other absentmindedly smoothing Sam's little dog. It appeared to be no worse for whatever ordeal it had gone through and showed no obvious signs of missing Sam – but that's a dog for you. Born survivors. Indeed, the dog seemed untroubled: it lay on its back on Nina's stomach without an apparent care in the world. Its forepaws were bent neatly forwards, its back legs splayed outwards and its little pink hairless tummy rose and fell rhythmically whilst Nina stroked it gently with the tips of the fingers of her free hand. The dog barely registered me coming through the hatchway and down the narrow steps where this cosy little tableau greeted me. A slash of sunshine was slanting through the open crack of the hatchway and Nina had put a warning finger to her lips to prevent me disturbing her new companion. The hum of people's voices on the bank and the occasional splash of a duck or a moorhen landing on the water nearby was all that disturbed the quiet. The boat's wooden veneer walls and ceiling contributed to the atmosphere of cloistered peacefulness.

'The dog warden was a sweetheart,' she whispered, waving me to sit on the other bed. 'He'd only just qualified with a zoology degree.' The dog raised his eyes to the back of his head to look at Nina as she continued in a hushed voice. 'Some children had found Eddie wandering around on an industrial estate near the canal. Their parents called Peter – the dog warden. There was no name tag or microchip, so he was planning to take Eddie to Birmingham tomorrow if nobody claimed the poor little thing.'

So far, I hadn't had a chance to say a word. Nina was clearly enthused by her successful search and captivated by the young terrier.

'But when I explained what had happened to Sam, Peter couldn't have been nicer.'

I reflected that an eager young graduate wouldn't have stood a chance when confronted with Nina's determined and attractively set jaw.

'I had to sign a form saying his owner had died and you were taking over ownership and that was that,' she whispered with satisfaction.

'What?' I forgot to whisper and Eddie turned his head to stare at this loud and unwelcome new intruder. 'What do you mean *I'm* taking over ownership? I can't have a dog.'

'Shhh...' she said. 'Don't upset Eddie. Of course you'll have him. I had to give your name because it's your address... your boat. And anyway, he'll be wonderful company for you. And a very good guard dog. Peter completely agreed with me. Now, I'd just love a cup of tea, but I simply can't move without disturbing him.'

Annoyed but powerless, I banged through the door towards the galley with enough force to leave it swinging several times before it settled.

CHAPTER SEVEN

I was having a lie-down while Nina continued to fuss over Eddie in her bunk when my mobile vibrated. The caller was Deb. This time, I decided to ignore it until the vibrations stopped. I didn't have the energy for her questions and I was still sulking about Nina landing me with the dog. I woke with a start an hour later at the sound of a commotion in the hatchway. Nina was talking to someone. The far door swung open and Sergeant Milk's big florid face appeared apologetically from behind it.

'Sorry to disturb you both,' he said, his voice sounding unnaturally loud in the boat's interior.

'Tea?' I asked, rising to rinse out the mugs in the sink.

The sergeant was busy examining the interior of the boat with interest; his large frame seemed to fill the small space. Nina had followed behind him with Eddie cradled in the crook of both arms.

'No, thanks. Look I won't hang about. I just wondered if you fancied coming out to help me look for Drood Cottage? I was about to go when it occurred to me that it might help if I took his dog along. I spoke to the dog warden and he told me it was here. I don't know who the lad was living with – you say he mentioned someone called Jazzer? Well, I thought they might not like having the police around so perhaps the dog and a civilian might help a bit... ' He tailed off, but I knew what he was getting at. 'And the little fellow might like a run in the woods,' he added, although it was already clear that Nina didn't need any additional incentive.

'Of course,' she said, eagerly. 'If they're anything like Sam they probably won't want to co-operate at all. But we've got to trace his family and Eddie might help to break the ice. We'll come with you, won't we, Jack?'

'I'm not sure it's a good idea to get you mixed up in this,' I said to her.

She stared back at me with unblinking eyes.

'Yes, well, this time I get to decide for myself and I'm coming, whether you like it or not. Eddie trusts me and he doesn't need any more strangers dragging him around.'

I opened my mouth to protest but the sergeant cut me off with a shrug.

'It's all right by me,' he said. I shook my head at Nina but she just tilted her chin upwards and poked a tongue out at me.

'Come on,' she said, 'We're wasting time.' I was quietly fuming to myself. Surely she could realise that I had good reason to keep her away from the investigation into Sam's death? Her apparent strength of character was clearly masking a fragile inner core if the scene at the theatre was anything to go by. But she was determined.

The dog warden had given Nina an old leather lead and collar that she slipped round the dog's neck. We returned to the sergeant's car and set off towards Wilmcote, Nina in the back with Eddie, and me in the front alongside the hefty bulk of the police officer and the remains of his most recent snack.

A local commercial radio station burbled quietly in the background, filling the silence whilst we made our way back to the village where we had moored overnight. I wondered who or what we might find at Drood Cottage and if there were friends of Sam there, how would they react to news of his sudden death? I also wondered about the mysterious Major Jones and the two men who worked for him at Chester Farm. They had denied all knowledge of ever seeing him before but they had certainly been in a hurry to drink up and leave the pub once they realised they were dealing with a police officer. I kept my thoughts to myself for the moment.

Once we reached the pub again, the sergeant slowed, dug a scrap of paper out of his pocket, muttered its directions to himself and headed off out of the village. We drove for a little while until we passed a small but neat sign in the hedgerow: Chester Farm. A long straight lane headed off at right angles to the narrow road we were on. The sergeant checked his mirror punctiliously and came to an abrupt stop. He reversed until the little car was sideways on to the drive and took a long look down it. But there was nothing to see. Just a long narrow stretch of tarmac ending in a hedge where, no doubt, the drive swung away in one direction or the other. The sergeant engaged first gear and we set off again.

'Should be about a mile from here,' he muttered. The sergeant took the winding lane slowly and sure enough a bridleway sign came up that pointed into the woods on the right. There was nowhere obvious to park on the narrow lane, so he drove on slowly for fifty metres until a passing place appeared. He switched off the engine, pulled out the small laminated sign saying 'Police Business' from the door pocket and put it face up on the dashboard again. 'Right then,' he said. 'Off we go.'

Sergeant Milk pulled a large pair of well-used black rubber boots from the car's boot and grunted as he put both feet into them. Nina and I exchanged glances at our trainers. Eddie was straining at the lead, whining with excitement. He seemed to recognise the sight of the path that sloped down through the densely packed trees.

The slope was steep almost immediately and there were the rotting remains of wooden planks and pegs that had obviously been used in an attempt to create steps in the steepest stretches. The path seemed pretty well used and the recent overnight rain had left it treacherously smooth and slippery. The sergeant led the way, Nina and Eddie following, whilst I brought up the rear.

As we walked, I wondered again what we would find at Sam's 'home'. Judging by the remoteness of the cottage and the effort required to reach it, the occupants wouldn't be used to visitors arriving unannounced.

Sam's lifestyle would suggest that his housemates might not welcome a visit from the police, let alone a whole delegation of strangers. It would be interesting to see how the taciturn coroner's officer would deal with them.

At the bottom of the steep valley's side we discovered a small metal footbridge with a gate at each end. The stream below was barely a trickle, but its soft muddy banks made us glad to use the bridge. The path rose steeply on the other side and the sergeant began to wheeze heavily as he pushed on his thighs to get up the incline. The hill began to flatten out after about five minutes and the path opened up into a track with knee-high banks of earth on each side and trees that sprouted at regular intervals. Someone had deliberately planted them many years ago.

I could smell the cottage before I saw it. The scent of wood smoke reached me before I glimpsed glass and red bricks through the trees. The sergeant caught sight of it at the same time, nodded and strode on. The cottage slowly took shape in front of us as we approached. It ran parallel to the track, roughly twenty metres to the side of it. It was two storeys high and largely made up of ancient red-coloured bricks on the ground floor with rotten overlapping timber boards making up the second floor. The end nearest us had a small ground floor window with a brown cloth hanging down inside it and a tree emerging from the apex of the roof above. Brambles ran right along the cottage's frontage, completely blocking one of the other two windows we could see. The roof, which sagged desperately in the middle, was missing slates in several places and the skeleton of the wooden roof joists could be seen at one point. Old ceramic pots, broken glass and the charcoal footprints of outdoor fires littered the approach to the building. It must surely have been the cottage of a gamekeeper at some point. I couldn't imagine why anyone else would live in such an isolated spot. There couldn't be any connection to electricity, although I remembered Sam had mentioned an outdoor tap that supplied cold water. It was probably connected to some kind of spring or borehole. A few more years would see nature completely reclaim the old building.

Having approached closer to the cottage, my nostrils now picked up a different kind of smoke. I had last smelt it whilst walking beside the canals of Amsterdam. Eddie had seemed to know his way along the path only too well, straining at the lead and threatening to pull Nina over at times in spite of his tiny size. Now he was desperate to pull us all closer to the cottage. Nina bent down and picked him up. She tucked him in the crook of her right arm and put her left hand under his chest whilst whispering soothing words in an attempt to calm him down. For some reason I had anticipated a greeting by more dogs, but the silence was all-pervading.

The sergeant led the way round to the rear of the cottage, paused outside a paint-blistered door and then banged on it with a clenched fist. 'Hullo. Anyone there? Can we have a word, please?'

We could immediately hear movement and indistinct whispering coming from a room above. The sergeant moved back from the door, looked up at a tiny dirt-encrusted window and went to speak again, before stopping himself suddenly and thrusting his hands in his pockets. There was the sound of footsteps coming down a staircase and the door slowly creaked open. The face that peered out was like an older version of Sam's – thin and white with mousy brown hair, a straggly moustache and a goatee beard framing a pair of thin, colourless lips. The man's hair was tied back in a ponytail and he appeared to be naked from the waist up – possibly even from the waist down; it was impossible to tell due to the angle of his body behind the door.

The man opened his eyes wide behind a pair of thin wire glasses, possibly to adjust to the daylight after the gloom of the interior, and they flicked rapidly between the three of us. His gaze rested on Nina and he gave an upward jerk of his head.

'That's Sam's dog.' The man had a Scottish accent and clearly wasn't disposed to be friendly to visitors.

'Was Sam your friend?'

The man ignored the police officer and kept his eyes fixed on Nina.

'Where d'ye get it then? Where's Sam?'

Nina looked like she was about to speak but the sergeant stretched out one of his hands in a gesture clearly meant to indicate that he would do the talking.

'The dog was found running loose. Look, we need to talk to you properly. Can we come in?'

The man smiled and shook his head.

'Okay. Maybe you could come outside.' The sergeant's voice was firm. It wasn't a question.

The man smiled again and closed the door. We looked at each other and waited for at least another couple of minutes. The sergeant was getting impatient but suddenly the door opened again and the man slipped outside, closing it quickly behind him. His secretive movements suggested he was anxious to keep us away from the contents of the house.

He was dressed in a long, baggy loose-knit cardigan and had a grubby pair of flip-flops on equally grubby feet, which poked out from the bottom of a pair of light cotton purple trousers. He looked back at the cottage briefly and then shuffled forwards 'Over here,' he said, jerking his head away from the cottage.

We followed him into a small clearing marked by the blackened remains of an outdoor fire and surrounded by a motley assortment of tree stumps, grey-white plastic garden chairs, the upholstered seat from a car and a rotten wooden bench. The man slumped down onto one of the plastic chairs and dragged on a small roll-up that he had concealed in the cup of one hand.

'So, where's Sam got to then?'

Sergeant Milk picked up the other plastic chair, placed it just a few feet directly in front of the man and sat down heavily in it. One of the legs looked dangerously close to buckling. Nina and I stayed standing. The sergeant fished out his wallet, flipped it open and showed the man his police warrant.

'Aye, I thought so,' said the man, his eyes narrowing into slits of hostile suspicion.

'Sergeant Milk. I'm afraid I have some bad news. Sam was found dead, drowned, in the canal between Wilmcote and Stratford yesterday.'

The man looked genuinely shocked for a split second before resuming his poker face. He glanced back over his shoulder at the cottage behind him. I thought it might be to hide his emotion, but I soon realised it was an involuntary check on whether the words might have been heard by whoever else was inside. He turned back to look directly at the police officer.

'Stupid wee bastard. He owed me money.'

I heard Nina give a short gasp of surprise, but the sergeant took it in his stride.

'Did he now? So, you weren't close friends then?'

The man sucked a remaining mouthful of smoke from the stub of the roll-up, gave up and flicked it into the ash on the ground.

'He stayed here sometimes. He owes me rent.'

'Do you know his surname?'

The man laughed sardonically. 'We're not that formal round here. Sam... we just called him Sam.'

Nina was curling her lip in visible dislike of the man by now but the sergeant pressed on in a neutral tone.

'We think he had parents or family in the Manchester area. We need to let them know. Are you sure you didn't ever hear him give his surname?'

The man shook his head with disinterest.

'Did he leave any documents here that might have his name on?'

He pursed his lips and shook his head again.

Sergeant Milk decided to change tack. 'So, can I ask what *your* name is, please, sir?'

A thin smile played at the police officer's form of address. 'My friends call me Jazzer.'

Sergeant Milk pulled out a small black notebook and pen from an inside jacket pocket. 'So, Jazzer, what would be your full name then?'

'Like I said, everyone calls me Jazzer.'

'I'm a coroner's officer, sir. In circumstances like this there will be an inquest. We need to know as much as we can about Sam and we want to inform his next of kin. I also need to decide whether you're helping a police enquiry or not. If not, you might have to come down to the station for a proper chat... or we might need to come back here with a few more officers and a search warrant. So, what's it to be, Jazzer?' The sergeant sniffed the air, slowly and deliberately.

The sudden change of tone and clear no-nonsense threat had the desired effect.

Jazzer looked back at the cottage again, his attention on whatever illegal substances would be discovered if the run-down building was searched. He shifted in his chair and his eyes darted between the three of us. As I followed his look back at the cottage, I thought I saw a pale face staring out at us from an upstairs window. But it was gone in an instant.

'James Mackintosh,' Jazzer eventually said, sulkily.

The sergeant scribbled the name in his book.

'And how long had you known Sam exactly?'

'A few months maybe.'

'And he stayed here – at the cottage?'

'Now and then. He'd walk into Stratford and sleep out there for a few days sometimes – usually after I got heavy about him needing to pay me some rent.'

'So, you own this place then, do you?'

We all turned our heads to look at Nina, who had virtually spat the question at him.

Jazzer stretched both arms out expansively, straightened his legs and crossed his ankles. 'None of your business, is it, darling?' he said with a humourless smile.

Sergeant Milk ignored the interruption. 'Had he signed on?'

Jazzer shrugged. 'He got some money from somewhere now and then. Not much though. Probably just begging – or something.'

Nina turned disgustedly and stalked back up to the main path, Eddie still under one arm.

'Did he ever talk about his family?'

'A few times, but just to say his dad was a right wee bastard and wouldn't care where he was now.'

'And you really don't know what Sam's surname might be?'

Jazzer just shook his head again.

Sergeant Milk closed his notebook. It seemed the investigation was over.

'Maybe the other person in the cottage might know something?' I said.

The police officer and Jazzer both looked at me. The notebook was opened again.

'So, Mr Mackintosh, would you mind asking your companion to join us?' Sergeant Milk said.

Jazzer gave me a hard stare and tipped his head back. 'What's he got to do with this?' he demanded. 'He a cop too?'

'This gentleman came forward to identify Sam and now he's looking after his dog.'

'The dog should stay with me.'

The sudden petulance in his voice made me smile.

'The dog is staying where it is,' said the sergeant firmly. 'So why don't you stay here and I'll ask your friend to join us. Just the one of them in there is there?' He moved quickly to the back door and thumped it again. 'Hullo! Whoever's inside, can you please open the door?'

Nina was still watching events from the path. She put Eddie on the ground but held him firmly by the lead and began to walk slowly back towards us. Jazzer glowered at me and I glowered back. The back door of the cottage swung inwards and this time a girl emerged. Sergeant Milk stepped back to give her more room but blocked her path to Jazzer.

She was tall and very thin, dressed in heavily ripped black jeans and wearing two dark lumberjack shirts, one on top of the other, which hid her figure. Her eyes were dark with make-up, in contrast to the unhealthy white pallor of the rest of her face. Her hair was shaved close to her head on one side. She exuded a sullen recalcitrance. I wouldn't have been surprised to learn that she was still legally obliged to go to school. She sniffed at very regular intervals, as though suffering from a bad cold.

'I'm Police Sergeant Milk. And you are?'

She ignored his question. 'Jazzer?'

Jazzer stayed in his plastic chair and feigned nonchalance as he studied one of the grubby rubber flip-flops that dangled down from a big toe.

'It's okay, Birdie. Sam's dead. Stupid wee bastard fell in the canal. They just want to find out where his folks are and let them know.'

Birdie showed no surprise at the news, which suggested she had managed to overhear all of the preceding conversation from her hiding place in the cottage. She sniffed, wiped her nose with the sleeve of the outer shirt and shuffled the big boots on her feet.

'Well?' said the sergeant. 'I've asked for your name.'

'Birdie,' she muttered.

'Your full name, Miss.'

She was trying to look past Sergeant Milk at Jazzer but the policeman stood resolutely in her way.

'Tell them, Birdie,' said Jazzer.

She sniffed again and then muttered, 'Suzi. Suzi Quattro.'

Jazzer snorted with laughter.

The police officer scribbled something else in his notebook.

'Right then, Birdie... or Suzi. Maybe we should continue this down at the police station in Stratford. I'll just call up a car to take you down there, shall I?'

The girl's face was tilted to the ground, but she shook her head and bit her bottom lip, defiance gone.

'Real name?' demanded the sergeant.

'Suzi Dickinson.'

'Age?'

'Eighteen.' The girl had replied so quickly that I was sure she was lying.

'And you knew Sam too?'

She muttered a confirmation.

'And have you any idea what Sam's surname was?'

'No.'

'Anything in there which might have it on?' Milk asked, gesturing to the cottage.

She shook her head.

'Any stuff he left behind last time he departed?'

'Dog food,' she replied. 'In a bag.'

'Any other bags? A rucksack? Papers? Anything like that?'

She shook her head again.

'Mind if I have a look?'

This time Jazzer leapt up from his chair and moved hastily towards the cottage. He put one arm round the girl's back and his hand on her shoulder.

'Yes, we do mind, don't we, Birdie? We've told you all we know so how about pissing off and leaving us alone now, eh?'

'Did Sam take drugs, Mr Mackintosh?'

Jazzer laughed. Suddenly he swung the girl around and pushed her firmly though the doorway with one hand on the small of her back. Then he turned to face us.

'Good luck then… keep the dog, why don't you? Save me feeding it. If you find his parents tell them they owe me some rent. Be seeing you.'

With that, he nonchalantly waggled some fingers in the pretence of a farewell gesture, slipped behind the door himself and slammed it shut.

Sergeant Milk sighed and closed his notebook.

'Horrible, horrible people!' exclaimed Nina.

'We'd better be getting back,' said the sergeant, packing his notebook into a jacket pocket.

'But you can't just leave it like that,' protested Nina. 'We still don't know Sam's surname and I bet they've got some of his stuff in there.'

Sergeant Milk bent down with a grunt and ruffled the dog's ears. 'I'm afraid there's no law that forces them to co-operate, Miss. There's been no obvious crime and if they don't want to invite me in... well, let's just say I'd need a good reason to invite myself.' He stood upright. 'There's nothing here to help us. Maybe the lad was signing on and someone at the benefits office will recognise the photograph,' he went on. 'I need a firm ID before we can get on with the inquest. Maybe he was reported missing in Manchester.'

The sergeant set off back down the path and Nina, Eddie and I followed him. None of us said anything until we got back to the car.

The meeting with Jazzer and Birdie – or James Mackintosh and Suzi Dickinson – had been very frustrating. I imagined they had been friends of a sort with Sam but there was no sign of that in their reaction to the news of his death. There was no sign of real distress, just a total unwillingness to co-operate with the police. Perhaps they had already learned of Sam's death. Or perhaps they were just dysfunctional junkies living off-grid and completely focused on themselves and feeding their addictions. But why had the girl tried to stay hidden? They were clearly hiding something, and I suspected it was more than just a stash of cannabis in a plastic bag under their bed. The brief exchanges had clearly troubled Nina whose face was fixed in a frown of frustration and annoyance. The sergeant, though, seemed largely untroubled as he pulled off his rubber boots and struggled to bend over and tie the shoelaces of his barge-like black shoes. Perhaps such frustrations were all too common as part of his daily round of duties.

'So, is that it?' asked Nina truculently as we all took our seats in the car.

'They're definitely hiding something,' I added lamely in an effort to support her.

The sergeant swung round in his seat to look back at Nina. 'Of course they're hiding something. I'll run their names and descriptions through our database when I get back and see if they've come to our attention before. We'd need some leverage to search the place but even if there is anything belonging to the dead boy there now, I doubt it will be by the time we call again.'

Nina shook her head in frustration and so we pulled away in a strained silence and with a sense of shared failure. Back in Stratford, the sergeant dropped us off at Shakespeare's statue and we were soon back onboard *Jumping Jack Flash*, the two of us huddled under blankets with Eddie in the bow.

'I am so angry,' said Nina fiercely. 'How could he just walk away from them with nothing?'

'He got their names in the end,' I said lamely.

'Big deal,' she snorted. 'It was Sam's surname we needed. His home address.'

'There is one other line of enquiry,' I ventured hesitantly. 'Chester Farm.'

Nina looked up sharply. I told her how the sergeant and I had met the two men from the farm at the pub and how they denied recognising the mobile phone picture of Sam.

'I didn't believe them,' I said. 'They couldn't wait to get out of there.'

'We have to go there,' said Nina firmly. 'Maybe he worked there and that's how they knew him. It's very close to the cottage. And if he did, maybe they'll have his home address in Manchester.'

'Maybe,' I said hesitantly. My impression of the two men was that they would be very unlikely to co-operate.

'So, come on, we can get a taxi out there. What's the matter?' Her brow creased in exasperation as she saw me wavering. 'Look, Jack. We owe it to that poor drowned boy to do all we can for him. You helped him once and we can do it again – one last time. No one else cared about him when he was alive, and they still don't now that he's dead. What was that line from your play? *They give birth astride of a grave, the light gleams an instant, then it's night once more?*'

I nodded, struck with surprise that she had remembered it verbatim.

'Well, if that's all there is to life, the rest of us have a duty to keep the light gleaming as long as we can.' Her eyes filled with tears.

How could I resist in spite of my misgivings?

'Come on then,' I said.

CHAPTER EIGHT

We quickly found a taxi in a town centre rank and described the route back out of town to Chester Farm to the young driver. As we turned into the approach to the farm I reflected that this was going to be interesting given the clear view of the locals that visitors were very unwelcome. Nina was in the back seat holding Eddie on her lap. At times the trees on either side met in the middle forming a green tunnel that felt oppressively dark, as though dusk was falling several hours before it should. The lane curved sharply to the right for the same distance again and then there was a sudden bend to the left as it resumed its original course. The dog-leg in the approach afforded the farm total privacy from the road.

A large three-storey Georgian house could now be seen square on in the distance. White plastic poly tunnels stretched away in countless rows on a hill behind the house. We were still too far away to see details, but the setting made the honey-coloured stone building appear as though it was placed in the centre of an enormous and unfinished painting on a stretched white canvas.

Three large notices were cemented into the grass verge in quick succession. The first one read: *Chester Farm Ltd – Soft Fruit. The Natural Way*. After another twenty metres another appeared saying: *Visitors Strictly By Appointment Only*. The third sign came shortly after. It read: *PRIVATE. NO TRESPASSING.*

Our driver turned his head to look back at us. 'Are they expecting you guys?' he asked in a slightly worried voice.

'Just drive on, please,' said Nina firmly.

The lane opened out into a large concrete yard separated from the house by a tall railing with two ornate two-metre-high metal gates. Two large warehouse buildings were sited off to the left, where a man in blue overalls was using a forklift truck to load covered pallets into the rear of a long, covered lorry trailer. I could see another man inside the trailer. I told the taxi driver to park alongside a rectangular wooden shed on the right of the yard. It had a sign saying '*Office*' above the door and another below it saying: '*All visitors MUST report here*' on the door itself.

I shifted in my seat to take in the details of the place. The whole site had a tidy, well-organised feel to it. There was no sign of the usual detritus found on farms. Discarded corrugated sheeting, redundant machinery and piles of unwanted rubble were conspicuous by their absence. The industrial units looked large and fairly new, as did the office. But it was the house itself that was a surprise. It could have come straight out of the glossy property-porn pages at the front of *Country Life*. It probably dated from the eighteenth century and boasted two rows of large casement windows subdivided into nine smaller panes on the first floor and twelve on the ground floor. An immaculately painted shiny black front door stood square in the centre of a portico flanked by flat ionic columns. The classical proportions were softened by some kind of rampant climber that covered the brickwork between the upper and lower windows. A knot garden of immaculately clipped yew hedges wove in and out of each other along the front of the house.

'Wow,' said Nina.

'So that's a ten then, is it?' I asked.

She nodded. 'Maybe even an eleven.'

The house was more of a manor house than farmhouse, which suggested to me that it had been there first, and the farm had subsequently grown up around it.

'You give Eddie a stretch,' said Nina, handing over the little dog. 'I'm going to ask some questions in there,' she added firmly, looking at the office. 'We won't be long,' she said to the driver. I thought about objecting but then realised that it might be useful to have a look around.

I put Eddie onto the concrete floor of the yard while Nina marched off. Some other dogs were barking somewhere. I thought again about following her but decided that she might have more luck on her own – especially if the men recognised me from the pub and associated me with the police. They were more likely to co-operate with an attractive and intelligent young woman on her own – especially one on a charitable quest, I thought.

Eddie gave no sign of having been here before, but was happy enough to trot along at my side as I wandered over for a closer look at the house. I started at the far left end of the railings, near to the trailer, and was conscious of the two men looking hard at me and exchanging words that I couldn't quite make out. I could see further inside the storage unit from this part of the yard, and alongside the boxes were several vehicles – a large lorry cab, a couple of quad bikes and three cars: a maroon Jaguar sports saloon, a silver Japanese hatchback and a blue Land Rover. My heart skipped a beat as soon as I saw it. Surely, this was the same vehicle we had seen taking Sam and Eddie away from the bridge near our mooring?

Somewhere inside the house I heard the loud jangling bell of an old-fashioned telephone, which rang four or five times before it was answered. I continued walking along the yew hedges in front of the house, past the steps up to a gravel path leading to the front door and on behind the office to the right-hand side of the house. There was a small stone path leading to the rear of the house, so Eddie and I followed it.

If the blue Land Rover suggested a connection between Sam and Chester Farm, then I doubted the two men from the pub would be willing to share what it was very readily with Nina. Perhaps a bit of freelance snooping was called for? The rear garden had an attractive expanse of stone terrace that ran along the rear of the house with steps down into a large fan-shaped area, which gave way to a smart-looking orchard. White picket fencing separated the garden from the poly tunnels. The garden had been meticulously planned: there were immaculate flowerbeds, carefully tended groups of shrubs and an occasional showpiece tree. Business must be booming at Chester Farm judging by the money and care being lavished on its main property and outbuildings.

Suddenly, I registered the presence of a woman kneeling at one of the flowerbeds. There was a metal wheelbarrow next to her, half full of weeds, and I could see a small trowel in her right hand. The sky was beginning to cloud over and it wasn't a particularly warm day, which added to the shock and surprise I experienced as I realised that the woman didn't have a stitch of clothing on except for a pair of red plastic clogs and some kind of headscarf. Her large round and very white buttocks rose and fell slightly on the heels of her clogs as she bent forwards and backwards to dig in the border.

I retreated quickly along the path by the railing, rounded the corner and made a beeline for the taxi, crossing the yard in front of the house just as Nina emerged around the corner of the office accompanied by a well-built man with a military-style haircut. It was one of the men from the pub. He seemed to be trying to hurry her back to the vehicle. Her body language suggested that she was bristling with stiff indignation.

'WHAT THE BLOODY HELL DO YOU THINK YOU ARE DOING?'

The bull-like bellow reverberated around the yard before I could locate its source. Dogs were barking somewhere close by. Then, all of us were transfixed by a figure in the open front door of the house.

'I SAID, WHAT THE BLOODY HELL DO YOU THINK YOU ARE DOING?'

This time, the question was twice as loud as the first time. But it wasn't the stentorian parade-ground delivery that was most astonishing. It was the fact that it came from a totally naked and barrel-chested man. Of course, my eyes were immediately drawn to his penis, hanging straight down under the roundness of a generous belly and between a pair of sturdy legs spread wide. Yes, he was definitely naked. But his maleness was dwarfed by the long barrel of a shotgun that lay in the crook of his right arm.

'YOU!' The man pointed a finger directly at me. I half-heartedly pointed an index finger at my chest in query. 'YES, YOU! IDIOT. COME HERE NOW.'

I swallowed hard and walked towards the man who I assumed must be the Major. The locals' sly comments about the Major's dress code suddenly made sense. As I neared the railings he marched down the short path from the house and arrived at its end at the same time as me. Close up, he seemed even more naked, if such a thing were possible. His hair was cut short in a military style and was the same salt-and-pepper colour as his generous nest of pubic hair. He had thick bushy eyebrows above heavily creased eyes, a boxer's flattened nose and a strong square jaw. One arm cradled the gun whilst the other was indignantly pointed straight at me. Major Jones was probably in his late fifties or early sixties, but he was a bull of a man and gave not the slightest hint of disquiet at his lack of clothing.

He looked down at me from the three steps that descended from the house into the yard and which reinforced his own considerable height. I felt rather small and ridiculous – which was frankly absurd, given that I was the one who was fully dressed. I looked nervously over my shoulder to see Nina and her escort hurrying up behind me. I now understood the mixture of fear and amusement the locals had shown when they had spoken about the Major. He jabbed a finger at me again.

'You were sneaking around my house. I saw you watching my wife in the garden.'

'I wasn't sneaking anywhere,' I said. 'I was just giving the dog a stretch.' Eddie was sitting on his lead at my feet, looking interestedly up at the naked man.

The Major snorted with disbelief and shifted his gaze to the younger man behind me.

'Who the hell are these people, Roberts? Why are you letting them wander round the farm?'

The man's voice was firm but respectful. 'I'm sorry, Major. This is the lady who I rang you about just now. I didn't know there was anyone else with her.'

The Major looked angrily at Nina, once again showing a total lack of embarrassment at her wide-eyed scrutiny.

'Perhaps you could put the gun away,' I suggested.

'And perhaps you can explain why you're snooping around my property without an appointment,' he snapped back.

Nina stepped forward. 'As Mr Roberts told you on the phone just now, we're trying to find out the identity of a young man called Sam whose body was found in the canal not far from here. It appears he has been living at Drood Cottage –'

'Yes, yes,' interrupted the Major. 'And as I told Roberts to tell you, we've never met him. Now, I think you and your nosy companion have outstayed your welcome.' He glowered at me again. 'Time for you to bugger off – and sharpish.'

The man called Roberts came forward and put a hand on my elbow. 'Come on now...' he began. I shook myself free – it was time to play a trump card, I thought.

'Just a minute...' I looked up at his boss. 'I think you may be mistaken, Major.'

Roberts put his hand back on my elbow, tighter this time, but then froze as the Major's face turned a dark red. He exploded. 'Mistaken? Just what the bloody hell do you think –'

I put up one hand, palm first. He obviously wasn't used to anyone challenging him within the boundaries of his mini-kingdom.

'Nina and I met Sam briefly but, after he left us, we saw him getting into a vehicle on the bridge at Wilmcote. I'm pretty sure it was the blue Land Rover parked in your warehouse over there. And whoever was inside seemed to know him.' I had the Major's attention now.

There was a brief silence, during which the Major and Roberts looked at each other.

'Roberts?' asked the Major.

Roberts looked unhappily around. 'Like I said in the pub – I've never seen the guy before.'

'What about the other man you were with at the pub?' I asked. 'Does he work here? Maybe he gave Sam a lift?'

'This would have been the day before Sam was found dead in the canal,' Nina added, twisting the knife.

The Major had heard enough. 'You've been told that Roberts didn't know the boy. Maybe Andrews gave him a lift. Maybe he didn't. Maybe it was another Land Rover. Plenty of them round here. He has never been to this farm. Never worked here. Got it? Now bugger off.' With that, he broke the shotgun and collected the shells in his other hand. It had actually been loaded. Then he swivelled 180 degrees, marched back through the glossy front door and forcefully slammed it behind him. I turned to Roberts who was looking distinctly unhappy.

'So, you weren't in the Land Rover we saw picking Sam up on the bridge?'

'No.'

'And nor was your friend Andrews?' asked Nina.

'No. Now you heard the boss. I'd advise you to bugger off before he lets the dogs loose.'

From their frenzied barking, they sounded as though they might be rather large. We strolled back to the taxi as nonchalantly as possible with Roberts snapping at our heels. Our young taxi driver's eyes were like saucers and he screeched out of the yard at some speed. We were about a hundred yards along the narrow drive before Nina and I exploded into simultaneous laughter that, in turn, prompted Eddie to bark excitedly.

'Hey man,' said the driver. 'That guy had no threads and a gun. A big gun. You're damn lucky I hung around for you!'

'Thank you,' said Nina. 'You'll get a tip.'

'Oh my God,' I said. 'Just what on earth was that all about?'

'It seems our Major and Mrs Jones are committed naturists,' Nina replied calmly. 'Roberts warned me about it in the office. He said that was why he would telephone him rather than invite him over to have a word.'

'Weird,' I said.

'Roberts didn't give much away. The Major and his wife run a soft-fruit business and Roberts is the site manager. He said they knew about the people at Drood Cottage but they didn't ever have anything to do with them. Said he'd never seen Sam out and about – which is surprising if the lad was wandering in and out of Stratford all the time or hanging around the village shop.'

'I'm certain it was the same blue Land Rover that picked Sam up,' I added. 'And I'm pretty sure it stopped for him and he had a conversation through the window at first. And if it was only one of them, why did Sam climb in the back? It didn't feel like a random lift for an unknown hitchhiker. And if it was just a coincidence, why pretend they hadn't seen him before?'

It was late afternoon when the taxi dropped us off at the basin. The driver had been shaking his head and muttering to himself for most of the return journey but seemed happy enough with his tip. The boat felt dark and chilly and so I busied myself lighting the woodburner while Nina fed the dog and made a pot of tea. Later, we walked Eddie to a nearby pub where we had beer with fish and chips and became slightly hysterical as we talked about our visits to Drood Cottage and Chester Farm.

'Oh my God,' Nina said, her eyes watering with laughter, 'I heard him shouting but I couldn't believe what I was seeing.'

'Yes, well, don't forget that I had just seen Mrs Major in the same condition,' I said.

'Gardening. In the nude? In September? Hardcore.'

'So, tell me,' I said, 'were you impressed by the Major's swagger stick?'

Nina snorted with laughter but then turned serious. 'Seriously, though, it was more than strange, wasn't it? That guy Roberts was lying. But why deny any knowledge of Sam unless he had something to do with his death?'

'And why go to such extreme lengths to dissuade visitors?' I asked. 'There's more to that place than meets the eye. But I don't think we got very far.'

'I agree,' said Nina. 'Neither at the cottage nor the farm. But we mustn't give up,' she said determinedly. I could only imagine that Nina's resolution was acting as some kind of distraction from the other matter which was disturbing her, whatever that was.

Back at the boat, having gone our separate ways to bed, I checked my phone before pulling out the laptop. The missed call from Deb reminded me that I needed to call her back some time tomorrow. She might have news of my money.

CHAPTER NINE

It turned out that I didn't need to ring Deb. She rang me. At six-thirty a.m.

'Ughhhhh. Bloody hell, Deb. What time do you –'

'Shut up, Jack. Pay attention. Are you paying attention?'

I sat upright and squeezed a palm into one eye. 'What is it? What's the problem?'

'Is she with you?' Deb was talking in an urgent whisper.

'Is who with me?'

'The woman you called Nina. Is she with you?'

'For Christ's sake, Deb.' I was also talking in a whisper, conscious of the need not to disturb Nina or Eddie on the other side of their door. 'She's still in bed.'

'But not with you?' Deb's whisper was ridiculously urgent and conspiratorial.

'No! In the spare room, not that it's any of your bloody business –'

'Shh. Can she hear you?'

'Deb. It's six-thirty in the morning and she's asleep, not unreasonably. Look, what is –'

'I know who she is.'

Now she had my full attention.

'Who? Nina?'

'Her real name isn't Nina.'

I looked at Nina's door but there was no suggestion of sound or movement behind it.

'Wait a minute.' I pulled on some jeans and a sweater and padded outside barefoot onto the well of the foredeck. It was bloody cold, a foot-high layer of mist was clinging to the surface of the water, like the dry ice on a rock star's stage.

'Are you still there?' hissed my ex-wife in my ear.

I stopped whispering and spoke in a normal voice. 'Yes. Now what the fuck is this all about?'

'I told you. I know who she is.'

Part of me told myself to hang up. Did I really care who Nina was? She didn't want me to know and we had rubbed along just fine in spite of that. Knowing her real identity was going to change things and I wasn't at all sure I wanted anything to change.

But I couldn't help myself.

'Okay. So who is she?'

'She's an army widow,' hissed Deb.

'Deb, you don't need to whisper.'

The urgent whispered tone continued regardless. 'Her husband was called Alan. He died not long ago in Afghanistan.'

'Okay. So, she's grieving and getting her head together. End of mystery,' I said.

'Shut up and listen to me, Jack. It's not as simple as it sounds.'

I sighed. 'I'm still listening.'

Suddenly, I heard Eddie's excited yapping, which suggested that Nina was on the move. Sure enough, a little brown blur of fur came shooting out into the bow area and danced excitedly around my feet. Eddie's bottom was wagging from side to side in an attempt to keep up with his tail.

'I'm sorry, Deb, I've got to go.'

'No, Jack – you need to hear this.'

'No Deb,' I said firmly. 'I really don't need to hear it. I don't need to know any more. Nina's waking up now.'

'Jack –'

'Bye, Deb.'

'Jack, buy a paper!'

I cut her off and looked up to see Nina walking towards me through the boat's central walkway.

'Good morning,' she said. 'You're up early. Could you take Eddie out for his business while I have a shower?'

I slipped on a pair of trainers, scooped up the dog with his lead and a plastic poop bag and headed off for some canine bowel emptying. I took Eddie down to the left of the theatre and he trotted happily alongside me on his lead along the riverside path. The early morning mist clung to the surface of the Avon; a pair of swans in mid-river could only be seen from the neck up. It was wonderfully quiet as I contemplated Deb's excited news and its implications. So, Nina was a war widow. Her disquiet at the theatre suddenly made complete sense to me. The actors had been dressed in modern combat fatigues and the scene had clearly acted as some kind of trigger which had released an emotional tsunami. And her trip to my bed that same night was clearly about meeting some kind of need to grieve, to reach out and remember how it was sharing a bed with a man who was now dead. Her clipped diction and privileged background suggested to me that her dead husband was almost certainly an officer. Yet I registered that Deb had also been trying to tell me something more when I hung up on her.

We doubled back towards the town along a lane that passed by the other side of the theatre. The shops and food outlets facing the basin were still shut apart from a newsagents. I tied Eddie to a drainpipe and moved into the shop's interior yellow light.

The floor had bundles of broadsheets and tabloids ready to be sorted for the early paper rounds but some had already been stacked on the shelves, their front pages screaming for attention. I cast a critical eye over a line of tabloids, imagining how I would have used a different typeface here or a differently sized picture there. One of them brought me up sharply. It was a photograph of Nina, glamorously made-up in a closely fitted wedding gown, holding onto a handsome soldier in peaked cap and full officer's dress uniform. They were looking out, with beaming smiles, from the bottom half of the front page. It was tempting to devour the story there and then, but I resisted. I snatched a copy from the shelf, paid for it and headed back outside. The iron of a nearby bench was freezing cold on my arse and the icy morning dew had soaked my feet but I barely noticed as I looped the dog's lead around one of my ankles and gripped the paper with both hands.

Above the photograph, which spanned three columns, the headline read:

FEARS DEEPEN FOR MISSING WAR WIDOW

I read on.

Relatives of a grieving war widow have appealed for her to contact them as fears grow for her safety.

Newlywed Angelina Wilde, 30, went missing shortly after receiving news of her heroic husband's death in Afghanistan. Captain Alan Wilde was killed during a fierce firefight as he attempted to rescue two injured members of his platoon.

'We are desperately anxious about Angelina,' said Mrs Wilde's elderly mother from her home near Salisbury, Wiltshire. 'She just walked out with a couple of bags and we haven't heard from her since.'

The attractive young widow left her family home during the night two weeks ago and there has been no sign of her since. A spokesperson for Wiltshire Police said: 'We are appealing for Mrs Wilde to get in touch and reassure her family and friends that she is all right. This is now being treated as a missing person enquiry.'

The couple were married just six weeks before Captain Wilde left for his second tour of duty in Bazra, Afghanistan with the Parachute

Regiment. 'It was a wonderful day and they were blissfully happy,' said a family friend. 'We thought Angelina was coping with the terrible news of Alan's death. Now we are all terribly worried about her.'

My phone rang. It was Deb again.

'Can you talk?' she hissed.

'Yes, Deb.' I sighed. 'I can talk.'

'You need to buy a newspaper.'

'I've read the paper.'

'Oh. Well? What are you going to do?'

'What do you mean, what am I going to do? It's her life. It's up to her.'

'But people are looking for her, Jack. They need to know that she's okay. Her mother needs to know.'

'How did you know it was her?'

'What?'

'How did you know that the woman who'd offered to help me with the boat and who called herself Nina was this missing woman from the paper with a different name?'

There was a cold prickle on the back of my neck which had nothing to do with the coldness of the morning. The line went very quiet.

'Deb? How did you know?'

My ex-wife sighed. 'I recognised her from the photograph.'

'What do you mean? How? You've never met.'

'I'm sorry, Jack.' Deb's voice had gone very quiet. Uneasiness bubbled up inside me. 'I asked Mary to go to Stratford and take some pictures of you yesterday. I wanted to know who this strange woman was.'

'What?' I exploded. The little dog whimpered at my feet. 'You sent Bloody Mary to spy on me?'

'I know, I know. I'm sorry, Jack. I was... we were married a long time. I wanted to know what this new woman in your life was like. I know I shouldn't have done it.'

I was genuinely speechless. My mind raced. Mary would have relished her undercover role. I pictured her in a headscarf and sunglasses, acting like one of the many tourists on the towpath, taking pictures of the narrowboats on the basin but particularly of the couple enjoying a cup of coffee together on *Jumping Jack Flash*. She had probably pretended to be taking a selfie, but switched the camera around. It made my flesh creep.

Deb's voice had gone very small. 'I'm so sorry, Jack. I'm ashamed of myself. I didn't want you to know. But when I read the paper this morning and recognised her, I had to tell you who she really is. The police are involved.'

'Priceless,' I said. 'Utterly bloody priceless.' Now I was just cold with anger.

'Jack –'

'Okay, Deb. Firstly, we are divorced. D'you hear me? You have no kind of stake in any of my future relationships. None whatsoever. So just... just back off. Secondly, you keep that bloody woman well away from me in future. You tell Mary that if I see her anywhere near me or my boat again, then she'll be going for a swim. And thirdly, you and her need to keep very quiet about this. It's up to Nina... Angelina... to decide what to do next – not you or your bitch of a so-called best friend. Okay?' I waited for an answer. 'Okay? Are you hearing me Deb?'

'Okay, Jack,' she said miserably.

'Right then. If we understand each other you can just fuck off.' A passing couple looked up sharply at me as they walked by but I carried on. 'What I do now and who I do it with is no business of yours or anyone else's – especially not Bloody Mary's. Understood?'

'But, Jack –'

'Goodbye, Deb.'

I hung up and furiously pushed the phone back into my trouser pocket.

'Jesus,' I exhaled, still shaking with fury. What could have possessed her to send her friend to spy on us? Could she really still be jealous after all we had been through? It was pitiful. Eddie was looking up at me and

I met his gaze. 'Now what?' I asked him. He cocked his head on one side but it remained my problem.

When we returned to the boat Nina was freshly showered, her black hair still glossy and wet. She had a half-full mug of tea in front of her, next to the remains of two boiled eggs. She gave me a smile and buried her nose in Eddie's fur.

'Oh, damp dog.' She looked up. 'So what's the plan for today?'

The newspaper was still carefully folded in my right hand. The front page was deliberately collapsed in on itself so that only the back page was visible. My resolve was wavering. Nina seemed so happy and normal. She sat there, looking clean and pretty and clear-eyed, petting the dog, sipping her tea and enjoying the prospect of another day in Stratford. It was just too tempting to pretend that I didn't now know what I knew. I didn't want to break the spell. I muttered something about needing to freshen up and went to the bathroom, stopping en route to hide the newspaper beneath the pillow on my bed.

'What's the plan?' she asked again when I came back.

'Completely up to you,' I said. 'I'd quite like to get moving again.' Suddenly, the centre of Stratford felt like a risky place to be. 'But I'd also like to see if the good Sergeant Milk has got anything new on Sam and we'll need to give him some time for that.'

She nodded. 'We can call in later today.'

'But we could maybe get out of Stratford for a while? Find somewhere nice to take Eddie for a walk?' I suggested.

She nodded brightly. 'Good idea. I'll go over to the tourist centre and ask where they suggest.'

'No,' I replied, sharply enough for her to register some surprise. 'Best if I go.' And so I did, before she could ask why. I couldn't tell her that I feared that her mixing with crowds of people who might have read the same newspaper as me that morning wasn't a good idea.

An hour later a taxi delivered Eddie, Nina and me to Burton Dassett Country Park, one hundred acres of ironstone hills as recommended by the Tourist Information Centre. A sign at the car park told us it had opened as a country park in 1971 and that we could expect good views from hills that rose to 203 metres above sea level.

'Come on, old man,' Nina called to me. 'Time to stretch those ancient legs of yours.'

We had been given a basic map of a circular route starting from the tiny village of Burton Dassett. Nina took charge straight away. But we didn't get very far before we swung off the path towards an ancient church. 'Wow,' said Nina. 'Twelfth century. There's supposed to be a holy well somewhere.' We found the well of All Saints Church very quickly and gazed down in awe at its mossy walls. 'So this was being built – or being used – more than 800 years ago,' I marvelled.

'Incredible,' agreed Nina, but she soon wandered away on her own, meandering around the ancient graveyard with Eddie on his lead, stooping to peer closely at the barely decipherable inscriptions on the lichen-covered headstones. My new knowledge about Nina's loss was prompting me to give her as much time and space as she needed, so I wandered into the church itself. The unique, dusty smell of bygone centuries hit my nostrils as soon as I lifted the bulky wooden latch. Although I could probably identify its component parts as damp stonework, aging Bibles, mouse droppings and dry rot, I wanted to believe it was the distilled essence of many hundreds of thousands of prayers, hymns and acts of devout worship. I could also tell that the church was much cherished rather than neglected. Fresh flowers adorned the wax-polished surfaces, and immaculate tapestry kneelers hung from the pews. Every detail suggested the building was still very much in use by people who loved it.

I sat down on a pew at the rear and stared at the primitive stained-glass window. I couldn't work out what scene it depicted but after a short while the colours seemed to fuse together and sent me into something of a reverie. Churches usually fill me with melancholy. The aura of happy events – christenings and weddings and Christmas – were somehow always swamped by the visible memorabilia of death that adorns the walls, floors and surrounding land. Now my thoughts wandered to Sam and what a waste it was of a young life. It was upsetting to think his family were still unaware of his death even though he had been escaping from them, or at least from his father. Hopefully the drink and drugs that had been swirling through his system had prevented him from suffering too much. Hopefully unconsciousness overcame him quickly in the cold, dark water. But my gut told me otherwise. A bright sunny day at a noisy outdoor lido pinged unbidden into my mind. I was four or five years old and had I slipped away from my mother, whose eyes had closed behind her wing-shaped sunglasses. I had walked down the wide and shallow concrete slabs that sloped gradually towards the pool until I got halfway along the pool's length and simply stepped off the side into the water.

I suppose I must have somehow thought the whole pool was the same depth as the shallow end, where I had been confined up until now. Even now, forty years later, I vividly recalled how the noise of the seagulls and people shouting was suddenly muted as my head slipped underwater. My feet scrambled to feel the solid floor of the pool beneath me; when it wasn't there I panicked. My weight and the force of the fall plunged me deep into the heavily chlorinated water until my body's natural buoyancy brought me back to the surface. Suddenly, the muted sound burst back into full volume, but I barely noticed as I opened my mouth to shout and my arms flailed in terror. My mouth filled with water and I sank back down again, not knowing how to co-ordinate my limbs to fight my way back to the surface. The soundtrack to my drowning was switched back to mute and I was lost once more, until my feet finally touched the bottom. I must have instinctively pushed myself back upwards. I remembered afterwards the vivid colours of the scene above water, with all the people noisily enjoying themselves, oblivious to my trauma just a few yards away. I think I sank a third time. I can't be sure. I might even have come back up and gone down for a fourth. I know my mouth was clamped shut but my lungs were about to burst. Then a hand grabbed my hair and yanked me up out of the water. A tall, well-built boy, about fourteen or fifteen years old, was standing next to me. I clamped myself tightly around his neck – which he clearly found either embarrassing or annoying because he pushed me roughly towards the pool's side, put both hands under my armpits and sat me there while I coughed and spluttered, my eyes streaming with water from the pool and hot tears.

'What the fuck are you up to then?' he demanded angrily.

I must have stuttered a thank you. I knew I had almost died and now this huge boy was being nasty to me. He frogmarched me back to my mother, who was still dozing. I had probably been away from her for no more than ten minutes. The boy told her what had happened in a priggish, condescending way and stalked off as she tried to thank him.

We packed up shortly afterwards and went home in a mutually guilty silence.

The sudden flashback to the fear I had felt, flailing in the water, powerless to breathe, made me convulse in a sudden shiver. However many drugs were in his system, Sam would have known what was happening. He would have felt that fear as the air left his lungs, unable to save himself. I was sure of it. But unlike me he had not been surrounded by clear water, a blue sunny sky and lots of people in vivid colours. His death would have been a cold, dark and lonely one and suffused with the pure undiluted terror. Poor Sam. Could he have been saved? If we had moored nearer would we have heard something? Could a passer-by in the right place at the right time have got him out? Could anything have prevented him filling himself with drink and drugs to the extent that he staggered off the towpath to his death? His mother was out there somewhere now, unaware of her son's fatal accident. The thought filled me with a deep sadness. My reverie was interrupted by the sound of the latch on the door being lifted again. Nina poked her head around its solid oak planks. 'There you are. Coming?'

We walked for an hour along a well-signposted circular route. The dog had clearly bonded with Nina and, unlike me, she felt sufficiently confident to let him off his lead. Her trust was repaid as he ambled ahead of us but kept looking back to reassure himself that we were still in sight.

'What were you thinking about in the church?' Nina asked.

'What were you thinking about in the graveyard?' I replied.

'You first,' she said.

I told her about my near-drowning as a boy. 'I was always falling into water as a kid. It became a bit of a family joke. I suppose I was a bit clumsy. But I remember ending up in quite a few streams and boating ponds. I never came close to drowning again, though. And I love swimming – I even did a scuba-diving course once.'

Nina seemed characteristically reluctant to talk about herself as we walked so I burbled on, filling the silence but burdened by my new knowledge of her circumstances.

'Of course, I was always going to be saved,' I told her. 'Although I didn't know it at the time. My mother later told me that I had been born with a caul.' She looked puzzled. 'It's when the inner membrane of the foetal sac still covers the baby's head, like a net, after they're born. And legend has it that anyone born with a caul, or even possessing one, will never ever drown.'

She looked across at me dubiously. 'Explain.'

'Oh, it's just superstition,' I said. 'David Copperfield had one too. His caul was advertised in the newspapers for fifteen guineas. He said something about sea-going people at the time must have been short of money or short of faith, or preferred cork jackets, as only one person came forward to buy it – and he only offered two pounds plus the balance in sherry.'

'Quite handy, not being able to drown if you live on a boat,' she said.

'It's all bollocks, of course,' I replied. 'I'm sure I can drown as easily as the next man.'

'Or Sam,' she said sadly.

'Or Sam,' I agreed.

We stopped to sit on a bench overlooking one particularly panoramic view and the dog snuffled happily around our feet. I thought about pressing her about her interest in the graveyard but decided to stay quiet. It suddenly felt all too clumsy and obvious.

'All this green will go brown soon,' she said. 'Autumn is such a sad time of year.'

'I love the smell of wood smoke, though.'

'Me too,' she mused. 'Let's light the stove on the boat again tonight. It'll be cosy.'

I nodded. 'Good idea. There's still some coal left. That'll do – plus takeaway pizza washed down with plenty of whisky.'

We finished our walk and I called our taxi driver as we returned to the spot where he had dropped us off. He reappeared within a quarter of an hour. I was resting my eyes as the car approached the outskirts of Stratford – but when we stopped at some traffic lights they opened with a jolt and I suddenly registered the car idling in front of us. It was the blue Land Rover from Chester Farm. There were two men in it and although I couldn't quite see their faces, they looked very familiar – stocky builds and short haircuts. It had to be Roberts and Andrews. They too seemed to be heading for the town centre. I looked to see if Nina had noticed but she was in a world of her own, gazing out of the side window. The blue square bulk of the Land Rover had pulled ahead of us, travelling slightly faster than the 30 mph speed limit so I had some forewarning when it pulled over into a kerbside parking space outside a small row of shops.

'Can you just stop here a moment, please?' I asked the taxi driver. I turned to Nina. 'I'm just going to get some whisky,' I said. 'You take the taxi on to the boat and feed Eddie and get the fire going. I can walk from here.'

I was out of the nearside passenger door and shutting it firmly before she could argue. I headed for a small grocery store, waving one hand in the air at her without looking back. Once in the door of the shop I glanced back to see the taxi pulling out and accelerating past the Land Rover, which was still parked by the kerb about five vehicles away. There was a collection of business cards and photographs of secondhand things for sale stuck to the inside of the shop window and I pretended to study them whilst looking through the glass at the Land Rover. A young woman had approached the vehicle almost as soon as it had pulled in and she was talking to the man in its front passenger seat. It was definitely Roberts.

The girl was wearing an oversized parka with the hood up, preventing me from seeing her face. I bided my time, willing her to turn around. Then, to my satisfaction, she tilted her head first to the left, away from me, but then to the right, towards me as though to make sure she wasn't being observed. The synthetic fur around the edge of her hood partially obscured her features but I could just make out the dark mascara around her eyes and her thin, white face. I realised that I had seen that face before at the cottage in the woods. It was Birdie, Jazzer's girlfriend and Sam's former housemate. My heart pounded as I retreated back out of sight but continued to watch through the shop's side window. Roberts had been lying. He *did* know the squatters in the wood.

The side window of the Land Rover had been rolled down to one third of its height and now, quick as a flash, I could see Robert's hand lift up over the window and give a small package to Birdie. She immediately transferred it into her coat and walked away, shoulders hunched, both hands dug deep into the pockets. The Land Rover pulled out into the traffic a few seconds later. I had witnessed a very similar scene just a couple of days ago. It had involved the same blue Land Rover and Nina had been with me at the time. Birdie had passed something through the window and taken something back just as Sam had done on the bridge near our mooring. The similarity between the two scenes made my stomach lurch. I couldn't let her get away.

I headed off after Birdie, keeping about twenty-five metres behind her. Her tall painfully thin frame was hunched over as she walked, fast and determined, head down, using the whole width of the pavement to overtake other pedestrians. Adrenalin coursed through me. Birdie was speeding up and I raised my pace to keep in touch with her.

CHAPTER TEN

Birdie walked the length of two streets before disappearing down an alleyway on her left. I slowed my pace as I approached the corner and peered around it. There was no sign of her. I panicked for a moment and then spotted a small pub further down – the Pig and Whistle. It was odds-on that she had ducked into its entrance. The glass windows either side of the door were frosted to nose-height so I couldn't see in. I cautiously pushed open the main door. I needed to stay hidden because I knew she would recognise me. But it was a risk I felt I had to take if I was to find out more about the connection between Drood Cottage and Chester Farm and Sam's death. The little entrance hall with its dirty tiled floor was flanked by two more internal doors with their own frosted glass. The right-hand one was labelled 'Public Bar' and one to the left was labelled 'Lounge Bar'. I headed left.

To my relief, I had gambled correctly. Birdie seemed a public bar kind of girl and there was no sign of her in the small lounge bar, which was overcrowded with cheap metal furniture and devoid of any other customers. I turned to the bar. There was a small hatchway in the rear wall lined with drinks and glasses and it gave me a clear view through to the other side. Birdie had sat down against the rear wall. Jazzer was sitting with her, his face cunning and his eyes alert behind the wire glasses. I watched as she took a swallow from his pint and they began an urgent conversation.

I shifted to obscure myself as much as possible as I ordered a pint from the young barman who had appeared to ask what I wanted. I was poised to move quickly if Birdie or Jazzer approached the bar to order more drinks. But, for the moment, it appeared that they were content to share the dregs of the pint glass in front of them. There was a low murmur of conversation from the other customers in their side of the bar and I could hear the tinny electronic bleeps of a fruit machine. Then someone put some money into the jukebox and a Judas Priest track began pounding out – I recognised it as 'Breaking the Law', and smiled at the irony. I didn't have a hope in hell of catching a single word of their conversation now, but I watched them intently for any clues.

Five minutes and a third of a pint later I heard the outer door of the pub swing open and shut and two young men joined them at their table. One of the men immediately got back up, approached the bar and ordered four pints of cider. He took a good long look around the room whilst he was being served and I could feel his eyes boring into me through the hatchway. I pretended to be engrossed in the remains of a horseracing paper that had been left on the bar by a previous customer. The newcomers were tall, skinny kids dressed completely in black, with plenty of metalwork in their ears, noses and eyebrows.

They didn't stay long. The boy who had bought the drinks took three pints over to the table and then came back for the fourth, a tight roll of what looked like twenty-pound notes in his free hand. He put the money down on the table next to his glass and it was almost immediately swept out of sight by Jazzer. At the same time, I saw Birdie's hand reach under the table and rest on the upper thigh of the boy who had sat next to her. I watched as his hand closed over hers – their eyes avoiding any contact with each other. Then Birdie withdrew hers and he dragged his hand backwards, transferring something into the pocket of his ripped jeans. Jazzer said something brief and both the boys stood up, downed the rest of their pints and walked out of the bar. Jazzer said something to Birdie and they laughed – the tension between them evaporating.

I decided I had seen enough. After checking that Jazzer and Birdie were staying settled with their fresh drinks, I swallowed the remains of my pint and headed for the door. As I walked back to the basin I thought over what I'd seen. It was pretty obvious that Jazzer and Birdie were selling drugs and that those drugs had been supplied by the two hard-looking men, Roberts and Andrews from Chester Farm. That would be why those same men had denied all knowledge of the occupants of the semi-derelict cottage on the edge of the farm's land. It was also highly likely that Sam had been part of the same distribution network in Stratford and was equally well known to them. They had almost certainly given Sam a lift into town on the day when I saw him climb in to the blue Land Rover. And he had probably bought drugs off them with the money I had given him. So, was Sam's death really an accident? Could he have been caught up in something dodgy and upset the wrong people? Or had he just taken too much of his own merchandise and walked off the towpath into the water?

I could take what I knew to Sergeant Milk. He might use it to revisit the cottage and try again to get Sam's full identity in order to find his family. Or he might simply hand it over to his drugs squad colleagues who would then begin their own investigation. I asked myself what I was most bothered about and admitted it was the thought of Sam's family being out there and not knowing about his death that concerned me more than some small-time drug dealing. Was I right, though? Even small-time drug dealers ruined lives.

My thoughts remained unresolved by the time *Jumping Jack Flash* came into sight. There was a welcome tendril of smoke coming from the small metal chimney pipe on its roof and the lit portholes and windows looked yellow, warm and welcoming. I stopped. The incident with Birdie and Jazzer had driven all thoughts of Nina out of my head, but they came crowding back in a rush now. Nina was no longer just Nina. She was Mrs Angelina Wilde, a young war widow and currently the subject of a countrywide police search and front page news. I now knew her story – whether she wanted me to or not – and I needed to decide what to do about that. It could only be a matter of time before someone recognised her or the police or the press tracked her down. She needed to be prepared for that.

I closed the hatchway quickly against the chill and found Nina curled up with Eddie in his usual position, prone on her lap.

'You jumped out of the taxi in a hurry,' she said. 'So where's the whisky?' She gave me a quizzical look. 'Good job we've still got half a bottle left.'

So I told her what I had witnessed in the street and in the pub afterwards. She listened in silence until the end.

'And you decided to leave me out of it and go off on your own again?' she said in irritation.

'We had Eddie with us. We would have been spotted. I'm sorry.'

She seemed to concede the point and acknowledge the apology.

'So, you think the two men from the fruit farm are dealing drugs and using Birdie and Jazzer to sell them in Stratford?' she asked.

'It certainly looks like that.'

'And maybe Sam was caught up in it too?'

'We saw him talking to someone in the same blue Land Rover on the bridge and then getting in – for a lift into town maybe.'

'Are you going to tell the good sergeant?'

'I don't know. On the face of it, it has nothing to do with Sam's death. He was coming back from town, high or pissed or both, and could have just wandered into the water. And we don't have any evidence of him drug dealing either. Just suspicions based on who he lived with and what we saw.'

Nina looked hard at me. 'But?'

'But he may have died indirectly due to their drugs and a lot more could go the same way, one way or another.'

She nodded firmly. 'You're right. We can't do nothing. We've got to tell someone.'

'Or get more evidence,' I said.

'Well, we can't do that now,' she said. 'And I'm starving after that walk. Some pizzas are keeping warm in the oven. You can have a shower if you want.' She uncurled herself purposefully, placed the dog on another soft chair and headed for our remaining whisky and some glasses.

The shower was a pretty pathetic trickle and its warmth was fading fast. I made a mental note to run the engine for a while in the morning to recharge the batteries. I mulled over what to do next – about Nina and also about what I had witnessed an hour or so ago. I put the first dilemma back in the 'too-difficult' file and made my mind up on the other.

After a generous glass of whisky, I realised that our walk had made me hungry too as we tucked into the pizzas. 'Cheers,' we raised our glasses. 'It was a good walk,' I said as we clinked them together.

'The dog is shattered.' Sure enough, Eddie was fast asleep, gently whimpering and with his legs twitching.

'So, the question is, do we think our trigger-happy naturist major is the mastermind behind all of this?' I asked.

'Well, it's hard to believe his two heavies are working all on their own.'

'And fruit deliveries could be a very convenient way of distributing drugs around the country,' I added. 'Not to mention the acres and acres of polytunnels. The Major could be growing the stuff in plain sight.'

'What do you mean?'

'Well, the police have got helicopters now with heat sensors which can track down mini drug factories in the roof spaces of houses. But on a farm like that, well, it's just another plant growing under plastic, isn't it? But a lot more lucrative than strawberries.'

'And they certainly seem very reluctant to entertain any visitors.'

'Yep... and maybe the whole naturist thing serves a purpose too,' I pondered. 'Sure, it may raise a giggle amongst the locals, but it probably helps to keep them at a safe distance.'

'So, what are we going to do then?'

'I don't know... so what you wanna do then?'

We both immediately recognised the beginning of the script from the *Jungle Book*'s vulture scene and giggled. As we shared our mutual passion for the movie and its wonderful soundtrack, I reflected on how easy Nina was to get along with and how she must be working furiously to compartmentalise her grief. I poured us both another inch of whisky.

'But what *are* we gonna do then?' she repeated.

'I think I should try to have a closer look,' I said. 'If this does turn out to be as dodgy as we think it is there could be a great magazine piece in it and frankly, I could do with the money.'

'Hmm. Not exactly the purest of motives,' she replied, taking a sip. 'And how would you take a closer look? You can't just waltz up to the front door and start spying on the big bare arse of the major's wife again!'

'No,' I admitted. 'I certainly saw more than I bargained for then. But maybe there's another way. It's obviously a pretty big place and there might be a back way into the polytunnels. If it is some kind of drugs factory I can take some pictures, get out and fetch the cavalry.'

We agreed to sleep on it, washed and dried the dishes like a long-married couple, listened to *The World Tonight* on the radio and turned in to our separate bunks. I quickly scanned the BBC's news website on my laptop but as I pressed the power-off button, I reflected that putting off the difficult conversation with Nina had been the right thing to do. She had relaxed after our walk and immersed herself in the debate about what to do about our suspected drug lord and his gang. However, I knew I was only putting off the inevitable. If Nina was to be properly prepared for the hue and cry that would inevitably follow the publicity in the newspapers, it could only wait until morning.

CHAPTER ELEVEN

I felt my phone vibrate under the pillow and checked my watch. It was just after seven forty-five a.m. and I sensed from a small breeze flowing past the bed that Nina was already up and having a hot drink in the bow of the boat. I blinked and brought my eyes into focus.

> Inquest opens at 11am today. Magistrates' Court. Sam now identified. Brian Milk.

I thought about this for a few minutes and then padded to the galley in boxers and a T-shirt and refilled the still warm-kettle. Nina poked her head around the door.

'Morning,' she said cheerfully. 'Looks like it'll be a nice day.' Her head retreated out of sight. She was humming quietly to herself. The temperature still felt distinctly chilly to me, but I decided to take her word for it.

The radio was on quietly in the galley and I turned up the volume as I heard the pips announce the start of the eight o'clock news bulletin. I was half-listening to the usual litany of job losses, government initiatives, opposition counterclaims and so on when the announcer's voice suddenly broke through with stark clarity.

'Finally, police are increasingly concerned for the safety of a war widow whose husband was recently killed in Afghanistan. Mrs Angelina Wilde went missing from her home in Wiltshire two weeks ago. Her

friends and family are appealing for her to get in touch with them or the police. Mrs Wilde is the widow of Captain Alan Wilde, who was killed whilst trying to rescue two injured members of his Parachute Regiment during a fire fight with the Taliban in Helmand province. The couple had only been married for a few weeks. And now the weather...'

I instinctively went to turn the volume down but pulled my hand back at the last moment. Perhaps she hadn't heard.

However, the air in the boat suddenly felt charged with a menacing static. I padded back to my bed and retrieved yesterday's newspaper from under my pillow. I took it out to the bow and sat down opposite Nina, who looked both simultaneously tense and numb. It was obvious that she had heard the news bulletin only too clearly.

'I'm so sorry,' I said and passed the folded newspaper to her with the picture uppermost. She stared into my eyes for a moment and then they flicked down to the paper and back up again. It was just long enough to register the wedding photograph on its front page. She read the article sideways, as though she couldn't bear to confront it head on.

Then she stood up quickly and in one movement turned to go back into the boat whilst extending her arm over the side. She dropped the newspaper into the water as she ducked down inside and I stooped to watch her back retreating behind the swing door to her berth at the far end of the boat. Eddie trotted happily along behind her, oblivious to the unfolding drama.

I looked over the side to see the pages of the newspaper beginning to fan out. The front page was uppermost, the photograph already beginning to blur as it floated just under the surface of the water. The whistle of the kettle brought me back to my senses. I ducked back inside, turned the gas ring off and made a fresh pot of tea. Clutching both mugs, I pushed open the swing door to find her sitting sideways on her bed, both knees raised, her arms clasped round them. The little dog's paws were on the bed as it stood hoping to be lifted up onto it.

I proffered one of the mugs and she reached out, took it in both hands and began to sip. I sat down on the bed opposite, adopted a similar seating position and began to sip my drink too. I let the silence stretch out between us for as long as it took. Her eyes remained downcast, avoiding mine and anything else in the little cabin as she continued to sip her drink. Eddie began to whine in frustration. She seemed to notice the little dog for the first time then, dropped one foot down under his tummy and lifted him up onto the bed where he immediately curled up to one side of her. The movement also seemed to prompt her to look across at me and I was appalled to see two large fat tears rolling down her cheeks. Instinctively, I began to move towards her, but she shook her head fiercely and whispered 'No, Jack.'

'Look,' I said, leaning forward from the edge of the bed. 'We can work through this. They just want to know that you're safe. We can tell them that via the police. There's no need for them to find out where you are if that's what you want. Just tell them you need some time and space. Just phone them... or the police. They're worried about you. It's natural.'

She stared at me, but I had no idea whether my words had sunk in.

'Nina... Angelina... are you hearing me?'

'I have to go,' she said. Suddenly she was all movement, flustered and fluttering like a small bird that had flown into a room and become trapped behind closed windows and doors. 'I have to pack.' She had already grabbed the army kitbag from under her bed and started bundling clothes into it. 'I have to go,' she repeated agitatedly. 'I have to go.'

I reached out and held both of her wrists in my hands.

'Just stop, Nina... I mean Angelina. Oh Christ, I don't even know what to call you.'

She looked into my eyes and whispered again, 'I have to go.'

'Where?' I tried to keep my voice low and calm. 'The whole country is looking for you now. I can help you with this. Why shouldn't you grieve in your own way? I can't imagine what you are going through now, but –'

'I have to run,' she interrupted. 'I have to get away.'

I pushed her hands together. 'No. You will have to stop running some time. Do it on your own terms – not theirs.'

No sooner had I said this than she convulsed into deep heart-rending sobs. She pressed herself to my chest, both her palms flat out in front of her with her wrists still held in my hands. Her crying seemed to go on for a lifetime but in truth was probably no more than a couple of minutes. Then, as she seemed to quieten, I spoke again as gently as I could.

'I can't begin to feel the grief and pain that you are going through, Nina. If you want to stay on the boat for a while you are more than welcome. Stay for as long as you like. But honestly, we need to tell your people – your mother – that you're safe. It's not fair for them to be worrying about you on top of their own grief.'

She pulled back sharply. 'Fair? Fair! I'll tell you what's not fucking fair, Jack, and that's Alan dying in some godforsaken backwater of a war that's just a joke. An unwinnable joke. Don't tell me what's fair.'

A shudder passed through her small frame almost as an aftershock from her sobbing. Then she went on. 'I knew he was dead before they knocked on my door. I knew as soon as I saw them getting out of the Land Rover at the end of our garden. I knew he wasn't coming home alive or with bits missing after some bloody roadside bomb. I knew...' She was back on the bed now, knees hunched up again in front of her with the whole of her arms wrapped around them. 'I knew, but all they could tell me was that he died doing his duty. He died a hero's death. He died soldiering; doing what he loved. He died trying to save his men. Well, he shouldn't have been doing *any* of that. He should have been living with me and loving me and living. He should still be *alive*.'

The last sentence came out as a muffled wail and she buried her face in the top of her knees.

'Angelina...'

Her head shot up. 'Call me Nina,' she said fiercely.

'Nina...'

'They couldn't hack it. Oh no. They wanted a brave little war widow who would cherish her hero's memory forever. They didn't want someone who was bloody *angry*, bloody furious and bloody critical of the sheer bloody waste – not just of Alan but of every other poor sod that comes back in bits, or doesn't come back at all. They said I was 'overwrought'. They said I needed medication or counselling or something to stop me upsetting the other men's wives. After all, she'd only been married for six weeks, hadn't she? Not long enough really to marry into the army. Not long enough to appreciate the funeral with full military honours. Not long enough to know what to say and how to say it – to his fellow officers, his men, his parents, my parents, his brother...'

Eddie, who seemed to have been cowed by the outpouring of words gave a little whine which prompted Nina to lift him up to her chest. She looked across at me.

'So, I packed Alan's kitbag and cleared out,' she said. The trauma now seemed to have given way to a steely resolve. 'And I'm not going back until I'm good and ready and until I know... until I know how to live the rest of my life. Now, this dog needs a walk and so do I.'

She swung up off the bed, pulled on a baseball cap with one hand and climbed the short flight of steps up to the back deck with Eddie on his lead. I decided to let her go – as if I had any choice in the matter.

I turned off the wretched radio, rinsed our mugs and put them onto their shelf. It was only then that I registered that the shelf had two small strips of wood to hold the cups safe, presumably when the boat encountered stormy waters. How silly to have this feature on a narrowboat. But there was no doubt that Nina was in the centre of a storm of her own. I went out onto the front deck to see the town centre slowly coming to life. The rush hour traffic was now bumper to bumper and I could see staff arriving to open up the row of shops opposite the basin. There was no sign of Nina and the dog. It was barely breakfast time but I felt desperately in need of a proper drink. Nina's raw emotional state had been difficult to witness and I felt I had been a less than adequate grief counsellor. But as a journalist I was on more solid ground. I knew for certain that the first thing to do would be to take the air out of the story before the press pack could get a scent of her trail. Nina was in no state to have the ladies and gentlemen of the press descending in their hordes in open competition for an interview and pictures. I started the engine to begin recharging the batteries, pulled out my phone and pressed the redial button for Sergeant Milk.

'Mr Johnson?'

'Sergeant Milk. Thanks for the text about the inquest.'

'It's just a formality. An opening. But you said you wanted to know.'

'Thank you. I thought you said it would be a week or so?'

'Aye, well, we had a bit of a break. I didn't hold out much hope but it turned out that his mother had reported him missing when he first walked out. His first name matched a couple of Manchester's missing person records and we narrowed it down. My opposite number there called on the family and confirmed it was him. We drove them down for a formal ID yesterday evening and then they went straight back.'

'What was his surname?'

'Robinson. Sam Robinson.'

'How did they take it?'

'Mum was cut up, but his dad was pretty unmoved. It adds up with what he told you.'

I decided to change tack.

'Look, Sergeant, there's something else I need to talk to you about. It's pretty urgent and I just need to get some off-the-record advice. Could you spare me ten minutes?'

'Okay,' he said warily. 'Come to the coroner's court at eleven. Shouldn't take more than quarter of an hour and you can buy me a quick coffee afterwards. That's the best I can do. Got to rush.'

'Right. See you later.'

I waited on the boat until ten, but there was still no sign of Nina and Eddie so I locked both doors and set off to find the courts.

CHAPTER TWELVE

A sign in the lobby indicated that Court 4 was being used for coroner's inquests that morning. I pushed open the swing doors into a surprisingly modern room with strip lighting and stripped pine panelling and furniture. The sergeant was already sitting at a table in front of the bench and nodded a cursory greeting at me. A middle-aged woman sat to one side of the bench, presumably the court reporter, but other than that the room was empty. I shuffled into a wooden pew and waited for something to happen.

After a few minutes, Sergeant Milk rose to his feet, said 'All rise, please' and a door behind the bench swung inwards. The coroner was a small, pudgy man with very little hair and a decidedly old-fashioned black pinstripe three-piece suit complete with silver watch chain. His face had a pasty look and his brow was already beaded in an unhealthy sweat as he sat down. His eyes darted quickly around the court as though its relative emptiness was an affront to his sense of self importance. He nodded at the sergeant who remained on his feet whilst we resumed our seats.

Just as Sergeant Milk was about to speak the doors banged open and a tall greying figure in an equally grey raincoat bustled in. He nodded apologetically at the coroner, sat down a few yards from me on the same bench and pulled an exercise book and biro out of his pocket. Press, I thought. The coroner tutted fastidiously and nodded again at his officer.

'Sir,' Sergeant Milk said. 'This is the opening of the inquest into the death of nineteen-year-old Mr Sam Robinson, whose body was found in the Stratford-upon-Avon Canal on September the twenty-fifth of this year. The deceased's last known address was Drood Cottage near Wilmcote, however his family has been traced to Manchester. He left the family home some months ago.'

'Thank you, Sergeant Milk. What is the pathologist saying at this stage?'

'His report is in your file, sir, but he has confirmed the cause of death as drowning. No witnesses have come forward. There were some marks on the body but, in the pathologist's opinion, these were most probably caused by passing boat traffic. The deceased had also ingested a large quantity of alcohol and drugs before he went into the water.'

'Very well, Sergeant, thank you. This inquest is opened and adjourned to a later date.'

'Bollocks.' The thin grey late arrival had said the single word in a whisper, but it still sounded loud in the largely empty room. The other four people in the court – me included – looked up at him sharply. He stared coolly back, the small line of his lips clamped shut under his angular cheekbones. The sergeant looked to the coroner for guidance, but he just huffily gathered his papers together and swept back out of the door behind him. The thin man rose to his feet and turned to leave too. Instinctively, I decided to follow him. I calculated that I could catch up with the sergeant later and ask his advice about how to reassure the Wiltshire Police in their missing person enquiry. But at the moment my curiosity was piqued by the man and his one-word exclamation.

I hurried out of the main door, brushing past a short, balding middle-aged man who must also have come into the room after proceedings had started.

'Excuse me.' I eventually caught up with my quarry in the lobby. 'Can I have a word?'

The thin man spun round, a black leather briefcase tucked under one arm.

'What is it?' He had the slight trace of a Birmingham accent.

'Why "bollocks"?' I asked.

The man gave a faintly rueful smile. 'And you are?'

'I met Sam, the dead kid, shortly before he died. I helped the police identify him. I'm just curious. Why "bollocks"?'

He closed his eyes and gave a long and tired-sounding sigh. 'Because it's the usual myopia of the authorities as to what is really going on.'

'Which is?'

'Look, Mr...?'

'Johnson, Jack Johnson,' I shook the man's hand even though he clearly wanted to escape. I was determined to find out what he thought he knew.

'Look, Mr Johnson. Nice to meet you and all that but I don't really have time to explain and so...'

'I'm press,' I said. It was a gamble, but if people are harbouring conspiracy theories, as this man clearly seemed to be, they usually welcomed the chance to bring them to a wider audience. Sure enough, he suddenly looked more interested.

'Press?' He was rising to the fly. 'What paper?'

'Freelance,' I said. 'But national.' It was sort of true.

He nodded slowly. 'Okay then. But it's complicated.'

'I'll buy the first Americano and a second if absolutely necessary.'

Now he smiled. He was hooked.

'Very well, Mr Johnson. I'm Professor Rob Parsons, Department of Psychology, University of Manchester. I'm a specialist in criminal psychology.'

'Step this way, Professor Parsons.'

We found a couple of small brown leather armchairs facing each other in the window of a nearby Costa and I supplied us both with two large coffees. Sergeant Milk strode past the window just as I was sitting down but he was staring straight ahead and didn't seem to notice us.

'So why "bollocks"?' I asked again, taking out a scrap of paper and a pen.

'You first,' said the professor. 'What's your interest in the case?'

I quickly explained how I had met Sam; how I'd pushed him onto the ground, felt bad about it, bought him lunch and paid him to tell his personal history before providing him with a shower and then watching him disappear in the blue Land Rover. I described how I had helped Sergeant Milk identify his body and briefly outlined the trip to Drood Cottage, carefully avoiding saying anything about a possible connection with drug dealers. Professor Parsons, however, wasn't satisfied.

'So, this boy was effectively living rough, with no money, but had somehow acquired large quantities of drink and drugs?' He was leaning forward, his eyes bright with interest.

'I gave him a bit of cash,' I admitted.

'But not much, surely? He may have been involved in some crime?'

I shrugged. 'Maybe. Probably. Who knows?'

Professor Parsons pressed both his palms onto the sides of his nose and gave me a long thoughtful stare.

'All right. I want your agreement not to publish anything without my say-so,' he said. 'This is a working theory at present and I'm not prepared for publicity until my research is complete.' He held out a bony white hand. 'Agreed?'

'Agreed.'

He gave a conspiratorial look around the coffee shop – a gesture that appeared faintly ridiculous to me. The rest of the clientele seemed to comprise young mums and harmless pensioners, but he lowered his voice nonetheless.

'Eighty-five bodies have been recovered from canals, rivers, lakes and ponds in the UK over the past five years. A disproportionate number of those were found in the Manchester or Midlands areas.'

There are a lot of waterways and people in Manchester and the Midlands, I thought to myself. So far, not so shocking.

'I know what you're thinking,' he said. 'Birmingham – more canals than Venice et cetera. But the geographical profiling is suspicious, to say the least. When you get into the detail, the bodies are mostly found in isolated and secluded areas – just like the spot where Sam was found.' I opened my mouth to protest but he raised a palm.

'Yes, yes, I know. If they were populated areas they'd most likely have been pulled out by some passers-by. But I think there's a pattern emerging that suggests some of these people are being helped into the water and probably prevented from getting back out – especially in the Midlands. There's been a sharp spike in the number of deaths by drowning this year for no apparent reason.' Professor Parsons sat back and took a sip of coffee, watching my face.

'A serial killer?' I asked in surprise.

'I think it's a distinct possibility.' He seemed remarkably matter-of-fact. 'It's too lazy to assume they've all just drunk too much or taken drugs and stepped into the water on their own. There are all types of drowning – wet drowning, dry drowning, secondary drowning and immersion syndrome – but the point is that homicidal drowning is regarded as being very rare, except in the cases of children. Why? It's because pathologists look for obvious marks of strangulation or a big bash on the head. But what about bruises or other suspicious marks and cuts? They're often dismissed as injuries sustained by the body in the water. You heard today that they're already blaming canal boat propellers or the canal walls for any marks found on Sam's body.'

I nodded. I was intrigued now.

'But even if they're not, and this is the point – if a person has been taking alcohol or hypnotic drugs –' he held up one finger – 'and he is taken unawares or rendered senseless and defenceless – ' he held up two fingers – 'and his head is submerged in the water for five to ten minutes.' He held up three fingers and then unfurled a fourth. 'Then virtually no marks of violence will be found on the body. Look it up.'

He wrapped the four open fingers around his coffee cup and took a big swig.

'And, of course, the longer a body is in the water, the faster the decomposition and the more difficult it is to say what happened. But they're all tidily filed away under accidental death. It's a lot quicker and easier, isn't it? I believe, given the sheer scale of the numbers, the high proportion that are found with drink or drugs in their bodies and the geographical patterns, that this cannot be correct in all cases.'

'What made you come here today?' I asked.

He shrugged his sloping shoulders. 'I read the local newspapers, watch the local news websites and follow up when my nose twitches. Sam fitted the typical profile of a victim of deliberate drowning to me. Now, having spoken to you, I'm even more certain of that. Young, vulnerable – maybe even suggestible and compliant.'

'But you can't prove it?'

'No. I can't prove a thing. But I look for patterns and I study criminal psychology. I'm not saying there's one weird madman or woman out there responsible for all of these drownings – although there could be. But I am saying it has to be a more common method of murder than these idiot coroners' inquests are suggesting and that more of these deaths should be properly investigated.'

Professor Parsons' prominent Adam's apple had been bobbing excitedly as he outlined his theory, but it came to a halt now as he sat back in his chair, crossed his left ankle over his right knee and drained the last of his coffee.

I was stunned. If Sam had been caught up in some kind of nationwide drug dealing operation, were there others who had got in too deep and paid the ultimate price? Was this their grim modus operandi for getting rid of people who stole from them or tried to blackmail them? If so, the lack of evidence had made it virtually foolproof. What if the professor was right and the sudden spike in numbers hinted at what was really happening?

'Will you go public with your suspicions?' I asked.

'Probably. One day. I've got a PhD student helping me with the research. But at the moment I'm trying to get the police to take this seriously without going public.'

'And?'

'And they refuse to even contemplate the possibility that all of these people aren't just walking into the water on their own whilst under the influence of drugs or drink or both.'

'But why won't they even consider it?'

Professor Parsons shrugged. 'No witnesses. No corroborating evidence. Not enough resources. They don't want people to panic. They don't want to upset the families. Laziness. Police budget cuts. Take your pick, Mr Johnson.' He leaned forward. 'Tell me. Is there anything else you know about this young man, Sam, which might make my theory more likely?'

I drained my coffee and handed him the empty cup. 'That'll cost you an Americano,' I said.

After he returned from the service counter with two fresh cups, I briefly filled Professor Parsons in on our visit to the cottage. Then I told him about Jazzer and Birdie and how I had subsequently seen them dealing in the pub in Stratford after the handover from the Land Rover that was being driven by the hard-looking men who worked at Chester Farm – and who, I was sure, had also driven Sam away from the bridge near our temporary mooring.

'So, you think he might have been caught up in some kind of drug dealing operation?'

It was my turn to shrug. 'Maybe. But I can't prove anything either.'

'But don't you see?' he asked eagerly. 'Drug dealers have other nasty habits. It's part of their job description. They could have helped him into the water. Have you told the police any of this?'

'No. But why would they do that?'

'Any number of reasons. He might have owed them money, or stolen from them, or been threatening to shop them. Who knows?'

I smiled at him. 'It's not exactly proof, is it, Professor?'

He shook his head sadly. 'You should tell the police what you know. Okay – there may be no connection with Sam's death, but it won't hurt to rattle their cage, will it? What's the worst that can happen? Some nasty people get asked some pertinent questions about how they're earning a living.'

'I'll think about it,' I said, gathering up my phone and wallet from the table.

'And you're a journalist, aren't you? I would have thought you'd want this to turn into a decent story.'

I gave a guilty nod.

Professor Parsons fished into his wallet and slid a business card across to me. 'Please let me know how things develop.'

I nodded again, slipped his card into my wallet and wrote my email address on a scrap of paer. 'Sorry. I haven't got any cards on me. Thanks for your time,' I said.

'Stay in touch,' he replied.

We stood and shook hands, then I sat back down and watched his tall awkward frame leave the coffee shop. Bloody hell, I thought. Could it be true? Had Sam been deliberately given an excess of drink and drugs and then drowned by the drug pushers? And should I take my suspicions to the police? What if he was one of many? I shook my head at the sheer scale of the story – if it was true. For the moment, I decided, my priority had to be Nina and working out what to do about the nationwide missing person's enquiry trying to find her. I had thought to consult Sergeant Milk on how to call off the police search as quickly and quietly as possible but now I realised it would be wrong to attempt this without consulting Nina. Maybe she had calmed down enough to talk it through rationally by now? I made my way back to *Jumping Jack Flash*.

The fisherman finished his sandwich, swallowed the last of his cup of tea and meticulously wiped the corners of his mouth with a clean and neatly ironed white handkerchief. The bench gave him a good view through the window of the coffee shop of the two men he had followed from the inquest. Attending had been a gamble, but he had been clever as usual, quietly slipping inside once proceedings had begun. He had been surprised and a little dismayed by the sparse attendance. He thought his handiwork deserved a larger audience and was worried about the increased risk of someone noticing him. But even if they did, so what? There was nothing to connect him to a young man's death on the canal just a few miles away from where he now sat. He would write about it in his journal that evening and, one day, it would be another detail that added to people's amazement at his audacity. He had been very satisfied with the comments made by the policeman. Once again, there had been no witnesses and no marks that aroused suspicion on the body. Everything was pointing to yet another very satisfactory verdict of accidental death or death by misadventure – depending on how seriously the coroner regarded the drink and drugs which his victim had taken.

He balled up the paper that his tuna sandwich had been wrapped in and carefully put it inside a litter bin next to his seat. Then he watched the two men stand up, shake hands and the tallest man leave the coffee shop. He thought about following him but then he saw the second man walk through the door. He was twirling some keys on a small cord with a large round piece of cork on it. The fisherman knew that boat owners used these cork floats to prevent their keys sinking to the bottom if they fell overboard. The man must be a boat owner. He waited for the man to walk past him, heading across the expanse of grass towards the canal basin. The fisherman rose to his feet and shuffled after him. Who was he and what was his interest in the dead boy? He had watched him engage the tall thin man who had said 'bollocks' at the end of the inquest's opening and then usher him into the coffee shop. They had clearly been strangers to each other before the inquest. It was all very intriguing.

The fisherman remained twenty metres behind the man as he followed him to the basin. The man walked across a small bridge and around the path to the canal boats moored on the far side. The fisherman watched as the man climbed onto a red-and-black boat and disappeared into its interior. That was interesting. The man had a canal boat and had also gone to the hearing. Why? He couldn't have witnessed anything on the night the boy drowned or the policeman would have referred to it. Perhaps he had found the body the following day? The fisherman sauntered over to another bench near a statue of Shakespeare and sat down. He pulled a tabloid newspaper out of one pocket of his coat and opened it out in front of him.

As he sat watching over the top of the newspaper, an older couple emerged from the boat next to the one the man had entered and seemed to be tentatively encouraging each other to approach their neighbour's vessel. The older man knocked on the hatchway and the man he had followed reappeared on the boat's stern deck. He watched as the two men spoke briefly to each other. The older man and his wife seemed to be trying to give the younger man a newspaper. The body language between the three people became stiff and uncomfortable, then the older couple went awkwardly back to their neighbouring boat.

The fisherman turned the pages of his newspaper without reading them and maintained his vigil.

Five minutes later a young woman appeared on the path and climbed up onto the stern of Jumping Jack Flash. The fisherman started as he realised two things in quick succession. The first was that he had seen her before, jogging along the towpath behind him as he had explored the stretch of canal looking for a suitable spot for a killing. He *remembered her vividly because she had been on her own and he had quietly hoped she might repeat her lonely run much later that evening. His second, even greater, surprise was that she was carrying the little brown terrier that had belonged to the boy. So, he thought rapidly, she was staying on the boat with the man from the inquest and they must have been moored somewhere near the location of his ambush. She had probably found the dog wandering along the towpath the following morning. His mind raced. What else did he need to know? Why had the man gone to the opening of the inquest? And what had he discussed with the other taller man in the coffee shop afterwards? Had the dog somehow given them a clue as to what had happened? Should he have killed it too? Or had they somehow known the dead boy? He realised he was being uncharacteristically irrational and he also knew he was being stupid loitering so close to the couple on this boat. He quickly folded his newspaper, returned it to his coat pocket and turned to walk away from the basin, back towards the town centre car park where he had left his car. He had a lot to think about. If he had lingered for another twenty minutes and seen the large bulk of the coroner's officer returning to climb clumsily on board the boat, he would have been even more troubled.*

CHAPTER THIRTEEN

I heard a ping to indicate an incoming text on my mobile as I walked back to the boat from the coffee shop. It was Deb.

> You've got to tell the police.

I calculated that if I didn't do something quickly, Deb or Mary might take matters into their own hands. It also occurred to me that Sergeant Milk had already met Nina and that it wouldn't be long before he read a newspaper or saw a missing person appeal on his police computer or on a poster at the police station. When I got back the hatchway was still locked and so I assumed Nina was still out with Eddie. I hoped her baseball cap would be enough to prevent her being recognised.

'Ah, hello there! Excuse me?' There was a knock on the hatchway. It was the older man on the neighbouring boat who had told me about the discovery of Sam's body. His wife was hopping nervously behind him on the bank by our stern. He had a newspaper in one hand.

'Yes?' I said, somewhat wearily, clambering up the steps from Nina's bedroom.

'Not our business, we know, but we wondered if you'd seen this?' He waved the newspaper apologetically. I could see it had been folded to show Nina's picture. 'You see we think it may be your... your...' His face twisted with embarrassment as groped for the right word.

'Lady friend,' whispered his wife from behind him. He pounced gratefully on the word.

'Ah yes... your lady friend. Seems she's gone missing and the police are trying to find her.' The man's body language was anguish personified. I imagined that the net curtains on his boat carefully matched those in the couple's immaculate bungalow somewhere in the suburbs of a Midlands town. Their early-retirement lifestyle was no doubt one of quiet self-satisfaction measured out in pots of tea, Radio Two and occasional 'adventures' on the boat that he had bought second-hand with the pot of cash that the government now allowed him to siphon out of his retirement pot. Only this one was turning into too much of a real-life adventure, what with a drowned body and now a missing person 'lady friend'. Whilst he relished the prospect of telling the tale to his friends at the bowls club, he was now crucified with a very English embarrassment at having to broach this awkward topic with his floating neighbour. Not knowing how to continue, he proffered the newspaper to me.

'Do take it,' he said. 'Or borrow it,' he added quickly, no doubt realising that otherwise he would have to buy another as a memento of this exciting turn of events.

I folded my arms and stared him out.

'Look, she hasn't gone missing, has she? She's on my boat, she's safe and well and she just wants some peace and privacy. We'll let the police know that's she's here later today, so can you just keep this to yourselves for now, please?'

The man nodded furiously, pink with embarrassment, whilst his wife gave me a sharp, suspicious look from over his shoulder.

'Yes. Yes, of course. Privacy. That's the thing.' He looked relieved as he pulled the newspaper back under one arm and turned to bustle his wife away. 'Let's leave them to sort things out, dear. Privacy, that's the thing.'

I sighed. Deb, Bloody Mary, Sergeant Milk and now the bloody next-door neighbours. It was time to take control of this thing.

Nina arrived five minutes later with Eddie. She came to the front of the boat and sat down, her legs stretched lengthways on another chair next to the kitchen table. The dog briefly jumped down to greet me and then quickly back up to stretch out on Nina's lap. She put a new neatly folded copy of the newspaper in front of her.

'Hi,' she said. 'How was the inquest?' Her tone was wholly matter-of-fact. All trace of the shock and anger of earlier this morning was gone. I sat down opposite her.

'Intriguing,' I replied. 'Good walk?' It had clearly helped her to calm down and regain some equilibrium. She just nodded and smoothed the newspaper with the palms of both hands.

'No unexplained injuries, no witnesses and it looks like he was pissed and drugged up. Time to call off the hounds?' I asked, changing the subject quietly and nodding to indicate the newspaper.

'But how? They'll still come after me, won't they?'

'Probably,' I conceded. 'And it won't take long. Even the neighbours have already seen the story and came to ask if you were alright. I was going to ask Sergeant Milk to let his colleagues know that you're safe and well and haven't been kidnapped. Hopefully they can tell your friends and family without giving your location away. But I can't guarantee it'll stop the hack-pack trying to find you. They'll already be mobilising to try and get pictures and an interview. It's just a matter of time.'

Nina nodded. She'd already worked it all out for herself. 'Unless...'

'What do you have in mind?' I asked.

'We could keep moving. We can turn around and head north. There are a few different ways we could go.' She pulled the little canal map book from under the newspaper and pushed it towards me. Sure enough, the canal network offered the choice of a couple of junctions below Birmingham and a myriad of options once we were in the city.

'Okay,' I said, spreading my hands on the table. 'Devil's advocate, okay?'

She nodded.

'We'll be going at less than four miles per hour – so it's not exactly Bonnie and Clyde getaway speed. And once the word is out,' I continued, nodding meaningfully at the boat moored alongside us, 'there will be no shortage of people who are only too happy to report the sighting of a boat called *Jumping Jack Flash* with the nice big painting of a jester on its side as it goes oh-so-slowly past marinas, pubs and homes in return for a tidy tip-off fee from those nice people at the newspapers.'

'So what?' she said defiantly. 'They might find us, but they can't make me talk. I can just tell them to bugger off.'

'You're right, of course. You don't have to talk to them – as long as you don't mind them hanging off bridges to get photographs of you and making up ever more lurid stories about you in the absence of anything from the horse's mouth. You won't be able to walk the dog, go for a run or even leave the boat. It'll be a floating prison.'

'They'll get bored eventually,' she said truculently.

'Maybe. Although it will take a while and once the daily rags give up it'll be the Sundays and the magazines who will dig in for a long-term exclusive. I've worked in this business, Nina. Trust me, it'll be a nightmare.'

'We can swap boats.'

I stared at her. She wasn't giving up on her escape plan and I had to admit, part of me was very pleased about that.

'We can,' I admitted. 'But we'd need to get back up to the boatyard at Wootton Wawen first and we can't guarantee that even the name of the new boat will remain much of a secret for long.'

The obvious solution, of course, was for Nina to leave me and head off by land to some remote and secret location. But for some reason she wasn't contemplating that, and I certainly wasn't about to suggest it.

'So what kind of lurid stories would they make up about me?'

'What?' The question threw me.

'You're the expert. What kind of stories would you make up?'

'Would *they* make up.'

'Okay. Would *they* make up?'

I thought for a minute. 'Well, for a start they'd put two and two together about you and me and make five – or even six. They'd say that the grieving widow was finding consolation – maybe they'd even call it romantic consolation – in the arms of a redundant and newly divorced journalist on board his appropriately named boat, the *Jumping Jack Flash*.'

To my surprise Nina giggled.

'Love-boat,' she said.

'What?'

'They'd call it a love-boat.'

'Yes,' I conceded. 'They probably would. And they'd go to my ex-wife for some character assassination and if she didn't oblige, her friends almost certainly would. Then they'd go to your friends and relatives for expressions of serious concern that I was taking advantage of a vulnerable and distressed woman.'

'Vulnerable and distressed *younger* woman,' she added.

'Younger woman,' I agreed sadly.

'Good story,' Nina nodded. 'But it wouldn't bother me.'

I pressed the fingertips of both hands into my eyes and cradled my chin in my palms.

'And it wouldn't really bother me,' I said, removing my hands and giving her a level look. 'Especially if it was true.'

She gave me a level look back.

'Look, Jack. It's your boat and I'm in your hands. But if you're really prepared to help me out I would like to stay on board for a few more days. We can head off first thing in the morning rather than sit here in the middle of Stratford. I'll take my chances with the press. But in the meantime, you're right. Eddie helped me do some thinking this morning and we need to get everyone to calm down – especially the family. Could you ask Sergeant Milk to pop over so we can chat it through with him?'

***

The generous bulk of the good sergeant filled the boat again as soon as he descended the steps. He had listened to my brief explanation on the phone and said that, whilst it was really a matter for his colleagues, he would be there in twenty minutes. Having settled himself opposite Nina with a cup of tea – milk, two sugars and two chocolate biscuits – he asked me to give them some privacy for ten minutes, so I took Eddie outside for a wander around the basin.

The temperature was falling along with the leaves on some of the surrounding trees, which had already turned from red to brown. Everyone scurrying past was well wrapped up in thick clothing, even scarves. It would soon be October and I hadn't given much of a thought to my own future over the past few days. I sat down on one of the cold metal benches while the dog snuffled near a waste bin. Would I buy the boat? Where and how could I begin to start earning a living again? When would I get the cash from Deb and how long would it last? Nina and Sam had pushed these thoughts to the back of my mind since I had collected the boat six days ago. And that's where they retreated again as Sergeant Milk loomed in front of me. He sat down next to me on the cold metal bench with one of his characteristically heavy grunts.

'Mr Johnson,' he said.

'Sergeant.'

'Well, I'm satisfied you aren't holding Mrs Wilde against her will,' he said with a half-smile.

'That's good to know.'

'And she wants to stay on board your boat.'

'That's okay with me too.'

'I should have recognised her. I read the papers this morning, but I was in a bit of a hurry, so it didn't register.'

'Well, you've found her now,' I said.

'Aye. We'll let her family know she's safe and well but that she's not ready to come home for now. They can spread the word.'

'And you'll tell the press?'

'We'll need to call an end to the nationwide alert.'

'But it won't stop them coming after her.'

'Aye, well, they won't find out where she is from me,' he said calmly. 'Poor young woman. She just needs a bit of time and space. We'll tell them that we're satisfied that she's safe and well with a friend and that she wants to be alone for the moment.'

'I suppose you deal with bereavement all of the time?' It was a statement of the obvious, but he was too polite to say so.

'Aye, well, yes. Comes with the job. Everyone reacts differently, and everyone reacts the same in a way. Shock, numbness, anger, grief.'

'And eventually reconciliation?' I asked.

'Eventually, yes, for most people. Like I say, it takes time and sometimes people need the people they love around them and sometimes they just need their own company... or even the company of strangers,' he added, meaningfully.

'Thanks for not persuading her to go home.'

The sergeant, who had been talking straight ahead, turned to look at me directly for the first time.

'She knows her own mind. But she's very grateful to you, Mr Johnson. She said you'd been very kind and thoughtful and treated her with respect.'

I laughed quietly to hide my embarrassment. 'To be honest, I just needed a pilot who knew how to handle that thing.' I nodded to indicate the boat.

'If you want my advice, sir,' he continued. 'You won't be getting too close to her. She'll be on something of an emotional roller coaster at the moment, but she'll be ready to rebuild her old life at some stage.' He rose to his feet with an even louder grunt and held out a hand.

'Listen to me, talking like some bloody agony aunt. Thank you for persuading her to call us, sir. We don't have the resources for unnecessary manhunts just because the bloody press thinks that it's a good story.'

I shook his hand, but he held onto it. 'And one more bit of advice, Mr Johnson. I wouldn't take too much notice of that other chap at the inquest today.' I started in surprise as he withdrew his hand and pulled on a pair of black gloves that had been in the pocket of his police jacket. 'No need to go upsetting families when there isn't a shred of evidence for what he says.'

'Professor Parsons spoke to you?' I asked.

'On the phone before the inquest. We know all about him and his so-called research. I saw you talking to him afterwards. Be a shame to give it a lot of publicity. Like I say, it'll upset a lot of families for nothing.' He turned his collar up. 'Good day now, Mr Johnson.' And with that he turned and lumbered back towards the town centre whilst I stared at his back and tried to absorb his parting words.

Nina came towards me as I pushed through the swing door. She leaned forward and gave me a peck on one cheek as she took the dog off me.

'Nice man,' she said with an ambiguous smile. I wondered whether she meant me or Sergeant Milk.

CHAPTER FOURTEEN

After a very late lunch of fried lamb chops, new potatoes and peas, I slipped out on my own while Nina headed below for a nap with Eddie. In a bookshop I bought a detailed Ordnance Survey map of Stratford and the surrounding area and went back to the coffee shop to study it. It didn't take me long to find Chester Farm in the centre of a large swathe of land that sat between a B-road and a small tributary of the river. I followed the tributary with my finger for half a mile or so until it joined the River Avon as it flowed down and on through Stratford. I picked up a few more things from an outdoor equipment and camping shop and returned to the boat where Nina had resumed reading a book on her bunk. She looked at my carrier bags but didn't comment as I passed her into the main cabin. She probably thought it was about time that I bought some new clothes. The evening settled into a comfortable silence; we read and occasionally helped ourselves to small whiskies and water. Nina turned in at about 10.30 p.m. after giving me a friendly goodnight peck on my cheek. She seemed to have calmed down a lot since the meeting with the sergeant.

I waited another hour and then quietly slipped on my newly purchased black walking trousers and black waist-length jacket over an old dark blue sweatshirt. I tied on a new pair of dark blue trainers, slipped my mobile into a buttoned pocket and grabbed my baseball cap as I tiptoed out of the front hatchway. I stepped down onto the pontoon as gently as possible so as not to rock the boat or wake

Eddie. I waited a moment but Nina's porthole remained dark and so I moved off.

I had noticed the small fleet of battery-powered pleasure boats the previous day. There were about twenty of them painted in a range of bright colours; each had room for four passengers on two small benches. A high wire fence and a padlocked gate prevented access to the pontoon around which they were clustered, but it was a quiet riverside spot and, after checking that no one else was on the towpath, I climbed up and over the gate, squeezing the tip of my new trainer on top of a small wooden sign that said, 'Strictly No Entry'. I rolled on my stomach over the steel tubing at the top of the gate and dropped down onto the other side. The pontoon bounced slightly on the water with the momentum of my fall and sent a gentle wave washing against the bank. I crouched low and clambered across two of the boats to a black one on the outer edge of one group. I quickly untied it from the others, pressed the little starter button next to the steering wheel and slid the throttle forward. It was almost completely silent but responded instantly, moving out slowly through the dark water into midstream, where I turned the bow to the right and began heading upstream, away from the town's lights.

I knew I would have to go for about two miles until I reached the mouth of the tributary, which would be on my left almost immediately after a small sewerage works that was marked on the map. The little boat crept ahead at a speed that was deliberately limited to prevent tourists enjoying themselves too much. At least it didn't seem to be fighting much of a current. I prayed that the battery had been well charged for the following day's business. There was just enough of a moon to see by and I was relieved not to have to rely on the torch on my phone. I realised now that I should have supplemented it with the little pencil torch from the boat and quietly cursed myself for embarking on this half-baked plan. After some time, the end of the dark mass of buildings on the bank to my right finally slipped past. I had been wary of a householder raising the alarm as they gave their dog its final wee of the day in the garden before turning in to bed. But no one appeared and, anyway, I would probably have just looked to them as a dark smudge in the middle of the narrowing river.

I smelt the sewerage plant before I saw it and felt confident enough to switch my phone's torch on. Another 'Keep Out' sign and barbed wire indicated I was in the right place so I swung closer to the bank and my light quickly picked up the entrance to the stream, which was about three metres across. However, a tree had fallen across half of it and I had to grab the branches of its crown and pull the small boat through the little bit of space that remained clear. Once through, my light showed the stream stretching off into the distance, bordered by dense trees and shrubbery. It quickly narrowed so that I had less than half a metre free on each side, but it stayed deep enough to float my borrowed boat. After about five minutes I felt the small boat's shallow bottom gently slide to a halt on the bed of the stream.

I risked my torch again and saw a little wooden jetty up ahead, stranded now by the silted-up stream. I pulled my trainers off, tied the shoelaces together and slung them around my neck. I stuffed my mobile phone firmly into the toe of one of them, and my socks into the other, avoiding my trouser or jacket pockets in case the stream suddenly went deep again. Next, I pulled off my trousers, looped them over my neck too and tied the ankles loosely in front of my chest. Finally, after a momentary hesitation, I pulled off my boxer shorts and stuffed them into my trainers too. There was no point in having wet pants if I didn't need to. Then I gingerly sat on the prow of the boat and, as it dipped with my weight, slipped down into the cold water. My bare feet went straight into mud and stopped sinking at the level of my knees. The water was now lapping around the level of my groin. I congratulated myself on my careful precautions. But the shock of the cold was more than enough of an incentive to begin wading quickly towards the jetty. I kept both my arms outstretched to maintain my balance, but I nearly lost my footing twice. Eventually, I hauled myself up onto the jetty. I sat on its edge and rinsed the mud off, wiped my legs and feet with a handful of leaves and then hurriedly pulled my boxers, trousers and trainers back on and stuffed my phone into my back pocket.

The jetty was short and balanced precariously on some old scaffolding poles, but it held my weight as I inched back towards the bank where, having crawled through a tangle of undergrowth, I could just see a small overgrown path. It ran just one way, further upstream. I switched off the torch and began to make my way along the path. It was hard going at first. It was clear that no one had used the path, or the jetty, for a very long time. But after about ten minutes the corner of a tall metal fence appeared on my right and I followed its line until I came across the first of a series of signs, all neatly printed with the words 'Chester Farm' and below that, 'KEEP OUT'. The bottom perimeter of the farm had looked a few miles long on the map and so far, I could see nothing beyond the fencing other than a thick line of trees. After five minutes of walking, the trees ended and another perimeter fence stretched away inwards. The trees were now replaced by line after line of white plastic semi-circular tunnels that rose to a height at least double my own and matched the height of the fencing. This fencing had a single strand of razor wire looping in and out of the topmost level of diamond-shaped spaces. It was clear that Chester Farm's unwelcome attitude to visitors extended around the whole of its perimeter. This in itself was strange. Surely, a typical fruit farm wouldn't invest in miles of expensive fencing of a type that could do justice to a prison or military camp? I was breathing fast now. This was going to be much more difficult than I had anticipated.

I thought quickly. There must be a door of some kind through the fencing to allow for the maintenance of the perimeter path, but I had come across nothing yet. My watch told me that it was half past midnight and scudding clouds kept obscuring the moon, temporarily casting me into total blackness. On the one hand, this meant I was less likely to be spotted but, on the other, I could barely see what I was doing and I longed to use my torch.

I continued along the fencing. This was fruit-farming on a truly industrial scale. The soft white glow of the polytunnels stretched on and on towards the darkened horizon. The land immediately beyond the fence seemed to slope upwards very gradually and I assumed that it then dipped down towards the farmhouse and its outbuildings. During our brief visit, the house had seemed to sit at the centre of a vast bowl of the large white caterpillar-like tubes. From my current position these contours would keep me out of sight of anyone in the house or the farm buildings and I could use them as a rough guide to navigate by.

Finally, after ten more agonising minutes, I came across a gate in the fencing at last. I was probably a mile from where I had started. It would be a long way back if I needed to get to my laughable little getaway boat in a hurry. A heavy metal chain was woven through the gate and the fence was secured with a heavy-duty padlock. If this was the weak link I had been looking for, it was about as weak as a silverback gorilla. The razor wire looked lethally sharp above the gate, a horizontal steel pole closely hugged the ground below and, in the middle, the padlock looked like it would be daunting even if I'd had housebreaking tools and knew how to use them. I cursed myself for failing to shop for some wire-cutters along with my new dark clothes. I cast around for inspiration, reluctant to turn back and almost equally reluctant to go on.

I could just make out some dark semi-circular shapes in the fields on the other side of the path. I walked along the hedge bordering the land until there was a bare spot where the chicken-wire fence was exposed. I vaulted over it by the fence-post and quickly headed for the shapes. Sure enough, they were semi-circular pig pens made out of corrugated iron. When I got closer, I could see one in particular that was in a bad way, peppered with rusty holes. Wide strips of black rubber hung forlornly at its entrance. They had presumably acted as some kind of windbreak. I felt the rubber. It was at least half an inch thick. I tugged a few bits free, a slightly desperate plan beginning to take shape in my brain.

Back at Chester Farm's boundary fence, I draped three of the rubber strips across my right shoulder and made to begin climbing the fence. With frustration, I realised that the toes of my new trainers were too wide to penetrate the fence's chain-link holes, making it impossible for me to ascend. I pulled them off for the second time that night and readjusted the heavy rubber strips on my shoulder. Then I poked my toes directly into the gaps in the fence. This time, I successfully began to move upwards. My climb was awkward due to the rubber mats balanced on my shoulder and painful thanks to the wire cutting into my fingers and toes, but at least it was an incentive to keep climbing as fast as I could. When my hands were just below the razor wire, I stopped, pushed both feet as far forward through the fence as I could and, clinging tight with my right hand, flipped the rubber mats forward and over the top of the fence with my left, spreading the mats out over the razor wire on both sides of me. The pain in my toes was now excruciating. I clumsily tried to reposition the mats and, suddenly, I was falling backwards. With one great effort, I managed to regain my hold. I was a bit shaken now and breathing very hard, but gave myself one last push up, so that my stomach straddled the strips of black rubber lying across the top of the fence and my legs dangled freely at last. The relief to my toes was enormous. Gingerly, I began to pull and twist myself sideways on the mats. I prayed the rubber would be thick enough to prevent the sharp points slicing through into my torso. I began to panic as I felt them moving with me until the points of the razor wire suddenly gripped them firmly into place. It was a clumsy performance but I somehow managed to swivel 180 degrees and soon my legs were hanging down on the farm's side of the fence. I was sure that my aching toes couldn't take the strain of an orderly descent and so I looked down, took several deep breaths and let go. I pushed out and backwards with my feet as hard as I could and hoped for the best.

I had intended to twist in the air in order to land on all fours but somehow I didn't quite manage it. Instead, I thumped onto my upper back from a height of more than three and a half metres. The breath rushed out of me in a single whoop and I lay spread-eagled for several minutes until my pumping heartbeat had slowed a bit. Even then, I stayed completely still and prone, my ears straining to hear anything out of the ordinary, any sign that I had been discovered. All I could hear was the unearthly screeching of a fox somewhere in the darkness.

I sat up gingerly and looked straight through the fence at the pair of brand new dark blue training shoes that had been placed neatly side-by-side on the ground. Bloody idiot. Why hadn't I thought to tie them around my neck again? I still had my socks on, although they had done little to protect my toes from the pain of climbing the wire. I had set out with just the vague plan to have a good snoop around the farm's polytunnels, anticipating that its back door would be far less secure. My plan was still the same, but I now realised I would have to be extremely quick and careful. These people weren't messing about and I would be trapped on the inside if I couldn't make it back to my improvised entry point. I remembered the dogs barking somewhere during our unwelcome visit and suspected they weren't likely to be over-friendly cocker spaniels.

'Onwards,' I muttered quietly to myself and moved off quickly in a crouch along the side of the nearest polytunnel. There was no obvious entrance – presumably you had to go to the very end to gain access. The tunnels stretched for as far as I could see in the darkness. I decided to take a shortcut. I tugged and pulled one side of the tunnel, where the plastic met the ground, and then flattened myself and wriggled headfirst inside through the gap I'd created. Instantly, the intense heat and overwhelming smell of hot plastic, fertiliser and plants hit me in the complete and utter blackness. I decided to take a chance and use my mobile phone's torch – I didn't have much choice. I fished it out of my back pocket, grateful for the trouser buttons, which meant that I hadn't lost it in the scramble over the fence. The bright white light showed me a wide path of packed earth stretching along the centre of the tunnel in both directions. On each side of the path ran a red hose that leaked water into the beds. The tunnel must have been five metres wide on each side of the path and strawberry plants on raised planters stretched into the distance. I switched off the torch, waited a few minutes for my eyes to adjust to the darkness again and then set off down the path, which I could just about make out at my feet.

Despite my fast pace, it must have taken me another ten minutes to reach the end of the tunnel where an unlocked plastic door took me out onto a road made of well-mown grass that led up the slope. The ends of successive tunnels flanked the right-hand side of the road. Crouched over, I ran along the ends of the tunnels, stopping and opening each door to briefly shine my torch along the interiors. After passing about fifteen tunnels I reached the top of the slope and saw there were roughly the same number again, sweeping down in parallel lines towards the silhouette of the farmhouse. I knew the risk of being discovered would increase the closer that I got to the buildings and the lights in the yard. I stared down at them for several minutes, watching and listening intently for any sign of life. Everything appeared to be silent and still. I kept going.

This slope was steeper than the one I had just come up and the first tunnel was also different to the others. My already racing heart began to gallop. This door was locked with a hefty chain and padlock and there was a 'Strictly No Entry' sign on it. I shifted round to the tunnel's rear perimeter, which was hidden from the house, and wriggled under it, just as I had done before.

Again, the temperature inside was stifling and it was pitch black. However, the pungent smell was very different from the fruits and vegetables housed in the previous tunnels. I recognised the sickly-sweet smell from my visit to Drood Cottage as well as my weekend in Amsterdam. Cannabis. This time I was more cautious before turning on the torch, and pulled the sleeve of my sweatshirt over my phone. The light was far weaker as a result, but it was still sufficient for me to see a miniature forest of waist-high plants stretching far into the distance.

Result! My suspicions were correct. It all now added up. The Major and his ex-army buddies were running a significant illegal drug operation under the cover of their fruit farm.

I knew that just seeing it wasn't enough. I needed proof. I unwrapped my sweatshirt from the mobile, switched off the torch and activated the camera button. The automatic flash was already on, so I pointed it down the tunnel and pressed the little white circle. There was a small delay while the flash registered that it was needed and then two successive bursts of light illuminated the path bisecting its river of green like a sudden flash of lightning. Then, I repeated the action for luck. Back in nearly complete darkness, I set off along the path to see how far it would stretch.

CHAPTER FIFTEEN

The path seemed to go on forever and the dense rows of plants on both sides were unbroken until I reached another wooden door. I grabbed a handful of the nearest cannabis plant and stuffed it in my trouser pocket before cautiously swinging the door back on its hinges. Instead of opening into the field, it led into a large square tent, not unlike an oversized wedding marquee. But there were no welcoming round tables, delicate gilt chairs and cascading flower arrangements in here. Instead I was confronted with long wooden benches with an assortment of chemistry equipment scattered along them: Bunsen burners, test tubes, glass jars and containers of all shapes and sizes. I had entered some kind of well-equipped and well-concealed laboratory.

'Shit,' I whispered to myself, casting my eyes around in disbelief. It no longer seemed as if I was dealing with a single tunnel full of cannabis plants hidden in the centre of a fruit farm. This was a more serious operation than I had anticipated. I didn't need to know much about the professional drugs scene to come to the conclusion that the Major and his cronies were producing something much more dangerous than ordinary weed here. High strength skunk perhaps? I had no idea. But I knew I needed to get out of here. And fast. These guys seemed to be major league players and I now knew for certain that my life could be seriously in danger. I glanced at my watch: 01:30. I quickly pulled out my phone again and snapped two pictures of the laboratory before sprinting through the far door and re-joining the tunnel.

I ran as fast as I could back through the cannabis – adrenalin rushing through my body alongside a sudden awareness of the scale of the gamble I had taken. The stupidity of my gung-ho adventure hit me with full force. By the time I was halfway along the second stretch of tunnel and the white semi-circular wall of the entrance came into view, my breathing was ragged with the unaccustomed physical effort and no small measure of panic. I just needed to keep going.

Suddenly, with no warning, I heard the high-pitched whine of an engine. It sounded like a quad bike. Terror washed through me. Someone was coming. The sound seemed to be coming from the far side of the tunnel that I was in, back where the grassy road swept down to the house and farm buildings. I listened for a second. The engine's whine was getting closer. I quickly calculated that the vehicle would be able to speed along the wide grassy tracks at both ends of the tunnels with ease. I needed to avoid being seen at all costs. My best bet was to wriggle from one tunnel to the next until I got to the boundary fence. Hopefully, they wouldn't have the manpower to search all of them.

I began to wade through the waist-high cannabis on my right, wriggled on my stomach out under the plastic wall, crossed quickly over the gap and immediately wriggled into the neighbouring tunnel. This one had a crop of knee-high plants in it that I failed to recognise. I immediately turned left and began running to its end, but the noise of the bike's engine seemed to be growing even louder. Suddenly it was joined by the sound of an alarm that someone had set off. It was coming from the direction of the farmyard. Any hope that the quad bike might be a routine night-time patrol was now abandoned. Somehow, they knew I was here.

The sound of the bike was closing behind me, getting louder by the second. I assumed it had entered the neighbouring tunnel, the one full of drugs, and was powering down its central path. How had they been alerted to my presence? Had I triggered a hidden alarm when I entered the laboratory? It seemed likely. In that case they knew exactly where I was – or where I had been. Would they stop to search for me there?

Or did they have cameras? They were ex-army – of course they bloody did. And guns. I swore at my stupidity. But I had to stay focused now to stand any chance of survival.

The quad bike seemed to be in the second stretch of the drugs tunnel nearer to me. It hadn't lingered in the central laboratory and it was coming ever closer. Suddenly, its throttle died back as it cruised just behind me in the parallel tunnel. I stopped still and crouched to hear what its driver did next. He halted in the tunnel almost opposite me. He was close enough for me to hear him speaking. I couldn't make out the words over the noise of the idling engine. There was a crackle of static and I realised he must be speaking into a walkie-talkie. Someone was replying to him. They could be guiding him towards me.

Then the penny dropped. I frantically scanned the roof of the tunnel. Sure enough, suspended in the centre of one of the metal hoops holding up the tunnel was a small camera, pointing away from me, towards the entrance door. A tiny light on it flashed green every few seconds. Someone must be in a control room watching the cameras, guiding the man on the quad bike. The man had stopped because, right now, I was in a blind spot. I looked back the way I had come but couldn't see another camera. I gambled that they would have most cameras in the drugs tunnel wouldn't bother monitoring a boring crop of new potatoes or whatever these plants were. But they had probably seen me escape under the plastic. As quietly as I could, I wriggled sideways out of the tunnel, crossed the small space of grass to the next one and wriggled under. I looked up to see another camera in the same position as the one in the previous tunnel. Thankfully this one was also pointing back towards the entrance. I listened for any change in the note of the quad bike. Although it was more muffled now with a whole polytunnel between us, it did not seem to be accelerating. I knew I couldn't reach the end of this tunnel without moving in front of the camera. But I also had to reach the perimeter fence and ideally the rear gate as quickly as possible. I would have to risk being out in the open at some stage.

I crossed the tunnel and wriggled back out again onto another grassy path dividing it from the next one. This time, though, instead of going under the adjoining wall of plastic, I began sprinting along the path, towards the end of the tunnels and the fence. The wail of the alarm was still shattering the silence of the night.

I reached the end of the tunnels. The quad bike still sounded like it was moving slowly but it was definitely travelling in the same direction as I had come. I swung right and began running full pelt down the grassy slope in the direction of the rear fence. The ends of all the other tunnels flew past me as the downward trajectory hurtled me forwards. I was desperate to get away and my next idea was inspired by that desperation. Ahead of me, right beside the fence, was a tractor with a digger bucket. I tumbled forward, my stockinged feet slipping on the grass as I slowed down and veered over to it. The front bucket had been left in the upright, horizontal position so that it formed a platform about two feet higher than the razor wire – surely, I could use this to get over the fence? Before I had time to work out the finer details, a pair of blazing headlights burst out of one of the tunnels above me. The bright white headlights of the quad bike were making a beeline straight for me.

I yanked open the door to the tractor cab and climbed up into it, closing the door behind me. I ducked down as low as I could, desperately hoping the man on the bike hadn't spotted me clambering inside the cab. If the bike stopped there was little doubt I would be facing the barrel of a gun in the hands of a trained soldier. It did stop next to the tractor, but the engine just idled over a few yards from where I was hiding.

'What have you got, Dave?' The man on the bike was shouting excitedly above the engine noise into his walkie-talkie.

He was so close to the tractor I could hear the metallic-sounding reply. 'Cinderella's still in the fucking building,' a voice said. 'I can see some trainers near the rear gate and some matting on top of the fence. It must be where he got in.'

Another voice now broke into the static.

'Right,' it barked. 'I'm in the Rover with the dogs. Where is the bastard?'

I recognised the gruff bark of the Major. The other man, Roberts, must be monitoring the cameras. I was practically hugging the floor of the tractor cab.

'Let the dogs loose by the back gate, Major. He'll have to head back there to get out.'

'On my way,' shouted the Major.

I heard another vehicle's deeper engine accelerating away somewhere over the hill. Meanwhile, the quad bike was slipped into gear and it too sped off towards the rear of the farm.

As its engine note receded I quickly raised my eyes above the cab door. I checked right and left before climbing back out and up onto the long bonnet of the tractor. I found a foothold and pulled myself up the bucket arm until I was lying, stomach-down on the flat top of the bucket. There was a gap of about a metre between the bucket and the fence and the drop to the other side looked terrifyingly high. This time I needed to try to avoid landing flat on my back. I stood up, nervously trying to keep my balance, then stepped back to the edge of the bucket. I took a couple of fast steps and leapt forward across the gap. I just cleared the razor wire and plummeted down to the ground, immediately rolling forward on impact thanks to some long-forgotten instinct that had been drummed into me during a schoolboy outdoor assault course. The momentum took me tumbling forwards until I crashed into the undergrowth of the woods surrounding that part of the farm. I picked myself up – I had to keep going. In the distance, above the continuing wail of the alarm, I could hear the excited barking of dogs. I prayed that my pursuers would think I was still inside the fence, hidden somewhere, trapped and waiting to be eaten alive.

I took a diagonal path through the trees, hoping I was heading back in the direction of the little jetty where I had come ashore. Sure enough, eventually I emerged onto the little path. Grateful to recognise my escape route, I crawled hurriedly back through the undergrowth, not even noticing the pain of brambles, branches and nettles on my hands and knees. And there was the little tourist boat waiting for me. I waded straight towards it in my hurry to get away, my feet squashing soft mud. I pushed the boat back towards the junction with the river until the water reached my midriff, then I boarded it clumsily and pointed it towards the safety of the open river. I heard the faint wail of the alarm stop but I could still hear dogs barking in the distance.

Relief flooded through my body. Slowly my breathing became less ragged. I knew I wasn't clear yet, but I wasn't trapped, or being hunted inside the farm's perimeter. The little boat was going even slower now. Its battery power was ebbing fast. If the dogs picked up my tracks they might still be able to catch me. I urged the boat on silently, glancing behind every few seconds to make sure that no one was following. Finally, as I made my way back past the sunken tree, onto the main river and past the sewerage plant, my heart rate began to slow. After a while I could see the dark buildings of Stratford loom up on the bank. The battery gave up just before I reached them. I could walk from here. I glided to the bank and tied the painter to the exposed root of a tree, patted the little boat thankfully and clambered up the steep and slippery slope before padding barefoot through the dark streets of Stratford, back towards the basin and *Jumping Jack Flash*.

As my body systems slowly returned to normal, I began to think more rationally about the implications of what I had seen. Once the Major and his merry men abandoned their search for me, what would they do? They'd go back to their cameras and try to identify their uninvited visitor. I had no idea how many cameras they had or how clear the images would be. So, let's assume the worst, I told myself, which was that they had a good clear picture of me. Let's also assume they recognised me from the visit I had made to the farm with Nina and Eddie. A scrawny-looking fox looked up from a discarded McDonalds box as I padded by, my cold bare feet making slight slapping noises on the pavement. The fox's long cool stare followed me unconcernedly before it returned to the remains of its fast-food meal and I returned to my line of thought.

So, let's assume they got a good picture and recognised me as the guy who was caught accidentally snooping on Mrs Major in the buff. I tried to remember our brief exchange word for word; I was pretty sure I hadn't mentioned being on a boat. Sure, I'd mentioned that we had met Sam and seen him go off in a blue Land Rover, but I couldn't remember giving them any clues as to where we were at the time. Their only likely line of enquiry was via Sergeant Milk. But surely they wouldn't dare to go asking the police questions about someone who might now have given him proof of what they were up to?

Proof?

'Shit!' I unbuttoned the back pocket of my sodden trousers and pulled out a very wet mobile phone. I had forgotten all about it in my anxiety to get away. I punched the on button but there was no response. 'Shit!' I repeated, only louder this time, furious at myself. Would it dry out sufficiently to come back to life, complete with its incriminating photos of the drugs tunnel and the laboratory? Or had I washed away the evidence? Silently cursing my folly, I trooped on through the empty streets and the intermittent pools of light and darkness between the street lamps. I was wet, cold, miserable and very worried.

I figured the Major and his men would steer well clear of Sergeant Milk – and I could warn him not to give them any information anyway. But if I did that he would want to know why. Should I tell him the whole story now? But then I would have to admit to trespass, and without the phone evidence it was hard to know what the police would do. But the Major wouldn't know what I had discovered. The Major couldn't gamble on whether I had any evidence or not. I put my hands in my pockets and felt the squishy wet cannabis plant that I had grabbed earlier. It wasn't much use as evidence either, I realised. I lobbed the soggy green mess over a passing privet hedge. No, the Major couldn't afford to gamble, which meant one of two things. Either he would quickly pull the plug on the whole enterprise and try to cover his tracks – unlikely given the sheer amount of effort and money he had obviously invested in it. Or he would try to track me down as quickly as possible and somehow shut me up – that wasn't a very comforting thought at all.

Bancroft Basin was silent and still in the moonlight, only the occasional passing car disturbing the peace. My watch now said four a.m. The dawn chorus would be starting shortly. What a night. I yawned till my jaw muscles cracked, crept along the pontoon to the bow of the boat and let myself into the main cabin as quietly as I could. It was too dark to see anything, so I felt my way along the sink cupboards and round to my bed where I sloughed off my sodden trousers and pants, pulled my jacket and sweatshirt off and prepared to slump naked onto my bed.

'Where the bloody hell have you been?'

The yellow light on the wall above my bed came on, temporarily blinding me. When I opened my eyes I saw Nina, sitting on the far corner of my bed with her knees pulled up in front of her and a blanket wrapped around her. I scrambled for a pillow to hide my modesty and held it sideways in front of me. 'Put something on,' she snapped.

I backed off into the shower room and grabbed a towelling dressing gown that I had 'borrowed' from the last chain hotel that I'd stayed in.

'Where the fuck have you been?' she repeated when I returned.

I perched on the side of my bed. 'Nina, it's a long story and I'm shattered. I need to go to bed.'

She folded her arms in front of her and glared.

'And I've been worried and sleepless for the last three hours. I came out for a glass of water and found you missing. So, if you think I'm just going to go back to bed without an explanation, you're deluded.'

I yawned again with exhaustion but realised that resistance was futile. I was coming to recognise a certain stubborn fixity to Nina's jawline. So, I briefly recounted the story of my night, described what I had found and outlined what I thought the consequences might be. She looked increasingly shocked as I told her my story, but stayed silent until the end. Then there was a long disquieting pause.

'But why?' she asked eventually. 'Why the bloody hell would you do something so bloody stupid and dangerous, Jack?'

'Well,' I said, 'we'd agreed to move off tomorrow to get away from any press interest in you and so I thought it was my last chance to find out what's been going on. What the connection with Sam was.' I paused. 'To be honest, I also thought there might be a good story in it – and there still might be if my phone dries out and ever works again.'

'A good story?' She was incredulous. Civilians usually are.

'Look, it's not just the drug dealing and the eccentric nudists, Nina. It's Sam too. If he *was* pushed in and drowned, then maybe his death is connected with this drug operation.'

'What? Where the hell did you get that theory from?' she demanded.

There was a scratch and whine from the other side of the door where Eddie seemed to be echoing the question. I told her then about Professor Parsons and his theory about a pattern of deliberate drownings.

'Oh great,' she said. 'So, you haven't just stirred up a hornets' nest of drug dealers who are going to come looking for you. They might also be in the habit of killing anyone who crosses their path? We've got to take all this to the police.'

'Take what?' I asked. 'Sergeant Milk warned me off causing trouble with talk of murderers. And there's no proof of a drug operation at the farm unless it's in that phone and I'm not waiting round here until it works or not. We head off first thing tomorrow as planned – after I've asked the sergeant to keep quiet about our address if anyone comes asking.' I yawned for what seemed like a whole minute. 'Now I have to sleep.'

A glowering Nina stomped off to her bed, kicking the pile of wet clothes on the floor as she went. Her door had barely stopped swinging before I fell into unconsciousness, sprawled backwards on the bed in my towelling robe.

CHAPTER SIXTEEN

I was woken just after eight by the hum of Nina's hairdryer in the main cabin. I peered around the edge of my bed and saw her hunched over the table, directing a warm blast of air at the innards of my mobile phone. I pulled my dressing gown together and padded to the shower, where I spent some time inspecting an impressive collection of cuts and bruises from the previous night and washing them under a trickle of water that was now stone cold. We needed to get the engine running again if we were to have any hot water. The overnight ban on using the generator had passed, so I fired up the engine and dried and dressed myself, shivering all the while. Then I padded back to the cabin and helped myself to a lukewarm mug of tea from the pot. The SIM card from my phone was sitting in a little china ashtray on the table alongside the remaining bits of phone. Nina switched off the hairdryer and replaced all the phone parts in a Tupperware pot of uncooked rice, which she sealed.

'I've been thinking,' said Nina. 'What would you do in the Major's shoes? You're worried that someone will blow the whistle on you. And you don't know where to start looking for that person, but you need to stop them going to the police.'

'So?'

'So, assuming they aren't all busy back at the farm dismantling the whole operation, they'll sit outside the police station from early this morning to stop you from knocking on the door.'

'Stop me?' I queried.

'Yes, stop you. If they murdered Sam for some reason, they're not going to pull their punches with us, are they? It sounds like a very big thing the Major has got going. He's got a ready-made distribution network all over the country under the guise of his fruit and veg business. And their laboratory suggests that they really mean business.'

I nodded my agreement. Nina went on.

'So, it's probably not a good idea to try to pop in and ask Sergeant Milk not to hand over our details to the nasty men. I don't think you'd ever make it. Ring him. Or better still *I'll* ring him. He liked me, and he'll think I'm just anxious to avoid being tracked down by the press.'

'And we get out of here,' I said.

'We do,' she nodded. 'As quickly as possible.'

I did a quick tidy-up while Nina went onto the boat's roof to make the call. Then I heard a brief altercation and raised voices. I shot up on deck as quickly as possible, my heart pounding with terror that the men from Chester Farm had discovered us already. But I found Nina wholly in command of the situation. She was standing with both hands on her hips and fiercely ordering two Chinese tourists off our boat. They had climbed on board without permission to take pictures of each other on the deck.

Within a short time we were casting off from the pontoon in front of a small audience of unabashed and uninvited guests and their friends. Nina had insisted we put on baseball caps and sunglasses and turn the collars of our shirts up to reduce the chance of anyone recognising us. She swung the tiller far over to execute a sharp turn to the right, backed up briefly and then we headed slowly under the road bridge and away from the basin. It felt a huge relief to be putting some distance between ourselves and Stratford. This time, despite our enforced slowness, there was a real urgency to our journey and we quickly settled into a rhythm of successive locks and bridges; me jogging on ahead to make sure the water was the right level and the gates were open for Nina to keep taking the boat forward without any time-consuming stops. Eddie seemed to enjoy watching the world go by, occasionally from the bow but mostly at the stern, close to his beloved skipper.

There was only one way out of Stratford by canal and so we had no option but to go back past the spot where Sam's body had been found and on through Wilmcote, in spite of its proximity to Chester Farm. It was one o'clock by the time we passed through the last lock of the Wilmcote flight and we both kept a nervous lookout for the Major and his men or the blue Land Rover. But all was quiet, and we motored on, eating a quick sandwich on the go and making faster progress in the long and largely lockless stretch of canal back to the boatyard at Wootton Wawen. It was mid-afternoon when we approached it across the little metal aqueduct. Nina and I briefly debated the merits of changing boats or calling in at the boatyard's office to ask them to stay quiet if anyone came asking questions. But we decided that it made more sense to keep our heads down and keep motoring. As getaway vehicles go, there were probably better options that an eighteen-tonne boat travelling at walking pace but we calculated that it could take us to very remote spots which no one could access from the land and where we could remain out of sight until our potential pursuers gave up. After all, we reassured ourselves, they didn't even know we were on a boat.

We passed a sign to a pub at somewhere called Preston Bagot but reluctantly pressed on, crossed another aqueduct and then hit a lonely stretch of land called Yarningale Common. There were no longer any pretty little barrel-roofed cottages nearby and the nearest road had swung inland, out of sight of the canal with woods that ran down to it on both sides. It seemed like a perfectly concealed spot to moor up, have a rest and take stock. And so that is what we did.

We had covered about nine miles since leaving the basin and I felt much safer now that we were out of Stratford and on the other side of Wilmcote. With the engine off, a comforting silence descended on our isolated mooring, which was broken only by occasional birdsong, the splash of a duck or moorhen and the engines of a far-off commercial jetliner. I opened my laptop and briefly caught up with my log. I fetched two bottles of beer from the little fridge and took them out onto the prow where Nina was sitting, barefoot and legs out straight on one of the two curved benches that faced each other. She took a bottle and we glugged happily in silence while I flicked through the little Canal Companion booklet to plot our forward route.

I traced the winding blue line across four pages. It took me onwards along the Stratford Canal and past the Kingswood Junction, which would offer us the chance to switch to the Grand Union Canal. However, my finger continued north, up through the Warwickshire countryside to the suburban fringes of Birmingham and on through King's Norton into the very heart of England's second city. It looked like one long day's journey, or an easy two days at most. Just as we were out of sight now, I thought we might be equally hard to find in the maze of waterways of such a major city. That should give us time before... before what? Before a gang of murderous drug dealers abandoned their search for a man who had broken into their farm at the dead of night? Before the press gave up looking for a grief-stricken young army widow? I knew in my heart of hearts why I wanted to prolong this journey rather than do the sensible thing – which, of course, was to abandon the boat and catch a train to somewhere a very long way away. And it was all to do with Nina. I had fallen for her deeper than the Mariana Trench and I was quietly desperate for the intimacy-inducing peril of our situation to be prolonged in our cosy little floating home. Of course, I realised the selfish stupidity of this even as I thought it. But I also knew it was the uncomfortable truth.

'Penny for them?' asked Nina.

I coughed with embarrassment. 'Oh, I was just thinking through the options for our route.'

I showed her the map and explained my reasoning for heading out of the countryside and into the city.

'And the chance to visit some nice shops and restaurants,' she added nonchalantly. 'Some retail therapy wouldn't go amiss.'

I nodded. 'Speaking of which, we're running a bit short on stores. There are a few paths that cross the common marked on the map. I think maybe we should walk Eddie into the village and stock up while we can.'

Disguised once more under our baseball caps and unseasonal sunglasses, we locked up the boat and followed the signposts of a ramblers' path towards Preston Bagot. Eddie scampered off his lead around our heels and, at one stage, Nina looped an arm through mine.

'It's quite exciting, being on the run like this,' she said. 'But you were a mad bastard breaking into the farm like that.'

'I know. Curiosity killed the cat and all that.' I gave her a sly sideways glance. 'But I'm glad you were worried about me.'

She snorted in disgust but didn't say anything, so I continued. 'I had no idea it would be as big an operation as it is. It's very clever, isn't it? Hiding in plain sight. I suppose cannabis is just like any other crop in a way – but a hell of a lot more lucrative than strawberries. And there's a ready-made distribution network too. It was the laboratory that puzzled me.'

'Why?'

'Well – I'm not sure you really need anything that size to process weed, do you? It made me think they're into other heavier stuff.'

'They didn't look to be short of money, did they?' Nina mused. 'The house, the lorries, the cars. It all looked pretty well funded.'

'Plus the security set-up; all the cameras and the fencing.'

'And presumably the whole naturist thing helps to keep nosy neighbours from popping in… and military know-how must come in useful.'

I remembered the knowing remarks of the pub landlord and the other locals. Nina continued: 'Alan never used to talk about what he'd do when he left the army. I think he'd have happily stayed forever. He was born to be a soldier, as everyone kept bloody reminding me.' At last, I thought, Nina seemed to be opening up to me.

'No retirement plans to go into drug-running like the Major then?' It was a crass remark, but I was trying to keep things light. Nina just shook her head, unlinked her arm and ran ahead briefly so that Eddie could chase her.

There was a small village store in Preston Bagot where we separated to stock up. At the front was food and drink, and in the rear was a small section crammed with DIY equipment. I added a medium-sized can of glossy black paint, a couple of brushes and some white spirit to my basket. Then we went on to a nearby gastropub called Crab Mill, a very smart converted cider mill, and sat in the beer garden nursing a pint of cider each. Although the late afternoon chill tempted us to retreat inside, we decided to avoid other people and instead ambled back to the boat where we companionably shared the cooking of two chicken breasts, finished a bottle of red between us and dozed to some classical music on the radio before turning in. I comforted myself that our day's exertions on the canal and the previous night's excitement would have exhausted a much younger man.

I checked the remains of my phone but Nina had warned me not to try to switch it on for another couple of days and so I resisted the temptation and went to bed. I watched jealously as Eddie trotted happily behind his new mistress to share her bunk for the night. There's no fool like an old fool, I thought sadly, or even a middle-aged one.

CHAPTER SEVENTEEN

I woke – rested and early – and reached for my laptop to check out the BBC News headlines, thankful for the owner's decision to install a WiFi hotspot as a bonus feature on a boat that he had struggled to hire out. Checking the headlines had become my regular early morning habit, quickly followed by a trawl through a few newspaper websites. Suddenly, I was sitting bolt upright. 'Fuck... fuckity fuckity fuckity fuck.' Sometimes I surprise even myself with my command of the wonderfully wide scope of the English language.

Staring out at me was a picture of Nina and myself on board *Jumping Jack Flash*. The photographer had taken the snap from the side, so that the painting of the jester was smack in the centre. Nina and I were sitting and chatting on the boat's roof, our legs dangling down either side, nicely framing the picture of the grinning jester in mid-leap. The boat's name was easily distinguishable, curving upwards below the jester with just a couple of letters at either end partially obscured by our feet. I clicked on the picture and expanded it. It had been taken in the basin in Stratford. Our heads were slightly turned inwards. It looked as though I was saying something and Nina was listening with a serious look on her face. My fingers raced to the accompanying story. The headline was sensational, and the story underneath brief, but devastating.

MISSING YOUNG WAR WIDOW FOUND SAFE ON CANAL BOAT WITH MYSTERY MALE COMPANION

The missing young war widow Mrs Angelina Wilde has been found safe and well and the nationwide missing person's police search has now been called off. Anxious friends and relatives had reported the 30-year-old missing after her army hero husband, Captain Alan Wilde, died following a fierce gun battle in Afghanistan. The couple had been married for just six weeks. Police have refused to give any details of Mrs Wilde's whereabouts, but it's understood she has been living on a canal boat at Stratford-upon-Avon with a mystery older man. Mrs Wilde and the unnamed man were photographed looking happy and relaxed on board the boat earlier this week (see above).

I slammed shut the laptop's cover and re-opened it. It was no good. The story was still there below the large colour photograph of Nina and yours truly. I grabbed my towelling robe and scrambled out of bed.

'Nina...'

She was sitting up and rubbing her eyes as I crashed through her swing door. Eddie gave a yelp of surprise from the bed.

'Ughh... what time is it? What's the matter, Jack?' she groaned.

I put the laptop onto her lap. 'Look.'

She read it once, then put the palm of one hand in front of her mouth and widened her eyes as she read it through for a second time. Then, just like me, she opened the picture and zoomed around it, first expanding the image of her face, then mine and then of the jester and the boat's name.

'Fuck,' she said.

'My words exactly.'

'How did they get this picture?'

'I haven't a – ' But I stopped short.

In fact, I did have a clue. My mind raced back to the call from Deb when she had admitted to sending Bloody Mary to snoop round the boat like a tourist and get a picture of her ex-husband's new companion. That's how Deb had identified Nina as the missing war widow before she rang to warn me. Had she taken matters into her own hands? I cursed myself for failing to let her know that we had called off the hunt by going to Sergeant Milk. Or, maybe she was still so sore and jealous that she just decided to flog her snap to the papers?

'What is it?' asked Nina.

I briefly explained how Deb had secured the picture and then recognised Nina from the wedding photograph in the papers that had accompanied the story of her going missing.

'But would she really have sold it to them?' she asked. 'She must hate you a lot.'

'Maybe it wasn't Deb,' I conceded. 'It could have been her friend Mary. She hates my guts – she'd love the chance to stir things up and make some cash in the process.'

'What do we do now?' asked Nina in a small voice.

I didn't have a clue. 'Cup of tea first,' I said, more reassuringly than I felt. I dressed quickly while the kettle came to the boil and Nina and Eddie joined me as I filled the teapot and splashed some milk into two mugs.

'The Major and his men might see this story and recognise you from the farm,' said Nina. It was more of a statement than a question, but I nodded in agreement anyway.

'Assuming they got a decent image of me on their CCTV cameras,' I added.

'So they'll know we were living on a boat in the basin at Stratford,' she continued.

'And they'll know the boat's name,' I said.

'But they won't know whether we went north up the canal or south onto the River Avon, Jack.'

'But they might get lucky and find someone who saw us leave,' I said. 'And they'll guess that we left first thing yesterday after the fuss the night before.'

'What would you do if you were them?'

'I'd put the two monkeys in two separate cars and have them drive along the river and along the canal to try to spot us,' I said. 'We're pretty safe here for the moment, unless they start exploring on foot. And, fortunately, I was a Boy Scout.'

'What?'

I grinned and ducked down into the cupboard below the sink before re-emerging with the paint and brushes that I had picked up from the village store yesterday.

'I came prepared.'

Working side by side, it took us just over an hour to cover the picture of the jester and the boat's name with the black gloss paint. It was thick, sticky stuff and it did a good job of obliterating the yellow and green that the jester's artist had used. The resulting black rectangle looked much newer than the faded red-and-black paint that covered the rest of the boat's upper structure, but at least it felt like part of the same overall colour scheme. We both jumped down onto the towpath and stepped back to admire our vandalism. There was no trace left of the picture of the jester or the boat's name.

'Seems a shame to see him go,' said Nina.

'His grin was starting to get on my nerves,' I replied. 'The fresh paint stands out a bit, but we'll just have to hope it does the trick.'

Nina nodded. 'I think it also means you're going to have to buy the boat now!'

I returned to the main cabin, perched over my laptop and opened my email. My fingers banged into the keyboard much more aggressively than usual.

Dear Deb,

Today's Mail Online has a story about the search for Nina being called off. This is because we went to the police and reassured them that she was safe and well – just as you asked me to. However, it also has a picture of me and Nina on our boat??? I assume they got this from you? I thought we were trying to be civilized? Sending Mary to spy on us was bad enough but flogging the picture is a new low. This is going to cause us real problems. I can't go into details – but our safety could be at stake. Please, don't speak to the press – or anyone else. This is v important.

JJ

ps any sign of the money?

Nina was watching me silently from the hatchway as I clicked on send.

'What are you doing?' she asked.

'Closing the stable door,' I snapped angrily. I swivelled the laptop to face her and she quickly scanned the sent email.

'Now what?' she asked.

'I think we sit tight for the moment and stay out of sight on the boat. There's a chance that the Major might not see the news story or even recognise me from the picture. We can't be seen from the road and we've done the paint job, so the boat is anonymous now.'

I was trying to sound more upbeat and optimistic than I was, but it seemed to do the trick.

'Okay,' said Nina. 'I'll just walk Eddie down the towpath and back. Won't be long.'

'Hat,' I said, throwing it to her.

Whilst she was gone I emailed Sergeant Milk. I was tempted to spill the beans about my night-time raid on Chester Farm and what I had found there, but in the end I doubted the police could do anything based solely on the word of someone breaking and entering into private premises – in fact, it might make things even worse for us both. So I simply attached the link to the newspaper article and asked him to let us know if anyone came asking about us and not to tell them anything. Then I settled down to study the canal network in Birmingham more closely.

There were no less than eight separate canals converging on the city, and our own, the Stratford, would join up with the Worcester &

Birmingham Canal after the King's Norton junction. This seemed to quickly lead into the very heart of the city centre. A spot of research informed me that an area around Brindley Place, Gas Street Basin and the Mailbox, a massive converted Royal Mail building, had a number of moorings ranging from twenty-four to forty-eight hours, and some longer mooring of up to fourteen days. My finger traced the return route of the Worcester & Birmingham Canal, out of the city and on down to Worcester, taking in the UK's longest flight of locks at Tardebigge along the way. I calculated it would take over twenty hours of continuous travel to reach Worcester and the River Severn – so perhaps three days? But it offered us the chance to double back and potentially wrong-foot any pursuers. The route also seemed to provide plenty of under-populated countryside to lose ourselves in.

It felt like a plan and I talked Nina through it after she returned to the boat with Eddie. I was delighted when she agreed – particularly because it meant she would be keeping me company for at least another four or five days. Deep down, I selfishly feared that she would think it was time to cut her losses and jump ship, abandoning me to the mess I had landed myself in and struggling to control the ridiculously long boat on my own. But she cheerfully agreed to push on and we set off across another aqueduct and under a few bridges and we were soon approaching the Fleur de Lys at Lowsonford, a pretty little country pub. Some people were already enjoying early lunchtime pints in the large garden by the canal and there were plenty of free visitor moorings, so we decided to call in, even though we had been chugging along for less than half an hour. After all, we agreed, the boat didn't have a name any more. We had nothing to worry about.

CHAPTER EIGHTEEN

Nina and Eddie claimed an empty garden table under a large weeping willow on a flat patch of lawn by the canal and I headed into the bar. Whilst I've had an enjoyable lifetime's experience of meeting different pub landlords, this one immediately struck me as a candidate from central casting. He had a walrus moustache and bushy side-whiskers but was carefully shaved below his bottom lip and on his chin. A large waistcoat, which had to be made-to-measure, stretched comfortably around an ample waist which suggested that he must have sampled more than his fair share of his own merchandise in his time. A floral shirt and a paisley silk cravat completed the ensemble visible above the bar. We exchanged some genial chit-chat as I placed our order. Then something strange happened. It was as though he had suffered a mini-stroke halfway through pulling my pint of bitter. His fist, which was clamped round the handle of the draught pump, stopped at forty-five degrees. He stared at me. His fist stayed there, whilst he continued to stare.

'On a boat are you, sir?' he asked.

I nodded, looking pointedly at my half-empty glass. Others might have called it half-full, but that wasn't my nature.

'Yes, moored up outside. We haven't come far, though – just up from Yarningale Common where we spent the night.'

He nodded, his hand staying stubbornly static on the beer pump.

'So you aren't on your own then?'

The penny dropped with a thud. I reminded myself that we were fleeing from some nasty people as well as the press. These weren't just polite enquiries. My stomach flipped but I tried to stay calm and just nodded at the glass.

'A full pint, please.'

The landlord moved his pint-pulling arm back into motion but gave me a knowing look.

'Ah yes, pint of beer and a half of cider, wasn't it?' he said, implying all too well that my order had betrayed the fact that I wasn't alone.

'That's right. Is something wrong?'

He rubbed his mouth vigorously with the palm of one hand and leaned forward conspiratorially as far across the bar as his stomach would permit. I automatically leaned inwards too, frightened about what I would hear.

'Man was here as soon as we opened this morning,' he said quietly. 'He had a newspaper photograph of you and a young lady.' He winked. 'He asked if I'd seen you.'

I took a sip of my drink, trying to stay calm on the surface. It seemed that the Major's men had moved very quickly indeed. 'And what did you tell him?'

'Nothing, of course. I hadn't seen you before now, had I?' The landlord's voice was a whisper and he looked left to right to make sure no one was listening. He was obviously relishing the situation.

'Did he say who he was?'

'He said he was a friend of yours. He was wearing motorbike leathers.' I swore inwardly. If the Major's men were on bikes they would be able to search the route of the canal quickly and much more easily.

'He left me his telephone number in case you turned up.' The landlord turned and pulled a scrap of paper off a shelf behind him before flattening it out on top of a small beer towel. I wondered if I might use this opportunity somehow to send the Major's men on a wild goose chase.

'Mind if I take this and ring it myself?' The landlord bent back to begin pouring the half of cider.

'No need to do that sir.' He nodded his head in the direction of the open window behind him which looked down and across into the pub garden. 'I think he's found you.' I had a moment of sheer panic. Was the Major's man already outside? Had he lingered at the pub? Was he already holding Nina captive?

I followed the landlord's gaze and burst out laughing with relief. Nina was sitting at a bench table under the willow tree and with her, holding Eddie up to rub noses, was my old and deeply unreliable friend Will Simpson.

'He's drinking cider too,' said the landlord. I nodded with resignation and he poured a third drink.

'Do me a favour,' I asked, sliding an extra twenty-pound note across the bar. 'If anyone else comes asking for us, you haven't seen us. The lady just needs a bit of privacy and time to grieve for her husband.'

The landlord wrinkled his eyes and nodded understandingly. Then he slid the note back towards me.

'Right you are, sir,' he said. 'No need for that. Mum's the word. I was in the military myself,' he said, before turning away to serve another customer.

'Jack, my man!' shouted Will as he saw me approaching the bench with three glasses cradled carefully between both hands. He stood and stretched his arms wide, exposing a band of flat stomach as his white T-shirt rose up from his heavy black leather motorbike trousers. A full-face crash helmet and a leather jacket were next to him on the bench. Of course, the tight-fitting T-shirt had been carefully chosen to flatter the bastard. It clung tight to Will's brown biceps and stretched across his sculpted chest. I put down the glasses and submitted to a brief and grumpy hug.

'You're looking older,' he grinned, releasing me and taking a big swallow of cider. 'And I've met the lovely Angelina here already,' he said waving his glass at Nina.

'Nina,' we both said simultaneously.

'Oh.' He looked momentarily baffled. 'Nina. It's just that the newspaper...' He tailed off in embarrassment. 'I'm really sorry for your loss,' he said to Nina. She gave him a brave smile and sipped her half pint of cider but didn't say anything.

'So, what are you doing here, Will?' I asked. 'Guilty conscience? Decided to keep your promise after all?'

Will's choirboy looks framed themselves into a sorrowful pose. As an actor, he had the full set in his locker and no qualms about using them.

'Yeah, I'm sorry about that, mate. I couldn't abandon Susie in the week of her professional debut. Anyway, I've got some work of my own now. And when I saw that picture of you in the paper I thought Wow! My old mate's shacked up with...' He caught Nina's eye. 'Er. Yes, well, what I mean is, I thought you might need some immoral support.' He took a swig of cider and gave us the benefit of his megawatt grin, which showed off his white and even teeth. 'And the truth is I need somewhere round here to stay, and you've got a bloody big boat, haven't you? I tried ringing your mobile but got nothing so I bombed down to Stratford from Bristol this morning and followed the canal. I knew I'd find you in a pub – or find a pub that would find you!'

I reflected ruefully that if my unreliable idiot of a friend could find us after just one morning on a motorbike, a determined drugs gang might not be far behind. I glanced over at Nina. Like most of the women who came into contact with Will, she seemed to be enjoying either his looks or his lively personality. Neither did it for me.

'Where are you working?' she asked him.

'Packwood House – a National Trust place near here. They're putting on *As You Like It* in the gardens, with yours truly as Jacques.'

'*As You Like It* performed in the real Forest of Arden,' said Nina.

'Clever girl,' nodded Will. I shook my head at his patronising tone, but Nina affected to be unconcerned.

'Yep, *As You Like It*, staged at Henley-in-Arden near the original forest.' He waved theatrically to indicate the woods on the other side of the canal. 'Why don't you come? Rehearsals this afternoon and first performance tomorrow evening.'

'Great,' said Nina, looking encouragingly at me.

'We need to get going, Will,' I said. 'And quickly – away from this road.' I gave Nina a meaningful look.

'Awww, c'mon, Jack.' Will turned his beseeching look on me. 'Besides, I do need a bunk for the night.'

I shook my head firmly. 'No way. Sorry. We're heading off.' I drained my glass and stood up purposefully. 'Good to see you, Will.' I held out my hand for a goodbye handshake, but he ignored it and scooped up his helmet and jacket.

'Let me just see this boat of yours then,' he said. Sometimes, I'm just too damn polite. We walked back past a little white lockside cottage and along the towpath to our mooring. As Will excitedly went ahead of us with Eddie, Nina pulled my arm and I fell back alongside her.

'You're worried?' she asked.

'If this idiot can find us so easily, anyone can,' I said, nodding at Will's broad-shouldered back and swaggering walk. 'We need to crack on.'

'Maybe,' she said. 'Or maybe we just hide up for a while? We're coming up to another quiet stretch with no roads anywhere overlooking the canal. Maybe they'll overtake us and then give up.'

I seriously doubted this but perhaps she was right. We couldn't outrun anyone chasing us, but we might be able to lay low for a bit and give them the slip. I doubted that the friendly pub landlord would betray us.

Aboard *Jumping Jack Flash*, Will peered into every nook and cranny of the boat. He registered the two used beds with a knowing wink at me.

'Very cosy,' he said. 'It's like caravanning on water. But you've got a spare bunk, Jack, so come on. Just one night until I get some local digs sorted out.'

Nina shrugged her shoulders. 'It's okay by me.'

Will whooped. 'Nice, nice lady! I'll get my bag.'

He was back out of the hatch before I could say anything, his bike jacket and helmet left on the spare bunk.

I glared at Nina.

'He's your friend,' she said apologetically. 'And anyway, he's quite nice and it's only for one night.'

'Quite nice?' I said in disbelief. 'Well, he's not sleeping there,' I said pointing petulantly at the spare bunk opposite hers. 'He can share with me.'

Nina gave a knowing smile and turned quietly to loosen the mooring ropes.

As soon as Will returned, she started the engine and we set off away from the pub and its busy car park into a long and heavily wooded stretch of canal. We moored up again after passing through two locks with Will scampering around uselessly in high spirits. I could see from the map that the busy M40 motorway and the Birmingham to London railway line ran alongside each other and were not far away. The low roar of traffic and the occasional whine of a high-speed train could be heard in the distance, but there was no chance of someone spotting us now unless they walked along the towpath. And the boat looked completely anonymous thanks to our recent paint job – although it still had its unique Boat Index Number on display. We'd decided that painting it out would make us more suspicious rather than less.

However, we would still be on the boat ourselves and potentially vulnerable if any towpath snoopers, which an old Canal Boat magazine told me were known as *gongoozlers*, came peering through our little round portholes. And so I persuaded myself that it might be a good precaution to get well away from the boat for a while. If anyone was looking for us rather than the boat, it wouldn't hurt to be with Will at Packwood House for the afternoon's rehearsal. It also wouldn't hurt to be disguised as part of a threesome rather than a couple. But beyond that, I was still racking my brains about how to stay one step ahead. If we didn't, the consequences could be disastrous. I had been stupid involving Nina in all of this drug-dealing fiasco – but I still thought I could protect her from any more unwanted attention from the press.

The map function on Will's smartphone told us it would be a three-mile, hour-long walk and so we set off on foot with Eddie trotting along happily, his crooked tail proudly upright like a little flagpole.

CHAPTER NINETEEN

There was little warmth coming from the sun but the sky was a lovely pale blue, interspersed with cotton puffballs of cloud and the vapour trails of jet liners flying into and out of Birmingham Airport. It almost felt like a midsummer's day. It was a pleasant walk to Packwood House, apart from a bridge the width of the M40 made of grey concrete slabs that took the canal and both of its towpaths directly underneath the motorway. Colourful splashes of indecipherable graffiti and the brutally straight lines of the tunnel made us feel as though we had suddenly stepped into a slightly threatening city centre environment. But the bucolic beauty of the canal quickly reasserted itself on the other side of the bridge and we strolled along, past a little cash-only canal shop where Will bought us all chocolate ice creams 'in lieu of rent' and then up the long flight of Lapworth Locks where we passed a waterborne traffic jam as boats waited between the closely packed locks to make progress in both directions.

We swung off to the right along a small road and quickly picked up the little National Trust oak leaf and acorn signs that showed we were close to Packwood House. The steeply pitched Tudor gables of the mansion and its tall chimneys could be glimpsed beyond the trees that lined the approach drive. A steady stream of visitors' cars passed us on their way to the car park.

To the left of the house, beyond an impressive yew garden, we found a small group of actors sitting in a circle on the ground next to a camper van. They greeted Will with squeals of excitement and it quickly transpired that he was part of a regular troupe which came together occasionally to perform *As You Like It* or *A Midsummer Night's Dream* in the parks or grounds of fine houses around the country during the spring, summer and early autumn months. They hardly needed a rehearsal, but a bossy young woman was insisting that they listen to her notes from their last performance in Bristol. Will joined the circle, after pressing a couple of free tickets into our hands. Nina and I peeled away to explore the interior of the house, after handing Eddie into the cooing care of an elderly lady volunteer by the front door.

The wood-lined rooms with their wall tapestries felt dark and cool after the light of the gardens. Sombre Tudor furniture lined the corridors. Dried thistle heads were perched on the seat of each chair to dissuade visitors from using them. We wandered from room to room, reading about Graham Baron Ash, a confirmed bachelor and heir to an industrialist's fortune who had created his vision of the perfect Tudor home between the world wars. Little cylindrical cushions were scattered in the rooms and embroidered with quotes about the owner, many of them from his intensely loyal butler. Nina began to speculate naughtily about Graham Baron Ash's sexuality, especially when she read an embroidered quote from Queen Mary, who had commented waspishly during one visit in the 1920s that, 'These bachelors seem to live a very comfortable existence.' Nina snorted when she read about the white Rolls Royce Baron Ash would order to fetch him at the house's 'Birmingham Entrance' and in another room she pointed me eagerly at an little information panel which talked about his fondness for the 'Follies', entertainments hosted by the squire which included a performance of *As You Like It* on the tennis court just before the Second World War. His fastidious interest in cut flowers and clothes was also remarked upon by Baron Ash's adoring staff.

'Honestly,' she said. 'Listen: "We hope to give you a glimpse into the mind of a wealthy perfectionist and idealist who remains something of an enigma today." Enigma?' she said loudly, startling a portly elderly volunteer who was watching us suspiciously from a dark corner. 'Well, we all know what that's code for, what with his prissy house flowers and his white Rolls Royce!' She was grinning mischievously and I rejoiced in the cheerfulness of her mood. But as I ambled behind her, I reflected that there was a brittle edge to her good humour. This desperate attempt by Nina to run away from confronting her husband's death must come to an end eventually. I worried that the new and very real danger of the drug dealers at Chester Farm might be making her slightly hysterical. However much I dreaded the moment, she would need to go home at some point, if only for her own long-term sanity.

We recovered Eddie and spent another hour wandering happily around the flower borders, an orchard and a wildflower meadow. Finally, we made our way towards an ornamental lake that had been emptied of water. Men in fluorescent yellow jackets were working on repairing a long dam. It formed part of a causeway that approached the house from a different direction to the main drive. We found an empty bench and watched the workmen for a while.

'You're still quite worried, aren't you?' she asked quietly.

I looked directly into those darkly beautiful black eyes. 'Yes, I am,' I admitted. 'We're in over our heads. It was bloody stupid of me to shake up that particular hornets' nest and I don't think the Major and his men are just going to sit back and do nothing about it. The worst thing is that I've put you in danger too.'

She patted my hand in sympathy.

'Poor JJ. But we're well away from the canal for now and the boat can't be seen from a road anyway, and we'll soon be lost in the centre of Birmingham. We've disguised the boat's identity and perhaps we'll be able to use those pictures of yours as proof if we can retrieve them. Then we can call in the cavalry. So don't worry about me. We're a team.'

'Nina,' I ventured tentatively. 'Maybe you should be thinking of going home?'

She stiffened immediately and withdrew her hand.

'Nope – not unless you're kicking me out,' she said firmly, her jaw clenched. 'Are you?'

I ducked the question. 'Your mother will still be worried about you. Especially if she saw that article and the photo.'

Nina shook her head. 'I've been messaging her,' she said. 'She knows that I'm not ready to come back yet. Hey!' she said suddenly. 'I wonder if your SIM card will work in my phone?'

'It's worth a go,' I said grudgingly. And all further talk of her leaving was suspended.

We wandered back to the lawn where the actors were still rehearsing some key scenes. They had attracted a small audience of visitors who stood on the edge of the action enjoying the free show. Will saw us approaching and held his thumb up with a grin. A natural show-off, he strode purposefully into the centre of the action and launched into his main soliloquy, 'All the world's a stage...'

The crowd chuckled as he threw himself into mimicking the actions of a 'mewling and puking' infant. Then he slumped, all too realistically, into the sulky slouch of a teenager, dragging his feet exaggeratedly as he crept, snail-like, unwillingly to school. The laughter increased in volume as he moved towards Nina and threw himself onto both his knees in front of her, clasping one hand over his heart and holding the other, palm outward against his forehead. He looked up longingly into her embarrassed eyes and pink-flushed cheeks.

'*And then, the lover, Sighing like furnace, with a woeful ballad Made to his mistress' eyebrow.*' He gave a deliberately overly dramatic shudder of his whole body and rolled backwards, springing up onto his feet. '*Then a soldier.*'

Will suddenly realised the potential impact of his next lines on the young war widow. His voice fell to a whisper. The impromptu audience sensed the change into a more sombre mood.

'*Full of strange oaths, and bearded like the pard, Jealous in honour, sudden and quick in quarrel, Seeking the bubble reputation...* '

Will turned away from Nina, his voice almost too quiet to hear.

'*Even in the cannon's mouth.*'

The lowering of his voice, his expressionless delivery and the abandonment of his clowning around somehow gave even more force to the words and Nina turned away with moist eyes. Will deliberately broke the mood again and resumed his clowning.

'*And then, the justice, In fair round belly with good capon lined…*' he continued with a renewed burst of energy. He stuffed a nearby cushion up his T-shirt and paraded pompously up and down, prompting the audience to break into laughter once again.

'Are you okay?' I asked Nina, now at the fringes of the crowd.

She nodded. 'He's good, isn't he?'

'No,' I said. 'He's a pain-in-the-arse show-off.'

She laughed, and we turned back to watch the rest of the scene and its poignant closing lines, which Will delivered with sensitivity in an old man's quavering voice.

'*Last scene of all, That ends this strange eventful history, Is second childishness and mere oblivion. Sans teeth, sans eyes, sans taste, sans everything.*'

He bowed low at the generous round of applause and then broke out of the action and looked at the bossy young woman director. 'That'll do, won't it, Annie? We can bloody well do this in our sleep.'

The director clapped her hands officiously and addressed the group. 'Yes, that's it everyone. Thanks very much. Back here at four p.m. sharp tomorrow for costumes and make-up. And the Trust has booked beer and curry for us at the Punch Bowl tonight.'

Will introduced us to the rest of the cast, who insisted that we join them. The company crowded into the camper van and a National Trust minibus which ferried us all the short distance to the nearby gastropub. It had a smart clientele judging by the Porsches and Range Rovers in the car park. Our group made its way straight into the garden where dinner was already waiting on an outside cooking range.

Will was always good company in spite of his unreliability and his fellow actors were all larger-than-life extroverts. Nina and I were thankful for the chance to lighten our mood and took comfort from being in the safety of a larger group. The evening progressed nicely with a hefty chicken curry washed down by large quantities of beer and cider that someone else was paying for. As darkness fell, the pub staff brought some more lights into the garden and we took part in raucous drinking games. Nina was surprisingly good at them. One vivacious young actress paid particularly close attention to Nina and me. Her questioning verged on the intrusive and I found myself wondering whether she had recognised us from the newspaper article.

A collective self-survival mechanism kicked in at about ten p.m. when the actors started slipping away to the guest bedrooms in the pub or to the little cluster of two-man tents in the adjoining orchard. Will lurched up behind Nina and me and slipped an arm around both our waists.

'Time for bed, me hearties,' he slurred. 'Thank God it isn't a matinee tomorrow. I hate bloody matinees – they do get in the way of a proper hangover.'

The three of us staggered back in the direction of the canal, giggling as we weaved unsteadily from side to side and talking the kind of nonsense which none of us would remember in the morning.

Although he was sheltered by the motorway bridge, the fisherman was once more dressed in his sinister cape. It hid his face and body very effectively from passers-by on both banks. He had been drawn to this location by its isolation from any nearby buildings. He had unpacked his seat and rod at the mid-way point under the bridge. A few dog walkers and a pair of joggers had gone by earlier, but it was now past ten p.m. and he hadn't seen anyone for a while. It was a good spot for a killing, he thought, noting the ugliness of the painted grafitti on the wall opposite him. The sides of the canal were smooth concrete and an exploratory poke with his rod showed that the water was unsilted and still deep at the sides. The cars thundering above made him smile at the thought of committing a murder just a few metres below so many thousands of people. The fisherman had asked for a week off work after his trip to Stratford because he had seen the couple from the boat again, pictured in the newspapers that morning. He needed answers to his questions. She was an army widow but the press didn't know or say who he was. The man had been interested enough in the dead boy to go to the inquest – and they were on a canal boat which had been moored in the basin at Stratford. He needed to find out more about them.

The fisherman had traced the canal routes from Stratford using his library of specialist books at home, calculated the speed of travel of a narrowboat and then assumed the couple would want to moor up somewhere nice and private. But it had still largely been chance that saw him stop in the large car park at the Fleur de Lys in the early afternoon and wander along the towpath in both directions for a couple of hours. When he saw their boat he quickly registered the fresh patch of paint covering the picture of the clown that he had seen on their boat in Stratford. At the time he had laughed at their pathetic attempt to hide its identity. But now, on reflection, he thought it seemed an extreme thing to do. Did they somehow suspect he was following them? Ridiculous. How could they? They knew nothing about him.

Knowing they weren't at the pub, and weren't aboard the boat, he had walked on and eventually settled himself to wait here patiently under the motorway bridge.

Everything comes to those who wait, he reassured himself. He had waited more than forty-five years to get even with 'the bitch' as he called her. Never to her face, but he never called her 'mother' or 'mummy' either. She despaired of his job in a garage bodyshop and the council flat in a run-down tower block where he lived on his own. She nagged him relentlessly about his lack of a wife and his failure to give her any grandchildren. The teasing of his workmates only added to his humiliation. He was always the butt of their banter, the victim of their childish humour, the socially awkward loner who took his meals early to avoid their cruel jokes about his height and his hair and his fishing hobby and his bachelor status. It had been much the same throughout his schooldays but now, now his life had real purpose. Now he had found a way to draw on his hidden strengths and demonstrate his true abilities. One day, they would all shake their heads in wonder at how they could have misjudged him so badly. But just as he was giggling quietly to himself at the prospect, he heard laughter, amplified by the concrete surfaces of the tunnel under the motorway. The fisherman glanced down at the hard steep edge of the canal in front of him with grim satisfaction and waited.

He looked quickly left and right and then across the water as two men and a woman appeared opposite. They were laughing and talking loudly, their arms linking and unlinking around each other as they swayed drunkenly nearer. The fisherman immediately recognised the man and the woman from the boat. The second man was absurdly good-looking and well-built and seemed to be holding court.

'Ah ha,' the newcomer shouted, pointing across the canal. 'Look. It's the Spanish Inquisition.' The fisherman guessed he was referring to the pointed hat of his cape. They all exploded with laughter. 'No one –' declaimed the man, one hand pointing upwards – 'no one expects the Spanish Inquisition… to be fishing on a canal at night!' They fell among themselves in their group, laughing again. The fisherman stayed silent with his head down, the fringe of the peak covering his furious eyes. How dare they mock him here, on the canal, where he was all-powerful?

'Hey, you!' called the man. His words slurred together. 'Haveyoucaugh'anything?'

I'd catch and kill you if you were on your own you bastard, thought the fisherman. But he did not reply. The man said something else to the couple that the fisherman couldn't hear, and they laughed again before staggering on and out of the other end of the tunnel. Their casual taunts had left him almost dizzy with rage and the nerve endings at the top of his spine seemed to squeeze his brain painfully, like a clenched fist. He would be avenged on those bastards with their casual good looks and their careless high spirits and confidence.

The fisherman quickly packed up his equipment and followed the group's noisy progress, stopping to see them climb onto the boat, unlock their hatchway after several mirth-filled attempts and disappear below decks. The lights came on for five minutes and then went off again. The boat was silent and dark now. The fisherman trudged back to his car wondering about a change in tactics. His victims would no longer be random strangers who passed him by chance, but specifically chosen targets that he would hunt down and drown. It was an exciting idea. He would explore the notion in his journal when he got home and begin to plan his next steps.

CHAPTER TWENTY

I didn't remember getting to bed, although I did remember insisting that Will join me in the double bed rather than invade Nina's space by occupying the spare single bunk in her room. He had been too drunk to argue and we both quickly fell into unconsciousness. I woke just after dawn without the slightest hint of saliva in my painfully dry mouth. I staggered to the sink for a mug of water, which I quickly gulped, refilled and glugged back again.

'Water,' croaked Will from the bed and I poured a mugful for him. He gulped it as greedily as I had, then turned over, groaned and pulled his sleeping bag back over his head. It felt like a woodpecker had nested in my forehead and was hammering away at a point somewhere behind my eyes so I climbed back over Will's prostrate frame into bed and dozed fitfully between occasional bouts of nausea for another couple of hours. This time it was Nina going to the bathroom that roused me. I forced myself up, climbed over Will and put the kettle on for a pot of tea.

'Morning,' Nina whispered, partly due to her own hangover and partly in deference to the sleeping form on the bed, before pouring herself a drink from the pot. Her black eyes were like dark pinholes and she drank some milk straight from the plastic bottle before swallowing a couple of white tablets. I grunted in case the effort of speech set the woodpecker off again and took two tablets from her proffered hand. I could hear a light rain falling on the roof of the boat. Nina opened the door off the galley to let some fresh air blow in and I could see the rain beginning to puddle in the well of the bow. There is a strange type of camaraderie amongst the hungover – a combination of shameless self-preservation and shared sympathy. When Will eventually surfaced the three of us spent the morning speaking and moving as little as possible until our heads and stomachs approached some kind of numb equilibrium.

Eventually, Nina had bravely put on her running gear and disappeared with the annoyingly clear-eyed and bushy-tailed Eddie for a kill-or-cure jog. When she returned, flushed and damp with sweat, hair wet from the rain, she was carrying a farm shopping bag, from which she tipped bacon and fresh rolls. Soon, the boat was filled with the smell of frying bacon. We slathered butter onto the rolls, smothered them with tomato ketchup and greedily demolished three each, all washed down with mugs of fresh tea. Our hangover cure was largely complete and we slowly began to exchange whole sentences with each other again rather than monosyllabic grunts.

'So, what are your plans now?' asked Will, wiping the cups and plates with a tea towel whilst I washed and Nina took a warm shower.

'It's complicated,' I said and briefly outlined the events of the previous seven days.

Will's eyebrows shot up theatrically when I told him of my night at Chester Farm, but he stayed quiet for once, listening intently until the end of my account.

'Bloody hell, Jack. I thought my life was complicated but these guys sound dangerous.'

'So, you see,' I continued, 'we think we're on the run, both from the Chester Farm gang and the press – but we're not quite sure! It wasn't exactly reassuring when you found us so easily.'

'I think you should go to the police with what you've got,' Will advised. 'Or think seriously about dumping the boat – or even tool up with some guns of your own.'

Sometimes, you were never quite sure whether Will was being genuine or performing lines imagined from a play.

'And you and Nina?' Will went on, with one upraised eyebrow. 'What's your exact status?'

'Well, er, ' I coughed. 'I'm very fond of her but there's nothing going on between us.'

'Yes,' he said. 'But you'd like there to be, wouldn't you, Jack?' Will had known me for a very long time.

Nina suddenly appeared. 'Like there to be what?' she asked.

I felt myself colouring as Will winked at me and stepped in smoothly. 'Like there to be a plan,' he finished for me.

'Ah yes,' said Nina, as though suddenly remembering that she had forgotten to do something. She retrieved her smartphone from her bunk and sat down at the table to replace her SIM card with my own. Will and I bent our heads closely over hers and sighed simultaneously when her prodding of the on-button failed to elicit any kind of response. We had agreed to give it at least another day before trying the card in my phone.

'Still no picture proof-positive then,' said Will.

Nina looked up at me quizzically and I nodded to indicate that I had told him our story so far.

'I think we'll press on up to Birmingham and then maybe go back down on a different canal to Worcester,' I said. 'We can lose ourselves in the city or in quiet places like this.'

'Until?' asked Will.

'Until we've been forgotten about and we can get on with the rest of our lives.'

The 'we' hung heavily in the air and I glanced awkwardly at Nina, but her face remained deadpan and she didn't comment.

'Look Will,' I said. 'I'm not sure we should hang around here any longer. D'you mind if we skip the play tonight?' He shrugged amiably.

'Not a problem,' he said. 'It might get rained off anyway.'

'It means you'll need to find somewhere else to kip.'

'Not a problem either. I'll bunk up with one of the others.'

'Thank you, Will,' said Nina. 'You will stay in touch, won't you?'

'Okay,' Will nodded. 'Here's my number.' He scribbled on a scrap of newspaper and handed it to Nina. 'You'd better have it as you've got the working phone. I'll be at Packwood for three days now but if you need me for anything, anything at all, give me a shout. I can get to you quickly if I have to, and I'm quite handy with a sword these days!'

He pulled on his leather bike jacket, stuffed his sleeping bag and other things back into his bag and scooped up his helmet. Then he rubbed heads with Eddie and gave Nina and me a hug before we said our goodbyes. He gave us both a final serious look from the towpath.

'Be bloody careful, you two,' he said, before striding off down the towpath to collect his bike.

Will's departure, the bacon butties and the waning hangovers had given us the desire to get going and we were soon passing under the bleak graffiti-lined motorway bridge. I had a pang of guilt; I vaguely remembered Will shouting at a harmless fisherman the previous night but not what he'd said. We continued onwards to Kingswood Junction where there was a small link to the Grand Union Canal. We briefly debated taking it and heading south towards London instead of Birmingham but just as quickly talked ourselves out of the idea. The rain continued to fall in a light mist, but our waterproofs worked fine and we felt comfortably unidentifiable under their generous hoods. There were a lot of locks on this stretch of the canal and we were kept busy, negotiating one after another before passing the lane where we had turned off up to Packwood House. I jumped back onto the stern after the final one and we motored on towards Hockley Heath. The afternoon had slipped by quickly.

I was aware of Nina watching me as I anxiously scanned ahead, looking for signs of anything out of the ordinary. I realised that I should try to reassure her rather than spook her. I thought for a few moments and then, as we passed one particular moored boat, I pronounced 'Hire boat.'

'What?'

I pointed to the boat we were passing. 'No flowers. No fripperies. Corporate paint job. Hire boat.'

'And maybe the company logo and its phone number also gives it away?' said Nina cheekily.

'Trippers,' I said mock contemptuously. 'Just hired out for a week at a time. Not like us real sailors.'

'Liveaboard,' said Nina, as we passed another moored boat. This one had neat piles of solar panels jostling for space on the roof with a satellite dish, carefully piled logs and colourful pots of geraniums. The bow and stern spaces were crammed with more flowers and a miniature kitchen herb garden.

'The names are the giveaway,' I said, pointing to *The Great Escape* lovingly painted on the side of the boat alongside the image of Steve McQueen on a motorbike. Others had clumsy jokes based on the owner's names, like *Ben's Blunder* and *Freda's Folly*.

'Look,' she said laughing. A sticker on one of the passing liveaboard's windows said, 'Adventure Before Dementia'. Everything was spotlessly sponged down and ship-shape, the ropes neatly coiled and the hinged TV aerials raised into position. 'Bet they drink from mugs labelled Captain and Galley Slave,' observed Nina.

'And the radio is permanently tuned to Radio Two,' I laughed.

'Or Classic FM.'

On we motored, calling out 'Tripper' or 'Liveaboard' as we passed each moored boat until we arrived at a new category.

'Wreck,' pronounced Nina.

We could only begin to guess at the personal story that might lie behind this neglected and mildewed hulk of a boat, its windows opaque with grime and its woodwork filthy and rain-streaked.

'Definitely empty,' said Nina, registering a pathetically optimistic 'For Sale' sign scribbled on a piece of paper that was propped up behind a grimy window. The phone number to call had been indecipherable for a very long time.

'The trouble is that some wrecks are actually still liveaboards,' I said.

Nina agreed with pretend seriousness. 'You're right. It's a fine line. It'll demand fine judgement to decide.'

We had both seen wrecks with signs of habitation; a sad thin trail of chimney smoke or a chaotic pile of detritus in the well of the bow. I imagined these as the last homes of lonely old bachelors, coughing and wheezing in the dampness of their disintegrating boats, marooned by engines they could no longer afford to fix whilst quietly drinking themselves to death. Once again, I wondered if that was to be my future.

I shook off the thought, and the mood lifted as we continued on our way, cheerfully categorising each boat that we passed – tripper, liveaboard, wreck, wreck, tripper, liveaboard. How should we label ourselves? I wondered. Target, sitting duck or deadaboard? I kept the thought to myself.

Our juvenile and judgemental game came to an end shortly after we came to a manually operated lifting bridge. Nina laughed as I quickly became breathless with the seemingly endless heavy turns of the windlass. The turns were equally heavy to lower the damned contraption and I counted 96 of them. Red-faced and gasping for air, I boarded the boat again and we quickly pulled into a small boatyard to refill our water tanks. When a second lifting bridge came up shortly afterwards, I handed the windlass to Nina. Annoyingly, she seemed to raise and lower the bridge with much greater ease.

We had been anxious about staying anywhere near the small suburban development of Hockley Heath, with its imposing Victorian Baptist church and confluence of roads. But we were losing the light and even immediately after Hockley Heath a road ran closely along one bank of the canal, which would make it easy for anyone in a car to cruise along and spot us. So we made our way into some visitor moorings just after the Wharf Tavern by the main bridge. We kept our waterproof capes on and our hoods up whilst we tied up between two liveaboards. It looked as though both were unoccupied for the moment, which suited us perfectly. We quickly secured the hatches and ducked down into the boat, pulling off our capes and changing into fresh, dry clothes.

It was tempting to explore the town, especially the Wharf Tavern and the nearby fish and chip shop. But I remembered how easily Will had found us at the Fleur de Lys and so we hunkered down inside, the log burner lit, some red wine poured and a casserole bubbling away on a gas ring as the rain fell outside. Eddie was stretched on his back, his front paws hanging bent in front of him, his ribcage rising and falling gently in his sleep. The herbal smell of the casserole mix infused the galley and saloon.

'What a very domestic scene,' grinned Nina, her legs tucked underneath her and a holidaymaker's well-thumbed novel in one hand.

I grinned too. 'We're definitely a liveaboard rather than a tripper,' I said.

'And will this really be your new life?'

'It's all I can afford.'

'Surely you could afford a deposit somewhere? Get a mortgage and a job.'

I grimaced. 'Been there, done that – a job maybe but never a mortgage again.'

'Won't you be lonely?'

Her question, however innocent and well-meaning, hinted at a future when Nina would no longer be sharing a boat with me. It left me slightly winded, like an unexpected punch to the solar plexus.

'I might,' I conceded. 'But I might meet someone. Or I might have met someone already.'

She looked at me steadily then. 'Jack...' she said warningly.

I held both palms up in a gesture of surrender. 'I'm sorry.'

Nina bustled over to the stove and gave the stew a stir. 'This is nearly ready,' she said in a very business-like voice.

I didn't dare to push it any further. The peril of our situation and the close confines of the boat had created an intimacy between us – but I still had no real idea how she might feel about me. Fond? Perhaps. I sighed. It was a word that could be applied to a pet dog. Perhaps Eddie and I had something in common when it came to Nina. In fact, I would probably come a poor second to the scruffy little terrier.

The fisherman had been waiting on the main bridge at Hockley Heath since lunchtime. He would continue to track the boat until he had his chance. As the afternoon stretched on, he risked wandering up and down the canal on both sides of the bridge whilst maintaining a constant watch on the canal's sparse traffic. If they didn't appear by evening then he would assume that they had moored further down or perhaps even turned off to join the Grand Union Canal. But he would find them. He had used a large black umbrella to keep the rain off as well as prevent anyone taking too close an interest in his features. The fisherman was back on the bridge by late afternoon, standing patiently under the umbrella and looking down the canal, when he recognised the red-and-black paintwork of the approaching boat. The couple from the newspaper were standing at the tiller in waterproofs but there was no sign of the other man. He watched closely from above, imagining himself as a magnificent and deadly bird of prey circling its target as they passed under the bridge and manoeuvred themselves into a mooring space between two other boats. He swore quietly to himself. He had hoped they would go on a little to find somewhere isolated. Isolated and vulnerable. But they had chosen to stay in the centre of the affluent little town. He shrugged. There was plenty of time. At least he knew which canal they were on and which direction they were going in. He would continue to stalk them and wait for his moment. This was much more exciting and challenging than waiting for random victims to walk past him.

CHAPTER TWENTY-ONE

The rain continued to patter onto the roof throughout the night and into a grey and chilly daybreak. The engine seemed to be charging the batteries efficiently and giving us hot water again, and the onboard WiFi was working, though very slowly. Nothing seemed to happen in much of a hurry on the canal. Nina gave Eddie a quick walk while I went through my regular routine of checking the oil and water levels and turning a little brass tap to re-grease the propeller shaft before firing up the engine. Hidden once more by our voluminous waterproofs, we cast off and headed for the bright lights of Birmingham. The next five miles showed plenty of bridges but no locks and so I ducked down out of the wet and flipped open my laptop to check the day's news.

My email traffic had slowed to a trickle since abandoning both work and marriage so I was surprised to see that quite a large number had piled up since I had last checked my inbox. Most of it, of course, was unwanted spam that had managed to sidestep the filters, but there were three proper emails, which I read in quick succession. The first was a reply from Deb to the angry message I had fired off.

Dear Jack,

I am really sorry about this. I confronted Mary straight after you wrote to me and she admitted selling the picture to a news agency – which is why it appeared in several papers and websites. I promise you that I honestly had no idea that she would do this. You know that she's never been your greatest fan and she saw the chance to cause trouble and

make some money in the process. We've had serious words about it but I'm afraid she isn't very sorry. I know I was stupid to ask her to go to Stratford and I'm truly sorry for that. But I still care about you Jack and I want us to stay friends if we can. At least she didn't give them your name. So, that's the bad news. But the good news is the solicitor has given me the final breakdown of the house sale etc after costs and the money will be transferred to our separate accounts. He says I need to get a signed receipt off you for your half, so we need to meet up. Don't worry – it can be brief and I don't think I could bear to meet your new girlfriend at the moment so please come alone. Please let me know where and when would be convenient.
Deb

I had always referred to Deb's friend as Bloody Mary and it had never seemed more apt. The woman had been paid blood money to plaster the picture of me and Nina across the whole of the British press. The chances of the Major and his men failing to identify Nina's mysterious companion as their night-time visitor seemed very remote. And now, to make matters worse, Deb needed to actually meet up with me. It wasn't a meeting that I particularly relished and I suspect that she felt the same. The second email was from Sergeant Milk. It had an official Warwickshire Police email address and was brief and business-like.

Dear Mr Johnson,

I hope this finds you and Mrs Wilde well.
I have two messages for you. I tried your mobile phone number but there was no answer.

1. As you predicted, a couple of reporters have been to see me to ask if I knew your latest location. The first one had been to the canal basin and the couple in the neighbouring boat advised him that the police

(me) had been to your boat. I told him I had no idea where you were. The second man brought your photograph from the newspaper in and asked if you had been in touch or if I knew where you were. I said no and that was that.

2. The mother of Sam Robinson has been in touch with me. I get the impression her husband isn't aware she has contacted me. I told her you met the lad briefly before he died and she has asked if she can meet you. I said you were travelling but I would ask. If you feel able to, it would be a nice thing to do.

Let me know
Sergeant Brian Milk

I was slightly reassured that the sergeant had not been inundated with reporters following up on the article – although it sounded as though our next-door neighbours at the basin had been more than a little forthcoming. I wondered whether they had seen us leave the mooring and heading north and if they had told the first reporter this. More worryingly, I doubted that the sergeant's second visitor was a reporter at all. It sounded like someone had been sent to check on whether we were at the station, whether there was any kind of investigation and to try to establish where we had gone. In which case, they had taken quite a risk. Hopefully they had been reassured and abandoned our trail. Hopefully...

The third email was from Professor Rob Parsons.

Dear Mr Johnson,

I hope you are well and continuing to enjoy your boating holiday.
I have been thinking about young Sam Robinson and our discussion after the opening of the inquest in Stratford.

It seems to me that his death is a classic example of the type of suspicious drowning which my research has identified. Once again, I believe, the police are jumping to conclusions that effectively blame the victim(s).

The location and time of the death, the injuries sustained and the profile of this young man all prompt me to think further investigations are called for in this particular case.

You indicated that he may have been involved in some kind of drug dealing operation and so this would seem to be a sensible place for the police to begin asking further questions. However, I do appreciate that you told me about your suspicions in confidence and I am now asking you to relay them to the police, which you may feel unable to do.

In any event, I am now hoping to give evidence when the inquest resumes in order to force the issue and this may give rise to some publicity.

I look forward to hearing from you.

Professor Rob Parsons
Department of Psychology
University of Manchester

Despite all the activity of the last few days, I confess my conscience had been nagging me over Sam ever since the professor had outlined his theory. I had little doubt that we had seen him with the Major's men in their blue Land Rover on the bridge. But they had denied ever meeting him. I had later seen the same men trading drugs with Jazzer and Birdie, who had shared a cottage with Sam. It was the same cottage that Sam had presumably been returning to full of drink and drugs when he had drowned. Where did he get the money from to buy drink or drugs? The tenner I gave him wouldn't have gone far and he owed Jazzer money. Had he been drowned after falling out with the others over money? Perhaps he had stolen from the dealers to feed his own habits and been found out? Or perhaps it was just a terrible accident after all? Perhaps he had slipped off the towpath and was too stoned or drunk to get back out. Whatever the truth, I agreed with the professor that the police needed to ask more questions – but why should they believe any of my theories without proof of the drug operation. And even if they might believe me, how could I alert them without putting Nina and myself in further danger? If these people had killed Sam, they could easily kill again.

CHAPTER TWENTY-TWO

We had been motoring continuously, free of locks, for about forty-five minutes. Through the portholes I had glimpsed banks lined with oak, alder, hazel and willow, and occasionally large, impressive houses came into view. No doubt their owners commuted into the city centre for well-paid professional work. It was all very la-di-da and when I went up on deck I asked Nina if she felt at home in such affluent surroundings. She poked her tongue out at me and then prodded her finger on the map at a spot where Birmingham's orbital motorway, the ever-busy M42, crossed over the canal. 'Elevenses,' she said.

I caught a whiff of baking bread on the breeze and, sure enough, some big signs appeared saying 'Wedge's Bakery and Delicatessen'. We moored up in the rain, cut the engine, locked the hatches on a forlorn-looking Eddie and walked a couple of hundred yards to a red-brick bakery on our right, just past the motorway bridge. It had a Union Jack hanging proudly over the front door and inside was an eye-watering display of fresh loaves of bread, sandwiches, pies, cakes, puddings and a range of meat, cheeses and olives.

Nina quickly filled and paid for a basket of provisions for the boat whilst I ordered coffee, orange juice and croissants for two in the small cafeteria area. I'd slipped my laptop under my arm as we left the boat and I opened it up to show Nina the three emails: ex-wife, police officer and professor.

She read all three before speaking.

'Interesting,' she said, stretching out the word. 'So your ex-wife commissioned the photo of us, and her friend sold it to the papers. I have no problem about not meeting her – though you might want to correct her about the "girlfriend" bit.'

'Well – I need to check the money is in my account and sign this bloody receipt. I want to draw a line under the whole thing now. So I thought I'd fix up to meet her at lunchtime tomorrow, somewhere in the city centre?'

'Good luck,' said Nina sardonically. 'What about the sergeant?'

I explained my theory about the reporter and the second visitor and she agreed with me.

'Even more reason to keep our heads down as much as we can,' she said, looking guiltily around our very popular eating place.

I nodded in agreement. 'But as to meeting Sam's mother, I'm not sure?' I framed it as a question rather than a statement and she looked thoughtful.

'Well, I think it would be a nice thing to do, as the sergeant says. You were probably one of the last people to see Sam alive and she probably just wants to speak to someone about her son.'

'Yes,' I said. 'Do you mind if I give her your mobile number via the sergeant? She lives in Manchester so you'll need to liaise on a place and time to meet us.'

Nina agreed and so we turned to the professor's note.

'It sounds a little like he's decided to use Sam's case to go public with his theory,' I said.

'But it's just a theory – even with a possible connection to drug dealing and Chester Farm there's no proof of anything,' Nina replied. 'And it won't make Sam's mum feel any better. He needs some more proof before he starts upsetting people.'

'I agree,' I said. 'But he won't get any if the police don't do a bit more investigation into suspicious cases. So perhaps publicity is the answer?'

Nina crossed her arms. 'But who says the cases are suspicious? The absence of physical marks could just mean that the marks weren't there in the first place. Accidents happen near canals – especially when people are pissed or stoned.'

'Well, anyway, regardless of whether it's a good theory or not, I still haven't got enough to go to the police – without the photos it's just my word about what I saw. And it could end up poking the hornets' nest even more.'

'So, we agree. We leave the professor to it.'

I nodded reluctantly. Deep down, I still wasn't wholly convinced it was the right course of action.

Our Canal Companion guide told us it was about thirteen miles to Gas Street Basin in Birmingham city centre. With no more locks to operate, we set ourselves the target of getting there that same day. There was much to see on both sides now as the built-up areas crowded in on either side. In some places the canal had been embraced by new housing developments. The balconies of spectacularly ugly brand-new apartments peered down onto the waterways of the city's eighteenth- and nineteenth-century commercial lifeline. Elsewhere the apartment blocks gave way to large houses with canalside gardens where many of the owners had boats moored up. At one stage we went under the electricity-powered Shirley Drawbridge, which, when raised, temporarily held up the road traffic. I had to insert a key that had come with the boat and press a button to start the automatic sequence. It began with flashing warning lights and a siren sounding. The amber lights prompted some cars to speed up and cross over the bridge before the lights turned red and the barriers fell. I watched drivers quietly fuming as they were forced to give way for *Jumping Jack Flash*. Suddenly my heart skipped several beats. Further down the queuing traffic I had spotted the bulky square top of a blue Land Rover. I ducked low instinctively and crouched down. The occupants of the first car in the queue looked at me curiously. But a closer inspection reassured me that this Land Rover was a different shade of blue from the Chester Farm vehicle and was occupied by a family. My pulse slowly returned to normal, but it showed how edgy I was. I didn't mention it to Nina.

It was a sudden and unwelcome reminder of the canal's proximity to the hurly burly of the tens of thousands of lives being lived along its route through the city. It was a strange sensation, being a part of something and yet apart from it at one and the same time. Inevitably the two worlds were forced to collide at times and not always amicably. As if in confirmation of my thoughts, a motorist lobbed an apple down at us as we pulled away from the bridge. It hit the boat's roof in front of me with some force and bounced off into the water. I didn't turn around but I confess I did raise a middle finger into the air.

We munched on our deli sandwiches but kept going, ignoring the heady attractions of a busy little suburb called Warstock and travelling through 275 yards of dank darkness at Brandwood Tunnel. A short while later we came to King's Norton Junction, which marked the end of the Stratford-upon-Avon Canal and the point where it met the Worcester & Birmingham Canal. The junction, which was overlooked by a large old junction house, was a very tight turn to the right with a bridge almost immediately after it. Nina had to reverse four times before we managed to swing onto the final stretch of waterway that led into the centre of the UK's second largest city.

Nina seemed confident at the helm in spite of the increase in traffic and the change in our surroundings, but when I offered to give her a rest on the helm she gratefully ducked down below. I remembered a travel article I had once subbed that had made fun of the comparison between Venice, surely one of the world's most beautiful car-free cities, and Birmingham, home of the industrial revolution and the automotive industry. Deb and I had been to Venice once, a ruinously expensive tenth wedding anniversary trip, but I couldn't see many similarities between the sights and sounds of the Grand Canal and the canal I was now travelling on. The article did, however, prove that the claim that Birmingham had more canals than its European rival was true – mainly down to the fact that Birmingham was 265 square kilometres in size, whilst Venice was just seven square kilometres. The city council apparently boasted a total of 114 miles of canals for Birmingham compared to just 28 miles for Venice. Of course, it was a hackneyed comparison and a daft article. The astonishing light of northern Italy, the flamboyant gondoliers, the highly varnished water taxis and, of course, the palaces and the Rialto Bridge all felt a million miles away from my current surroundings. But still, I felt there was something awesome about the energy and the skills of the men who had built this canal network and delivered an industrial revolution in the process.

As we passed through Bournville and alongside Cadbury World, commuter trains would occasionally hum past. Those Herculean efforts of the canal builders had eventually been usurped by the railways and then by the undisputed champion of Birmingham's later development – the combustion engine. We continued past the university buildings and the botanical gardens, catching glimpses through the trees and undergrowth that lined our route.

It was late afternoon and the rain had stopped before we slowly manoeuvred past the rear of the Mailbox, where we felt dwarfed by surrounding office tower blocks. Both Nina and I had previously visited the city centre on foot so we were already familiar with the area around Gas Street. The Mailbox was an old Royal Mail depot, now converted into a huge modern-looking building decorated in red cladding. Its designer shops, offices, apartments and the BBC studios loomed over us, next to an even taller geometric building called The Cube. The time of year meant that there were lots of empty moorings but a friendly shout from one boat drew us towards one in particular. Nina ordered me to drop some fenders and our new neighbour – a grinning, sandy-haired man in his late thirties – grabbed one of our lines, pulled the bow into the concrete towpath and tied it up for us whilst I did the same at the stern.

'You'll be okay here for a couple of weeks,' he said, with the slight hint of an Australian accent. We shook hands and introduced ourselves while Eddie bounced excitedly around our ankles.

'Pleased to meet you,' our new neighbour said. 'I'm Pete, Peter Andrews. I hope you haven't come for any peace and quiet!'

'It doesn't seem too bad,' said Nina, cocking her head to one side to concentrate on the hum of traffic and the far-off sound of a jet.

'It's the bars and restaurants,' Pete said, waving a hand vaguely at the surrounding buildings. 'It gets pretty lively at throwing-out time – or maybe it should be called throwing-up time?'

He brought three cold cans of beer onto our boat and we sat companionably while he explained how he had been living on his boat for nearly three years whilst holding down a job as a video editor at the BBC's Midlands headquarters.

'The nice thing about living here is the neighbours keep changing,' Pete said. 'Bloody good job in some cases. The mooring restrictions mean I have to keep moving around the city, of course, but I've got it off to a fine art now.' He explained that enforcement officers from the Canal & River Trust ensured that nobody could outstay their welcome on any particular mooring so he was forced into a state of semi-perpetual motion. I realised I would have to do a lot more homework before I found myself somewhere permanent to live if I bought *Jumping Jack Flash*.

'We were at Pebble Mill previously,' he said, meaning the BBC studios. 'Well, I wasn't. But if I wasn't living here I'd be commuting for bloody hours. Gets a bit damp and chilly in the winter but it could be worse. And the cycling keeps me fit.'

We both warmed to Pete immediately. He was open and friendly and had provided a welcome human dimension to our daunting entry into the heart of this seemingly vast and impersonal metropolis. We answered his questions about ourselves with as much vagueness as possible and allowed him to assume we were a couple without correcting him.

'Well, I must be going. See you two later maybe,' he said cheerily and scrambled back down into the depths of his scruffy liveaboard, which was called *Mary-Lou*.

As the offices emptied and the bars and restaurants became busy, we discussed the risks of being recognised and agreed we were as close to anonymous as we could be amidst the crowds of people and boats. So we retreated to the outdoor seating area of a nearby tapas bar with good guest WiFi and I tapped out some emails while Nina watched the world go by.

Dear Deb,
Phone's broken.
Good news re money.
1pm in Birmingham tomorrow? Steakhouse at top of The Cube?
Jack

Dear Sergeant Milk,
Thanks for the email. We are now in Birmingham.
No sign of the press yet so thank you very much!
We're happy to meet Sam's mother. Can she text us to fix a time and place?

Regards
Jack Johnson

I decided to leave the professor's email unanswered for now but attached Nina's phone number to both of the other emails and pressed send. Later we wandered around the city centre streets, the conference centres and the big open squares until we accidentally drifted onto Broad Street. Despite being early evening, the drunks already staggering, fighting and vomiting along its neon-lit length made it feel like a combination of a scene from *Blade Runner* and Hogarth's cartoon of Gin Street. We fled quickly and made our way back to the boat.

CHAPTER TWENTY-THREE

The view from the restaurant on the twenty-sixth floor of The Cube was spectacular. The canal boats far below in the basin looked like colourful toys. I had arrived early and alone for the one o'clock table. I had a very dry Vesper martini in order to prepare myself properly for our meeting. This place, part of a chain run by a celebrity chef, wasn't cheap and Deb wasn't exactly in my good books. But, I had been delighted to see how healthy my bank balance was for the moment and I had booked the table in a moment of largesse. I decided that we owed it to ourselves to make a small dent in the financial proceeds of our twenty-year marriage and use the meal to draw a final line under it.

I had to admit, Deb looked great when she arrived. She was wearing a new clingy dress and her hair had been freshly highlighted and styled. She gave me a strong hug, sat down and eyed the lemon peel in my empty glass.

'Needed the strong stuff, huh?' she laughed, before telling the waiter 'We'll have two more of those, please.'

'You're looking great,' I said and meaning it. 'Special effort to remind me what I'm missing?'

'Oh, Jack,' she sighed. 'Let's be nice, shall we?' She peered out of the window, down into the basin. 'So which one is yours?' she asked. I pointed it out. There was no sign of Nina on it at the moment.

'You should recognise it from the photo that you asked Mary to take.'

'I said I was sorry,' she said. 'I couldn't help myself – though God knows why. And I honestly didn't have a clue she was going to flog it to the press.'

'Yes. You said,' I replied grumpily.

Deb decided to change the subject.

'So, tell me all about it,' she prompted. 'You and Mrs Wilde...'

'There is no *Me-and-Mrs-Wilde*,' I replied. 'We're just helping each other out. Right place, right time.'

Deb's blue-green eyes, which I knew so well and which knew me so well, locked onto mine but I refused to blink. She pursed her lips knowingly.

'Hmmm. I'm not sure I really believe that, Jack.'

I was about to snap back angrily when the waiter materialised with our drinks. I sat back in my chair after he left.

'To be honest, Deb, it doesn't really matter what you think, does it?'

Her eyes filled for a second and she leant forward, blinking rapidly, to sip her drink. It was only a moment but it gave me pause for thought. We had both worn each other out over the divorce and perhaps it was time to put things on a new footing. We ordered our food and then I began to tell her about the last few days. She listened intently as I described Nina's fragile state and her ferocious desire for space and privacy. I told Deb about the incident at the RSC and how we had asked Sergeant Milk to call off the missing person's search. I told her how much Nina loved running and how she had tracked down and adopted the little dog Eddie, and I described Nina's well-founded confidence with the boat. Finally, I confessed that I had no idea how long she would be staying with me, or what any kind of future plan looked like save for travelling south towards Worcester. But I deliberately avoided telling Deb about Sam Robinson or Chester Farm. I could not trust her not to repeat any juicy tales to Bloody Mary who would broadcast them far and wide. Nevertheless, the first course came and went, and it seemed that I had been doing all the talking. Deb had come to Birmingham by train and so we agreed to split a bottle of Chablis after the martinis ran out.

'I think you're smitten, Jack,' she observed as our main course arrived.

I was sufficiently relaxed by then to shrug my shoulders helplessly and confess, 'Maybe – a bit.'

I expected cynical laughter, but instead, touchingly, she covered my hand with hers on the table and gave it a squeeze. 'Poor Jack. I hope it works out.'

'How about you?' I forced myself to ask.

'Oh,' she said, removing her hand. 'The odd Tinder date, you know. Nothing serious. Let's just move on, shall we?'

Deb reported back on our network of friends, although I could only really report on Will as he was the only one I had seen since leaving home. It made me realise, somewhat sadly, that most of our friends were Deb's rather than mine. We passed on puddings and after the plates had been cleared away Deb reached into her handbag and put a white envelope and a pen on the table.

'You need to sign,' she said. 'There's a pre-printed receipt in there.'

I sliced the envelope open and signed the slip of paper. It somehow felt more final than signing the divorce papers.

'Thanks, Deb,' I said.

'It's not that much to show for twenty years, is it?' she said sadly.

I was determined that we shouldn't become maudlin in drink and begin the endless round of analysis and recrimination that we had rehearsed too many times before.

'Time to go,' I said firmly, and signalled for the ruinously expensive bill. 'This one's on me.'

'We're splitting it.'

I decided not to argue. Deb seemed slightly unsteady as we emerged into the fresh air and I offered to walk her to the station but she declined the offer.

'No,' she said. 'You get back to Mrs Wilde. I hope it all works out for you, Jack, I really do.'

We hugged each other tightly before she broke off quickly and turned away, hiding her face as she tottered away from me. I watched her go, and my old life with her.

I turned to go too and climbed a flight of steps to an upper level where I saw our neighbour, Pete, coming out of the rear of the Mailbox. There was a tall man in a suit and tie with him and as soon as Pete saw me he raised an arm. I veered reluctantly towards him where he pumped my hand and then introduced his friend.

'Jack, this is Ben Taylor,' said Pete. 'He's a TV reporter for BBC News,' he said, nodding back at the building they had come from.

We shook hands. The reporter had a carefully shaped quiff of black hair and a long narrow face with a beaky nose that probably looked very telegenic on the box but seemed a bit horse-like in the flesh. He confirmed this impression by flaring his nostrils and opening his eyes wide to stare at me.

'Pleased to meet you, Jack,' he said. I recognised the professional ease with which he had quickly established our relationship on first-name terms. I noticed uneasily that he was still gripping my hand after the brief up and down motion had stopped by mutual consent.

'Do you think we could sit down and have a chat?' he asked, fractionally tightening his grip.

I retrieved my hand. 'Err... why?' I was suddenly suspicious about this supposedly chance meeting.

'Well, we were just on our way down to your boat,' said Ben Taylor smoothly.

Pete had the grace to look embarrassed as he explained. 'I thought I recognised you and Nina,' he said apologetically. 'I checked it out this morning in the papers and then I mentioned it to Ben.'

I nodded with sudden understanding. They were bloodhounds on the scent of a story.

'Can I buy you a drink?' asked the tall TV reporter, waving his hand at a group of tables outside a nearby bar. 'Or maybe we can go down to the boat and say hullo to Mrs Wilde too?'

I nodded to the tables and waited while Pete scurried away for drinks. I was still a bit befuddled from the lunchtime alcohol and ordered a pint of iced mineral water, hoping it would help me to sober up quickly.

'So,' Ben said, 'to cut to the chase, I'd like to interview Mrs Wilde about her husband's death and the nationwide search for her – and I'd like to interview you about what you're both up to now.' I gave him a hard stare.

'No way,' I said. 'You're not going anywhere near Nina and you're not going to tell your grubby little story.'

Ben Taylor rubbed his chin. 'Pete tells me you're a journalist too, Jack,' he said.

'Yep – so I know how it works and I know the story you're after,' I replied. He shook his head firmly.

'With respect, I don't think you do. We're TV – not the tabloid press. The interview would be about Mrs Wilde's husband's death in Afghanistan. Does she think the cause is worthwhile? What does she think about the sacrifices that the Forces are making? My news editor wouldn't want it to be about anything else.'

'Yeah, sure,' I said, sipping my drink while Pete sat back and listened to our exchange. 'And even if Nina agreed to such an interview – which believe me she won't – then the subtext will be why this grieving young war widow has so quickly shacked up with another man on a canal boat and who exactly is he?'

The TV reporter shook his head again. 'We can't stop the viewers speculating – but we won't go there,' he said firmly.

'Yes, you can stop any speculation,' I said. 'By not doing the story.'

His ingratiating smile suddenly took on a hint of menace.

'Well. Obviously, we want to do the story. But even if we don't, someone else might. Someone with fewer scruples, who doesn't see the bigger picture in the way that we do.'

This was undoubtedly a threat. If he didn't get the story, Ben Taylor would make sure his mates elsewhere did – probably in return for a decent tip-off fee. This would bring the pack to our door and cause a noisy fuss that we needed to avoid at all costs. But the same would surely happen if Nina and I were broadcast on television into tens of thousands of sitting rooms across the West Midlands. It was Catch-22. I was seething with anger at the smug bastard sitting opposite me. I thought fast. In the end, there's only one thing a journalist cares more about than his or her story – and that was a better story.

'Okay. Listen up, Ben,' I said. 'First I need to tell you that Mrs Wilde is an intensely private person. She is very much in mourning and the reason she has left home for the moment is that she needs some space and time to get her head straight. You need to believe me when I say there really isn't a cat in hell's chance of her agreeing to speak to you on camera. She's barely spoken to me about her husband's death in a whole week. So if you think, for one second, I can persuade her otherwise, then you're wrong. She won't talk to you or to the newspapers. You're wasting your time trying.'

Ben Taylor opened his mouth to reply but I shushed him with an upraised forefinger.

'However, we value our privacy – and not for the grubby kind of reasons that might be bouncing around in your vivid imagination. Look, all this is off the record – I'm in no way giving you a quote on our relationship – but if you must know, we were strangers who are now friends and that's the sum of it. Okay?'

Taylor nodded although his arms were folded stubbornly and his body language said, 'I'm listening to you but I'm not letting this story get away.'

I sipped my iced water before I spoke again.

'I'll tell you what I'm prepared to do. I'll give you a different story – a much better story – if you agree to leave us alone. I guarantee you'll rate it more highly than an interview with a war widow who has temporarily run away from home. You'll be telling this story before the newspapers get even a sniff of it.'

Taylor leaned forward with interest. 'What's to stop me doing both stories once you've told me?' he asked nastily.

I briefly considered adding a touch of red to his flared nostrils but sat on my hands.

'Your professional honour – plus the fact that you'll put our agreement in writing and I'll play merry hell with your bosses if you break it,' I said. 'Oh, and I'll probably break your head as well.'

He sneered. 'I don't respond to threats.'

I spread my arms in a placating way. 'I'm not asking you to. I'm just asking you to trade a crap story that's inconvenient to me – to us – for a better one that isn't.'

I knew he'd go for the bait. What journalist wouldn't?

'Tell me the story and then I'll sign the agreement,' he said.

It was the best I was going to get.

'You're witnessing all this,' I said to Pete and he nodded. To his credit, he still looked slightly guilty and miserable.

'Okay. A few days ago, the body of a nineteen-year-old boy was fished out of the canal near Stratford. His name was Sam Robinson.'

'Hang on,' said Taylor, opening a notebook and beginning to scribble.

'An inquest has been opened and adjourned,' I continued. 'He had drink and drugs in his body and it looks like an open-and-shut accidental death.'

Taylor looked up and opened his mouth to protest but I shushed him again.

'Just listen, okay? Deaths by drowning like this happen all the time, right? Someone under the influence slips off the towpath into a canal or down a riverbank and drowns. Well, there's a professor of criminal psychology who's about to go public with his theory that many of these deaths aren't accidental, or suicides – but could be out and out murder.'

Taylor looked up at me sharply.

'Yes. Murder. By a serial killer, or maybe by a number of killers. The professor has been researching the patterns and the profiles, and the medical science, and he's convinced about this.'

'Is it true?' asked Peter.

'Who knows?' I said. 'But that's his theory.'

'Doesn't matter if it's true, it's still a story,' Taylor said hungrily.

'Of course it is,' I agreed. 'It can't be proven one way or the other at present. But if a distinguished academic says it's possible...'

'What do the police say?' asked Taylor. I could almost see the bait hook now protruding through his long lean cheek.

'It'll be your job to ask them. I doubt they'll be very happy about being accused of failing to properly investigate dozens of potential murders.'

'What will the families say?' Taylor was thinking out loud now, following the threads of the story, trying to predict where they would go.

'They'll be upset, angry, confused – all those things,' I said.

'Who's this professor?'

I took his notebook and wrote in capital letters: Professor Rob Parsons, University of Manchester.

'I can't guarantee he'll talk to you,' I said. 'But I'm pretty sure he has decided to go public with his theory when the dead boy's inquest resumes. You need to get him talking exclusively to you before then. He says there's been a very unusual spike in the numbers in this region over the past year.'

Taylor nodded confidently. We both knew the sudden increase in drownings would be a significant element of the story.

'And, if she agrees, I may also be able to put you in touch with the dead boy's mother.'

Taylor looked at me greedily. 'You're right. It's a better story.'

I nodded purposefully down at his notebook. 'So, write down our agreement and sign it – now.'

The TV reporter bent his long frame over a blank sheet and scribbled some sentences before signing it with a flourish, followed by his email address and his mobile phone number. He gave it to me and I passed it straight to Pete without reading it. 'You read it and sign it too – as a witness,' I said.

Pete did as he was told and then gave the paper back to me.

'Now,' I said, pocketing it, 'I don't want to see or hear from either of you ever again. If you go back on your agreement, I promise you'll regret it. Now I must go. I feel in need of a shower.' I got up and walked away, back towards the boat, without a backward glance. But as I walked I reflected that I wasn't much of a journalist. I should have told or sold the story for myself. But it had been my only bargaining chip to keep the pack away from Nina and I had no regrets.

As I stepped into the cabin Nina was on her bed reading a book but put it down as Eddie gave me a little bark of welcome. She gave me a sympathetic look.

'How was it?'

'Oh… you know. It was okay. But I had an interesting meeting on the way back.'

I sat on the other single bed and told her about the ambush by the BBC men and how I had hopefully seen them off. Nina listened carefully without interrupting me.

'Jack, are you sure about this?' she said after I finished.

I shrugged my shoulders. 'Look, I don't feel great about it, but it was the only thing I could think of to steer them away from you… from us.'

Nina nodded. 'I'm really grateful to you.'

A ping from Nina's mobile phone interrupted the moment. She fished it out of her back pocket.

'It's Sam's mum,' she said. 'Mrs Brenda Robinson. She wants to get a train down to New Street tomorrow morning. Are we able to see her about eleven o'clock? She says she'll be on her own.'

I pulled a face. It wouldn't be a pleasant conversation, but it had to be done.

'Okay. We'll both do it.'

Nina nodded and bent over her phone to send Mrs Robinson directions to the boat.

CHAPTER TWENTY-FOUR

'Hello. Is anybody there?'

The quaveringly plaintive voice fetched me from inside the boat. A thin pinched woman in her mid to late sixties was standing on the towpath by the boat. She was clutching a shiny black handbag with both hands; she held it in front of her, as if for protection. A patterned silk scarf was tied under her chin.

'Mrs Robinson?' I asked.

'That's right.' She nodded gratefully. 'Mr Johnson?'

I jumped down and shook her hand awkwardly. Nina had come out behind me and followed suit, but instead of shaking hands she gave the woman a comforting hug and said, 'We're very sorry about Sam.' The woman was clearly touched by the gesture and swallowed gratefully.

'Let's go and get a coffee,' said Nina, linking her arm through one of Mrs Smith's.

I locked Eddie in the boat and caught up with them as they found a table in a nearby coffee shop. I ordered and collected two cappuccinos and 'a builder's tea, please', and we settled into a quiet corner.

'It's very good of you to see me,' said Mrs Robinson in her quiet voice; it had a slight Welsh lilt. 'The policeman said you met Sam before he... before he was found.'

I was about to speak when Nina put a hand out on my arm to restrain me. The woman was looking down, unaware of the gesture and she continued to talk without meeting our eyes.

'Sam is, was, our only child, you see. He was a dear little boy, but he was always very private. He was a bit of a loner. He didn't like sport. His pa always wanted him to be a boy's boy, you see. He hated it when Sam got into his teens. They wound each other up the wrong way. Sam didn't do well at school and he fell in with two or three others who weren't very good for him. They'd skip off and spend all day smoking and listening to music.' She swallowed hard. 'Then he started stealing things from shops, you see, and he was brought home by the police once or twice. My husband went berserk at Sam, but it didn't help at all. I tried to keep the peace between them but it was so hard, so very hard.'

Nina exchanged a look with me. I just shook my head and we allowed the sorrowful monologue to continue.

'When Sam finished school he just… drifted away from us,' she said sadly. 'We didn't know where he was sleeping, and he wouldn't say. But he came back to see me sometimes. He wouldn't see his pa. He brought me a lovely box of chocolates once.'

She darted a quick look up at both of us. 'I'm sorry. I just needed to tell someone. My husband won't even hear his name in the house.'

Nina put a comforting hand on her arm and whispered, 'It's okay. Go on.'

'I worried about where he was getting his money from,' she said. 'Then his father came home and found he'd been sleeping in his shed and went for him. They had a massive row and it all came out. It was horrible.'

She dabbed her eyes with a paper tissue from her bag.

'He was shouting at us – saying horrible things about how he sold himself to other men in Canal Street. He blamed his pa for everything. I don't know why – he just did. And then he ran out and we didn't hear from him again. After a month I reported him missing, but he must have come down here. My husband says he was on drugs, but I don't know how he knew that. I just knew he was my little boy. He needed help and…'

Mrs Robinson began to sob silently into her tissue, her shoulders shaking uncontrollably. Nina moved alongside her and put an arm around her.

'Shhh, now, shhh,' said Nina. 'It's okay, let it all out.'

We were attracting looks from several of the other tables. I glared around protectively.

'I'm so sorry,' hiccoughed Mrs Robinson. 'Please tell me how Sam was when you saw him.'

'I met him in a village shop in Wilmcote,' I said. 'He had a little dog with him, Eddie. We're looking after it now.'

She nodded gratefully. 'Could I see it?'

'Of course,' said Nina.

I decided that Sam's mother didn't need to know about her son's begging or my suspicions about his involvement in some kind of drug dealing network. So I chose my words carefully.

'I bought Sam lunch in a nearby pub and he came back and had a shower on our boat,' I said. 'Then I saw him hitch a lift and that was the last we saw of him.'

'That was kind of you. Did he say anything?' asked Mrs Robinson quietly.

'Not much,' I said. 'He told me he was living in a run-down old cottage with a couple of friends.'

'Do you think his friends would see me?' she asked hopefully. Nina shook her head at me and I tried to be as gentle as I could. 'We've been there,' I said. 'I honestly don't think they'd be very welcoming.'

Mrs Robinson nodded sadly. There didn't seem much more to say so Nina stood up purposefully. 'Come on, Mrs Robinson,' she said. 'Come and meet Sam's dog.'

Sam's mother walked between us to the boat and as we sat over a second cup of tea, she stroked Eddie on her lap.

'He's a sweet little thing, isn't he?' she said. 'Sam always loved animals, but his pa didn't ever want a pet in the house. It's nice to think he had a little friend when he was away from home.'

'Would you like to keep him?' asked Nina in a quiet little voice. I looked at her in surprise and admiration.

'Oh no! No thank you. My husband would be very cross,' she replied in a panicked voice.

'There's one other thing you should know,' I said tentatively, after a long silent pause. Mrs Robinson and Nina both looked up at me curiously. 'As you are aware, Sergeant Milk and the pathologist think Sam's death was an accident. But there is a remote possibility that it wasn't.'

'Not an accident?' she asked, perplexed.

Nina gave me a warning frown.

'Well, there is a university professor who believes that some people are being deliberately drowned in the canals,' I said. 'People are especially at risk if they have taken drugs or drunk too much.'

'Drowned on purpose?' She covered her mouth in horror. 'But who would do that? It's pure evil, that is.'

'Look, Mrs Robinson, I'm not saying that is what happened to Sam but I know there's going to be some publicity about this professor's theories and it's best that you and your husband are prepared for it.'

'But why on earth would anyone want to kill Sam?'

'We don't know,' said Nina. 'If they did, they may not have had a reason... and it was very probably just a terrible accident, like the police say it was. Jack's just saying that you need to be prepared.'

Mrs Robinson handed Eddie back to Nina and stood. She looked as if she was in shock or possibly denial.

'You've both been very kind,' she said. 'I must go now. My husband doesn't know I'm here. I told him that I've gone shopping for the day, but I don't think he believed me. I just needed to see someone who had seen Sam.'

We all shook hands quite formally and then I helped her off the boat and watched her bustle away, her bowed and anonymous figure quickly vanishing into the crowds.

The fisherman had lost track of the couple from the paper and their red-and-black painted narrowboat. He had followed the canal into Birmingham as closely as he could in his car, but it was impossible to see long stretches of the waterway from the road. They could have moored up anywhere and anyway, he thought to himself, they would be surrounded by lots of other people in the city centre. It would be impossible to get at them there. Angry and frustrated, he had returned home and studied his map books. Fine, he thought to himself, if the trail has gone cold, he'd just go fishing again. He decided to try a lonely looking spot near Droitwich Spa, which he could reach easily off the M5.

The fisherman arrived at Hanbury Wharf just before nine p.m., parked in a public car park by the entrance to the smart-looking Droitwich Spa Marina and walked past three locks along the towpath of the Droitwich Canal all the way up to the Eagle and Sun pub, where it joined the Worcester & Birmingham Canal. With a bit of luck, the couple he was stalking would eventually come back out of Birmingham on this route – and then he would kill at least one of them. In the meantime, he needed to recover his composure with another demonstration of his power, his skill and his experience.

He slipped past the pub, crossed the canal on the road bridge and walked along the towpath to Bridge 36, which was picturesque, dark and quiet. He didn't want it to be too quiet, though. With pubs to both sides of him, there was always the chance that someone would take a shortcut along the towpath after they'd had a few too many.

Gratifyingly, a man came past just after the fisherman had set up a rod. He looked to be aged somewhere in his late sixties or early seventies and his ruddy complexion, rough clothing and mud-caked boots suggested he was some kind of farm worker or labourer. He stopped as people often do and asked the fisherman if he'd had any luck. 'Not yet,' grunted the fisherman. The man fished in his baggy corduroy pockets for a tin and made himself a roll-up, which he lit with a cheap plastic lighter. He tried to start a conversation, but the fisherman deliberately stayed quiet. He didn't want to give this man anything to talk about with his friends in the pub. Eventually, the man got the point and moved off towards the Eagle and Sun after he'd finished his cigarette.

Now it was all about patience, the fisherman thought to himself, hunching his shoulders and beginning his wait. Would the man pick up a friend at the pub? Could he even go back a different way? The fisherman could never predict what might happen, but he knew he had to be ready in an instant. When the old man did reappear two hours later, he was on his own and singing quietly to himself, but the words were slurred. 'Farewell and adieu, to you fair Spanish ladies, Farewell and adieu to you ladies of Spain.' The fisherman quickly checked in both directions, but the old man, with his frizz of white hair above a heavily sun-creased face, was the only person in sight.

'Still 'ere, are you?' he said, expelling fumes of strong rum. 'Caught anything then? Nah... and you won't neither.' He hawked phlegm into the water and then he deliberately spread his legs wide and clumsily began unbuttoning the flies of his thick baggy trousers.

The fisherman watched the man swaying backwards and forwards. The tips of his heavy boots were inches from the corrugated metal edge of the canal lining. He grunted with the effort of staying upright. After a few seconds a weak trickle of piss hit the water and he chuckled to himself. 'Won't catch anything now either,' he said.

The catch net hit the man in the small of his back with considerable force. Both the man's arms began to windmill as he realised he was being pushed forward into the water. His head turned sideways towards the fisherman and his mouth opened, but nothing came out. The strong metal hoop of the net was still pressing firmly against his back. Then the fisherman reached along the handle with his right hand and gave it a firm push forward. It was enough to send the old man head first into the water. The splash sounded as disconcertingly loud as it always did. The fisherman got up quickly, ready to place the net over his victim's head and onto his shoulders but he was already too far away, halfway across the canal.

The fisherman panicked for a few seconds. Would the man be able to struggle across to the other bank? No, he was splashing ineffectually. He was old, drunk and weighed down by heavy clothing and boots. The fisherman watched closely as his victim's arms became weaker and the white-haired head sunk slowly below the water. Nothing broke the surface and the dark ripples quickly dispersed. The canal became glassy smooth again.

'Adieu to you too,' the fisherman whispered. Then he pulled a scarf up over his face, gathered his equipment and walked back down the dark towpath to his car.

CHAPTER TWENTY-FIVE

It was dark outside and the screen of my laptop gave an eerie glow to the interior of the boat. Nina and I were watching as a well-groomed female presenter turned to camera as the opening titles of the programme finished. The director did a fast mix and the presenter gave a welcoming smile.

'*Good evening,*' the presenter said, before adopting a more serious face. '*A leading criminologist has warned that a sharp rise in deaths by drowning on the West Midlands' canal system may mean that a serial killer is on the loose. Latest figures show that the number of such deaths has risen sharply. There have been twenty-four deaths by drowning in the last twelve months.*'

A map graphic of a network of blue canals with white crosses scattered across it appeared on screen.

'*They appear to be widely distributed across a number of different canals in both populated and rural locations.*' The camera cut back to the presenter. '*However, police have dismissed the warning by Professor Rob Parsons of the University of Manchester as unsubstantiated scaremongering. Ben Taylor has this report.*'

The presenter in the studio was immediately replaced by an image of a canal towpath. The camera was tilted up to show Ben Taylor's tall frame walking towards us as a narrowboat passed him going in the opposite direction.

'*On a bright autumn day like today, the canal is a picturesque place where people come to relax by boating, fishing, hiking and cycling.*'

The camera cut to a close-up of the reporter's beaky face. '*But is there something much more sinister happening on the West Midlands' canals and waterways?*' The shot cut to a tall thin man in a suit, sitting in an office with rows of books behind him. '*Distinguished criminologist Professor Rob Parsons of the University of Manchester explains his theory.*'

The professor was talking to a faceless interviewer to the side of the camera. '*I just don't believe that this sudden and unusual spike in the number of deaths in the canal system can be easily explained away. Canals are not places where people generally commit suicide and if the person has taken drugs or alcohol, it is very difficult to identify any signs of violence on the body.*' The picture of the professor was replaced by shots of a canal passing underneath a road bridge. His voiceover continued over the pictures.

'*There are miles and miles of isolated canals and waterways in the Midlands and it would be quite easy for a killer to pick on lonely and isolated individuals. In my opinion it doesn't make any kind of sense that we have gone from an average of just five drownings a year over the past five years to a sudden spike of fifteen in twelve months.*'

The camera now cut to the reporter, Ben Taylor, who was looking back at the professor. Ben Taylor leaned forward intently. '*But you can't categorically prove that any of these drownings were anything other than accidental, Professor Parsons?*'

Now both men were in shot.

'*No. I can't,*' admitted Professor Parsons as his name appeared on screen beneath him. '*But my research indicates common factors such as the locations and the condition of the victims. And I think the spike in numbers speaks for itself.*'

A picture of a teenager laughing at the camera replaced the professor and Taylor's voiceover continued. '*This is nineteen-year-old Sam Robinson from Manchester, who is the latest person to drown in the region's canals.*' The camera slowly zoomed into the photograph, focusing on the boy's eyes. '*Sam's body was found in the canal outside*

Stratford just over a week ago. A coroner's inquest has been opened and adjourned. It found high levels of drink and drugs in his body. Professor Parsons believes that Sam's death, like many others, needs to be fully investigated. And so does his mother.'

Sam's mum appeared on screen, perched nervously on the edge of an orange sofa. As she started speaking, her name appeared in a caption along the bottom of the screen: Mrs Brenda Robinson. 'We just want to know what happened to our Sam,' she said in a quavering voice. 'It's just horrible to think his death might not have been an accident. Why would anyone do such a thing?'

The camera lingered for a second on her as she began to sob. The image cut back to Taylor again, walking towards the camera on another length of towpath. 'Why indeed?' he asked. 'Could there be an extremely disturbed individual on the loose who gets his thrills from random killings on our canals? And how does the boating community feel about this theory?'

There was then a short sequence of vox-pops. A girl in her twenties sitting on a canalside bench tossed her long blonde hair, excited to be on camera.

'Oh, it's terrible,' she gushed. 'I think people will be careful not to be on their own by the canal until this person is caught.' Next, a man in blue overalls looked up from the engine bay of a narrowboat. 'There's no proof that this pusher-guy exists, though, is there? You can prove anything with statistics, can't you?' A middle-aged couple appeared, pushing a lock gate closed with their bottoms, side by side. 'It's very worrying,' said the man. 'Yes, very worrying indeed,' his wife agreed.

Ben Taylor appeared on screen again. This time he was standing on the rear balcony of the Mailbox, with the canal basin framed behind him. 'If there's even a remote chance that there is a 'Pusher' haunting our canals, as Professor Parsons claims, police across the region will need to answer some difficult questions before people will feel reassured. Ben Taylor, BBC Midlands Today, Birmingham.'

The picture cut back to the studio, where the presenter was sitting behind a shiny black mirror-glass table with the programme's logo reflected in it. A large, heavy-jowled and grey-haired police officer in uniform sat alongside the presenter, two meaty fists resting defensively on the table to either side of a sheet of paper. '*I'm joined now by Detective Chief Superintendent George Chisholm, from West Mercia Police. What's your reaction to Ben Taylor's report, Chief Superintendent?*'

DCS Chisholm's body language suggested exasperation but his answer was calm and considered. '*Each individual death of this sort is thoroughly investigated before we pass the file on to the coroner. I am sure the Warwickshire Police will do the same about the case in your report.*'

'*Yes, but you must concede that the sudden rise in the number of people being found drowned in our canals and waterways is striking – and worrying?*'

The police officer tilted both palms slightly upwards towards the camera and looked the presenter square in her eyes. '*We have found no evidence whatsoever that any such deaths in the last year were connected in any way.*'

'*Really, Chief Superintendent? Had you actually been looking for any connection between the deaths before Professor Parsons spoke exclusively to our programme and raised his concerns?*'

'*We had been made aware of the professor's theories,*' said the police officer. '*And we believed that they would cause additional grief and unnecessary suffering to the families and friends of the people who have accidentally drowned.*'

The presenter leaned forward.

'*I'm sorry, but I must press you, Chief Superintendent. Are you saying that you have carried out a review of the fifteen deaths by drowning that took place over the past year in the areas covered by three different police forces and that you are now dismissing the professor's claims?*'

The DCS involuntarily clenched both fists in front of him.

'We haven't carried out a review as such,' he conceded. 'But we've spoken to our coroners' officers and we are satisfied that there were no signs of foul play in any of the individual cases, and there is no sign of them being connected. More to the point –' he stabbed the desk with the forefinger of his right hand – 'the coroners themselves were satisfied.'

The presenter leaned forward again. 'So, do you now think there should be a thorough-going review of all the drownings in the last year, Chief Superintendent? In case there is a so-called "Canal Pusher" on the loose or just to reassure people?'

'I repeat,' said the police officer, his lips tightening, 'each case has already been rigorously investigated. However, if anyone has evidence that any of these deaths were anything other than tragic accidents, we would always ask them to come forward and speak to us.'

The presenter smiled with self-satisfaction. 'And we'll need to end it there on your appeal for help. Thank you, Chief Superintendent.'

DCS Chisholm gave a furious look at the glossy-haired woman across the table. He'd had no intention of appealing for anyone's help when he had entered the studio. The presenter turned smoothly from him and spoke to the camera. 'And in other news... '

I clicked to pause the programme.

'God knows how they tracked down Sam's mum,' I said. 'Taylor turned the story round very quickly.'

'But surely,' said Nina, 'If there was any truth in any of this, then there'd be some kind of evidence. Someone who saw something... or someone who managed to get away?'

'You'd think so,' I nodded. 'But not necessarily. I think the strongest argument is the unusual spike in the numbers. It's hard to think of another reasonable explanation.'

'So,' said Nina slowly, 'do you think Sam's death might not be connected with Chester Farm?' Her eyes were wide. 'D'you think he could have been killed by this... Canal Pusher?'

'Maybe. Or maybe he just fell in,' I said. 'Who knows? What I do know is that the professor's theory is going to cause a stir.' I expect all the papers will follow it up now.' I yawned and stretched. 'We move on at dawn.'

CHAPTER TWENTY-SIX

The BBC News report and the noise from the city centre bars and restaurants kept me awake until the early hours. I tossed and turned in my sleeping bag, occasionally hearing little whines and snuffling from Eddie, who sounded as though he was having no problem sleeping. Nina had trained him to sleep on the bunk opposite hers and he usually stretched out luxuriously in the middle of the blanket until he was allowed to join her in her own bed in the morning. Lucky dog.

My thoughts kept drifting back to the Major's drug operation as I tried to work out how much of a continuing threat he might be to Nina and me. All of Nina's attempts to get my mobile powered up again or my SIM card to work in her phone had come to nothing. I tried to put myself in the Major's place. I estimated that the scale of the operation at Chester Farm and the value of the crop in the ground would be worth many millions of pounds. He was nobody's fool if he had built an operation that big, and his men, who were clearly ex-military too, seemed highly competent, fit and sure of themselves. But, as the days had gone by and the roof hadn't come crashing in on their criminal enterprise, surely they would grow tired of trying to find their mystery night-time visitor? I seriously hoped so. I remembered their grim faces and the terror of my frantic night-time escape from the men and their dogs came back to me.

And now there was something else to think about. Was the professor right? Was some kind of psychopath stalking the canals of the Midlands and getting away with murder by targeting lonely and intoxicated individuals? I pictured Sam's face snarling into mine and then crying with self-pity; then I saw him white and bloated on the mortuary slab. These images and my fears swirled round and round without ever landing, like a commercial jet in a holding pattern above a busy airport. Eventually, exhausted, I managed to bring myself into land for a fitful few hours of sleep before dawn, when Nina gently shook me awake with a mug of steaming coffee and a couple of digestive biscuits.

'Come on,' she said, breaking off half a biscuit to feed to Eddie. 'We shouldn't stay here a second longer. Crack of dawn, you said. I'm taking Eddie for a quick walk and then we're off.'

Nina disappeared with the little terrier while I tried to wake myself with a trickle of lukewarm shower water and a cleansing wet shave. My watch said 07:30 as I strapped it to my wrist.

Once again, a layer of mist was carpeting the water in the basin and the sky seemed to mirror it with a continuously unbroken ceiling of low-lying grey cloud. It wasn't a sight to make the heart leap with joy, but it helped to hasten our departure. When Nina returned we bustled about, untying the boat and manoeuvring it free of our neighbours. The thoughts of my restless night were still fresh enough in my mind to prompt a quick but careful survey of our surroundings, but I could see no one taking a particularly close interest in us. Indeed, the steps and pathways around the pastiche warehouse buildings of the basin were remarkably deserted apart from an occasional early morning commuter hurrying past on their way to work. Our engine sounded abnormally loud when it burst into life and settled into its regular rhythm. I saw Pete's face appear briefly at one of his portholes before guiltily ducking back out of sight.

Nina took the helm without any discussion and pivoted the boat in a circle to retrace the course we had taken to come into the centre of Birmingham. It was astonishing how quickly the city's buildings were lost behind thick screens of trees, bushes and undergrowth. We passed a couple of floating narrowboat restaurants which were closed and moored up for the winter, and pressed ahead as intercity and commuter trains regularly ran past us, their noise joining with the rising level of rush hour car traffic. Birmingham was busily coming to life.

The absence of locks on this stretch meant that I could busy myself in the galley and we were soon enjoying bacon sandwiches smothered in ketchup and washed down with tea as we stood at the stern of the boat. I took the tiller while Nina concentrated on her breakfast. I now felt reasonably confident steering the lengthy boat and Nina no longer needed to keep a watchful eye on me all of the time. However, I reflected, it would still be a very tricky proposition to manage *Jumping Jack Flash* wholly on my own – largely because of the locks which seemed to demand a minimum of two people to navigate through them quickly and efficiently. I had to decide whether I wanted to buy the boat and, if so, find somewhere I could moor up more permanently and begin to start thinking about earning a living again. Would Nina feature in some way in this vision of my future? I pushed the thought away for the moment.

The steady noise of commuter traffic reached us from the unseen roads as we slipped slowly past the university buildings and the outskirts of the Bournville chocolate-making estate. My little guidebook told me that Cadbury's had once boasted its own fleet of narrowboats and an internal railway system. Now, the only sign of life was an occasional cyclist-commuter who chose the safety of the towpath to get to work rather than risk the car-choked arterial roads that led into and out of the city centre. There was a handful of visitor moorings near the Bournville site behind a padlocked gate; a couple of boats had decided to stay overnight, defying the dire warnings not to leave any valuables on board due to 'thieves operating in this area'. I slowed from a fast walking pace to a slow one in order to prevent our wash from disturbing their lie-in and Nina nodded approvingly.

'You're getting the hang of this,' she said, feeding a final scrap of bacon to an eager Eddie.

We reached the large junction house and the soaring steeple of the nearby church at King's Norton, but this time we passed under the bridge, ignoring the turning immediately to the left which led back onto the Stratford Canal. We kept going straight ahead, continuing along the Worcester & Birmingham Canal. If anyone was still trying to trace us, I hoped the switch of canals would throw them off our trail.

It was 9.30 a.m. by now and my close study of the canal maps the night before had shown me that it would probably be lunchtime before we reached a very scary-looking flight of locks at a place called Tardebigge. There were no less than thirty locks stretching for four miles, which would lower us more than two hundred feet. It could take a whole day to get past them, so we had agreed to find a quiet and isolated mooring with no road nearby and tackle them the following day. Nina was mildly excited at the prospect of meeting this formidable challenge, whilst I, who would be running ahead and dealing with the gates, regarded it as more of an exhausting ordeal to be survived.

But before we could moor anywhere we first had to navigate all 2,493 metres of Wast Hill Tunnel, the longest on this canal. Trees and vegetation tumbled thickly down the steep slopes on either side of the tunnel entrance; its pitch black semi-circle above the water was reflected below to create the illusion of a single dark circle. The towpath stopped at the mouth of the tunnel and the light on our bow shone on the red engineering bricks that glistened with damp above our heads. Nina had taken the helm and we quickly realised that the pinpoint of light up ahead wasn't the end of the tunnel but the light of an oncoming boat. She throttled back and edged as close to the right-hand wall as she could. It was going to be ridiculously tight, but the tunnel had been built to allow two boats from opposite directions to pass – just.

The ghostly face of a young woman at the tiller of the other boat advanced on us, and as we came alongside each other we could clearly see through the wide rectangular windows into the well-lit interiors along the length of her boat. The woman called a cheery good morning to us, but as soon as we passed each other, the pitch black of the tunnel once again stretched out before us – this time with no hint of daylight in either direction.

'My God,' said Nina, in awe of the back-breaking labour that must have gone into creating this impressive feat of engineering. 'It's incredible.'

'A perfect place to get lost from the world,' I reflected.

'You're welcome to it. I can't wait to get out,' she said, shivering at the cold and the dark. The temperature seemed to be dropping fast as we penetrated further into the heart of the tunnel. Eddie seemed to share her view; the dog was whining unhappily at her feet.

According to our map book, there was a suburban housing estate somewhere on the hill that rose up above our heads with a big modern pub and a fish and chip shop, but down here it was hard to imagine all those thousands of lives being lived above us as we moved slowly forward in complete and utter isolation. I was suddenly fearful of our engine failing and marooning us deep in the bowels of this hill. The little tugs that had pulled horse-drawn boats through this tunnel had given up their trade a long time ago and it would be quite an operation to pull us out. I decided to keep this thought to myself and peered forward, searching for the real light at the end of the tunnel. Eventually, after about twenty long minutes, it appeared, but it took us another ten minutes to emerge fully into the daylight.

A while later we decided to risk stopping at a small place called Hopwood to pick up some newspapers. We wanted to see if the BBC's report about a possible 'canal pusher' had been picked up by the rest of the press. I jumped ashore as Nina brought us up to a visitor mooring and, after trekking to the Hopwood Park service station on the nearby M42, I was back an hour later. The shops there had furnished me with an armful of national dailies and two reheated Cornish pasties for lunch.

We went down below to the main table and grabbed a bundle of papers each. Nearly all of them covered the story on the inside pages and repeated the main points of the BBC broadcast, although some in much more lurid language. Many carried the photograph of Sam, which had probably been obtained from his mother, and one carried a photograph of Mrs Robinson and her husband framed in the doorway of their modest Manchester home. Professor Parsons was also pictured and extensively quoted. One of the more serious broadsheets also carried an inset story about a spate of young male drownings in Iowa, which had been called the 'smiley face murders', on the basis that if it could happen in America, it could happen here too.

The BBC report had been broadcast the previous evening and most of the newspapers seemed to be relying on the same news agency copy for their coverage. Many were peddling the line that the police 'were appealing for help' and considering a full-scale review in the light of the professor's comments. This was all in spite of an official police spokesperson's attempts to calm speculation. Some of the papers threw up theories about the motive for any possible serial killers; most of them settled on the idea of a loner with a disturbed personal history or a sick thrill-seeking monster. A few local MPs had jumped on the bandwagon to express concern at the sudden peak in numbers and called for the police to review their case files. One was even asking for extra police patrols along canals.

After reading the papers, we had set off again. The rolling countryside and panoramic views were peaceful enough, but I was keen to put as much distance as I could between ourselves and Birmingham now. I certainly didn't want to get caught up in the story about the 'Canal Pusher' and I didn't trust the TV reporter not to come looking for us, fishing for a juicy follow-up angle. I was also, I admit, still scared witless that the Chester Farm gang could trace us and I also suspected that some sections of the press wouldn't give up on trying to get an exclusive interview with the attractive young army widow who had left home in such strange circumstances. And so we beat on, not quite boats against the current, but trying to escape being borne back ceaselessly into the past.

The fisherman was also bent over a pile of that morning's newspapers. He was exultant. Famous at last! And he had even been given a name: the Canal Pusher. At last, he thought, the dozy bastards had woken up to his achievements. Seven drownings in ten months – although the authorities didn't know that, of course. He had recently stepped up the frequency of his attacks as he had grown more confident of his methods and eager for the thrill to be repeated. But there was no reference yet to the old bastard he had drowned the night before. He hugged himself with glee. The Canal Pusher! And yet all they had to go on was a rise in the number of canal drownings, he told himself. No survivors. No witnesses. No medical evidence. His crimes were flawless. Of course, the police were still trying to deny his existence. That both angered and pleased him. Perhaps he should do something to embarrass them? He would think about that. But for the moment, their lack of curiosity suited him. He looked forward to returning to work the following week and hearing his so-called workmates discussing the story. The only disappointment was that he had lost track of the couple from Stratford after his last sighting. No matter, he thought to himself. They'll turn up eventually and when they did, he'd be ready.

CHAPTER TWENTY-SEVEN

My anxiety to get away meant that the last thing I wanted to hear was our engine suddenly splutter and cough alarmingly. Nina put down her half-eaten pasty and throttled back so that we were barely moving forward. It reduced the frequency of the spluttering but something was clearly wrong. I opened the wooden panel that concealed the engine and stared at it stupidly. The fan belt looked okay and there was no obvious sign of damage, but the engine had clearly developed some kind of breathing problem. I returned to the tiller and shrugged hopelessly at Nina, who was looking at the route of the canal in our little book.

'There's a large-looking marina just after the motorway,' she said. 'Looks like we'll have to stop there and get help.' I quietly wondered to myself whether anyone could have tampered with the engine but quickly dismissed the thought as paranoia.

A small aqueduct took us under the screaming lorries and cars of an M42 road bridge; the speed of the motorway traffic was a stark comparison to the snail's pace of our arrival at Alvechurch Marina. A smart complex of buildings rose up behind an impressively large fleet of hire boats and other moored visitors. We made for a pontoon next to a large workshop where two boats had been craned up onto dry land and another could be glimpsed inside a large white plastic tunnel. Nina brought the struggling engine to a stop while I tied us up to the moorings and a middle-aged man in denim overalls and a lumberjack shirt appeared, wiping his hands with an oily rag.

'That don't sound too good,' he observed.

Nina fixed him with her most charming smile. 'Hullo... can you help us? It just started to cut out on us about a mile ago.'

The man climbed on board, restarted the engine and listened, tilting his head and his little ponytail of black and grey hair to one side.

'Sounds like a fuel problem. We're a bit busy at the moment but I'll have a look. Come back in an hour.' He clearly didn't want us anxiously peering over his shoulder during his investigations and so we were dismissed to dry land while the mechanic fetched a toolkit and an apprentice.

Nina and I strolled uphill towards the village centre with its shops, pubs and takeaways.

'Whatever it is,' I muttered, 'I hope it's not going to be too expensive.'

'... or take too long,' added Nina. 'Have you decided to buy it, then?'

I gave her a sidelong glance.

'Probably. I've developed quite a liking for the canals. The idea of just moving on if I get bored with somewhere is really appealing, although I'll need to find a job too.' There was a silent pause. The unspoken topic of Nina's own future plans lingered tantalisingly in the air between us. I was still too scared of forcing her into a decision to leave and so I changed the subject. 'How about a bit of shopping for dinner?'

We swung into a little grocery store after tying Eddie up outside and stocked up on some cans of ruinously expensive food for small dogs, a couple of sirloin steaks, salad ingredients, a decent bottle of red, gin, tonic water and an expensive bottle of single malt whisky called Caol Ila. The clinking weight of the carrier bags and the walk back down the hill made us both slightly breathless by the time we reached the boat.

We entered through the bow, dumped the bags and made our way back towards the engine bay where the mechanic and his apprentice were bent over, their heads in the engine's innards. The older man straightened up with a grunt.

'It's the fuel, all right – looks like it's been contaminated. Probably rust and gunk from the tank,' he said. 'We'll polish it and change the filters.'

'Thanks so much,' said Nina whilst I simultaneously asked, 'How much?'

The man smiled at her, then narrowed his eyes at me and shrugged.

'Two hundred quid... two-fifty, maybe.'

'All right,' I said. 'How long?'

'Rest of the afternoon. I reckon you'll be stopping here tonight.'

I cursed under my breath.

'I also reckon a couple of mugs of tea might go down well... and some biscuits if you've got them.'

The beefy young apprentice grinned, Nina bustled away to put the kettle on and I went outside to sulk. I had hoped to make a start on the enormous flight of Tardebigge Locks today, but they would have to wait for tomorrow now. I felt very vulnerable in such an easily accessible and well-populated place but there wasn't much I could do about that now. I hauled the pile of newspapers onto the boat's roof and leafed through them again. One was a local paper that I had ignored the first time around as it didn't have coverage of the so-called Canal Pusher, but picking it up now, a small inside story caught my eye.

MAN'S BODY PULLED FROM CANAL

The body of a 72-year-old farm worker has been recovered from a stretch of canal at Droitwich.

A hiker found the body of Mr Albert Thomas in reeds at the edge of the Worcester & Birmingham Canal near Hanbury Wharf. It is understood that Mr Thomas, a widower, was a regular customer at the Eagle and Sun and had been drinking at the pub on the night before he was found. Landlord Mr Bill Sutherland said, 'Albert had been coming in here for a few pints every night of his adult life. Everyone knew him; he was a bit of a character. He would always walk back to his cottage along the towpath. We're all very upset.'

It's understood that Mr Thomas lived alone. Police say there are no suspicious circumstances and the coroner has been informed.

Yet another victim of the Canal Pusher? The local newspaper was a weekly and it had only just managed to squeeze the story into that morning's edition. The body must have been found very early for them to manage it. There was no reference to Professor Parsons' theory that had been picked up by all of the national dailies. But could there be a connection? A seventy-two-year-old man, who obviously liked a drink, had wandered into the canal on his walk home in the dark. It sounded like yet another tragic accident on the Midlands' waterways. But was it just supposed to appear that way when, in fact, it was much more sinister? This man had been walking back from that pub his entire life – why had he gone into the water now? I thought again about Sam. The flurry of coverage of the professor's theories had caused me to revisit my suspicion that his death was in some way connected with Chester Farm. Maybe there was no connection at all? Maybe he had been the victim of this Canal Pusher all along? Or maybe Sam had just wandered into the water, just like poor old Mr Thomas, his mind befuddled and his co-ordination shot by too much drink? I shook my head. Maybe I was letting my imagination run away with me? Whatever the truth, Hanbury Wharf, the site of the latest drowning, was on our route south into Worcester and I decided I would be keeping a sharp lookout as we went past.

Nina and I lazed around on the boat until the end of the afternoon when the engine suddenly burst into life again. It seemed to be running smoothly and after five minutes of chugging away, the older mechanic reappeared.

'Seems to have done the job. You'll need to come over the office and settle up.'

'Thank you very much indeed for your help,' gushed Nina.

'Yeah, thanks a lot,' I said.

'Don't forget to bring your wallet.' The mechanic grinned. I followed him off the boat and into a very tiny and grubby office which was strewn with all manner of paperwork. The office was off the main workshop, which was strewn with machinery in the same way. He sat down at the chaotic desk, cleared a space and laboriously wrote out a bill in spidery joined-up handwriting before passing it to me.

'Two hundred and fifty pounds, plus VAT.'

I gulped. With those kind of costs, my money from Deb wouldn't last long.

The mechanic saw my expression, sat back and stared hard at me.

'Took longer than I thought, two of us. That's what it is. It's all there,' he said, nodding at the bit of paper in my hand. 'Labour, parts and VAT.'

I handed him my debit card, which he manoeuvred through his machine.

'I'll waive tonight's mooring fee,' he said, as I punched my code in.

'That's good of you,' I muttered miserably as I retrieved my card, scribbled my name on a receipt pad, took the top copy and stuffed it with my card into my wallet. 'Thanks for sorting us out so quickly,' I turned to the man to say goodbye but he had already reached for his telephone and was rootling around in the papers on his desk.

CHAPTER TWENTY-EIGHT

It was a cold but dry daybreak that saw us motor out of the marina and through some steep cuttings. There was just the faintest lingering smell of wild garlic on the air. We went through the Shortwood Tunnel, thankfully much shorter than the previous day's experience, but we were travelling too early to encounter any other boats coming the other way.

Eventually we emerged from another tunnel at Top Lock, the highest step of the famous Tardebigge flight. It was a particularly deep one. A helpful little plaque told us the chamber was fourteen feet deep and had replaced a lift at some stage. Like all of the locks on the canal, it had a triangular black and white warning sign on the big square wooden beam of the gate. The sign showed a cartoon canal boat tipping at an unhealthy angle into the water and was accompanied by the warning: 'Keep boat forward of cill marker.'

I thought back to that first day of boating, when Nina had explained to me that the cill was a little ridge of brick, rock or cement just under the water when the lock was full, but which quickly became visible as it emptied. Failure to keep the boat sufficiently forward of the cill marker would mean that as the level of water fell, the stern of the boat would come to rest on the ledge, whilst the bow would continue to fall, leaving the boat stranded at a perilously steep angle. It seemed a lifetime ago. We had negotiated many locks and many dangers together since then.

One evening, Nina and I had combed YouTube, chuckling condescendingly at video footage of various careless or inexperienced boat skippers who had failed to follow the instruction to keep forward of the cill marker and ended up needing a major operation to recover their badly smashed-up and waterlogged boats. One click too far, though, and our mood had become serious when we discovered that in a few rare cases, such accidents had caused deaths and serious injuries. The carnage cause by a 'cilling', which was the name for such an accident, would be considerable in a deep lock such as this one. Nina called up to me at ground level as the boat disappeared, breaking my reverie.

'One down, twenty-nine to go!'

I quickly calculated that this was going to be much more tiring for me than for her and resolved to suggest we swap places at the halfway mark.

It took us almost six hours in the end to work our way steadily downhill. Oddly, the lack of oncoming traffic at this time of year also slowed our progress, as there was no one to helpfully leave the next gate open for us to enter. Nina sportingly swapped places with me at the halfway point. We moved relentlessly forward, chamber to chamber, ticking each one off as we went. Having rested briefly for an hour for lunch, we finally emerged into a pound with moorings for half a dozen boats in the gap between Tardebigge Locks and the much smaller flight of Stoke Locks. We had already descended 217 feet that day and the next flight would take us another 42 feet lower. It was four p.m. and we both felt badly in need of a rest. I'd noticed a pub called the Queen's Head near to the bottom lock of the epic flight. I knew that my first pint of beer was going to taste exactly as it should to the deservingly thirsty. However, it was not to be.

A woman on a small road bridge was staring down at us as we negotiated the last lock of the day. I thought she was just a curious onlooker until I looked up as I was tying up and saw her sauntering towards our boat. I returned to the stern where Nina was stowing the windlass safely in its plastic holster.

'Hullo, there,' called the newcomer as she came alongside us on the towpath. She looked familiar somehow. I guessed she was in her mid-thirties. She had corn-coloured hair cut in a bob and wore a little black dress that was gathered by a shiny belt at her waist. A small expensive-looking handbag was slung over one shoulder. Her hard eyes glittered eagerly from behind a large pair of designer glasses. Her face, artificially taut and stretched, looked hungrily up at us. Suddenly, I realised who she was.

'Petra Barker,' I said quietly.

Nina looked at me sharply and the woman also turned to stare up at me. The bank was slightly below our deck, so she had to stretch a hand up awkwardly over the stern rail.

'I see I need no introduction. Very pleased to meet you, Mr...?'

I ignored the outstretched hand and the invitation to name myself and turned to Nina.

'Petra Barker is a feature writer for one of the Sunday magazines,' I said to her. 'Although she doesn't look much like her photo by-line.' I recognised her primarily from her frequent appearances on television discussion panels, where she specialised in a particularly vicious and waspish right-wing view on most issues. The woman moved her hand towards Nina: her bright red painted fingernails reminded me of talons on a bird of prey.

'And you must be Mrs Wilde?' she said with her famous gravelly voice.

Nina stepped back away from the hand.

'What do you want?'

Petra Barker allowed her hand to drop to its side whilst quickly pulling the other up to the side of her face. She clicked her finger and thumb three times next to her ear for no apparent reason. It was as though she was peremptorily summoning a waiter. It suddenly dawned on me that she was signaling to a snapper and sure enough, twenty yards behind her, I could see a man's head and the dark circle of a telephoto lens popping up above a hedge.

'A photographer,' I said urgently to Nina. 'Down below, quick.' I shoved her down through the hatchway before turning to snarl down at Petra Barker, 'We have nothing to say so you can piss off now.'

'Come, come, Mr Johnson. All I want is a civilised chat. And I have come a long way.'

I had been about to follow Nina, but the use of my name halted me in my tracks.

'It is Mr Jack Johnson, isn't it?' she purred. 'You're probably wondering how I know that and how I found you, aren't you?'

I stayed still in spite of my better judgement.

'Well,' Petra Barker said, folding her arms in triumph. 'First of all, I know a nice young actress who is quite keen to build her profile with my help. She recognised you and Mrs Wilde when you joined them for a spot of Shakespeare and she gave me a ring. It was so kind of her. And then, of course, I had one of my researchers ring every marina along every canal near Stratford and offer a modest cash reward for a sighting of you both.' She spread both arms out from her side. 'And so – tah-dah – here I am!' She looked very pleased with herself.

'You've had a wasted journey, Barker,' I snapped. 'Nina... Mrs Wilde doesn't want to talk to you.'

'Look, Jack, you've been in the business.' She saw my surprise. 'Yes, dear, I've done my research and I know all about you, Jack. Your ex-wife proved to be very loyal and silent on the subject, but her friend who sold us the photograph of you both in Stratford was much more forthcoming. Anyway, you know that wherever I go, others will follow. Let me do a sympathetic feature and get it all done and dusted in one go. We can offer a nice fat facility fee in return for some lovely cosy pictures of you both on board the boat. I promise, it'll all be very pleasant and understanding.'

'No deal. Now bugger off.' The photographer had emerged from his hiding place and was brazenly out in the open now, shooting pictures of our encounter. The star columnist's bright red lips tightened into a thin line.

'You need to think again about this, Jack Johnson.' She spat my name out. 'I've got more than enough on you both to write a feature – with or without your co-operation. But if I have to do it without you, it'll be far less sympathetic. And you won't get a penny.'

Without missing a beat, she bent down and kicked off a pair of red-soled high heels to reveal her black stockinged feet. She moved to put one of them on the boat and stretched a taloned hand up for a rail to pull herself up on board.

'So, don't be a silly boy, Jack. You just pop back downstairs and ask Angelina – or Nina, was that what you called her? – to put the kettle on for a nice little chat.'

I glanced down the hatchway and saw Nina's frightened eyes staring up from the bottom of the steps where she had been kneeling to listen to our exchange. She was looking up at me like a cornered animal, her eyebrows furrowed and her head shaking violently from side to side.

I turned back to see that Petra Barker had almost hauled herself up onto the stern, although the tightness of the hem of her dress was making it difficult. I was really angry now. Too angry to think clearly but angry enough to grab the bucket of canal water that I had scooped up earlier in the day to wash down an oily mark left by the mechanics. I lifted it clear over Barker's head and emptied the greenish, brackish water over her in a single rush. She half-gasped, half-screamed and fell back onto her backside on the towpath, both legs splayed out in front of her. I calmly dipped the bucket off the stern on its rope, let it sink and then pulled up another twelve litres of dirty canal water.

'You were trespassing,' I said, as coolly as I could. I was still boiling inside. 'But feel free to have another go.' I raised the full bucket of water to chest height.

'YOU BASTARD!' she screeched from her prone position, her hair plastered to either side of her head. 'YOU FUCKING BASTARD!'

I shook my head sadly. 'I think you need to go and dry off before you catch a cold, Petra.'

'I'll make you very sorry you did that,' the journalist spat, as the photographer hurried forward to help her to her feet. She shook off his hand angrily. 'And you'd better hope you got that,' she snapped at him.

'Every frame,' he grinned, no doubt thinking that Petra Barker's colleagues in the newsroom would appreciate the pictures every bit as much as the readers.

I waved a hand. 'Bye-bye, Petra.'

I continued to watch as she bent to snatch up her Christian Louboutin shoes and padded wetly away to a black SUV, which then drove off at speed.

Nina emerged through the hatchway and almost knocked me off my feet as she threw both her arms behind my neck and gave me a very tight bear hug.

'Jack! Thank you, thank you, thank you.' She loosened her grip to look me in the eyes. Her own were glistening. 'Oh my God. Did you really do that?'

'Hmmm… that water smelt a bit. I wouldn't fancy sharing a car with her all the way back to London.'

Nina burst out laughing; her mood had shifted in seconds from terror to triumphant joy.

'My hero! You deserve a drink, Jack. We both do.' Then she released me and vanished again, reappearing a few minutes later with two beakers of Navy-strength gin and tonic, which we used to toast our triumphant repelling of the unwelcome would-be boarder. We moved onto the foredeck, refreshing our drinks on the way. We were quickly a little bit drunk on victory and gin. I was caught up in Nina's happy mood as she laughingly recreated the scene.

'Did you *see* her hair?' Nina said. 'She was like a drowned rat. Serves her right. I hated the woman. D'you think they'll run a picture of it?'

However, as Nina prattled on happily, I knew all too well that I'd opened a new can of worms. I tried to warn her.

'Pah! What can she write?' she asked petulantly. 'She's got nothing. We didn't talk to her, did we?'

I knew that small detail wouldn't make a blind bit of difference to Petra Barker, but I didn't want to spoil the celebratory mood so I held my silence. Later, after dinner and a shared bottle of wine, Nina took herself off to bed, after rewarding me with a chaste goodnight kiss on the cheek.

'My hero,' she said again, waving a hand above her retreating back.

CHAPTER TWENTY-NINE

MISSING WAR WIDOW IN FAMILY 'KIDNAP' FEAR screamed the headline of the Page Three lead story. Petra Barker had decided to avoid the ridicule of a photograph of herself sitting prostrate and drenched, and had instead opted for a shot of Nina looking diminished and frightened whilst I was standing in the foreground, angrily pointing at something or someone in front of me. A small but glamorously unrealistic head-and-shoulders drawing of the columnist accompanied the story and her prominent by-line read: 'by our star columnist, Petra Barker'. She had clearly decided to slum it by writing for the daily paper rather than the glossy Sunday magazine which accompanied its sister paper. The lack of a full-scale interview had made that inevitable. Nevertheless, she had obviously enjoyed wielding her poison pen in revenge for her drenching.

The family of the missing war widow Mrs Angelina Wilde say they are seriously worried about her safety, I can exclusively reveal, after my revelations about the violent older man who is now sharing her life.

Mrs Wilde's disappearance prompted a nationwide police hunt, which was called-off after she was found on a run-down canal boat with a stranger not previously known to the young widow. Mystery has surrounded this man's identity until now, but I can reveal he is Jack Johnson, an unemployed 45-year-old divorcee. Mrs Wilde's heroic husband, Major Alan Wilde, 32, died only weeks ago in an ambush whilst serving his country in Afghanistan. Stricken with grief,

Mrs Wilde left her home in Wiltshire after his funeral and has not been seen by her worried family and friends since. A nationwide police search for her was eventually called off after she was spotted on Johnson's canal boat in Stratford-upon-Avon.

I spoke to her anxious mother (pictured right) in the sitting room of her comfortable Hampshire home. 'I am so grateful to you for tracking her down,' her mother told me, clutching my hand in both of hers. Spritely 70-year-old Mrs Jill Aston added, 'But who is this man she is with? It's almost as though he has kidnapped her.'

Mrs Aston has only been in contact with her daughter via brief text messages. I was able to reassure her that Angelina is alive and still on board Mr Johnson's boat. After tracking the couple down to their hiding place near Stoke Wharf on the Worcester & Birmingham Canal, Mr Johnson attacked me, swore at me and prevented me from speaking to Mrs Wilde.

'I am very worried by what you have told me,' Mrs Aston revealed to me. 'Angelina is in a very fragile condition after Alan's death and I shall be asking the police to make sure this man isn't holding her prisoner against her will.'

This newspaper has now passed on my revelations to the police who have promised to investigate.

Johnson's boat, which looks tatty and run-down, has suffered engine problems and had to call into Alvechurch Marina for emergency repairs. A mechanic who worked on the boat said: 'She was very nice, but he was much older than her and very short-tempered.'

Johnson's ex-wife has refused to discuss the reasons for their recent divorce but a close friend of the couple, who declined to be named, told me, 'Jack's a nasty man and I'd be worried about any friend of mine who ended up with him.'

For more, see my column, this Sunday, on the blood-price our loyal army families have to pay.

'The bloody bitch,' I said, slamming the flat of my hand on the paper.

Nina, whose face had turned grey, shook her head from side to side and said in a small voice, 'Kidnapped? How can they write such things?' She closed the paper and picked up Eddie from the seat alongside her.

'By getting your mother to say the word and putting it in inverted commas,' I said.

Nina shook her head disbelievingly. 'I need to get some air.' I went to join her but she pushed me back gently. 'On my own, please, Jack.' Then she climbed out of the door in the bow and her footsteps and Eddie's scampering claws disappeared out of earshot.

I put my elbows on the table and covered both eyes with the heels of my palms to help me think. The article had blown our cover into tiny pieces. It gave the Major and his goons my full name and even our location should they want to come after us. I recalled now that the woman at the local newsagent's shop where I had picked up the papers that morning had given me a puzzled look of recognition. Suddenly, concerned for Nina's safety, I hurriedly locked both entrances to the boat and set off along the towpath after her. I found her sitting on a bench outside a little shop called Little Shop, which was nestled beside by a bridge. It seemed to be a chandlery selling bits of brass, rope, coal and Calor Gas bottles to passing boat owners. Eddie was on her lap, as usual, and I gave him a pat as I sat down beside her.

'I've been thinking,' I said.

'Me too, Jack.'

'I don't think it's safe for you to stay with me any more.'

'The article.'

'It's all bollocks, of course. But if the Chester Farm mob are out looking for me, they'll have a very good chance of finding me now. I don't want you to be around if they do.'

She nodded sadly. 'Probably time to go home and face the music then.' Her voice trailed away.

'We can ask about a taxi,' I said, indicating the inside of the shop.

'No. Not yet,' she replied quickly. 'I'll help you get to a mooring in Worcester. I can get a train from there.'

'But, Nina –'

Her mouth clenched in the stubborn look I had come to know only too well; her jawbone tight beneath the smooth skin of her face.

'No buts. You can look for a mooring and a job in Worcester and I can melt away from there.'

'But it's two days to Worcester. They could easily catch us,' I said anxiously.

'So, we need to move even faster, Mr Johnson. Come on, old man.' She yanked me to my feet and strode off determinedly in the direction of the boat, Eddie scampering happily at her heels. I sighed and dutifully followed Eddie.

I couldn't deny I was relieved that she was not leaving me at that instant, but I was worried that she had made the wrong decision.

There was open farmland and far-reaching views on both sides of us now and rushes lined the banks, giving it the appearance of a tranquil river rather than an old industrial waterway. By lunchtime we had reached Hanbury Wharf and I dug out the local newspaper article about the elderly farmhand's drowning and showed it to Nina. We saw the tattered remains of some blue-and-white police tape that was still tangled in a bush. It was next to a small road bridge, shortly after the turn off onto the Droitwich Canal and the Eagle and Sun pub, where it seemed that poor old Albert Thomas had enjoyed his last drink. Nina shivered at the sight and we sped up a little. Once again, we enjoyed a long lockless stretch that felt very remote from the rest of the world in spite of being sandwiched between the high-speed railway and a motorway. The sight of thousands of people flowing past us each hour at twenty times our speed only made me enjoy the passing woodlands and the soft waving reeds on the edges of our route even more – especially as I knew we were now sharing our last journey together.

Nina had refused to let me take the tiller since leaving Stoke Wharf and the knowledge that this was probably her last full day on the boat also seemed to make her appreciate her surroundings even more. She sipped a mug of coffee with her left hand, whilst her right hand made minute adjustments to the course of the boat stretching out in front of her.

'I am grateful to you, Jack,' she suddenly volunteered in a quiet voice. 'I just needed to get away from my situation and being on this boat has given me the space to get my head right.'

'It's only been a fortnight,' I said carefully.

'Yes, but it's been a very different way of life and I needed that. I feel I can go back and make my own decisions and not have Mummy, or the army – or anyone else for that matter – get in the way of my future.' She paused and took another sip. 'And I'm starting to face up to the fact that Alan won't be part of that future. At least I think I am.'

'I'm sure you are,' I said squeezing her hand on the tiller. 'You're tough as nails really. But if you ever need a friend, you can call me at any time.'

Nina squeezed my hand back. 'Dear Jack. Another place, another time...' Her voice trailed away. Then she grinned. 'But you'll always have Eddie to remind you of me.'

'What? Oh no, you can't –'

'The ship's all yours, Captain,' she said, smiling naughtily before vanishing below decks, deaf to my objections about the long-term ownership of the dog.

We nervously travelled through a small hamlet called Dunhampstead. A small boat hire company was based there and I remembered that Petra Barker's research assistant had telephoned marinas across the canal network to offer a reward for sighting us. But as we passed the line of hire boats waiting for their customers, I realised that perhaps

Petra had done her worst and could do no more. I didn't want anyone else ambushing us, though, so we hurried past the little place with its craft shop and inviting country pub. The map showed that we were now entering a very sparsely populated stretch of canal with few roads near it or crossing it, and just the Birmingham to Bristol trains thundering close by. We agreed to find a hidden mooring if we could, and do the final stretch into Worcester city centre on the following day.

A place called Oddingley looked promising, with little more to show for it than an ancient manor house, a church and a level-crossing keeper's cottage. We passed by them and agreed to stop shortly before a long bend in the canal, which preceded a winding hole. There were no rings set into the towpath, so Nina pulled out some mooring pins, which she instructed me to bang into the earth at forty-five-degree angles. It was now three o'clock and, through the pale afternoon sunlight, we could just see the humpback whale-shaped silhouette of the Malvern Hills on the horizon. Streaks of white cloud stretched long and thin above them. Even the benign weather seemed to be ready to co-operate with our last full day together on the water.

The Canal Pusher had spent the day in an agony of frustration. He had seen the newspaper article by Petra Barker and it had renewed his determination to track down and investigate the mysterious Mr Jack Johnson as soon as he possibly could. He now knew that Johnson had been talking to Professor Parsons after the inquest hearing in Stratford. He recognised him from his photograph in the papers. He was amazed that the professor had revealed the existence of a 'Canal Pusher' but he still couldn't fathom out the connection between Johnson and the professor. Had Johnson been on the canal that night and seen something of Sam's drowning? Had he shared what he had seen with the professor? If that was so, then Johnson could have vital evidence for the police. Vital evidence that could lead straight to the Canal Pusher being caught.

The newspaper had placed Johnson and the woman near Stoke Wharf after calling in at Alvechurch. So, they must now be heading south towards Worcester. He traced a stubby nail-bitten finger along the route of the canal, past Hanbury Wharf where he had drowned the old man just a few days ago and on to Dunhampstead. He calculated that they would have left early that same day in order to escape the attention of any more reporters but he doubted they would want to do the full eight and half hours it would take to get to Worcester and the River Severn. So, he thought, they would be mooring up somewhere between Tibberton and Dunhampstead.

At last, he felt he was closing in on them. And all thanks to the Petra Barker article. They had left the safety of their well-populated city centre mooring and if his calculations were correct, they would be moored up in a much more lonely and isolated spot. With a bit of luck, he could strike at his first ever pre-selected victim. Could he even see off both of them? He tingled with excitement at the prospect – even though it would most likely confirm the professor's theory and begin a police manhunt for him.

He changed into his fishing overalls, folded his rain cape, packed the car and drove for an hour until he reached the long straggling village of Tibberton, where he parked in a quiet side road near a cluster of modern houses. Then, his rods and keep net slung over his shoulders, and carrying his box-seat, he set off along the towpath going south. The tightness that sometimes gripped the back of his head had returned and he knew it would remain there, making him slightly nauseous and dizzy, until he could release it with a rush of adrenalin and an overwhelming sense of achievement.

He spotted the red-and-black boat after less than half an hour of walking. It was moored on the same side of the towpath that he was on and he could see the couple moving about on the stern. What to do now? It was one thing to know where they were, but another to find out exactly what they knew. But he didn't need to know, he reminded himself. Not if they were face down under the water.

He sat down on his box and brought out the crumpled copy of that morning's paper. He re-read it twice. It was a sly piece, he thought. The woman clearly wanted to imply that the man Johnson was a nasty piece of work. At least they hadn't blabbed anything to her, he thought. It was past seven now and the light was starting to fade. He needed to think this through carefully. The map showed him a pub nearby and so he walked past the couple's boat, his cap pulled down over his eyes, and across a pedestrian bridge into the tiny hamlet of Oddingley.

The Canal Pusher was famous now. He almost expected all eyes to instantly turn on him as he opened the door of the Fir Tree Inn. With a start, he noticed a sign above the pumps that read: The Murderer's Bar. But the handful of drinkers and card players just looked up briefly at the plump bespectacled figure in his fisherman's gear and returned to their muttered conversations. He collected a pint of lager and a packet of cheese and onion crisps and settled himself and his gear around a small table in one corner. A display of framed newspaper cuttings and sepia-tinted prints lined the walls and an account of 'The Murder' explained the curious name of the bar. He began to study them.

In 1806, the story went, the hamlet's rector, Reverend George Parker, had been shot and then bludgeoned to death whilst walking in nearby fields. Apparently, he had been a bit too enthusiastic when collecting tithes from the locals. Three local farmers called Clewes, Banks and Barnett, and a farrier named James Taylor, had hired Richard Hemming, a carpenter from Droitwich, to kill the rector.

The Canal Pusher forgot his pint and read on, fascinated.

Hemming hid in a hedgerow and shot the rector but was foiled when a villager recognised him as he fled from the scene. Hemming managed to get away all the same and was never seen again. It was assumed that he had fled abroad. However, nearly twenty-five years later, as a barn was being built nearby, a skeleton was found in a shallow grave. Hemming's wife identified her dead husband from the clothes and a carpenter's rule.

The Canal Pusher was now kneeling on his seat, facing the wall and eagerly reading. The landlord nudged a regular at the bar and pointed to the back of the transfixed fisherman with a grin.

Clewes, the former owner of the farm where the skeleton had been found was arrested and tried. The subsequent trial created enormous interest across Worcestershire, with crowds jostling for admission to the city's Guildhall where it was held. It transpired that no less than six men had clubbed Hemming to death to prevent him implicating them in the rector's murder. But by the time of the trial, the ringleader, Taylor, had died. Clewes was eventually found guilty as an accessory after thirteen hours of deliberation by the jury.

The Canal Pusher read on eagerly to the conclusion.

The judge had refused to accept the jury's guilty verdict. Clewes had not been charged with being an accessory so the judge declared he *was not guilty. The bells in the nearby church were rung in celebration when he returned to Oddingley, much to the displeasure of the rector at that time.*

The Canal Pusher sat back down and took a big satisfied swallow of his drink. It was fate. He had wandered by chance into a pub with a 'Murderer's Bar' and read a story about two murders on the very doorstep and nobody had ever been convicted. Was history about to repeat itself? He considered whether one day, in another two hundred years, someone might read similarly yellow newspaper cuttings about himself. It was a kind of immortality, he thought with a self-satisfied smile. But his work wasn't finished yet.

He finished his drink and crisps, gathered up his equipment and left the pub, trying to avoid the landlord's eye as he went. The evening had darkened considerably as he re-crossed the canal and settled himself down between the bridge and the moored boat. He dropped a bait-less float in the water, pulled up his collar and sat watching the boat's stern. A yellow light glowed up through the hatchway and he could hear the man and woman talking in low voices as they moved about inside. He could occasionally hear the dead boy's dog give a high-pitched bark. He hoped the events to come would be a high point in his journal.

CHAPTER THIRTY

I confess I was feeling pretty maudlin by nine that evening. We had continued to work our way through the bottle of single malt that I had felt rich and reckless enough to buy in Alvechurch. Nina had been matching me glass for glass, but with single measures compared to my doubles. We tried it neat, we tried it with a cube of ice, we tried it with a splash of water and then we repeated our cycle of important research all over again. Nina had heated up a ready-made lasagne and I had loaded coal into the little stove in honour of our last night – and so that we could leave the bow doors open to the star-studded night sky without getting too cold. In spite of the heat from the woodburner, Nina went to fetch a big, baggy orange and brown jumper. The strong smoky taste of the whisky had numbed my cheeks and blurred my senses but God, she was attractive, even with the shapeless woollen creation that now enveloped her. Her knees were drawn up in front of her with the jumper stretched over them, creating a small hammock on which Eddie was curled.

'That reminds me,' I said, apropos of nothing, as is the way when drink has been taken. 'The dog.' I waved a forefinger vaguely in its direction. 'The dog goes with you tomorrow.'

'Oh, Jack, you know you love little Eddie. He'll be company for you and he's a very fierce guard-dog.' She wagged a finger from side to side back at me. 'You know you can't be too careful and there are lots of nasty people on the canals, aren't there, Eddie?'

'Nope,' I said, shaking my head for emphasis. 'That was the deal. The dog goes with you.' I splashed another inch into my glass and half an inch into hers, followed by two splashes of water from a little blue-and-white striped milk jug.

She pushed her nose into the fur of the dog's shoulder and breathed in deeply.

'I do love him dearly.'

'And I love you dearly.' I hadn't meant to say the words out loud, but they came out all the same. 'Sorry,' I said with a stupid grin and I put the palm of one hand to my lips. 'Didn't mean to actually say that.'

Nina looked blearily sorrowful at me. We were both very pissed.

'Ahh, poor JJ,' she said in a cod-Irish accent. 'You're a lovely man, so you are. My heroic rescuer. But I've had it with that love thing.' She wagged her finger from side to side again for emphasis. 'Nope. Never again. Too, too painful. I shall die a little old widow so I shall.'

'But you're young and lovely,' I said. 'You'll meet someone again and be happy.'

She greeted this pronouncement with a sudden hiccough. She opened her eyes wide, giggled and covered her mouth. 'Oops... drunk too much of this... ' She picked up the bottle and tried to focus her eyes on the label '... of this Cowl Eeela.'

'Me too,' I conceded. 'I need some air.'

In order to give my head the benefit of the cold night air, I stepped unsteadily across onto the towpath and wandered along the length of the boat, past the stern. I could see the dark pointed hood and shapeless cape of a fisherman hunched over his rod up towards the bridge. It was vaguely familiar. I called out a slurred 'good evening' but got no response. The cold night air gave me the sudden urge to empty my bladder. I decided not to pee into the water in case it scared the fish away. And so, turning towards the hedge, I unzipped my fly and gratefully let loose a fierce jet of urine at a point midway up the foliage.

I had just finished and was fumbling at my fly when I became vaguely aware of movement behind me. I made to turn around, but I was too slow and clumsy. Suddenly, I felt my head jerked violently backwards and then a net of some kind being pressed into the flesh of my face. Panic surged through me.

'What the –' But I couldn't finish. My arms were pinned to my side by something hard and metallic. My feet were still free and I staggered to retain my balance as my whole body was physically dragged backwards across the towpath. I thought briefly about just collapsing into a heap, but instinct told me to stay upright. It was the wrong call as the attacker was able to continue pulling my whole body closer to the edge of the canal. The net was cutting into my nose and cheeks with real force.

Somehow, I found my voice and shouted something incoherent. My mind was somersaulting in terror, but shock and alcohol were paralysing my ability to control my body. Before I could process what was happening, I was falling through the air. I automatically took a huge gulp of oxygen. Somehow, I knew what was coming next. My body plunged into the water with an almighty smack.

The first sensation to hit me was the cold. The second was the blindness. It was pitch black. To my horror, my heels had met the corrugated iron banking and a viciously powerful final tug had pulled me backwards into the water. With relief, I felt the pressure of whatever was pinning my arms lessen slightly. But now I was struggling to breathe. Whatever had been pressing down on my arms was on my shoulders and something was twisting and tightening around my neck. Its downward pressure was forcing my head under the water.

In a flash, my brain went back to the moment I had nearly drowned as a boy, desperately trying to find a way to save myself. But, this time, there was no glaring sunlight above the water to guide me upwards, no burbling noise of other people shouting and laughing around me – and no young saviour to bring me back to the surface. There was just inky icy blackness and the only noise was of myself, drowning. I felt totally and utterly unable to help myself as whatever was around my neck squeezed the air from me.

Then my feet felt something hard on the bottom of the canal. Almost simultaneously, the downward pressure suddenly stopped. With all my remaining strength, I pushed upwards and, jubilantly, I broke the surface – my head back, my mouth outstretched. I gulped, coughed and spluttered, desperately trying to clear the water from my mouth and nose. I looked up at a shapeless figure on the bank and registered a commotion in the water alongside me.

'Jack! Are you all right?'

The shapeless figure was Nina, still dressed in her big baggy jumper. The splashing next to me was a struggling and gasping man. I seemed to have sobered up in record time. Adrenalin was coursing through me, tightening my arteries and making my heart pump furiously.

'Get the torch,' I shouted hoarsely, and reached across to the other man in the water. I grabbed one of his flailing arms and pulled him towards the bank, hooking my other hand onto the top of the canal's metal edge. A bright white light suddenly illuminated us both from the towpath, momentarily blinding me.

'Jesus, Jack,' said Nina urgently. 'I saw it all from the boat. He just yanked you in with his net.'

I turned back to the man spluttering beside me, balled a fist and drove it into his nose, which made a crunching noise. Then I somehow managed to get both hands on the bank and lever myself over the edge onto my stomach. I stayed on all fours and retched for a while before Nina pulled me to my feet and turned the light back onto the man, who was desperately trying to stay above water but swallowing a lot of it too.

I kept the torch on him and sent Nina back to the boat for a coil of rope. We hauled him up onto the bank and, as he also knelt on all fours, his waterlogged plastic cloak clinging to him, I kicked his arms away so that he collapsed onto his already bloody nose with a painful grunt. He was short and podgy with hardly any hair. Mid to late forties or early fifties I guessed. Once he was down I sat on the small of his back, pulled his arms behind him and tied them together as tightly as I could with the rope, before looping it around his ankles and tying them together too. He didn't say a word throughout the whole process. Nina had been holding the torch steady as I finished the task.

'Get your phone,' I gasped at her. 'Get the police here.'

Nina did as she was told, returning with a couple of blankets. She wrapped one around me as I shivered uncontrollably next to the prone figure of the man who had tried to drown me. She draped one over him too.

My attacker's head was turned to one side, looking up at us both from the ground. 'Who are you?' I asked.

'You'll find out,' he said quietly. And then, in spite of the hopelessness of his hog-tied position, he gave a smile that I can only describe as one of extreme satisfaction.

The headlights and blue flashing lights of the first police cars illuminated the other side of the canal within a matter of minutes. Uniformed officers were the first to arrive and after I described the man's murderous ambush, they were quickly joined by a trio of detectives in civilian clothes. The uniformed officers untied my knots with some difficulty, replaced them with metal handcuffs and led my attacker away over the bridge to one of the patrol cars. I was allowed to shower and change into dry clothes on our boat whilst Nina described what had happened to two of the detectives. Then we locked the hatchway with Eddie inside and we were both ushered into separate cars and taken to a stately home and estate which had been converted into a large police headquarters. Astonishingly, it was less than a mile away from our mooring.

Half an hour later, I was greeted in a comfortable interview room with soft seating and subdued lighting by the large frame of Detective Chief Superintendent George Chisholm. I immediately recognised him as the studio guest from the television news programme. One of the detectives who had come to the boat stayed in the room to take notes. Chisholm sat opposite me, in the centre of a large blue sofa. He stretched both arms out expansively along the backrest.

'Well, Mr Johnson, it appears that we all owe you a debt of gratitude for staying alive.'

'Thank Nina,' I replied. 'She saved me by pushing that madman in. Is it him? The Canal Pusher?'

DCS Chisholm wrinkled his nose in distaste at the label. 'It's possible, I suppose. But given how much publicity there was yesterday, he could just be some kind of copycat who wanted to share the limelight. We'll find out soon enough.'

'Is he talking?' I asked.

'Not yet,' admitted Chisholm. 'But I get the impression he's bursting to at some point. He's drying off at the moment and the duty lawyer is on his way. Now, we shall need a full statement from you and Mrs Wilde about what happened tonight.'

'There's something you should know first.'

'Go on.'

'I saw you on the television.'

The memory clearly wasn't an enjoyable one for the Chief Superintendent, but he shrugged as if to say 'so what?'

'It was me who leaked the professor's theory to the BBC,' I said.

DCS Chisholm sat upright. This towpath altercation, or attempted murder, or whatever it was had just become much more complicated. I was not a random victim of a copycat.

'I think you'd better explain yourself, Mr Johnson.'

The junior police officer turned to a new page and began scribbling as I talked. I described how I had met Sam before his death and then heard the criminologist's theory after the opening of the inquest. I told them about how Nina had volunteered to help me but then been harried by the press. Finally, I told them how I had traded the story about a possible 'Canal Pusher' for Nina's privacy.

'Hmm... quite a coincidence then that you should be attacked in such a way this evening,' said DCS Chisholm, thinking out loud. 'Are you sure you have never seen your attacker before?'

I did in fact have an uncomfortable sensation that I had seen the fisherman before but I couldn't place the location or time.

'Please think hard about that. It could be important.'

I nodded and DCS Chisholm left. Shortly after, I was collected by a police doctor, who wanted me to take precautions against catching Weils Disease from the canal water. I was returned to the interview room and Nina joined me shortly afterwards. We compared notes but did not learn anything new. The night dragged on and she fell asleep on my shoulder.

The Chief Superintendent returned with a female officer about an hour later. He looked rattled as he pulled up a hard chair and sat down in front of us.

'Any more thoughts about whether you might have seen him before this evening?' he asked.

I shook my head apologetically but brought it up sharply when Nina suddenly said, 'Packwood House!'

'What?'

'It was him! I'm sure of it. Don't you remember the fisherman Will shouted at, under the motorway bridge, when we were coming back from Packwood House?'

We had all been full of drink at the time, but I could picture the hunched and seated fisherman on the other bank in his strange pointy-headed cloak. We described the scene to the Chief Superintendent who scribbled in his own notebook this time.

'All right then. I'll need you to add this to your statements and then we'll take you back to the boat. We've got your phone number, Mrs Wilde, and we'll need you to let us know where your final mooring is in Worcester, sir.'

I looked hard at him. Chisholm's manner had changed and I wondered if, in fact, the professor had already been proved correct that night. If the Canal Pusher had indeed been caught red-handed there would need to be a detailed reinvestigation into all of the canal deaths of the past year and beyond. He was going to be very busy with a lot of explaining to do. I was exhausted but still curious.

'Has he said anything?' I asked. 'Could he really be a serial killer?'

We all stared at DCS Chisholm's tired grey face. 'He's being… forthcoming,' said the Chief Superintendent ambiguously. 'But we've got a hell of a lot of checking to do.'

He stood up to indicate he wasn't going to be pushed into making any further comments and so we shook hands.

As we were driven the short distance back to the boat, I reflected on my decision not to tell Chisholm about Chester Farm. Was I right to stay quiet? There was no obvious connection with the drug farm, the events of tonight and the Canal Pusher, especially if it was him and not the drug dealers who had killed Sam. The chances of that being the case seemed to be narrowing by the minute. No, I hadn't told them because I still had no proof. I needed to be 100 per cent certain that if I called in the authorities they could quickly close the whole thing down. I would not risk any chance of frustrated and vengeful criminals dogging my every step. I wasn't keen on spending the rest of my life looking over my shoulder.

It was four o'clock in the morning and we were both like zombies as we moved around each other to prepare for bed. But as she passed my bunk with a pint-sized glass of water I put out one hand and caught hers.

'Thanks,' I said. 'You rescued me tonight.'

She squeezed me back.

'Payback time.' Then she smiled and padded back behind the swing door to her bunk.

CHAPTER THIRTY-ONE

I woke after midday and lay back with my head on the pillow to take stock in the light of day. It was a Saturday but our long lie-in was due to exhaustion rather than simply marking the start of the weekend. Eddie's patience had run out and I could hear him scratching and whining at the stern hatchway. I raised my hands close to my face. They were shaking slightly; I assumed it was some kind of delayed shock. I could remember all too clearly the impotence I had felt as I was violently pulled across the towpath and into the cold water. And yet, my attacker had seemed so pathetic in the flesh. He must have been furiously determined to summon up such strength. He had been agonisingly competent with his keep net, I thought. Experienced? Perhaps it wasn't madness to assume I had come face to face with a serial killer, after all. I shivered uncontrollably and headed for the kettle.

Nina's face peered up from her pillow, white and round-eyed as though she too was slowly coming to terms with the events of the night before. I pressed a mug of tea into her hands and then I showered while Nina took Eddie outside, armed with a poo bag. When she returned she blearily stumbled into the shower to try to wake up properly under the trickle of warm water. I had more tea waiting when she emerged in a pair of close-fitting black trousers and a light blue denim shirt that I hadn't seen before. Her shiny black hair was still wet and scraped back in her usual ponytail.

I had my laptop open.

'Anything?' she asked, taking a huge swallow of tea and stifling a yawn.

'Nope – nothing yet. They've kept it quiet so far. But it won't be long.'

'Probably best to get away from this spot then?' she asked, fishing out her mobile to check for herself.

'Slave-driver,' I muttered, grim at the thought of saying goodbye. But she was absolutely right. We didn't want to be around when the press posse arrived at the probable location of the Canal Pusher's capture and arrest.

'There's one last thing to do though,' she said. 'Come on. One for posterity.'

I followed her up onto the stern where she scooped Eddie up to head height and framed a selfie of the three of us with the canal stretching out behind us. She turned the screen to show me the result. Nina and Eddie looked great. I looked at least ten years older – unsurprising after a night of too much whisky and almost being drowned.

I suddenly realised that I hadn't got any pictures of Nina. I didn't want my only memory of her to be a crumpled newspaper photograph.

'Can you save it on my laptop?' I asked.

'Okay,' she said cheerfully. 'You get us going then. What's your password?'

I gave it to her, then I started the engine, untied both lines, pushed out the bow with one foot and strolled nonchalantly back to the stern to step on board, take the tiller and put the boat into forward gear. My confidence in handling the boat had grown immeasurably thanks to Nina's patient instruction and sure-footed example. Suddenly there was a loud shout from below.

'Jack! Jack!' There was no sign of any oncoming boat so I quickly slipped back into neutral and nudged the boat alongside the bank again. Alarmed, I didn't wait to tie her up but hurried down the steps and through the boat's central walkway. Nina was at the table, the lid of the laptop up with a cable connecting it to her mobile. She was staring hard at something. Oh God, I thought. Not another bloody newspaper article. What would it be this time? I quickly bent my head down alongside hers. There, on the screen, was a brightly illuminated row of cannabis plants stretching as far as the eye could see under a bright white tunnel of plastic.

'Bloody hell,' I said. 'The photos! They must have automatically backed-up to the Cloud and synched with the laptop immediately after I took them. We've had them all along. What a bloody idiot.'

'What shall we do with them?'

I took over the little mouse-mat and swiped sideways with my forefinger. The second picture largely repeated the first, whilst the third and fourth showed the large well-equipped laboratory. I zoomed in and out. Bingo! The flashlight had worked well even though it had nearly got me killed, and the pictures were as clear as daylight.

'Can you get the boat back under control?' I said. 'I'm going to take out some insurance.'

Nina gave me a quizzical look but did as she was asked. A few minutes later I re-joined her at the tiller.

'Who did you send them too?' she asked.

'Chisholm. His busy morning just got a whole lot busier,' I said.

We motored on around the right-hand bend, past a seventy-foot winding hole and onto a straight stretch past a village called Tibberton, with a row of boats on permanent and visitor moorings. We played Liveaboard, Tripper or Wreck for one last time as we passed each of them in succession. It was one o'clock as we entered a cutting, ducked under the M5 and approached the six-strong flight of Offerton locks. As I strolled along the towpath to prepare each lock for Nina and the boat's uninterrupted progress, I saw crowds of people walking in the same direction as me on a nearby parallel path. Many were wearing blue and yellow tops or similarly coloured baseball caps: Worcester Warriors fans on their way to a rugby match at the nearby Sixways Stadium. I could see the nearest stand rising impressively above the trees. There were hundreds of supporters, smiling and walking along in family groups and in ones and twos. An excited buzz came from the crowd and, looking up, I could see the floodlights towering above the bulk of the stadium. It was a happy sight that lifted our spirits on what was likely to be a sad day.

But the smell was even more satisfying to contemplate. I sniffed hungrily as a waft of freshly fried onions and burgers drifted into my nostrils. I was starving after the exertions and excitement of the previous night. My stomach gave a sympathetic rumble. We hadn't had breakfast and it was now lunchtime. I turned back and signalled Nina to move in to the bank between locks thirteen and twelve. We still had two left to go through but there was no way I was passing up this opportunity. Nina looked puzzled but obediently steered over to a temporary mooring where boats could wait for other traffic to come through the next lock.

'Match day burgers coming up,' I grinned. 'Onions and ketchup?'

'Yes, please. And a sausage for Eddie!'

'Back in a minute,' I said, trotting off into the crowd as it meandered towards the beer and food stalls around the edge of the stadium. I joined the end of a short, cheerful queue and saw that a large metal sign gave kick-off time as 2.30 p.m. The fans around me were still quite early. A team mascot dressed like a Roman Centurion with oversized foam muscles walked up and down the line, waving his plastic sword excitedly and adding to the happy and expectant atmosphere.

Fighting my way back through the oncoming fans wasn't easy and I hopped across to the towpath as soon as I could, two containers of burger and chips, and one hot dog pressed to my chest to keep warm. There was no sign of Nina or Eddie on the stern platform, so I assumed she was inside, preparing plates, knives and forks. I wished we had some cold Champagne to wash down our last lunch together. It would have felt like a nice way of marking the moment properly. I knocked jovially on the side of the boat twice.

'Knock-knock,' I called out. 'Luncheon is served, m'lady.'

The top of the hatchway had been pushed back. I pulled open the doors to the steps and looked down, both my hands still occupied with the food pressed to my chest. Staring back up at me were the two menacing black circles at the dangerous end of a double-barrelled shotgun.

CHAPTER THIRTY-TWO

At the trigger end of the gun, and holding it at a steep upwards slant, was Major Jones. He was sitting on Nina's bed.

'Good afternoon, Mr Johnson,' he said with a grim yellow-toothed smile. 'Please don't be tempted to run away. There would be unpleasant consequences.'

I leaned further in through the hatchway and saw Nina opposite him at the far end of the other bed. Roberts, the man who had met us at Chester Farm, was sitting on the same bed with his back to the headboard and his knees raised. He also had a shotgun and was resting it on his knees. It pointed at Nina's very rigid back. A golf bag stood incongruously between the two single beds with a handful of clubs protruding from it.

Nina looked up at me. She was holding Eddie firmly on her lap. I immediately recognised the stubborn expression; the one that clearly signalled, 'Don't mess with me'. There was no sign of the terror she had shown when Petra Barker had come calling. This latest outrage wasn't about trampling carelessly over her grief at her husband's premature death. This wasn't personal. I looked into her liquid black eyes and registered that they were flashing with anger rather than fear. She was quietly seething. I resolved to try to follow her example and prayed for a fraction of Nina's courage in the face of the sinister silver-grey steel and highly polished wood of the shotguns.

'Good afternoon, Major,' I replied, relieved to hear there wasn't any trace of a tremor in my voice. 'I nearly didn't recognise you with your clothes on.'

Nina snorted and I saw Roberts raise an eyebrow in surprise. Sure enough, this was the first time we had seen the Major fully dressed. He was wearing highly polished brown brogues, green moleskin trousers and an expensive-looking crew neck jumper, from which poked the collar of a white check shirt. He could be any other well-heeled country squire – apart from being some kind of drug crime lord.

'I inherited this gun from my father, Mr Johnson. He died ten years ago but every time I fire it, I feel it still has some of the force of his personality. It's a twelve-gauge and loaded with single lead slugs. That is a very powerful combination which can do a very great deal of damage to human flesh and bone.'

'I'm sure he'd be very proud to know his son had become a low-life drug dealer,' I said as coolly as possible. Roberts's eyes flitted nervously between me and his boss. He was clearly unused to anyone speaking to the Major with such civilian insolence, but his gun stayed steady and trained on Nina's back. My voice may have been steady, but my stomach was doing somersaults. This was the reckoning I had feared ever since my midnight visit to Chester Farm and once again I inwardly cursed myself for placing Nina in real peril. Why hadn't I insisted that she leave the boat when she could? A blind man could have found us after the newspaper article by Petra Barker.

'Watch your mouth, Johnson,' snapped the Major angrily, raising the two gun barrels higher for emphasis.

Nina gave me a brave smile of encouragement in the gloom of the cabin.

'And is it just drug dealing?' I asked. 'Or do you and your boys dabble in the occasional killing as well? You were clearly lying when we came to your farm. I saw Sam getting into the blue Land Rover with your goons the day before he was found dead a short distance away. What happened? Did he help himself to some of the merchandise from your grubby little operation or keep some of the cash for himself?'

Of course, it was equally possible that our nocturnal visitor from the previous night had been responsible for Sam's death – but it wouldn't hurt for me to explore the other option. Well, I hoped it wouldn't hurt.

The Major recovered his composure and answered smoothly.

'As I said, I don't have a clue about your dead little friend,' he said tersely. 'My men knew him slightly from some additional unsanctioned activities of their own – which have now come to an end.' Roberts avoided his boss's eye and looked down guiltily. It sounded like the Major's men had been running some kind of localised side-business on the Major's doorstep. 'But they assure me they had nothing to do with his death.' If the Major was telling the truth, Sam's real killer could now be in police custody. Or it was an accident after all? As if reading my mind, the Major continued.

'But you should be aware that I have had to kill for my country in the past and I am quite prepared to do so again in order to defend my interests.'

Nina turned her head towards the Major and spoke for the first time.

'You kill people all the time,' she said quietly, 'or just ruin people's lives by turning them into zombies.'

The Major kept his eyes on mine but replied to her in a bored voice.

'Indeed. The high-strength skunk and spice that we produce is extremely addictive and valuable because of its exceptional quality. It creates its own demand. But if you had lived in 1920s America, wouldn't you have said the same about booze-runners, Mrs Wilde? I am merely meeting a demand for a product that happens to be illegal at the moment. But will that still be the case in twenty, thirty or forty years? If you go to the cinema now, you can watch movies that celebrate the daring and clever entrepreneurs that kept the speakeasies of America supplied with drink. Cannabis is already legal in some American states. It's just a matter of time before it's legal across the world. In fact, even our own government now allows it to be grown under licence as a cure for epilepsy.'

I laughed out loud. 'You really are preposterous,' I said. 'A middle-aged nudist who grows and sells vast quantities of lethally addictive psychedelic drugs whilst his wife gets on with gardening in the nude.'

'That's enough!' growled the Major fiercely, his eyes narrowing into slits. 'Sit down on that top step before I blow your head off your fucking shoulders.'

I did as I was told, putting the cooling burger boxes down onto the step in front of me. There was a scratch and whine from behind the swing door where Eddie was asking to join the party – especially now that he could smell cooked meat.

'I know that you visited my farm at night and I know where you went and what you saw. You were very lucky to get away with your life that time. Did you really think that we'd stop looking for you? I need to know exactly who else you have told and what you plan to do with your knowledge because I have a very great deal of time and money invested in my business and I don't plan to throw it all away just because of you.'

I folded my arms onto my knees and leaned forward.

'My knowledge?' I asked. 'Oh, it's much better than that, Major. You see I also have photographic proof from inside your drugs tunnel. I had my camera-phone with me, see?'

Even in the gloom of the interior, I could see the muscles in his jaws clenching and unclenching as he stared unblinkingly at me. I took a deep breath and continued.

'And you should be aware that those pictures have been emailed to a friend – only this morning, in fact – along with explicit instructions about what to do with them in the event of anything happening to me or Nina.'

Nina was staring hard at me. She knew that I had sent the pictures to the Chief Superintendent, but I thought it best not to mention the police at this point. I needed to buy time and not make them too desperate.

'You're lying,' he snapped back. But I could see the doubt in his narrowed eyes.

'Hullo down there – excuse me?' The voice from the towpath was clearly directed at our boat. The Major and Roberts instinctively ducked their heads at the sudden intrusion. They exchanged quick looks and the Major held out a flat hand to his man, signalling him to stay calm, stay quiet and not move. The Major moved across to look out of the side of the small porthole but kept his gun trained on me as I replied.

'Hullo, there.' I stretched my head up and backwards to look around the door. A large-stomached man in a Warriors rugby shirt and pink knee-length shorts was standing on the path by the stern. He had a small boy on his shoulders and his hands were clamped around the child's ankles. The boy was four or five years old with an angelic face below a shock of curly blond hair. He too was in a replica Warriors' rugby shirt. I glanced at both the guns again which were trained on us with renewed emphasis. I had to get the boy and his father to go away.

'Sorry to trouble you, like,' said the man with a broad Black Country accent. 'My boy here loves seeing the canal boats and asked if he could have a look around inside one?'

I didn't need to look down to know the end of the shotgun barrel was now pressed firmly against my balls.

'No, I'm sorry,' I called back as emphatically as possible. The man's friendly smile collapsed into a hurt look. 'My wife isn't dressed at the moment,' I added lamely.

'Oh, right,' said the man. 'No problem. Just thought I'd ask, like.' He shrugged and turned away to join the line of other rugby fans slowly filing past on the track just beyond the towpath. The pressure on my groin eased and I ducked my head back down into the boat.

'That was sensible, Mr Johnson. Now you need to act just as sensibly and show me,' said the Major.

'What?'

'Show me the email and the photographs you attached to it this morning.'

'Or what?' I asked. 'You'll fire a shotgun just metres from a rugby crowd? The police would be here in seconds.'

There was a long pause whilst the Major weighed this up.

'You're right,' he said. For one ridiculous second, I thought he had given up. But my relief was short-lived.

'It's too busy to talk properly here. So, here's what you will do. You will move the boat on to a quieter spot where you will open up your computer and we'll see exactly what we are dealing with.'

This was not what I wanted. If the Major discovered I had sent the pictures to the police, he would feel backed into a corner. I couldn't see him doing anything except cutting his losses and making sure there weren't any loose ends lying around – loose ends like me and Nina. Moving to a quieter spot would give him the chance to interrogate us about the fictitious friend's identity and location as well as dispose of us as he wished. I nodded at Nina.

'It takes two to get through the locks,' I said.

'Nice try.' He chuckled nastily. 'Roberts will help you and I shall keep Mrs Wilde company, so please don't try to run away, Mr Johnson. As I've already said, there would be very nasty consequences.' He stood up and squeezed past the golf bag to stand by the swing door that led to the rest of the boat's interior. He swung the barrel of his gun to point at Nina.

'All right, Roberts.'

Roberts applied his safety catch before putting his gun, stock first, into the golf bag alongside the woods and the irons, and then he fitted a long woollen club cover over the end of the barrel to disguise it. It was a clever way to transport two lethal weapons through very crowded public areas. Then he climbed out of the hatchway to join me at the tiller. I handed him the windlass.

'If the water in the lock is the same level as ours, you just need to open the gates,' I said pointing at the next lock with a road bridge just beyond it. It was full of cars crawling slowly towards the parking around the rugby stadium.

'If it's not the same level as us, you need this to open the paddles in the nearest gates and get the water level to the same as ours.'

He nodded without saying anything and jogged off towards the lock. I fired up the engine and undid the mooring lines. I could see Roberts pushing open the nearest gates, so the water level must have been ready to receive us. He watched me closely, perched on the lock gate's big black-and-white painted wooden beam. I eased the boat forward and Roberts heaved the gates closed behind us. I ordered him to close the paddles and then move forward and crank open the paddles on the far gates and he sauntered forward to do as he was told. He was good at following orders, even from someone he might be about to kill.

I could just see Nina from my position at the tiller, but the Major was standing too far back to be visible. The water began to bubble noisily as it escaped from the lock into the canal beyond the gates. Without looking behind me, I eased the throttle into reverse for a couple of seconds and then back into neutral. The stern slowly edged backwards so that the large rope fender bumped slightly into the gates behind us. We began to descend below the top of the lock's walls. Then there was a slight bump as the stern of the boat came to rest on the cill, which was still hidden below the waterline.

I was about to take a huge risk, but I couldn't see any other option. Roberts was now unarmed and off the boat, and I had to hope that the sudden movement would take the Major by surprise and somehow disable him. But I was all too aware that this desperate measure meant that I was gambling with our lives. Nina was the one inside the boat with a 12-gauge shotgun in an experienced soldier's hands trained on her. What was the alternative though? As soon as we were in a quiet spot, away from the crowds, what was to stop the Major and his man finishing us off?

Almost immediately the boat began to slope forward and I heard something smash in the galley. I gripped the tiller with both hands and braced my feet either side of the hatchway as the long roof of the boat quickly began to slope away in front of me whilst the stern stayed motionless, stuck high and dry on the cill. There was more crashing from the galley and I heard the Major shout something that I couldn't make out above the noise of Eddie's excited barking.

Suddenly, there was a deafening explosion and the roof of the boat seemed to peel upwards just a few metres in front of me; a single gaping hole with ragged metallic edges opened up. Nina's outstretched hand appeared in the slanting hatchway and I grabbed it with one of mine. I crouched to pull her up and out with as much force as I could bring to bear. I looked down over her shoulder as I did so, but I could see no sign of the Major or the golf bag. Nina looped both arms round my neck to stop herself from slipping backwards.

'He just toppled backwards through the door,' she said breathlessly. 'The gun went off as he went through it. Eddie's still down there with him.'

'Come on! Quick!' I urged. The boat was now dipping steeply. I could see a white froth of water rushing over the bow and into the boat through the bow door and the forward windows. The Major's muffled shouts could be heard from the far end of the boat.

'Roberts! Roberts, help me!' I looked up over the top of the lock wall. Roberts's shocked face was looking helplessly down at us from one side of the lock.

'Come on,' I said urgently. I pulled and then pushed Nina along the sloping outside ledge of the boat towards a wet, rusting and slime-covered metal ladder on the wall of the lock. Nina clambered up it with me closely behind. On the far side of the lock Roberts stared back at us. He was in a quandary: rescue his boss from inside the stricken boat or get at us by crossing over.

Jumping Jack Flash was a sad sight, its stern and rudder were now clearly visible resting firmly on the stone ridge by the lock gates. The long black metal hull sloped downwards until it met the new, much lower level of water that was still rushing into the front part of the boat. The galley and saloon must be awash by now and filling fast.

'Jesus, Jack,' said Nina.

'I'm sorry – I had to do something,' I said, keeping my eyes on Roberts all the time in case he decided to prioritise us above the Major. Instead, he looked anxiously over his shoulder and then jumped down onto the sloping roof at the stern, falling forwards on all fours before clambering down through the open hatchway and making his way forward into the boat's interior. The Major's furious shouts could still be heard along with Eddie's furious barking.

'Eddie's still down there,' shouted Nina.

A small group of rugby fans was starting to gather on the far side of the lock. Presumably they had heard the sound of the shotgun cartridges blasting through the boat's roof and as they approached slowly, they could also see the boat's predicament. I shouted across to them.

'Call the police, please. As quick as you can!'

Even as I said the words I could see two uniformed officers running up and pushing through the small crowd. One of them was already speaking into a walkie-talkie.

I pointed down at the boat and shouted to them.

'There are two men inside the boat. They've got guns. They're dangerous!'

A new air of urgency gripped the crowd and many of the fans began to shuffle backwards while the police officers quickly conferred. One of them began ordering the rugby supporters to move even further back whilst the other crept slowly on hands and knees towards the edge of the lock and peered down at the boat. He took in the gunshot hole in the roof of the boat and continued talking into the handsfree mouthpiece of his radio. There was no sign of activity from inside the boat apart from Eddie's barking. Police sirens screamed on the road bridge just beyond us. The crowd of onlookers had swollen considerably but it was moved backwards as four firearms officers with bulletproof vests, black woollen caps and menacingly short, matt-black guns ran up to us. They must have come directly from the nearby police headquarters, whilst the uniformed officers must have already been on duty for the rugby match. One member of the firearms squad, who was wearing sergeant's stripes, pulled me back from the edge.

'Talk to me,' he ordered crisply.

'They're drug dealers,' I said simply. 'They took us prisoner but we've escaped and they've got two double-barrelled shotguns.'

He nodded grimly and silently signalled his men to the four corners of the lock. One of the unarmed officers pulled me and Nina further back so that it was only possible to see the very end of the boat's sloping roof at the stern and the hatchway.

A fire engine and ambulance were inching their way down the track through the fans. They stopped as close as they could and their crews waited in the background, in case they were needed. Nina had linked an arm through mine to watch the drama unfold. The firearms squad leader now had a small megaphone in one hand.

'People inside the boat. You are surrounded by armed police officers. Throw your weapons overboard and come out very slowly.' A tense minute passed with no reaction from inside the boat. The officer was about to use the megaphone again when the head and upstretched arms of Roberts appeared in the hatchway.

'I'm coming out,' he shouted. 'Don't fire.'

'Bring out the guns but hold them by their barrels,' the officer ordered.

Roberts ducked back down below before re-emerging with both shotguns held high in the air by their barrels.

'Throw them overboard.' Roberts hefted each of them in turn over opposite sides of the boat where they clattered against the wall of the lock and fell into the roiling water below.

'He's broken his leg,' shouted Roberts, both hands now flat on the top of his head, like a military prisoner-of-war. Roberts clambered along the boat and up the ladder where he was immediately spreadeagled on the floor by two of the firearms officers, handcuffed and led away. He passed close by and shook his head at us ruefully. Meanwhile one of the firearms officers climbed down onto the boat and edged cautiously towards the hatchway. He said something indistinguishable down into the boat. Then he edged down the hatchway's steps and disappeared from view, his small black machine pistol suspended from a strap across one shoulder and pointing forward. A minute later, the team leader's earpiece crackled into life, and he nodded and waved forward some firefighters and paramedics where they had a small conference.

It took fifteen minutes before the firefighters emerged with the white-faced Major who was strapped tightly to a stretcher. They manoeuvred it awkwardly through the hatchway of the steeply sloping boat and then pulled and pushed it vertically up the lock ladder. A medic followed and then another firefighter appeared, holding a sorrowful and drenched little brown dog in his arms. Nina ran forward to take Eddie from him.

A marked police car took Roberts away and the Major was loaded into the back of an ambulance where a uniformed police officer joined him. Both vehicles struggled slowly back through the milling crowd of rugby supporters who had stayed to watch the incident unfold. Many had been videoing it or taking photographs with their mobile phones.

One of the uniformed police officers had assumed overall charge whilst the Major was being treated in the boat, but he snapped to attention when he saw Detective Chief Superintendent Chisholm emerging from an unmarked police car. The Chief Superintendent had a quick word with the sergeant and then made straight for me and Nina. He looked very tired and put one hand on the back of his grey-haired head as he spoke.

'Shotguns fired, and a narrowboat involved. I thought there might be a decent chance that you two were involved,' he said with the slightest hint of a smile. 'I suppose this is all connected with the email and photos that you sent me this morning?'

'Yes, it is,' I said. 'They obviously tracked us down thanks to Petra Barker's piece in the paper. Just like the Canal Pusher did.' Chisholm winced once again at the nickname. I thought to myself that he'd better get used to it as it was going to haunt him for a long time to come.

'Aye. Well, you should have told us about this a lot earlier. Or even last night would have been helpful.'

I shuffled my feet uncomfortably. 'I didn't have any proof until Nina found the photos on my laptop this morning,' I said lamely.

'Warwickshire's drugs squad raided the place half an hour ago,' Chisholm went on. 'I'm told there was one man left on guard called

Andrews who gave himself up very quickly. The tunnel and the laboratory were all there just as you described as well as a barn stuffed with the product.'

Behind us, the remaining police officers were dispersing the crowd and dealing with the first newspaper photographer to arrive on the scene. Nina squeezed my arm and, for the first time in a fortnight, I felt a great weight lifting from my shoulders. Chisholm looked down at the wreckage of *Jumping Jack Flash*.

'You were lucky to get out of that alive,' he said with a shake of his head.

'What about the guy last night?' I asked. 'Was he a copycat?'

Chisholm looked hard at me, weighing up how much information to share. Then he shrugged. 'Confidentially, we found a kind of journal at his flat in Birmingham. It's extremely detailed. It says he killed Sam, as well as an old farmhand near Droitwich earlier this week and five others over the past year – seven in total since he began.' He shook his head sadly. 'We're still checking all the details.'

'So, the professor was right all along?' said Nina.

'Looks that way,' admitted Chisholm grudgingly. 'Seems that our man wanted to be famous. And he will be – for a few days. Then he can spend the rest of his sorry life asking himself if it was worth it. I don't think he'll find it very easy in prison.'

'But there's no connection between the Chester Farm gang and the Canal Pusher? Sam's death wasn't down to the Major and his drugs operation?'

'It doesn't look like it. Sam was just in the wrong place at the wrong time. And it seems that you two have also managed to be in the wrong place at the wrong time twice. Nice going.'

I reflected that Chisholm and the police had reasons to be pretty satisfied. They'd arrested a serial killer and broken a network of serious drug dealers within the space of twenty-four hours, largely thanks to Nina and me acting as human bait. But Chisholm didn't look very jubilant about it. He looked tired and over-burdened.

'We'll need more statements from you about all this,' he said, nodding at the boat, 'and everything else that went on in Stratford. It's quite a mess. Is it your boat?'

I shook my head.

'Not yet.'

'Well, whoever owns it – I hope they're insured,' he said, stooping down to rub Eddie's ears affectionately. The small dog lay in Nina's arms, which were still covered in mud and slime from the lock ladder.

'You'll both need to come down the station again. I'll leave an officer to guard the boat. You'd better come with me.'

EPILOGUE

It was my turn to have Eddie in the front basket of my bicycle. His head happily pointed forwards and his ears flapping in the wind. We were following our usual route along the towpath, one in front of the other, towards the city centre. She had a small overnight bag in the front basket of her own bicycle.

We'd had a short tussle over ownership of Eddie during our parting at Worcester Foregate railway station on the day after the Major's ambush, but I knew I would lose as soon as I saw the telltale set of her jaw.

'If you have someone to look after, you're more likely to look after yourself,' she had said firmly and I had meekly taken the loop of the dog lead from her. And then she had gone, after a tight hug and a clipped, 'Goodbye, Jack – stay in touch.' It could have been a scene from *Brief Encounter*, but without the billowing clouds of smoke from a steam train.

Jumping Jack Flash had been pumped out and pulled out of the lock at Sixways by a crane and loaded onto a long lorry trailer. Then she had been dried out and refitted – all, thankfully, at the expense of the previous owner's insurers. I bought her for a discount on the original price and used some of the money I had saved to commission an artist who repainted the grinning and leaping jester on her side alongside the neat new lettering of her name. It was good to see Jack Flash back, although his crazy smile still reminds me of our dramatic fortnight together whenever I see it.

The trip south and then west through Banbury, Oxford and Newbury had been slow and very hard work on my own but I had managed it without too much fuss. I stayed closely in touch with Nina throughout my trip, sending her daily email-postcards. She replied to them almost instantly with frank accounts of her attempt to rebuild her life with the support of her family and friends. She was more open with me in writing than in person and I took enormous care with our correspondence. A new permanent mooring had been difficult to procure, but the small floating village of people moored on the Kennet and Avon Canal at Bath was welcoming and full of advice. Eventually, whilst walking with Eddie, I spotted a private mooring at the end of a large and impressive garden and so I knocked on the door of the mansion it belonged to. The owner was a newly divorced investment banker of roughly my age. We hit it off and I am now paying him a monthly rent for a prime location in the city centre.

My cycle commute to the *Bath Chronicle* takes just under fifteen minutes. Eddie comes with me and has been welcomed as the office pet. He spends most of the day being cuddled on someone's lap or lying quietly on a very comfortable bed under my desk. I correct copy, tweak press releases and design the layout of pages for its weekly publication. It's a poorly paid but unpressurised job that has also allowed me the time and space to work on my book about the Canal Pusher.

I needed Nina's input to help fill in some of the blanks. And so, we continued our email correspondence, building up the story of our shared experience together and filling in some of the spaces of our unexpressed feelings at the time. It seemed easier to be honest with each other in writing and it turned out to be a cathartic process for us both. When we first met, we had both been badly bruised and at a critical crossroads in our lives. I think we came to appreciate how we had helped each other to find a new way forward.

But I also needed more background information about the people who had nearly killed us. The Canal Pusher, as the newspapers dubbed him in a frenzy of excited coverage, was only too pleased to plead guilty and was given seven concurrent life sentences. They didn't bother charging him with my attempted murder. He didn't just confess to the murders, he bragged about their execution as well as his cleverness at eluding any kind of suspicion for so long. I suspect that Detective Chief Superintendent Chisholm's career will never really recover from the newspaper's need to blame someone for failing to pre-empt or follow-up on Professor Parsons' theories. However, Chisholm remained friendly to us and he even let me read a full copy of the Pusher's journal as part of my research. Nina and I were relieved that we didn't need to give evidence due to the guilty pleas, but we met up again at Bristol Crown Court for the sentencing and enjoyed a friendly supper with Chisholm, who paid the bill.

The Chester Farm drugs gang also delighted the newspapers in their turn. The press carried lurid tales in the aftermath of the police raid on the farm and the discovery of an estimated ten million pounds' worth of cannabis, plus the laboratory in the polytunnels. They described the army background of the Major, Roberts and Andrews, who had all served together, and they excitedly repeated the locals' gossip about the Major and his wife's naturist lifestyle. One young lad came forward to describe how a naked Major had ambushed him as he cycled along the farm's rear perimeter fence and fired both barrels of a shotgun in the air above him. The boy's mobile phone picture of the furiously naked man shouting and pointing his gun at him made the front pages of almost every newspaper in the country. In all of them, the Major's groin was heavily pixelated.

Although all three men pleaded guilty to the illegal cultivation and distribution of drugs, the Major and Roberts denied charges of attempting to murder Nina and me. We thought we would be summoned to give evidence but in the end the Crown Prosecution Service settled for admission of guilt to a lesser charge of kidnapping. We were both relieved to escape the publicity that would have come with any court appearances. The Major was sent down for twenty years whilst Roberts and Andrews escaped with ten years each. There was no evidence to prove that the Major's wife knew what was happening on her doorstep. But her hopes of rebuilding the farm's traditional business of soft fruit rather than hard drugs are likely to founder as the police begin seizing 'proceeds of crime' assets.

The lack of a full-blown court trial in both cases has meant that there's been no shortage of interest in my book-length account of what really happened. There's a gratifying auction going on amongst the Sunday newspapers for exclusive extracts and pictures from my forthcoming book, and the fees being discussed should keep me on my mooring and Eddie in dog food for a long time to come. Nina has offered to proofread the final draft. I think she just wants to check how I have portrayed her – which is fair enough.

We brought our two bicycles to a halt on the towpath. Nina leaned forward and brushed my cheek with her lips.

'Thanks, Jack. See you again in a fortnight.' Then she leaned forward again and rubbed noses with Eddie. 'Be a good boy.' I liked to think this was aimed at us both.

'Take care, Nina,' I said.

She set off again, waving one hand in the air without looking back. I watched her diminishing form as she disappeared around a bend in the towpath. I checked my watch. She would still have plenty of time to get to the station and catch the train back to her flat in Salisbury. I would see her again soon.

Then I turned to cross the bridge, following the direction of Eddie's nose as it pointed the way into the city for another day's work.

Author's Note

The idea for a serial killer who pushes people to their deaths in canals was prompted by newspaper coverage of a spate of drownings in the canals and waterways of Greater Manchester. The *Daily Star Sunday* first published a two-page article in 2015 which cited sixty-one such deaths over the previous six years. At the time, Professor Craig Jackson, a criminologist from Birmingham City University, said that all of the cases were unlikely to be accidents or suicides. Since then, rumours of a serial killer stalking the city's canals have spread around the world, despite repeated denials from Greater Manchester Police. Fortunately, a novelist does not need to separate fact from fiction and so I have developed this story into one about a single serial killer stalking the canals of the West Midlands region. Whilst every single character in *Canal Pushers* is a figment of my imagination, I have tried to be as faithful as I can to the geography and features of the canals that Jack and Nina travel upon. Almost every lock, bridge, pub and mooring that is mentioned in the book can be visited by anyone who chooses to do so. However, there is no such place as Chester Farm and I am certain that the soft-fruit growers of Warwickshire are all fine, upstanding and law-abiding individuals.

I would like to thank Jeremy Clapham, Stuart Makemson and Matty Smith for their diligent proofreading and expert advice on all boating matters in the book. I am also grateful to Michael Pearson at J.M.Pearson & Son Ltd for their kind permission to replicate maps from their excellent 'Canal Companion' series of guidebooks. They have been an excellent source of information for myself, Jack and Nina. *Canal Pushers* and the Jumping Jack Flash series would never have left its mooring without the initial encouragement of Emma Holtz and

Emily Freer at Orphans Press. But it is the launch crew of Orphans Director Helen Bowden, Publishing Manager Joanna Narain and my expert editor Debbie Hatfield to whom I owe most thanks. Thanks to everybody at Orphans who have worked on the book, especially to Chris Knight for his cover design and Scott Myers for the atmospheric photography. Thank you also to Professor Craig Jackson for reading an early proof copy. Finally, I raise a gin and tonic in gratitude to the 'Besties', the group of close Worcestershire-based friends whose encouragement and support has been unstinting and to Helen, my wife and best friend, to whom this book is dedicated.

Coming soon...

RIVER RATS

A floating village.
Corrupt property developers.
What trouble awaits Jack and Nina
in historic, picturesque Bath?

Available where all good books are sold